GOD'S ANGRY MAN

A novel by Leonard Ehrlich

God's Angry Man

BY LEONARD EHRLICH

With a Foreword by

CLIFTON FADIMAN

The Press of THE READERS CLUB

NEW YORK

PRINTED IN THE UNITED STATES OF AMERICA

Foreword

LEONARD EHRLICH'S GOD'S ANGRY MAN appeared almost a decade ago. At that time I was of some slight assistance in furthering
its publication. (As Mulvaney might say, "I was an editor wanst;
I was rejuced aftherward, but I was an editor wanst.") Now here
I am doing the job all over again. This performance I am prepared to repeat regularly every ten years until a sufficiently large
number of Americans have read and been moved by this passionate novel of the life of John Brown of Kansas and Harper's Ferry.
A man in love with a book is like a man in love with a woman:
he is not truly happy until he has introduced her to all his friends
and forced them to admire her qualities. (This often turns him
into a crashing bore and even more frequently loses him the
woman.)

Not that at its first appearance GOD'S ANGRY MAN was without friends! On the contrary, I have known few first novels that
met with a more generous, though well-deserved, press. "A novel
with fire and flame in it," wrote Harry Hansen, "a glorious out-
burst of literary fervor." "A magnificent book," was the opinion
of Waldo Frank. Stephen Vincent Benét—who did a pretty imposing job of resurrection on John Brown's body himself, you
remember—called it "a remarkable and able first novel." *The
New York Times* man's verdict: "A work of art, powerful and
exciting." Lewis Gannett in *The New York Herald Tribune* sum-
marized it with terse accuracy: "It is the almost miraculous
achievement of Mr. Ehrlich's novel that he succeeds in reflecting
at once the glory and the savagery that was John Brown."

These comments were typical. But the public, for its own
unfathomable reasons, did not respond. Seven or eight thousand
people bought the book. This is a pleasant sale for a first novel,
but it was not good enough, I have always thought, for Mr. Ehrlich's. An attempt at a reprint edition was no more successful.
Still, *Paradise Lost* had a hard time finding its public, too, and it
took *Of Human Bondage* more than a decade to hit its stride.

I am not, it will be understood, comparing Mr. Ehrlich to either Milton or Somerset Maugham. I am merely pointing out—well, you get the idea, I'm sure.

It is the notion of the Selecting Committee of The Readers Club that GOD'S ANGRY MAN is just about ready for a large and appreciative audience. During the last ten years we have had dozens of novels exploiting our country's past. A few have been good, most bad. Whatever the merits or defects of this flood of historical novels may be, they have done one thing: they have re-awakened permanently our interest in the dramatic possibilities of the great chronicle of America. That reawakened interest should work in Mr. Ehrlich's favor.

But if his book were merely another historical novel, however accurate and "exciting," we should not feel it fair for us to propagandize among the members of The Readers Club. To my mind GOD'S ANGRY MAN is more than a good historical novel. For me it is worth a dozen of *Oliver Wiswell,* much as I admire Mr. Roberts' narrative skill and conscientious scholarship. It is worth a gross of *Gone With the Wind,* a book which found its proper avatar in the heaven of Hollywood. These best-sellers—and others like them—have given legitimate pleasure to many hundreds of thousands of readers. I do not believe they are literature.

GOD'S ANGRY MAN is literature. It is literature because it moves us not by the exciting power of its episodes (though it tells one of the bloodiest, tensest, and most powerful stories in our history) but by two rarer qualities: the quality of moral passion, the quality of tragic imagination. These are the qualities of Greek tragedy, and there is something classical about the life, the suffering, and the fall of John Brown, as Leonard Ehrlich presents them.

Aristotle tells us that poetry is more "philosophic" than history because its statements are of the nature of "universals" whereas those of history are "singulars." Most of the current historical novels are only history rewritten. They are effective and picturesque rearrangements of events ("singulars," to use Aristotle's jargon) through which one or more banal love stories are threaded to give the effect of a "plot." But Mr. Ehrlich's moral passion and tragic imagination lend to his "singulars" (which may be found in any good history book) a breath of the universal.

Here is the tale of a man of great stature, like the heroes of Greek tragedy who, again like them, falls because of a fatal defect of character—in his case, the defect of fanaticism. His life is grand; it has a grand meaning; and his fall is grand; and has a grand meaning. He is John Brown, Abolitionist; but he is also the type of all furious enthusiasts of boundless energy and intense, narrow vision. Such men usually die violently, or are killed because they are dangerous. But the lives of such men have incalculable consequences. In one way or another their souls, often for evil as well as for good, go marching on. In this sense GOD'S ANGRY MAN is a tragic poem, though written in prose. It is not a reordering of historical events, but a transmutation of them, so that they move us beyond their immediate and temporally limited application. This makes Mr. Ehrlich's book literature.

These are very big words and, as I read them over, they seem to be too orotund. Still, I will let them stand. But, whether this interpretation of GOD'S ANGRY MAN be cogent or not, the book will stand as a superb job of straight, suspense-filled narrative. It is full of characters difficult to forget (some of them very unpleasant, indeed) and episodes of battle, murder and sudden death. The life of John Brown forms a natural drama. It is difficult, let us admit, for anyone to make it sound dull. Mr. Ehrlich makes it magnificently engrossing.

But I must at once make clear that I do not consider GOD'S ANGRY MAN a masterpiece. It is often too consciously "impressive." Mr. Ehrlich like many young writers of great talent is afflicted at times with the specialized color blindness that prevents him from seeing when a patch is purple. He took four years to write his book, and perhaps it shows the strain. It is over-careful. The rhythms, though beautiful, are too sedulously elaborate. The story once in a while labors under the weight of too much intensity.

These are defects. But they are the defects of a large talent, not a small one. They do not prevent GOD'S ANGRY MAN from being a passionate and beautiful book. At a moment when we are all examining the meaning of the words liberty and freedom, and asking ourselves whether we are willing, as one angry man of God was willing, to suffer and die for them, this novel makes fateful and timely reading. It is for these reasons that I commend it to you.

CLIFTON FADIMAN

Author's Note

THIS WORK is a *novel,* not a biography or a history. But this is not to say that it is a flight of "fancy." Throughout, it moves scrupulously within a frame of historical fact. The main lines of the narrative are those of Oswald Garrison Villard's monumental biography (to which an unpayable debt is hereby recorded)—save that herein certain lesser events have been telescoped in the interests of dramatic continuity, and occasional letters are either composites or mosaics of John Brown's most vital and moving utterance. The names of certain minor characters have been slightly altered—first, to avoid confusion where repetitions occur in the nomenclature of the Brown family; second, so that freedom might be gained to work out their destinies more richly. But nowhere has their essential spirit been distorted; the historical originals can be easily discerned. The episodes dealing with Thoreau are written almost entirely in his own words, gathered from his journals and speeches—with the idea of presenting as directly as possible his very thought and emotion. There is little included which he did not actually say and think; and nothing which he might not have said and thought.

L. E.

Principal Persons in the Narrative

Owen "Oaken" Brown
Ruth Mills Brown }*the parents of John Brown*
Sally Bool Brown: *his step-mother*
JOHN BROWN
Ann: *his sister*
Dianthe: *his first wife*
John Jr. ⎤
Jason   ⎟
Owen   ⎬*John Brown's children by Dianthe*
Frederick⎟
Ruth   ⎦
Hen Thompson: *Ruth's husband*
Will Thompson   }*Hen's brothers*
Dauphin Thompson
Mary: *John Brown's second wife*
Watson ⎤
Salmon ⎟
Oliver ⎬*John Brown's children by Mary*
Annie ⎟
Sarah ⎟
Nell   ⎦
Wealthy: *John Jr.'s wife*
Ellen: *Jason's wife*
Bella: *Watson's wife*
Abbie: *Salmon's wife*
Martha: *Oliver's wife*
Abraham Lincoln
Frederick Douglass
Robert E. Lee
Jeb Stuart
Thomas Wentworth Higginson
Thoreau

John Brown's Harper's Ferry Raiders: { *sixteen white men and five Negroes*

Contents

THE FIRST PART

The Assassin

THE SECOND PART

Though Faint, Yet Pursuing

THE THIRD PART

Old Miners Will Come at Once!

THE FOURTH PART

War into Africa

THE FIFTH PART

O to Struggle!

THE LAST PART

We Shall Walk through the Valley in Peace

Action from principle, the perception and the performance of right, changes things and relations; it is essentially revolutionary, and does not consist wholly with anything which was. It not only divides states and churches, it divides families; ay, it divides the individual, *separating the diabolical in him from the divine.*

THOREAU

GOD'S
ANGRY
MAN

The Assassin

THE
FIRST PART

CHAPTER I

How Are You All on the Goose?

THEY WERE hunting John Brown as they hunted a wolf. They wanted him dead or living, better dead—a gray, gaunt man, almost sixty, with intense eyes, a mouth that was bitter, and seven huge sons. He walked with a long springing step and an inward air, his right shoulder thrust forward as though to meet life full on. He had a power of quickness and no fear; knew how to fade in a swamp or ride like a wind through hills; and he would stand and shoot against twenty. He could be tender with a sick lamb, and he could take men from their beds at night and kill them. "Right is everything, God is a god of wrath," he said, and took five men from their beds and killed them. It was near the Marais des Cygnes water, in the wild Osawatomie region of Kansas. There was a clear spring moon up and soft spring air and a host of warm stars, and that, the twenty-fourth of May, 1856, was the night he did it, using sabres to make silent work. Later, someone said to him, "You should have let the two Doyle boys go. They were slavers, but they were so young, only boys."

He answered: "Nits grow to be lice."

A year before he had knelt weeping, by a boy's grave in the mud of Missouri. His grandchild lay there, stricken by cholera on the way out from the East, and dead at four; and the old man with the grim face had carried the remains to Kansas that they might be buried closer.

"Right is everything," John Brown said, using sabres to make silent work of it.

He had been in a field with two of his sons, Jason and Frederick, planting corn. All about them—beyond the stone row where the rifles stood, beyond the low rude house and the failing peach trees—was a wide land lonely without towns, Kansas land in a vast roll, spreading in rise and fall out to a dimness merged with sky. The spring was settled now; the wild geese were passing. They flew high over in miraculous triangles formed clean and perfect, calling harshly that winter was gone, and the uncertain early season; that a gentler time was here. Now the warm winds from Mexico would hold sway and the bite from Dakota would be sheathed; now the weather would not drop from a good warmth at noon to zero cold in the starlight. Game was returning; small antelopes were shadows moving in the sallow distance, and the sage hens mottled the prairie.

The old man and his two sons sowed the corn. Jason, called "Jay" in fondness, save by his father, was in his thirties, a big man with a gentle mouth and importuning eyes, ringed darkly. Frederick, the younger by a few years, made a strange figure, shaggy and gleaming in the sun, with his bright blue shirt and yellow hair stiff to his shoulders. He had prodigious strength and was wrong in the head, and he could be gentle as a child. His eyes were pale and cold, like blue stones in icy water. Sometimes they would deepen, and a bewildered anguished look would come to them, so that he seemed to be weeping without tears. Of all the family he was loved the most, and yet perhaps the least, because there was pity in their love. Now, in the field, he muttered as he worked and his face held a kind of racked vacancy.

The old man went hard down the line, driving himself; but his heart was not in the planting. He moved, sowing the seed; his hands knew the way of it, but his thought was beyond. All his life he had spent in the service of the earth, close by beasts and free growing things; the best of his strength he had given to it. But now, in the evening of his time, he was restless, the soil was not sufficient.

The day before, Jason had been tending the fruit trees, brooding over the stunted growths. "They told us it was a rich land," he said bitterly. "They said it would be a good life."

The old man answered with harshness: "You didn't come for rich living. You came to fight for Kansas. You came to keep slavery out."

"I want to work and grow things! I want my Ellen and young Tom to live quiet!"

"Give up your ideas. You'll have to fight if you want to live at all. They'll not spare you here. You'll need to be a man, or you'll go under. You'll need to stand hardness and be ready to give as hard as you get. Don't hope for happiness. Who are you? Who are you to hope for it? Jason Brown who wants to grow things and live quiet? Well, there's slaves in the land, there's

≡＊6＊≡

humans held in bond. Only remember that, not your peach trees."

They worked at the planting, and the guns were against the stone row. A year ago the Brown boys had been on their new claim but a day, they were clearing ground, when a group of horsemen came up. They were rough men, in boots and flannel shirts and wide hats; armed heavily with rifles and knives. A dark, shifty-eyed man—he was Martin White, a preacher; they would remember him—called sharply:

"How are you all on the goose?"

The oldest son, John, a hot proud fellow, answered up: "We're from Ohio, we're Free-State. We're Abolitionists, too. How do you stand?"

"You damn nigger-stealers, you'll find out soon! You won't last long!"

The horsemen wheeled and were off in a cloud. From then on the Browns kept their guns close. It became not a rare thing to find a man dead in a field, shot through the heart as he worked a plough. In the beginning the dead men were all Free-Staters; soon there were pro-slavers among them.

So with guns close the three Browns planted corn, each in his own way—poor Fred in emptiness; gentle-faced Jason with hunger for a rich crop, with slow careful fingers trembling a little; the old man, far gone in thought, busied more with some seed in his mind. The afternoon moved on; the sun went lower, throwing a harsh lemon glitter over everything. Then from the north young Noah Fraze came riding down hard.

"They're burnin' Lawrence!" he shouted. "We're goin' to help! Meet at the Forks quick 's you can!"

When night fell upon that day, thirty-four men from the Free-State settlements of the Osawatomie region were gathered at a point along the California Road. The Browns were among them; six huge sons, and the old man dark as thunder. Soon they were moving forward in the darkness—a silent body of men, with fear at their hearts and bitterness. Lawrence was taken, Lawrence their chief town was being razed to the ground. Seven hundred men, a violent drunken mob; guerrillas from the Platte country, cut-throat Kickapoo rangers, scum from Missouri; were looting under Dave Atchinson, a former Vice-President of the United States. They had wrecked the Free-State presses and dumped them into the river; shot the post-office and meeting-hall full of holes with a cannon; were firing homes. Atchinson, inflamed with

≡ * 7 * ≡

drink, had made a speech before sending his wild crowd against the town:

"Boys, this is the happiest moment of my life! We'll enter damned Lawrence and teach the damned Abolitionists a Southern lesson they'll remember till the day they die! Be brave, boys, be orderly, and if any man or woman stand in your way, blow them to hell with a chunk of cold lead!"

That was the word a rider had brought. And now the violence would spread. Now it was no longer furtive: a man shot down in a field; another's throat cut as he came out of his barn. This was open war, brutality banded, murder organized. The Osawatomies went grimly in the dark, thirty-four men. Atchinson had seven hundred. Somehow they must help. There were Free-Staters in lonely places from Lawrence to the Cygnes water. Nor must they let the danger reach their own doors; the walls within which were their women and young ones must not go down in flames. They went forward steadily; soon a moon rose to light the way. There was little talking.

Near midnight a beating of hoofs sounded up the road; and Adam Hosmer, sent out early to scout, came riding back, dusty and peaked and savage. It was true, he said. It was true, damn them. He'd seen it himself, the sky was red with fires. And there was no use moving ahead, he said; the bastards were holding Blanton's Bridge. The Osawatomies were outnumbered twenty to one, and with the pass guarded it was suicide to go on.

There was a quick parley. They would halt. They would camp for the night, and await reinforcements from the outer Free-State settlements. A fresh rider went back swiftly along the way, bearing the message. In an hour most of the worn little company were huddled in sleep about the dying hill-fires.

Old Brown did not sleep. He sat alone in the night stillness. A Bible, faded with damp and handling, was in his bony hands, unopened. He was never without it, carried it always in the pocket of his linen coat, just above the long bowie-knife in his belt. He read from it each morning, and each night; but he did not need to read, because he knew its every word. Now, sitting by the embers, with a tattered straw hat, and his toes showing through worn boots, he looked like an aging farmer in straits. Like an aging farmer he looked—until you saw his face; the bluish eyes with something hawk-like showing, and something faintly

≡＊8＊≡

sad; the iron thrust of his jaw and the mouth drawn in bitterness. Then he looked like something more, there was some vitalness in his face—soon they would call it madness—some urgency you could not grasp to put into words, but you felt it. Now, by the embers, in the midst of his sleeping sons, he brooded:

Something must be done. Something must be done. And quickly, or Kansas and the cause were lost. Quickly; for a force of evil was spreading through the Territory like a pall. These wide plains, swept now by the winds of God, plains this very moment stretching free beneath the light of His stars and moon, would soon be given over to ungodliness. Slavery was taking root, from the South the poisonous growth was spreading; and soon here too in its shadow black men would be prostrate, soon here their groans would sound and the clanking of chains. It was the sum of all iniquity, it was the deepest shame of men. What must be done? Peace would not avail, nor an appeal to justice. There was no peace in Kansas, it lay agonized; there was no justice, the law itself was the prop of bondage. Patience, firmness at the ballot-box? That was a mockery too. Guns swept elections here; and the slavers had more guns. What was left then? What was left, old Brown called silently to the night stillness. . . .

God was left.

God.

The Lord is a man of war: the Lord is his name. Thy right hand is become glorious in power. Thy right hand, O Lord, hath dashed in pieces the enemy!

God, the old man thought, a wild fullness running on him. God and one man could overturn the universe! They were burning Lawrence to the ground, but there were two sides to the question, there was still a remnant in Israel! Was there oppression in the land? Then with Him in their hearts they would fight oppression! Was injustice framed into the law? Then they would fight the law! Did the government enforce it? Then with God's strength they would resist the government! There was a higher law, he had a book in his hand which gave it:

Because I delivered the poor that cried, and the fatherless, and him that had none to help him: I put on righteousness and it clothed me: my judgment was as a robe and a diadem. I brake the jaws of the wicked and plucked the spoil out of his teeth!

The wildness mounted in the old man's heart. His eyes

≡ * 9 * ≡

burned in the dark with sudden unfelt tears, and the whole surrounding night seemed a single vast presence, a Oneness breathing a Word:

An eye for an eye, a tooth for a tooth!

CHAPTER II

I Am Bounden to No Man

MORNING CAME, with no word yet from Osawatomie. The hours
passed; gloom was heavy over the little company. The men hung
about strained and restless, sharing their vague deep fears in low
speech. Then at noon a sudden excitement ran through the camp.
Old Brown was leaving, old Brown was turning back with four
of his boys and squat Hen Thompson, the young fellow who was
married to his daughter Ruth. Jim Townsend was driving them
in his wagon back to the rough wood country. And big Wiener
was going too, riding his dun pony; Wiener the Austrian with
the blotched face and the pig-eyes. Then something was up, ran
through the company. Old Brown wasn't running out of a fight.
If he was leaving, it was only to get in deeper. But he was silent
as death, saying only "My plans are my own."

Soon the wagon was moving slowly from the camp, Townsend driving, a thin man, with a scraggly black moustache. Brown
sat hunched up by the other's side, staring straight out. The
young fellows were crouched in the wagon-bed on a pile of old
two-edged sabres. Wiener was outrider. (He had a snarly brutish
look; his upper lip, slashed once in a brawl, was drawn back from
his teeth.)

All afternoon the wagon creaked along through the flatlands.
It was hot; they were without cover and a burning sun was on
them. The team raised dust in yellow clouds, choking them. They
were thirsty, but there was no water. Nobody spoke much. Wiener, riding a good way ahead, often looked back, as though he
were impatient for them to get on. They could see his red spattered face and the graven leer.

The sun slowly went lower, laying a sullen glow over the sallow fields, hurting their eyes; and they came to the end of the tame land, to the beginning of the Osawatomie country. They turned off the main way and as the day deepened they were full in a wild timber region, following a bad narrow road with holes a foot deep in places and big rocks jutting. Then old Brown took the lines; he knew the country best. After a good spell he drew up—it was black night by then, no moon out, no stars—in a deep gully. They jumped down from the wagon. The heat had gone with the sun; a sharp wind was blowing in from the prairie; in an hour they would be shivering with cold.

They camped in the gully, eight of them. Before they turned in for the night seven heard a low burning voice in prayer, ending:

For the Lord your God is a God of gods and a Lord of lords, a great God, a mighty and a terrible, which regardeth not persons, nor taketh reward!

They slept—those who could sleep—in the thick grass under the willows; without a fire, the old man ordering it so, lest they be seen.

The day came up (they would remember it always) ashen, with a boding sky and mists scudding before a wind. They ate meat strips and hard bread and washed them down with water from the nearby creek. Then they began the long wait. There was a whole day to get through; the old man said it would be night work.

He was very still. (But not with the impassibility of Wiener. The Austrian sat on a log, smoking his pipe, drawing with succulent, deliberate gust; and a yellow wetness was gathered in the corners of his mouth. His hands were steady as stone.) The old man's was a leashed stillness, the stir in him showed only in the eyes. His was ice covering a ferment. He was sitting on the ground near the stacked rifles, reading from the Book with bent head. He looked like an aging farmer in straits; until you saw his face, and then he looked like something more; there was some vitalness you could not grasp to put into words; but you felt it.

His boys felt it. He had given them the word and there they were waiting with guns and bowie-knives and two-edged sabres. They knew now for what. But they had not known in the beginning, and had waited so then too; great fellows, each of them; men in their own right, doing his bidding; challenging, true, his

≡ *11* ≡

secretiveness, and questioning, some of them, his ways, but in the end doing the bidding.

There was Owen up at the end of the ravine with his young brother Oliver, keeping a watch. Owen was thirty-two, the third son, big and hard as oak. His left arm was withered, it had been so from birth; he could fell a ram with his right. He looked, more than any of the others, like the father, had the same sharp nose, small high head and the great width between austere eyes. Only the mouth was different. It was softer and sometimes went into a smile.

Owen was deepest under the sway of his father. There was nothing he would not do at the old man's word, nothing. And it wasn't as if he were a lack-brain, like poor Fred, or weak-willed and quick to bend to another. For he had a strong mind of his own; could think matters through, come to his own way of doing things and stay with it stubbornly—except when his father's way was different. If there was something pitiable in the sight of the huge man-son yielding his being to the old man's call, so too was there something high and uncommon in the submission. For, having so much of eagerness, so much of a reckless ardor, it could not be called servility. It was devotion, rather, instant and unthinking, which, showing in a man otherwise strong-willed and even arrogant, held a kind of religiousness.

Owen, like all his brothers, had long ago rejected old Brown's God, a god who thundered through the Testament and was mighty in wrath and avenged. They had his hard-headed skepticism, but not the intense core of belief, the touch of mysticism which gave vitality to his trust in a living One. He could say: look to God and keep your powder dry; but Owen was careful only to have dry powder. The old man had an intuition bright and gleaming as the very water of life: the Lord, he said, directed him in visions what to do; Owen had never heard His voice.

But that was not all. Owen had Puritan blood, generations of it. This heritage gave him a distrust of dogma—and the hunger to believe in something, someone. He had no creed, but he had the old man. He had left the church by which his people had set store for two hundred years, but he possessed still the sense of childhood, the sense of godhood in father: the being who to childhood's eyes was the doer of all things; he who brought food, made light and warmth, the punisher of guilt and the voice of wisdom. John Brown had been such a god to his children. To Owen he was still.

≡ * 12 * ≡

There he was now, the son of Brown, standing guard at the end of the ravine. He would follow the old man anywhere.

Poor yellow-haired Frederick would too—like a child. He was moving back and forth in the gully, swishing with his red-topped boots through the high grass, or walking suddenly on tiptoe with his head half-cocked over his shoulder, as though he feared some lurking thing. He could not be still. Now he sat down near his father, staring till the old man looked up; now he went to Wiener, who ignored him. Soon he was by the two young fellows, Salmon Brown and Hen Thompson, watching them sharpen the double-edged swords. They were drawing them hard against rocks with quick strokes, sparks leaping.

"They'll do the job now!" said Salmon eagerly, rubbing his finger along the blade. He trembled a little as he spoke, but with excitement, not fear. Things would be happening soon, and he would be in them. Different from the stodgy life back in Ohio, the work on the farm, day in, day out, always the same and nothing stirring. This was a job for men; and he felt a man, wanted to do a man's share. Wasn't he going to turn twenty in a few months? A job for guts it would be, and he would be there, helping. The old man would never be able to say to him as he had said to Jay: "You've no guts for a man's work!"

Squat young Thompson felt his own blade. "Mine's ready too," he said; then, nervous as a cat, called in a taut high-pitched voice:

"Sakes, Fred, stop starin' that way! Do somethin', will you, only stop starin' at me!"

"Salmon's is ready too," said the giant, as though he had not heard. "And yours is ready. Should I tell father? There's two sides to this question, father said. Something's got to be done or we'll all be slaughtered. And who'll be right then?" His eyes took on a wild life. "Answer me that, Hen! Who'll be right then? Who'll be wrong if we slaughter them first?"

"Quiet, Fred." Salmon rose and put his hand to the giant's arm. "You'll have father up at you in a minute. You know his orders about quiet."

He ought not to be here, thought Salmon. The excitement is bad for him. Might bring on one of his bad fits. Look at him now, his face all twisted up, mumbling to himself. But you couldn't say anything to the old man. "Send him back," Oliver had pleaded that morning with their father. "Send him back, it's a crime to keep him! We know what we're going into. Fred

≡*13*≡

doesn't. You oughtn't drag him in!" But there was no gainsaying the old man. He wanted Fred there. "Fred's staying, there'll be work for all." And Fred had stayed. Now look at him, mumbling, twisted.

The great fellow pulled himself irritably from Salmon's hand. "I'm all right, now! Don't be watchin' me!" He bent and picked up a sabre from the ground. "You're sure they're finished? We'll need 'em sharp, won't we though!" He began to wave the sabre in the air.

"Put it down, Fred."

It was Oliver, speaking in a low firm voice. The giant turned and stared at him, the sabre held in mid-air. Then he lowered it. It was always Oliver who could quiet him. Oliver was only seventeen, the youngest. He was lithe as whipthong, and hard. (Two years back, in the little mountain community of the Adirondacks, he had thrown ten strapping lumberjacks one after the other in a meet-all wrestling match.) But the look of him was different from the others, save in his bigness. He had white skin and deep black hair; he had soft ways. It's my mother in him, old Brown used to think. He had her eyes, slow brooding eyes; and the old man cherished the dark boy.

But Oliver had a spirit which had never been in her, something jealously proud, almost tigerish. It would not let him be, he too had a driving need for dominance; and the boy contested the sway of the father over himself and the others with a bitterness that at times was almost hatred.

"I want to live my own way, not yours!" he would fling fiercely at the old man. "Guts, guts, you're always saying, and yet you'd have us follow you like sheep! Let live, father, let a man go his way!" And the boy would try to meet without flinching the old man's cold bluish-burning gaze, but he never could, the other's will was stronger. Even as he struggled he knew that he was lost.

"Put the sabre down," the boy now said in a low voice. The yellow-haired giant put it down, meekly.

Eight men were waiting in the ravine. Jim Townsend was the eighth. He was sitting in the wagon; thin, with a scraggly black moustache and frightened eyes; thinking:

It's like a bad dream. Why am I here? I don't want to go out and kill. I don't want to be in your schemes, Brown. I didn't leave the East to come to a bad end. The farm there was flinty and grudging, Brown, but we lived, Millie and me and the kids. I'll die out here, Brown, let me go! I don't want a bullet, I don't want to swing from a hemp rope! I want to sow my corn, and tend the three new sheep I just bought. I want to get the kids and Millie going happy in the new place. I don't want to kill anybody, Brown!

But they had to kill, the old man kept saying. "There are two sides to this question," he had said last night. They were sitting in the darkness, in the tall rustling grass. "Theirs and God's. I'll put the fear of God in them!"

God, the old man talked about, as though he were speaking of someone in the ravine, or someone back in the settlement, waiting.

"You can't do it, father," young Oliver pleaded in a strangled voice. "You can't kill 'em in cold blood. You'll be as low as the things you're fighting against, you'll stain yourself and all of us."

"Then I'll stain myself . . . Oliver, do you see this book here? It's guide enough. It tells about Gideon who drew a sword at the Lord's word. I'll stain myself like Gideon did!"

There was no speaking against him. He had his way of saying things, saying them with a burning till you weren't sure of your own side.

"What's Gideon to us?" the boy cried. "It's a crime, it's murder! This isn't Gideon's time! It's the nineteenth century!"

Then Townsend could see the passion in the old man's face, even in the darkness he could see it.

"The nineteenth century! The nineteenth century! You fool! Does God reckon what century it is? Do men change in their hearts? Do you think right things change to wrong or blood turns to water because a minute of His time passes? Do you see like I do a curse laying over the land, do you see a million black people lower than beasts in the field? There'll be no peace in Kansas, none in all our country till the slave sin is wiped out! And it'll be wiped out in blood!"

There was a low ringing in his voice that was like a knell for Townsend. A terrible feeling of helplessness went over him. This old man would go on to do the deed. He would do it, he would make them all do it.

God he spoke of, and right, and slaves. What were they to him, Townsend? Words, only words, not touching all that meant

≡ * 15 * ≡

most. He, Townsend, had a wife and three children. He had a place to look after. What were niggers alongside them? What did he care whether Kansas came in free or not free, whether pro-slaver Ruffians rode down from Missouri and swept the elections with a show of guns? He hadn't got his corn sowed and the spring was going fast. Winters out here were bad enough even when you had food; bitter cold they were, cutting you in two and terrible for health, with sickness coming on, chills gripping you, and fevers. Rob had gone last winter. He would have been ten now. They had to bury Rob under the snow. . . . And now Millie was not well, with the new one coming. That mattered, not the niggers; looking after the place mattered, looking after the kids, and Millie dreaming and heavy with child. And there was old Brown speaking, with everything black around, no moon, no stars showing, only blackness and a chill wind against them and a voice like a flame, like a cold flame burning:

"And now? Peace we have, eh?" (Dark Oliver had said fiercely: It'll spread like fire, you'll have killings back at us!) "A fine peace we have now! Let's have killings. Without bloodshed there is no remission of sin!"

"Haven't you any mercy? You're not even going against them in a stand-up fight!"

"Mercy! Stand-up fight! Did Reese Gill get mercy? Did Brackett get a stand-up fight? Hacked like pigs they were, mangled so you couldn't know them! And what mercy did Charlie Dugg get? Shot down like an animal! And for what? For staying to his rights when the Ruffians cut wood off his claim. And yet you'd bawl for mercy!"

Then young Oliver said in a passionate voice: "There was a man named Christ, father. There was a man named Jesus Christ. Was it killings he was for?"

The words quivered up to a silence. Then after a moment there came low from the old man:

"I don't keep you, Oliver. If you don't see right in my ways, you can go. You can all go. I don't keep you. . . . Only . . . only you mustn't judge me. Do you hear? You mustn't judge me. . . . My God will judge me."

And so the night wore on; with the old man speaking in fever; with Oliver desperately holding athwart, but always with lessened conviction; the rest silent chiefly, some sickened deeper with qualms, some wrought to a blood heat, and all sensing the futility of seeking to turn Old Brown from his plan. It was very late when the last words were said. The old man spoke:

"I've no more to say. I don't keep any of you, remember I don't. But tomorrow we go ahead. . . . What will you do, Oliver?"

There was a silence. Then the young fellow said, as though he were tearing it from himself:

"I stay."

And now it was the day; now they were waiting through the slow hours; and to Townsend, sitting in the wagon-bed, it was like a bad dream.

"You've got people in Osawatomie, Townsend," the old man said. "My boys have too. Once and for all we've got to strike a blow for them. We've got to strike it hard and first, before it falls on them."

A blow? On the kids, on Millie? Then he would fight, Townsend would fight. He didn't know anything about such things, had always been careful to go his own quiet way. Oh, they had lied to him, back in the East, that man who talked to him about Kansas had lied to him. A place for honest people wanting to work, he had said. A place for a good free life, with rich growing and a kind climate, and everybody minding their own affairs. Oh, what a lie. The very first year they were out, there was hell-heat in summer, with drought and an evil sun coming up every day red as blood; and the first winter, the one they buried Rob (O Christ, O young Rob!) it was twenty-four under zero, with fevers bringing people low and other sicknesses they had no names for. Then next summertime there were insect plagues, some that poisoned green things, others like the chintz locusts that ate four acres of sorghum in a single night, leaving a smell stinking to the sky. A kind climate, a rich growing, and all of it a lie. And the awful lie about peace and each keeping to his own affairs. Here was he who had never been in fights going out to kill! It had to be done, said old Brown who had eyes like flames and looked like a farmer and sometimes when you caught him right was like one of the thundering old men you read about in the Bible. It had to be done if their own families were to live. Well, then Townsend would go with the old man. His insides shrank at the thought, but there was Millie in her way, and his every cent sunk in the claim, and the kids wrapped in his heart. He was afraid, but he would fight.

≡＊17＊≡

The old man had come to him in the camp of the Osawatomies. "I'm Brown," he said. "John Brown. I want to talk to you, there's no time to lose."

"To me?"

"I want your horses and wagon, Townsend. I want you to drive me back."

"Why, are we all going back?"

"No, I'm going. And my boys. We've just got word that there might be some trouble in the settlement. . . . You've got a family back there, haven't you? Well, who's watching them? There isn't a man in the whole place. We were fools for all coming. Do you know Dutch Henry? Do you know Wilkinson and the other devils? They won't stop at much. They've got to be watched and I'm going back to do it."

"That's right, Brown! That's right!"

"Walking's too slow. Will you drive us back?"

"Sure, sure!"

"Good . . . and quiet, Townsend. This is only between you and me." The old man's eyes were glittering. "Get your team fixed up and ready to go in ten minutes. And remember, no talking."

Townsend hurried to the tethered grays cropping near the trees. He was in a panic. His hands trembled as he got the horses teamed against the wagon. In a few minutes he was ready, waiting with restless fear. Soon Owen Brown and Frederick came up to the wagon. The yellow-haired fellow clumsily held before him in his arms a pile of sabres. He dumped them into the wagon-bed and clambered up ponderously; he sat down on them. Owen followed, saying:

"They'll be along in a minute, Townsend."

A group of Free-Staters in the shade of a tree watched with curiosity. One of them called artfully, "Say, Fred, looks like business!"

"Yeah, there's two sides to this question, the old man——"

"All right, Fred," cut in Owen quickly. "All right. . . . Sure it does, Ashby. That's what it's going to be, business."

More men came around. Soon there was a little crowd. Then Oliver, Salmon, and Hen Thompson came through and climbed silently to the wagon-bed. A murmur went about the onlookers. Wiener rode up on his dun pony. Then the old man brushed through the crowd in his dirty linen coat and forlorn straw hat, rolling up some things in a bundle. A man pulled at his arm.

"Say, Brown, where you goin'?"

The old man looked up and said harshly, "My affairs are my own. I go when I choose. I'm bounden to no man."

Another said, "Watch out what you do, Brown. Don't get us into more trouble."

"That's right," another urged. "You want to do things with caution or. . . ."

"Caution!" old Brown called out in sudden anger. "Caution, sir, I'm eternally sick of hearing the word caution! It's nothing but the word of cowards!"

He moved brusquely to the wagon, the men falling back out of his way; threw the bundle among his sons and climbed up like a cat to Townsend's side. He stood there and looked down upon the men who had warned him.

"Caution!" he cried again. "The cowards back in Lawrence were cautious, so cautious they didn't fire a shot to keep Atchinson out! Caution? Guts, I say! Something's going to be done now! They'll not go on with impunity forever!"

There was a brief silence in the crowd, then a rising murmur. His words stirred them, restless with the long waiting; and a sense of their wrongs at the hands of the pro-slavers came over them. Some began to call in approval.

Brown sat down next to Townsend. He looked around sharply, seeking his son John. He saw him; their eyes met with a flash of understanding. Jason, by his brother's side, kept his head turned from his father's gaze. He was pale and his lips were dry. He kept putting out his tongue to wet them.

The old man called, "All right, Townsend, start 'em!" Townsend whipped up the grays eagerly, and the wagon began to creak forward. Wiener rode alongside. Now the onlooking men were in a ferment. In that instant, as the wagon moved out, all their hopes of safety, of well-being, seemed somehow to hover about it. There was hard old Brown, the feeling ran among them, going out on a secret errand with his husky boys and bloodthirsty Wiener; there was fierce old Brown turning back with bowies and two-edged sabres, bent on striking, they were sure, some sudden desperate blow for the Free-Staters. A cheer trembled on the lips of a few, was caught by others, sent back swiftly until the whole crowd took fire, roaring out encouragement. They did not stop until the wagon and its outrider had passed from sight over the dip in the road leading back to Osawatomie.

Later the eight men camped in the gully. Then Brown told them his plan; and there was the pleading of Oliver against it, and the old man flaming with Scripture known by heart. There was the startled silence of the rest who felt his power, each of them, felt it like fire and granite. And in the end there was Oliver's "I stay" rending him as he said it; and a troubled sleep in the damp whispering grass under the willows.

All these things Townsend remembered now, sitting in the wagon-bed, thinking:

It is like a bad dream.

Slowly, unbearably, the hours crept to their end. There was no curve in the day to ease the restlessness of the waiting men; no rise of the sun to height and then the waning that would give them a sense of passing time. The day was dead gray, each moment of it; it stood still under a blanched sky. They had only the writhing weight of their thoughts.

"Jesus!" cried Hen Thompson suddenly. "I can't stand this waiting!"

"We'll wait," said the old man, gray as slate.

It was five o'clock. Wiener took a piece of cold meat from his bag and began to chew on it. He crunched the bone, with a pant and a sucking like a dog's. They listened, watching him as though his sucking were significant. When he finished the first piece, he took another and began upon it. Then Salmon snarled:

"Quit it, will you, Wiener! Quit your slobbers!"

"Huh? Don't you like it? Maybe I'll use a gold fork for you. Are you scared? I'm hungry, see?"

Six o'clock came. The air had been turning warmer; now suddenly the mist began to fade and clear blue patches showed through. Soon there was a great swept twilight sky, and over the western trees a deep rose flush from the departed sun. Oliver stared into the glow and passed a trembling hand over his forehead. A little later full night was down over the gully and a great warm star was low in the sky. There would be a moon.

They waited, watching the old man's every move. They were near the end of endurance. But he sat, still and smoldering. In good time, he thought, he would say: Men, get your arms. In good time, in His time, the Lord's work would be done.

≡ * 20 * ≡

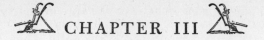

CHAPTER III

Judah Bleeding in the Snow

TOWNSEND'S WAGON had creaked out of the camp, with Wiener outriding. Soon after, there sounded a great clattering of hoofs along the Lawrence road, and a cavalry detachment swirled up in a yellow cloud. Lieutenant Church, U. S. Army, called, "Break up this camp."

The Army was in control now, he said, Atchinson had been commanded to cease hostilities, the pro-slaver forces were disbanding. Get back to your homes, he said, everything is quiet again.

Quiet? What about Lawrence, bitterly asked John, old Brown's first son, who was leader of the Osawatomies; how about Lawrence? Would the town spring up from the smoking ruins, would the presses leap back from the river, and the dead move living again? Everything is quiet now, the Army is in control, John repeated bitterly. But they made sure to keep well out of sight until it was too late to help. All right, they had a government which was on the side of the slavers; they would turn about, they would go back to the settlements. But this wasn't the end, he said, feeling a hopeless rage within; this was only the beginning. They could stand only so much, they had reached the breaking point. Lieutenant Church shrugged his shoulders. He had his commands. Move on, disband, get back to your homes. Everything is quiet again.

Quiet, thought John uneasily, giving the word "march" to the little company. Quiet . . . ? There was an old man out somewhere with wrath and two-edged sabres. Let's get home, the son thought, let's get ready to defend our homes. What were they doing now, his brothers and the old man; had they struck already? I'm scared for what might come, he thought, remembering black-eyed Wealthy and young Johnny back alone at the settlement.

The company had cheered old Brown as he rode out with his boys in Townsend's wagon. One man had not. Jason Brown had not. Look, he had thought, there goes the wagon, and how will they return, with what guilt? They won't tell me anything, they say I have no guts for a man's work. And I don't want guts, not if it means hardness and blood. Oh, what a devil eggs him! He thinks it's God, but it might just as well be the devil. He and his God, scheming together, he and the destiny he talks about, the destiny laid down for him since the beginning of time. How the thought drives him, how it bodes evil for all of us! There are my brothers riding out with him now, dragged into his mad schemes. They won't tell me anything, but I know my father. He'll drag us into some wildness, he'll kill our peace.

These had been Jason's thoughts as the wagon creaked from the camp. Now as he trudged in the dust back toward Osawatomie, they were still in his mind, magnified with brooding. But there was far more than this moment's fear and its presentiment of evil to plague him. For here was a man with a deep illness in him. There was stuff for ague and ache in the limbs and throats that felt sore. They had names for such ills, you could feel them and say: "Here it swells" or "This is the pain" and rubbing would help or thick burning medicines. But Jason had none of these, his was not of the body; and he would have stared if someone had told him he was sick. But old Brown unwittingly told him that very thing a thousand times, and never dreamed that his own share in the son's illness was great:

"You have no guts for a man's work."

There it was. He had no guts for a man's work. To be a man in old Brown's world you had to bear a cross, there needed to be some stringency in living. From their childhood to that very day the shadow of his narrowness had hung over them, killing laughter and ease in living. When Jason was eight, he had a cherished companion, Judah, a beautiful young gray shepherd-dog. After a time Judah grew fond of a neighbor's children, romping with them away from Brown's hearth. One day the tight-lipped father dragged Judah into the snow-filled backyard, and before the horror-stricken boy, shot the dog through the head. "Your beasts have got to be faithful, else they have no right to live," he said as the magnificent young creature writhed to death. Then it lay still, blood staining the snow whiteness crimson; and the boy felt such a revulsion that all the day he was trembling and faint. For months he was sick with grief, the sense of his father's heartlessness growing dreadfully in him all the while. As the years passed and he came into manhood that sense stayed with him. Voiced again and again with unrelenting grimness, he heard these words, the old man's lodestone for conduct: *Let the grand reason that one course is right and another wrong be kept continually before your mind.* He never forgot the words—nor Judah bleeding in the snow.

There it was then, his illness which no medicine could help. He was not formed for bitter living, and all the living he had ever known had been bitter. He did not have his father's grain for suffering; he had need for tender ways and amenities, for humane graces and the placid flow of time. He had been an eager boy; now he was crushed and wasting. "I expect nothing but to endure hardness," said old Brown; but the wintry negative which alone could give texture to the gray man's days meant the slow dissolution of the son's.

It was the struggle to break free, to somehow find his true way, that had brought Jason to Kansas. All the Browns were migratory, restless. The old man had lived here, there; in the East, in Ohio; in a mountain region under the shadow of peaks, by the side of a river in a lowland. He had grown crops and tanned leather; had been a breeder of blooded horses and had nurtured vineyards. He was a Puritan in rigor, but not in love for an unchanging hearth. And the sons shared this restlessness. But in Jason, added to it, was the need for escape. When their uncle, the Reverend Samuel Adair, wrote from Kansas that the country was glorious—he had been there for a month in the springtime—that life was bountiful and there was a chance for a man with willingness to go far, the Brown boys decided that they would leave for the Territory. For Jason the name "Kansas" came like a wind of hope, it gave a sudden lilt to his depression. Maybe, he thought, he could live contented there. It would be a new start, he would re-shape the welter of his life. There was nothing good in Ohio to keep him. At that very time a drought was grievous upon the land, full over the middle north, such a drought as even the oldest settlers could not remember. Each day they went out hopelessly to the fields. The air was glazed with heat. A dry breath rustled through the shrivelled maize; and all day long there was the mournful patter of wizened fruit falling from their boughs among the dead leaves. The cattle and sheep, fed now on dried hemlock buds and green stalks failed of corn, were falling in their tracks, not to move again. Twice, to add to the calamity, summer frosts nipped the vegetable beds which with nursing might have survived. They would lose almost everything, it was certain.

That was the way things were in Ohio when Adair's letter came. So they would move, the Brown boys decided; and hope for the new life lightened their gloom. Come out to Kansas, they urged the old man. He refused. He had lost things before, knew the feeling of it. "I'll move back to Elba," he said. Elba was in the Adirondacks. They had lived there before coming to Ohio; it was a bleak mountain place, fierce in winter. When they urged him again, with that strange desperate secrecy which he had always for them, he said, "I've got plans. Other plans." They could see that in some grim way he was glad for the change. Often during the last years he had said, "I'm keeping my affairs ready to wind up at a minute's notice. I'm getting on in years. Maybe some day soon, there'll be a duty calling. I want to be ready." So he was wasting nothing in regret for the drought. Life was as it was. You fought it tooth and nail and no quarter asked —you worried only about your eternal soul. The drought was bad. Well, he was going back to the East. He had his plans.

If Uncle Adair's letter set Jason to dreaming of better times in Kansas, it served to excite the others in a different way too. For as John said, "things were in a heave"; something big was in the air, the whole country was stirring. To glowing accounts of the climate and rich soil of Kansas, Uncle Adair added: "Good true men will be needed out here." And they knew what that meant. A bill had just been passed, the Kansas-Nebraska Bill. It left to settlers in Kansas and all Territories the right to decide whether slavery was to exist in their regions or not. There would be a struggle, good true men would be needed. Such an appeal, added to the restlessness of the Brown boys and the meagreness of their living in Ohio, was irresistible. For this question of the black man's bondage was for them a living question. From the earliest days they could remember it had been set before them by their father, darkly, hatefully. They had a heritage of free men, he would say. They heard often how a Peter Brown had come to America with the Mayflower company in a small vessel, to worship God after the bidding of his own soul. In the family album it was written that John Brown's grandfather had died "in the War for Independence, a Captain of the Ninth Company or Train-band 9, in the 18th Regiment of the

Connecticut Colony." And in Ohio a huge straight old man of eighty-four was still living, "Oaken" Brown, John Brown's father; who would say, his grizzled white head high:

"I am an Abolitionist. We are not loved by many, that I know. But I have no confession to make for being one. Since my childer days I've helped black men get free of that curse. I'm near the end of my days and I think I shall die an Abolitionist."

He was so full of a fierce independence that even in this long wane of his life he would not live with his own children, lest he burden them; and worked with beautiful and pathetic pride a tiny farm with the aid of a young colored boy whose freedom he had bought. He had been a leader in the shipping of slaves to Canada along the Underground Railroad route and loved to talk of old days. In his failing mind he told again and again the same stories of slave-running.

"I have no hatred to Negroes," he would say to the black boy who listened in patient stupidity. "When a child four or five years old, one of our neighbors had a slave brought from Guinea. That was the year my father was called to the army. It was in 'Seventy-six. He was called and soon left his work undone and my mother to be a widow. Well, in August, a good neighbor, except that he shouted oaths with gout-pains . . . his name slips me . . . well, he let my mother have the labor of his slave. Captain John Fast of West Simsbury, a good man save that he kept poor souls like you low in bonds . . . Captain Fast, he let my mother have the help of his slave to plough a few days. I used to go out in the field with Sam, and he carried me on his back and I fell in love with him. Aye, fell in love with him, with his back like a tree and good warm singin', but he worked but a few days and went home sick with shivers, and quick as you can wink, almost, he was dead. When they told him he would die Sam said he was goin' home to Guinea and wanted vittles put up for the way. As I recollect it, that was the first funeral I ever attended in the days of my youth." Then: "Since then I have been an Abolitionist. I am so near to the end of my life I think I shall die an Abolitionist."

And there, strongest force in their lives, was old Brown himself.

So it was decided. They would leave for Kansas. In the fall of that year, old Brown, away from home, wrote to them:

". . . and if any of my family are disposed to go to the Territories with a view to help defeat Satan and his legions in that direction I have not a word to say; but I feel committed to operate in another part of the field. If I were not so committed I would be on my way to Kansas already. One thing I do not fear to advise and urge, and that is the 'habitual fear of the Lord which is the beginning of wisdom.' Commending you all to His everlasting mercy, I am your father . . ."

He did not linger in Ohio. He sold his Devon cattle, settled accounts, and by the winter's end, was back in the Adirondacks. Ma Brown, his son Watson, and the two little girls returned with him.

In April, Owen, Frederick and Salmon left Ohio for Kansas. They were to get things ready. They took eleven head of cattle and three horses to Chicago by water, drove them through Illinois to Missouri and crossed. By the end of the month Owen was writing to his brother John back in Ohio:

". . . And Fred and Salmon say too they never was in a country that begun to please them as well. And I will say that the present prospect for health, wealth and usefulness much exceeds even my most sanguine anticipations. I know of no country where a poor man endowed with a share of common sense and with health can get a start so easy. If we can succeed in making this a Free State a great work will be done for mankind. . . ."

In a few weeks the two older brothers, John and Jason, were on their way with their families. John had Johnny, an only boy who was six; Jason two solemn little fellows, Austin five, and Tommy four. The Browns had sold out completely. "A new start," Jason had said to his young wife, Ellen; "a new start altogether." With her warm eyes in an eager face she smiled up at him: "A new start, Jay. Things are going to be different from now on. Something tells me. We'll start new altogether." So Jason took only a box of fruit trees—he dreamed always of great full orchards which would be his own—and some grape vines. And John left everything too; everything except his buxom black-haired Wealthy and their young one, and the new plough he had bought the year before and hated to let go.

They got nicely to St. Louis. The long train trip which to others might have seemed uncomfortable and tedious, was for them, in the flush of anticipation, all very exciting; a let-down from the strain of the bitter drought time. John was enthusiastic, like a boy; in high fettle he would say again and again as the train bore them slowly south and to the west: "Things look good to me, Jay, things are going to turn up good, you watch," and Jason too was in a stir, in spirits unusual for him. "We'll start right in hard," he said. He saw rolling prairies, rich land without end and gentle wooded streams. He saw in prospect their cattle roaming in great herds; fields of grain bending beautifully rich in the wind and sun; and best of all a precious peace in living. And the two women were like young girls on a lark. They whispered, and laughed together at little nothings. They scolded the children endearingly. They were very happy. They were going to Kansas for a new start.

Then came the boat trip along the Missouri to Kansas City. There were no railroads west of St. Louis; you went by water or stage coach. In this season the water was very low in the river-bed; the going would be bad. But the stage would cut deeply into their funds, scarce enough. Ellen, who burnished plain things to a kind of beauty with the quick fine glow of her spirit, said: "I'd rather, anyway. It'll be fun going by boat. It's cooler and there's always interesting things to watch."

Thus, when the little river-steamer "New Lucy" wheezed out from the St. Louis landing at the fall of an early May night, the Browns were aboard. They stood on deck by the forward rail, watching as the boat swung full into the Missouri, prow westward and with a harsh steady clanging of bells. A glow was at the hearts of the elders as the shore slipped back. They were getting nearer to Kansas. The boat-trip, a short run by stage, and then at last they would be there. "A new start altogether," Jason had said, his gentle tired eyes brightened with hope. He stood now with his hand on dark sturdy little Austin's head.

"It's up that way, boys," he said, pointing into the river dimness. "The Territory lays up that way."

Austin followed with his eyes the father's pointing. He had a serious face. "What's the Territory mean, Pa?"

"It's Kansas, son. It's where you're going."

"Isn't it nice from here, it's beautiful!" said Ellen, tremulous, bending to kiss the head of sleepy freckled Tommy. "Look, Tommy, look! Do you see shining there, like candles and lamps?" Shoreward there were lights, colored lights, green and blue and red slipping from moored boats and landings into the water. They gleamed from the windows of houses set in the wooded heights along the river-edge, more showing each moment here and there in the dusk, like early stars in the sky. The Browns stood watching, a glow at their hearts.

Later while Ellen and Wealthy were settling the boys for sleep in the small tight berths, the two brothers sat outside on the narrow deck, talking. The box of fruit-trees and the small plough were outside the cabin door.

"Believe me," said John, putting out his foot to the plough, "I'm itching to cut this into good loam." He went on: "I guess the boys are heavy in hay cutting about now. Owen said it was rich for miles, that it'll keep the stock winter-fed. He was figuring like this—hay got in by the boys all these weeks to stock up heavy against the cold season, and ground clearing, and maybe a few fences put up if there's time. Then when we get there with the plough we'll cut in for about twelve acre of sod corn. We'll have to work fast. Old settlers tell the boys you ought to calculate on having planting all done by middle spring. It'll be middle May when we get there. But we'll get white beans going and a vegetable patch, mebbe, case the corn fails. . . . But you know, Jay, I've got a feeling about things. Corn's not going to fail, nothing's going to fail for us this time. It's about our time, eh Jay?"

Jason smoking his pipe nodded dreamily.

The next night it was different.

"Don't tell anything to the girls," said John in a low guilty voice. "There's no use scaring them."

Jason sat with restless hurt eyes. Was that, he thought, what they could look forward to? They had come with a plough and hope for peace. The brothers, taking a turn about the narrow deck, had seen a violent swaggering crowd, heavily armed. They were men from the South, it was in the sound of their talk; they were pro-slavers and it was plain they were not going to Kansas to furrow and seed and grow. The brothers, walking about, had come across a man sitting in a chair tilted back against a cabin wall. His feet, thrust into the narrow space between wall and railing, blocked their way. He looked up at them insolently as they waited, making no effort to move. He was hatless and had matted red hair.

"We'd like to get by," said John pleasantly.

The man deliberately spat tobacco juice over the rail, then stared brazenly at them. "Whar ye frum?"

"Say," said John slowly. He had a bad temper, easily aroused. "We only asked to get by. What's all the fuss for?"

"Whar ye frum?"

"Come on back," urged Jay in a whisper, pulling his brother's sleeve. He could see a flush reddening up the other's neck.

"Let go, Jay. . . . We're from Ohio, if it means anything to you. I'd ask where you're from, only I don't give a hog's snoot. Let's get by."

"Ye don't, huh?" the stranger said, ugly. "Ye damn Yankees, ye'll larn fast——"

John's foot came out in a quick thrust. It caught the angled leg of the chair which shot upward from beneath the red-haired man. He went crashing down, his head banging against the wall. A bottle beneath the chair was smashed to pieces, corn whiskey dribbling from it along the deck. The man scrambled up in a rage. "Ye god damn . . . !" He was a duck-legged fellow, with weak glassy eyes filled now with venom. In the light from the lantern above the cabin door he blinked wildly, like a bloated rusty owl confounded by the sun.

"Ye northern scum!"

But the brothers were imposing in their hugeness.

"Git by! It won't make no difference! Ye'll never git to Kansas to steal niggers! Ye wun't live to git thar!"

"There's no use worrying," said John again, just before the girls came out.

"You shouldn't have done it. We can't get into any trouble with the girls and the kids along. You know we can't."

"I couldn't take that ruffian's spittle."

"Did . . . did you hear what he said . . . about not reaching Kansas?"

"He's a slaver, sounded like a Missouri man. They hate Northerners worse than snakes. But don't worry, he was just a bullying kind, a big talker. Nobody'll bother us if we mind our own affairs." With a feeling of guilt John saw the other's pale face.

Like the old man, Jason thought, just like the old man. He didn't see an end to a matter, only the moment's passion. And Jason had a sudden sense that every outcropping of the father's ways in the sons somehow troubled peace, had a consequence of unrest.

≡ * 29 * ≡

"It was long getting them to sleep," said Wealthy as the two women came out to the deck. "It's stuffy as a hay-loft, without the sweetness."

"We took a turn around," said John. "Nothing much doing."

"Austin wasn't so well," said Ellen, a little anxious. "His face was hot. His eyes didn't look right. They were too shiny."

"Don't fret yourself so!" scolded Wealthy. "It's only the air change. He'll be hopping around tomorrow smart as a squirrel."

Jason sat without speaking. He was thinking of the plough and the fruit-trees and "You wun't live to git thar!"

"Only three days more," said Ellen brightly, putting out her hand to Jason's.

"It's slow moving," he said, gloomy. "You can almost feel the bottom cutting through mud."

"Yes . . . the river's low. . . . But we're going steady, Jay. It'll only be three more days."

"I don't like river water. . . ."

He's feeling low again, thought Ellen sadly. There's no staying gladness in him.

"I always get the feeling there's something sick about river water, something dragging up and laying over you. You can smell it like the three dead moles we pulled up out of the well last summer."

"You're silly!" said Wealthy sharply. "Quit talking that way! Why it's grand out!" She breathed deeply. Upon their faces the air was soft with full spring. Beneath them the water was at its ceaseless murmuring. A whistle brooded far away in the river distance, rending faintly the young night.

"Rivers are like us," said Jason slowly as the sound died. His pipe had gone out and he held it limply in his hand, spilling the ashes. "Like people. They aren't all the same. . . . There's the Hudson. Clean. Fresh. Good to sit by or swim or ride down it. Others are like this Missouri—mixed up, with sick smells and crazy lights goin' in 'em."

If ever it occurred to him to simulate for Ellen's peace of mind a light-heartedness he was far from feeling, he never acted upon the thought. So long had he been yielding to melancholy that he had come to need her anxious solicitude to give him a sense of justification. Thus, though he would have thought it contemptible to tell her outright of his fears, he did not hesitate to brood now in a way that shattered her tranquillity far more than any forthrightness could have done. If he had told her of the scuffle, young Ellen would have answered in some fashion: "Don't worry, Jay! He's just a boaster! You meet that kind all over, up North too. Don't worry," and though she would have been more than a little frightened within, the mere fact of her speaking thus bravely upon a definite untoward circumstance would have bolstered her and tightened the marrow of resistance which was deep and certain beneath her gentle exterior. But this vague grieving of his—she could seek to meet it with patience and the strength of her love, but ever futilely, ever with the slow unperceived diminution of her own vitalness.

"It's a pity, John," said Wealthy firmly, later. Jason and Ellen had gone in. "It's your own brother, but I can't help saying it. It's a shame for him to act so. Elly tries so hard, but he bears her down."

"Jay's not well," he said.

"Then why doesn't he act like a manly body? . . . If you ask me——"

"I'm not asking you!" he said with sudden sharpness. She stopped, offended. Quickly he was regretful. "Wealthy," he said, his voice almost a pleading. "You oughtn't blame Jay. I'm sorry for Elly too. But there's things beyond a man. Jay can't help himself. He's not well somehow. . . ." He hesitated, averting his eyes. "It's in him, that way of seeing things dark. He can't help it, Wealthy."

"There's more in a man's liver," she answered in a dudgeon, "to make him see dark than in his head. If he'd take a mighty physic regular and put his shoulder to working and have a smile and jokes for Elly, he'd be all right. And I mean it!"

"You go around in circles, Wealthy. Smiling don't make you well. It's being well that makes you smile. No, and it's not Jay's liver, either. He's strong as iron. . . ." He shook his head. "No, Wealthy, he needs pitying. You oughtn't judge him severe."

"Well, he won't get pitying from me! You've stood trouble too, all of us have! You've got to meet it head on and no weeping! A man has to be a man!"

"I know, Wealthy."

He sat saddened, unlike his wont, thinking: Ah, Wealthy could talk. People could talk and in a way be right. Yet, you couldn't get around blood and what you were made of. Blaming

≡ ＊ 31 ＊ ≡

Jay was like scolding a tree, sprung with a blight, for not being proper. Aye, Wealthy could blame, not knowing. But he, John, knew. About Jay, and the blood he came from; about the warp that was on them all from their mother's strangeness—Dianthe Brown, untimely dead these many years—and the dark twist that had been in her poor head. How get around that, wife Wealthy? How could he himself be sure that the ravening ills of his young days would not return again? How, Wealthy, understand, not knowing? Hush, Wealthy, hush, we're only human.

Late that night Ellen awoke from a troubled sleep. The tight little room was oppressively hot; a curious offensive odor thickened the air. Her head was aching from the staleness. Then in the dark she heard young Austin whimpering from his shelf-like berth. No wonder, she thought, it's so heavy in here; and slipped from the side of Jason, deep asleep. She opened the door wide; cool fresh river-air flowed in, grateful upon her. Outside it was very still; there was no sound of living things, only the faint susurration of the unsleeping river. She breathed deeply; and went back. Still the boy was whimpering. A little worried now, she sought his berth, feeling her way in the darkness. Her bare feet slithered in something slimy, and her flesh tightened at the cold touch. Again the bad odor smote her nostrils, filling her, freshened only an instant ago by the lustral night, with a sudden nausea.

"Mom!" the boy called. She groped for him. First she touched tiny Tom, drowned in sleep; then found Austin and was gripped convulsively by his small hands. "Mom!" His mouth brushed her cheek moistly, like the nuzzling of a little animal; his breath was oddly cold. She slid her hands to his face and was frightened by its clammy throbbing feel. His gown was wet to her touch. Trembling, she fumbled about the small table and with difficulty set the lamp burning. By its fitful light she saw his gray face, his teeth clicking with chill, and the slobber he had spewed upon the floor.

"Oh my bunny!" she whispered in consternation. She held him close, her lips upon his hair, murmuring to soothe him.

"Look Mom, I couldn't help it." The little fellow showed her his smelly stained gown, shame upon his face.

"Oh my bunny, you're sick!"

"I hear noises, Mom."

"It's nothing, it's nothing, Mom's here."

"I'm cold, Mom."

Finally, afraid, she woke Jason. He got up with a scared face, and bent over the boy. "What's it, son, what's it?" he kept repeating, rubbing the moist little hands between his own huge ones. After a while, struck by a sudden thought, he lifted Tommy from the other's side and laid the sleeping chit in his own berth. With his shirt he mopped up the vomit from the floor and flung it through the door over the boatside. He gave the boy some tepid water from the table-jug. Then, helplessly—it was the first bad illness come over either of the two boys—they watched through the dim hours; till outside, the river-gulls began their calling, half-jeer, half-moan. Soon the first grayness of day came; then the sun; and they saw that the boy was worse. A pain was cutting through his vitals like a stab; he gave out fluttering breaths. Panic-stricken, Jason called Wealthy and John.

"Sakes!" the black-haired woman exclaimed when she saw the youngster. "Why didn't you rouse me?" Her heart constricted. "Get Tommy out of here! Get some fresh water! Some brandy! And quinine too! The captain will have 'em! Hurry!"

Jason sought out the captain of the "New Lucy." He was a small hairy man, wearing a black cap and a soiled buff satin vest over a black sweater.

"No, there ain't no doctor on this here boat."

"My kid's awful sick!"

"Keep him close. I don't want no plagues runnin' through my boat."

"Plagues! What do you mean—plagues? . . . He's just sick, that's all! No plagues! He's got pains in the stomach! He'll be all right!"

"People been known to croak. . . . Where you from?"

"We're going to Kansas. From Ohio."

"Huh, might have known it. You damn Yankees come down here bringin' brats and stuff fer settlin'! You ain't got any right down here, and mark me you'll find worse bearin' ahead of you!"

"I don't want to quarrel, captain! My kid's sick!"

"Well . . . you can have quinine—" his eyes went sly—"at ten dollars. Two pills, that'll be twenty dollars. . . . Keep him close. Don't want no plagues runnin' through my boat."

Evening came again; again the room was strange with candle-shadows. Often outside a boat whistle mourned, now far,

≡ ∗ 33 ∗ ≡

now close; once there was a flurry of sound from a passing craft—
laughter and calls and the ringing of bells, fading quickly. Jason
and Ellen watched in terror over Austin. Wealthy was by them;
John was in the next room with his own youngster and Tommy.
The sick boy seemed to have no pain now, only a consuming
thirst. A blue pallor was over all his body, thinned unbelievably
during the brief time of his prostration; and his breath still came
in icy gasps. But at about midnight the little fellow seemed to
slip into a deep slumber, the first in thirty hours.

"Look!" Ellen whispered, her eyes lighting. "He's sleeping,
Jay! He's sleeping!"

"It's the quinine, Elly! It's helping him, like the captain
said!"

Tears sprang in the girl-wife's eyes. "Lord God, forgive us if
we have done wrong things! Father in Heaven, let my boy stay
alive!"

In the morning Austin Brown was dead of cholera.

"You bury him tonight, or he goes overboard," the captain
said brutally. "It's the rule of the river. I'll stop for a half-hour,
and for stoppin' it'll cost you a hundred dollars." He smirked.
"He can go overboard for nothin'." (God damn you, he thought,
it's one less of you.)

So they buried him on the outskirts of a little Missouri town
during a terrific thunderstorm. In a streaming darkness broken
only by jags of lightning, Jason and John dug a grave; while
Ellen holding a wet snuffed pine-torch, Wealthy, and the two
frightened children, stood by, weeping. Then, the young body
wrapped in its death mould, the Browns crept back stricken to
the landing. There was nothing to return to, only a black river
and the wind mourning and the rage of the storm. The "New
Lucy" had gone, "servin' the damned nigger-stealers right."

They made the rest of the journey by stage. They were almost penniless; they had lost the plough and the fruit trees. A
few weeks after their arrival John was writing to the old man:
". . . and we have among us five Revolvers, 1 Bowie-knife, one
middling good rifle, 1 small pocket pistol and 2 slung shot. Send
us guns at once, Father. We need them more than bread." In
October the guns came—and old Brown with them, bearing from
Missouri the exhumed remains of Jason's boy. He found his
family living in tents, shivering before small fires in the early

winter winds and icy rains. They were enfeebled by ague and chills; the crops that had been raised were not cared for; there was no meat, little sugar, and nothing to make bread with save corn ground by great labor in a hand-mill two miles off. It was the "new life" for which Jason Brown had left Ohio, it was "a new start, Elly, a new start altogether."

* * * * *

And now on this day, a year later, a man with a gentle mouth, importuning eyes, and "no guts," Jason Brown, was trudging in the ranks of the Osawatomies, through the yellow choking dust, back toward the Free-State settlements. "Move on, disband," Lieutenant Church of the Regulars had commanded. "Get back to your homes. Atchinson's forces are dispersed. Everything is quiet again."

But somewhere out in the Kansas wilds there was an old man with wrath and two-edged sabres. In good time, he would say: Men, get your arms. In good time, in His time, the Lord's work would be done.

CHAPTER IV

"A Mighty and a Terrible, Which Regardeth Not Persons"

NORTHWARD THROUGH the woods he led them, a ghostly company moving in the soft night with sabres and guns and knives. They came to a narrow run of water. It was shallow, thigh-deep; and quickly they waded across. The woods began to thin out; soon they got to a clearing which rose very slowly to a good height. They followed it up, swishing, though they tried not to, through the tall grass. It's a ripe time, thought the old man, throbbing. Even the grass is good. We'll have to be on the move and there'll be food for horses. It's a ripe time, ready for a reckoning. To them he called back in a low voice:

"Slow now, we're getting close!"

They were near the top of the rise. Ahead of them a small cabin was dark against the pale spring sky. They came up to it like shadows. There was no light showing. The old man stood before the door, listening. Then he rapped twice on the timbers, hard with the butt of his revolver. The sound rang hollow in the stillness, and a quiet followed. Again he rapped. This time they heard a sliding noise by the wall to the left. They scattered back hastily. They knew the noise. It was a rifle being rammed through chinks in the logs.

"We can't take chances," whispered the old man. "Shots will stir up the place. We'll have to move on."

"Let's get 'em out!" said Wiener low and savage.

"Drive 'em out!" echoed Salmon, the sabre trembling in his hand.

"We move, I say! If we wanted a fight we could have stayed with the men. There's different work to do. Quiet now, and follow me!"

Again they were moving in the night. Now the strain was intense. Drive 'em out, thought Salmon, quivering, that's what the old man ought to do. Like Sam Burns was tellin' me. You light candle-wick in oil and throw it in a window, then you can see in and they can't see through. We could drive 'em out.

Soon they were approaching another cabin with stealth. The Doyles lived there, Oliver remembered, sickened. There were three sons about his own age. Then suddenly, as if to add to the terror of the night, something hurtled through the air, crashing with terrific force against Frederick. It was a huge bulldog, a snarly slavering beast. It did not bark as it leaped twice, thrice at the giant. He swung frantically with his sabre, missing. The dog turned upon Townsend. The thin man shot the sabre out in a blind thrust. The animal went down writhing. Owen was upon it swiftly; in an instant it lay still, dead. Townsend shuddered. He could feel the cut of the sharp steel against flesh, against bone, the sickening rip of it. He saw blood on his blade, and his body went cold all over; a monstrous burning flared in his head.

"Wiener!" old Brown whispered. "Owen! Oliver! Come on! The rest wait here!"

≡ * 36 * ≡

The four crept to the cabin door. The old man listened; then rapped with the gun butt. A moment passed, with the faint murmur of voices within. Then a gleam of candlelight showed through the chinks. A man's voice called thickly:

"Who's thar?"

"Strangers. Friends of Wilkinson, Allie Wilkinson. Can you tell us how to get to him?"

"It's a hell of a hour to come visitin'! . . . Wait a minute, 'n I'll tell ye."

Soon the door was opened, and a stocky man half-dressed and bare-footed stood sleepily before them. "Pullin' people outa bed," he grumbled, with heavy eyes. ". . . Yeah, I know Wilkinson. Ye git thar by followin'——"

"Move in!" Old Brown jammed his revolver tight against Doyle's heart. The other, fuddled, stared stupidly at the weapon.

"Move in! Quick!"

Doyle slowly stepped backward. There was no fear in his face, only an irritated astonishment. "I'll be damned!" he said. Old Brown and the three others pressed into the rude room. There was a wide bed on the farther side. An elderly woman watched them from it. She was muffled beneath the bed-clothes, only her graying head showing. Two little girls cowered in a bedstead. The strange men with their gleaming arms looked fearful in the dim candle light.

"Who are ye?" the woman called in a fright.

"We're from the army," said Brown harshly. "From the Northern army! No resisting now!"

"My ol' man ain't done nothin'! Ye daren't hurt 'im! Ye haven't the right!"

"What the hell do ye want here?" cried Jim Doyle.

"Make your peace with God, Doyle."

A tall blond young fellow came in from the next room. He was in ragged underclothes.

"What the hell's goin' on here? Say, Pa . . ."

Owen covered him with his revolver. "Get up against the wall."

"For God's mercy!" the woman began to wail. "Ye can't harm 'im, ye can't. Didn't I tell ye, Jim, oh, didn't I tell ye what ye'd be gettin' fer yer course? Now they'll end ye!"

She stormed in the bed, keeping the covers about her. The little girls began to whimper. Then two other boys in rough shirts and drawers came into the room, frightened. One was about twenty, the other sixteen. In an instant they were backed against the wall with their father and brother.

"Ye murderers!" screamed the mother.

"Hush, Mahala, hush," said Doyle, white to the eyes.

"You're pro-slavers, Doyle," said Brown. "You've——"

"Ye Abolitionist bastards!" the blond fellow said in a rage.

"Wiener. Take him out." The Austrian, his pig-eyes glittering and the mouth in its graven leer, prodded the blond fellow toward the door with his revolver. The boy went out, flinging over his shoulder:

"Ye Abolitionist bastards!"

"Now you, Doyle." Old Brown nodded to Owen. The woman jumped violently from the bed. She was short and fat, in a woolsey bed-dress.

"Oh, leave 'im be, for God's mercy."

Doyle, shoved ahead by Owen, called back: "Hush, Mahala, hush."

"Don't take 'em all!" she pleaded. "Leave me Willy! He's only a baby! Don't take 'em all!" She grasped the old man's arm convulsively. He looked at her grimly; then at the boy. After a pause, he said:

"Get to your room, William."

The boy crept back with stricken eyes, his dirty drawers flapping about his thin white legs. Old Brown prodded the second son forward. As they went out Oliver heard the weeping of the little girls in the room behind and the mother's long quivering moan.

O my God! thought Townsend a few minutes later, coming down the road from the Doyle barn with Hen Thompson, each leading a horse. O my God, they've done it!

In the moonlight, two hundred yards beyond the house, they had stood about the pro-slaver and his two boys. Doyle had been white as death, but silent. The younger son pleaded: "Ye can't do it, fellers! Ye can't kill us like this!" The elder son half-wept with fury: "Ye bastards! They'll get ye fer this!" Oliver was back a little from the group, his sabre held limp in his hand. Fred, staring wildly, was by his side. He held a burning pine-knot. Owen and Salmon were close, waiting. Wiener held his blade poised; he watched old Brown with lustful eyes.

"You're going to be an example, Doyles," the old man said.

≡ ∗ 38 ∗ ≡

"You'll afflict men no longer."

"Don't do it!" pleaded the younger.

"Ye bastards!" raged the brother. "Ye God——"

The old man nodded sharply, fiercely. Wiener and the waiting sons leaped forward, the sabres flashing murderously. Doyle went down immediately without a sound, pierced through the heart by a thrust from the Austrian. The older boy fell, his head hacked open from top to chin. The younger Doyle writhed in anguish as they cut at him, but he did not go down quickly. His night-shirt reddened as he swayed. Then there was a single sickening slash heard above the others, the sound of flesh ripping; and the boy, his eyes twisting crazily, toppled to the ground. They stood above him, panting, their faces ravenous, like beasts; while blood oozed from his mouth and head to the tender young grass.

O my God! thought Townsend, coming down from the barn, leading a horse.

"Come on!" said the old man. "There's no time to lose!"

He led the way. Soon they were in the woods again, following a trail. Fred's eyes were drawn again and again to Salmon's sabre. Once he bent a little, touching it; then he drew his hand away in a jerk as though it were a venomous thing. He shuddered, wiping his fingers on his shirt.

"You did it in cold blood!" called Oliver suddenly. His voice was hysterical; the words writhed up in the night. The old man kept going relentlessly.

"In cold blood!" Oliver called again.

This time his father halted and turned in low wrath: "How long will you vex me? I do it with all my heart, you blind one. *For the Lord God is a great God, a mighty and a terrible, which regardeth not persons!* Are you afraid? Then go home. Go home or be still. I am not afraid."

Again they were off feverishly through the moon-filled woods. It was not yet midnight. Again they came to the edge of a small clearing. A shack loomed in the dimness. A dog began barking.

"Careful now!" cautioned the old man as they moved up silently. "They may be ready."

O my God! thought Townsend. He recognized the place. They can't do this. Why, I know Busby. He was kind to us the year we came out. He helped us with seed and food when we were hard against it. He's for slaves, but he was kind to us! Townsend's heart beat to bursting as they drew very close. He must do something. He couldn't let this happen to Busby. He would shout, he would warn them somehow. Then even as the thought formed itself, he was conscious of a sudden hasty scattering about him. He stood bewildered alone before the cabin. He heard a sliding sound in the chinks of the logs and it meant only one thing to him. They knew then, he thought, inside they knew and would protect themselves. He felt a sweeping joy— and the following instant there was a flash, and a roar in his ears and something tearing terribly at his body. Townsend writhed to the grass, shot through the vitals with a charge of slugs.

You're dying, Townsend. Oliver has slid forward to the cabin and dragged you back, but it's no use, you're dying. He'll stay with you the rest of the night, trying to stem the blood; he'll watch over you, staring blindly after you've stopped moaning, after your life has flowed to the grass. The others will go about their black work again, leaving Oliver and you in the woods with the horses. But you won't know these things, you'll only know the gnawing agony in your inwards, you'll only moan and pray for death to come quick. Good-bye Townsend, thin man, with a scraggly black moustache and frightened eyes. You'll never tend those three sheep you just bought, you'll never again see the kids wrapped in your dimming heart, you won't ever see Millie again, Millie dreaming and heavy with your baby, Millie who was mother to Rob buried under the snow last year. O Christ, Townsend, you only wanted to be quiet and to get the loved ones going well in the new place, you only wanted to be happy, all together. O Christ, the tears go slowly down your thin face in agony and bewilderment. Die, Townsend, die in the night with slugs in you, and a huge dark boy crying by your side.

Up at Potawatomie Creek—it was midnight—Dutch Henry, pro-slaver, lay face downward in the shallows. By morning the water would wash out some of the brains from the clefts in his skull, and carry the blood away from the stump of his left arm.

"A fine hour to wake people up!" the voice behind the door grumbled. "Follow the road straight through till you meet the creek. That's Henry's crossing. Get across and the first house you hit before——"

"Come on out and talk!"

". . . What! . . . The hell you say!"

"Come out and show us the way. You'd better."

There was a silence inside. Then: "Say, boys, my wife's sick. Take it easy, will you? I'll tell you all you want to know."

The door opened a little and lamplight shone through. Instantly Brown pushed in, revolver in hand, followed by the rest. Wilkinson was a tall man with a hooked nose and eyes that were too close together. He was wearing a long sacklike sleeping gown. His wife, a faded little woman, lay in bed. A gray cat was curled in the corner of the room.

"Get your clothes on, Wilkinson."

The tall man gulped: "What for? What. . . . You're old Brown! I know you! You're old man Brown!"

The little woman scolded: "Why did you open, Allie? I told you not to open!"

"What do you want with me, Brown?"

"Get your clothes on. Hurry up."

"I'm a sick woman, Mr. Brown! Don't take Mr. Wilkinson away! I can't stay alone!"

"She's sick, Brown. Let me stay till I can get someone in to watch her."

"Get dressed."

"I won't run away, Brown! I'll be here tomorrow, any day you say. Only she's sick now and I can't leave her!"

Brown pulled the old straw hat lower over his eyes. He looked at the woman.

"You have neighbors."

"Oh, but I can't get them!" she cried. "I can't get them now!"

Dianthe, he thought, looked like her before she died.

"It matters not," he said.

"You have no heart in you, Mr. Brown!"

I have God in me, he thought.

"Come on, Wilkinson," he said. "Your time's up."

The tall man began to fumble desperately with some clothes on a chair. A wet drop was glistening in the end of his nose.

"Your boots!" the woman cried. "Don't forget your boots against the damp, Allie! And put something over you. You know the night air's bad for you!"

"Move out, Wilkinson."

They pushed him, half-dressed, toward the door.

"What are you going to do, Mr. Brown?" the woman called fearfully. "Where are you taking Allie?"

They went out, closing the door behind them.

"Henry, you and Fred get the horses from the stable. Look for saddles."

They hurried Wilkinson away, back toward the woods. Hen Thompson and Fred stood still, watching.

"I saw a saddle inside, Fred. Get it. I'll get the horses."

Fred opened the door and went in slowly. The thin woman was sitting up in the bed, weeping.

"Oh!" she cried when she saw the giant. "What have you done to Allie?"

"It's nothing," he said sadly, like a child who is grieved by an elder's weeping. "He'll be back soon."

"Don't leave me here alone! I'm very sick!"

He shook his yellow head. A wetness came to his eyes.

"They won't let me. Father won't let me."

"Fred! Fred!" It was Hen calling low outside. The giant went to the door, the saddle forgotten. The woman's anguished eyes followed him.

"Father won't let me," he said again, lifting the latch. Now a tear went down his face. "But don't be afraid. It's nothing. He'll be back."

The night's work was over. They were on horses, riding hard back to the ravine. Oliver had Townsend, dead, stretched over the pommel before him. Fred was up on Allie Wilkinson's shave-tail pony.

Clomp, clomp, clomp, the hoofs beat from the soft spring earth into Owen Brown's head. It's horse-thievery, he thought, remembering the hacked Doyle bodies in the road, but our lives aren't worth a bubble without them.

I told her it's nothing, thought the yellow-haired giant, whimpering softly, and now there's blood on Wiener's sword and Wilkinson's dead in the bushes.

You murderers, you murderers, Oliver Brown wanted to cry out to the night, God's will is done, God damn you murderers!

They'll all be against me now, thought the old man, but I had no choice. My heart was sick doing it. I didn't do it for revenge. They had to suffer because they were evil, not because they tormented me. It's better that a hundred evil men should die, than one man fighting for right. They'll all be against me now—but it was ordained, I had no choice.

CHAPTER V

The Fugitives

AT DUSK of the Sabbath day they slipped back to the Free-State camp, now by the Ottawa Creek. There were no cheers for their return as there had been for their going; a hostile ominous silence met them. Then Harley Williams, a lean man with heavy jaws, said darkly:

"Brown, move out quick. I'm captain here now, not your son. You murdered those men. You've put all our lives in danger, you've killed our last hope for peace. So get out quick or we'll hand you over. Stay clear of us from now on, do you hear, Brown? Stay clear of the settlement. We want none of you."

"We aim to stay clear," the old man said harshly. "You can go back to your homes. Shiver behind your doors, bow in the mud. We'll stay clear and fight. We'll give 'em blow for blow."

Then in the falling darkness, Jason, white and quivering, came to face his father.

"Did you kill those men on the Potawatomie?"

"I approved of it."

"Then you murdered! There's a sin on you!"

"God is my judge."

Jason turned, trembling as though with a mortal chill. He found Fred off on the side, staring with the eyes of a wild lost soul. He gripped Fred's shoulders.

"Fred, do you know who killed those men?"

"I can't tell you. Father won't let me."

"Did you help, Fred? Did you do it with your own hands?"

"No! No! I swear, Jay! When I saw what manner of work it was, I couldn't do it!"

The yellow-haired giant put his hand over his eyes. He began to weep.

≡∗43∗≡

And now the hunt was on. From Osawatomie to Palmyra the roads were lined with posses looking for a gray gaunt man. With the boys and the Austrian he made for the cover of the wild wood region, to stay low and secret for their lives. And southward John and Jason were riding fast on a single horse toward Osawatomie. Late that night the two fugitives reached a cabin. They knocked on the door.

"Who's there?"

"Jay and me!"

"Go away! We can't keep you here!"

"You've got to let us in, Uncle Adair!"

"We can't! Our lives are threatened, every minute we expect to have the house burned down over our heads!"

"Uncle Adair! Here are we alone. We've eaten nothing all day. Let us lay on the floor till morning . . . in the outhouse . . . anywhere!"

Then they heard their Aunt Florilla's voice.

"Did you have anything to do with the murders?"

"No, no! Jay didn't, I didn't!"

"Then come in. But we risk our lives in keeping you."

They gave the brothers a blanket on the floor by their bed; the four spoke in low fearful tones.

"Uncle Adair, I'm afraid for Elly and Tom! And I can't go near them, I might bring something terrible on them! Tomorrow, go for them, will you, Uncle Adair? Get them away from the settlement. Let them stay with you, let them stay here!"

"Get Wealthy, too," pleaded John.

They waited in the dark, listening, dreading to hear suddenly the beating of hoofs. They could not sleep; John lay groaning through the night. Once he said to his aunt:

"Florilla, I'm going mad! I feel I'm going mad!"

"Hush, you mustn't speak so! Things will be better."

In the still gloom of the earliest morning they heard a sound outside.

Adair crept to the door with a rifle. Then a low urgent knocking came.

"It's Owen! Let me in!"

"Get away! Get away quick as you can! You endanger our lives!"

"Only for tonight!"

≡＊44＊≡

"Not for a second! You're a vile murderer, you're a marked man!"

"I intend to be a marked man!"

They heard him riding away. Again there was a black breathing stillness, desperate as a nightmare. John began his groaning anew.

"I'm going insane, Florilla!"

When day came, the eldest son of Brown was insane.

CHAPTER VI

The Moon Is Not Up

CLEAR UPON the still Kansas night they heard the hoofbeats. The old man stood rigid as a startled hawk. Then he moved through the sedge, saying swiftly, "There's three, get to cover! Hold your pull till you're sure they're hostile! Maybe it's Owen with friends!" Friends, thought Oliver desolately, kneeling low in the muck behind a tangle of swamp creeper; friends, maybe it's the Doyles on a visit, maybe it's Mrs. Townsend coming to thank us! Frederick crouched by his side, uttering strange wild little sounds. They waited in the damp darkness as the beating came slowly closer and more insistent. Then suddenly it died, and the swamp immensity weighed upon them. Now they were quivering, but steeled too with a desperate icy anger. They would be dangerous, like beasts cornered. They knew there was no quarter for them.

The silence broke. Eastward there was a faint snapping, there was movement in the swamp. The sound rose nearer; a crashing of bodies through brush. Again it ceased sharply. In the stillness following they heard a muted twisting call, like an unknown bird's, twice drawn out. It was Owen's. His brothers knew it; it had sounded up in boy-games long ago, a quaver through the peaceful woods of a Pennsylvania farm. All this day they had been waiting for him in the gloom and the mists, silent almost as the marsh creatures peering invisible about them; their weapons close and the horses ready saddled. Since the Potawatomie blood they had gone forty hours without food; they dared not shoot game. "Owen, we need supplies," the old man had said, and the third son, without a question, rode off, only waving once his withered left arm.

Now he slipped in from the blackness, a sack hung over his shoulder. A man followed, leading two other horses. Brown met them, his rifle clutched tight; he peered with fierce distrust at the second man.

"What's this, Owen? Who is this?"

"It's Bondi. He gave me stuff." All the outlawed men were in close, watching intently.

"What do you want, Bondi?"

"I hope to help."

His words moved soft as honey, slow after the fierce questioning. He was small and frail; his eyes gleamed. It was not easy to tell whether he was young or old. He wore no hat, had thick dark hair almost to his shoulders; in the dimness his brow shone strangely white. They knew him, he ran a Free-State store near Lawrence.

"What gain are you expecting, Bondi?"

"None."

"We're hunted. If you're caught with us it will mean your life."

"I knew it when I came," he answered. ". . . I have nothing left. They have stolen everything, all my goods. My storehouse is ashes. My cabin is ashes. I have a grievance, you may trust me. . . . I will fight too. I was in uprisings in Hungary. I have thrown away my life many times to be free. You may trust me."

The old man was searching the thin high-cheeked face, thinking swiftly: We can move quicker with few. But I've got to think of later. Now we're hunted, we have to stay low, even our own are against us. But soon the slavers will tire, they'll find others to hound. Then we'll come out again to strike at them. I'll need men then. Some of these will go to their death. There must be fresh ones for the work.

He said harshly: "You can stay, Bondi. But understand me. There's one leader here. John Brown. You do as I say in everything, you take orders." His eyes bored into the other's. "We're struggling for a reason. Not for your hurt, not for mine. Not to be revenged for a grievance. There are humans low in bond. . . . You can stay. But remember that."

"Yes," Bondi said slowly. "I know your meaning. In Hungary to be free I was in uprisings. . . . My race, we have been slaves, but we have always been free. It is different with these people. Inside they are slaves, inside they have nothing to free them. . . . I know your meaning. You may trust me."

Wiener was fingering the sack greedily; it held four loaves of bread, a cloth poke stuffed with clabber, and a large flask of rum. They devoured the food in the dark, not risking a fire.

In the earliest hours of the morning the flight to a secret place began. "You should not stay here," Bondi had said to the old man as they ate. "They will find you here, they will search the farthest, the most wild corners. You must hide so close that they will not dream of looking. I have such a place. I have concealed my goods there often, so none would know. It is by the Ottawa creek, near a great oak killed in a storm. Come with me. If we are not betrayed we shall be safe for a long time."

There was no moon up, the blackness would conceal them. Cautiously they moved from the marshland, out upon the dim roads, a line of men and boys going two by two. For many hours they rode; now, near dwellings, furtively leading their mounts afoot, now in the open country giving rein and furious spur, thudding the prairie swells in a swift mass. They passed a region they knew—the Marais des Cygnes. Northward a little was Jim Doyle's empty cabin and the shallows that held Dutch Henry's blood.

CHAPTER VII

The East Is Away from the Sun

"Go NORTH toward Palmyra," Adair said to Jason. "Give yourself up to the Regulars." A cavalry patrol had passed that way yesterday. They'd be beating the whole bush region, the brothers were sure to meet up with them. They'd be arrested, but it was safer, there would be no violence.

≡ * 47 * ≡

"You'll go for Elly, Uncle Adair? You'll keep 'em safe?"

"I'll go for them. I'll do my best."

"Good-bye, Florilla."

She thrust a leather kit into Jason's hands. "There's bread and meat. . . . God watch over you both."

The two brothers rode off on the single horse, into the still wan crack of day, John delirious and mumbling terribly as they went. Suddenly, when they were beyond sight of the cabin he stretched forth his hand from behind Jason and violently pulled in the animal.

"Get down! Two's too heavy!"

He was a fearful sight with his hair all disheveled and the ragged golden beard and in his eyes the glint of the madman, hard and cunning.

"For God's sake, John!"

"Get down, I say! Quick!" he raged.

Jason gripped his shoulder. "John, for God's sake, listen to me! It's our only chance! If the Ruffians find us they'll kill us! We've got to get to the soldiers!"

The older brother's arm came out in a swift thrust. He drew it like a steel band across Jason's throat, then with a strangling heave toppled the other savagely to the ground. Jason lay stunned and white. The maniac reined the stallion in till the great creature stood high on its back hoofs, wildly pawing the air.

"They'll never get me! I'm going to raise the Osawatomies to fight 'em! I'm captain!"

Jason rose, weak with the shock, and watched his brother go crashing wildly through the timber. It'll be his end, they'll hang him, I'll never see him again, he thought. Then he turned and went on, trembling, northward toward Palmyra. The dawn was spreading down cool and gray. A pure white mist was afloat in the trees. From the low yellow furze glistening with dew the crimson-eyed wrens gave forth their little scolding sounds. The freshness of spring was over all the woodland; and in gentle Jason's heart was a black depth of fear.

For hours he kept going furtively through the wild brush. From time to time he crept the quarter mile to the right where the wide trail ran, so that he might keep his bearing and also catch a glimpse of the blue coats that would mean his salvation. Save for a snip at the Adair place the night before, he had not eaten for almost two days. His throat burned for water. He began to feel a faintness; the leather jacket of bread and meat was hung on the stallion. A sharp pain caught steadily at his back, his left leg was stiffening; John had flung him to the ground like a sack of flour. A great wilderness sun was beating down; and now the ague which had stolen into his blood during the first months of living in tents on the wet Kansas lowlands, began to ravage his body. Waves of chill and burning surged in him, blue motes swirled in his eyes. And all the time habitations and the sound of humans had to be avoided. Once, as he scrambled through densest brushwood to skirt a homestead, a great sheep-dog came snarling at his back. He beat it off with a thick gnarled bough, and once in the clearing ran till he felt his heart would burst. Then blindly he threw himself to the ground in a deep copse and lay panting and helpless. He felt as one dead and did not care; and consciousness fled.

When his awareness returned there was a gloom like night about him. He had no power in his limbs, he could not move. He groaned and closed his eyes, and thought: I'm dying. Then as he lay, there came the sound of voices in a distance. They're hunting me, he thought, it's the end. Soon very close there was a crackling and a swish, steps on the forest bed. He shrank in to himself, he was one point of ice. Voices sounded up, going by. They were high and young. The voices faded and silence came. Three lads hunting 'coons.

Now the remembrance of small Tom quickened in him, and Elly. He must move on, he must live. He wrenched himself to his knees. He crawled out of the brake. It was not night, it was the dim green stillness before night; low in the western trees the sun was flaming down. He stood up swaying, his head in a mad whirl. I've got to get to the road, he thought desperately, trying to keep his senses; I'll die in the woods if I stay the night, maybe I'll meet friendly ones, they'll give me food, the east is the road, the east is away from the sun. His eyes sought the dying flame; he turned and went staggering: the east is away from the sun.

Down the trail in the dusk they clattered toward him. They're Free-Staters, he prayed. In a moment he was standing in their midst, a lone man and twenty dusty riders.

"Who are you?" the horseman with the black hat called.

"I'm . . . looking for the regulars."

≡ * 49 * ≡

"Who are you?"

"I'm from Osawatomie. I'm . . . Jason Brown."

Twenty guns came up clicking; there was a spatter of murderous oaths.

"We been looking for you, Brown!"

"I've done nothing."

"Hand out your arms, quick!"

"I haven't got arms."

"Get ahead of the horses."

It was the order for his death, they would riddle his back. Jason felt the strength of desperation. He stood up straight and his haggard gentle face pleaded for him as he cried:

"I'm Jason Brown, I'm a Free-State man and what you call an Abolitionist! But I've never hurt a human being, I never was in a killing! If you want my life for that, don't shoot me in the back! Here's a mark for you!"

He ripped open the bosom of his shirt, and waited. Slowly, one by one, the guns dropped down and rested across the saddle-bows. Only the man with the black hat kept his levelled. He was Martin White, the preacher. "You damn nigger stealer," he snarled. "I've got an itch to put a bullet in you." But Jason only stood, his hands at his breast.

"You'll hang, you northern scum! You'll hang in Paola!"

They drove him at a run three miles through the dark. When he fainted they slung him on a horse and tied him with ropes. An hour later the cavalcade rode into Paola. The town was filled with two hundred pro-slavers, searchers for the Potawatomie murderers.

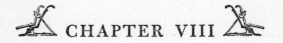 CHAPTER VIII

Let the Full Heart Pour

BONDI SLIPPED in from the dense brush. Old Brown was standing by the fire. A pot hung over it; he was stirring a rabbit stew with a bough. Oliver and Hen Thompson lay on the blue blanket on the grass, beneath a tree casting shade. Wiener was watching the old man stupidly, leaning hungry upon his rifle. Restless Frederick moved about in his high red boots, now aimlessly near the stack of rifles, now by the stamping whinnying horses picketed at the clearing's edge. Bondi came to the fire; they all watched him closely.

"Well, Bondi?" rapped the old man.

"There is nothing new. They seek us still."

Oliver called up: "Is there any word about John, about Jay?"

"Adair says he has not heard. Your brothers' people are in the blockhouse at Osawatomie. They watch there night and day, they fear an attack. . . . Your uncle speaks bitterly. He says you have been the ruin of all. . . ."

"Leave off, leave off!" the old man broke in harshly. He bent to draw the skillets of coarse flour from the blaze.

"I have a letter for you. Adair said it was from the East."

Brown straightened in a flash. Instantly Oliver and Hen Thompson leaped up. The old man tore open the envelope and began to read. The two young fellows watched him, they watched his eyes. He handed the letter to Oliver and began to dribble a snip of molasses into the canteens to sweeten the bitter creek water. The two read together, their eyes moving hungrily. Then Hen Thompson shoved his hands deep into his pockets and shambled back to the blanket. She must be carrying by now, he thought, dropping. Oliver stood looking at the fire, still and moved. The old man thrust the green bough into the meat for testing; Wiener's ugly mouth hung wet at the gurgling savor.

Soon the stuff was ready; first they ate greedily, half-starved, then with the slow grudging absorption of men who do not know when they will have food again. "Oliver, Wiener!" Brown said; they had scarcely finished. "Take the watch, send them in." The Austrian and the youngest son went off, carrying rifles, the one eastward through the timber, the other toward the creek-bottom.

Oliver was a hundred yards along his pathless way when he heard the old man calling after him. He waited, in a restless gnawing mood.

"You took the letter," the old man said, striding up. "Leave it to me."

≡ * 51 * ≡

Oliver drew it from his pocket and handed it over. His father turned without a word and began to go back.

"Wait!" Oliver cried. He walked up close, slowly, the old man watching him with stern impatient eyes.

"Well?"

The dark powerful boy stood confused before him, his head lowered; he thrust his boot at a scatter of bracken.

"I . . . don't know," he said. "I just . . . just wanted to talk to you."

"Here I am."

". . . Oh, I guess nothing. . . . I guess about them . . . home."

"What about home?"

The boy was pale. "Nothing," he choked. ". . . I guess . . . nothing." He turned suddenly and went off in a rush. The old man stood looking after him, fumbling the letter in his nervous bony fingers.

I'm getting out, I'm getting out, thought the boy; I'm sick to hell of hiding like a rat! I want to walk roads with my head up! I want to see a tree again without thinking it's made to hang from!

What a weariness comes on me, thought the old man, dropping heavily to the scarred gray slab of rock. It was beyond the camp, in a dense solitude. Such places always drew him; still and beaten, they drew him like a lodestone. There a man could wrestle and fight his mortifications through, be with his Maker. Now he sat bowed, his face in his hands, and a darkness rode his spirit.

The boy went stumbling through the underbrush, his knuckles white upon the rifle: You lay awake at night and every sound makes you shiver, like someone crying, and you can't forget for a minute, Townsend bleeding in your arms, and the Doyle fellows—what's it for, damn him, who are we helping? . . . His heart is like iron and we're all pawns for his deviltry!

The boy was lonely, the old man thought, I could see it in his face, and yet I had nothing to say to him and I chilled his

≡ * 52 * ≡

warmth. He is dearer than any, he has my mother's life again, and yet we are distant as death and shut off. . . . I am utterly alone, it bears me down.

Then the gray eyes with their scorn seemed to search him out, and in his thought the boy groaned: Christ, I can't run out on the old man, they're all against him! But what's it for? You kill and you hide like rats and you bring your own to ruin. . . . Christ, I'd fight to my last if my heart was in it, they all know I would, but what's it all for, what's it mean alongside the letter from home, Watson's letter? They had a fierce winter, they near starved. The babe near died of cough, and Annie's so skinny you can see her bones. The house is like thatch against the cold, and Ma's low with drudging. He says prospects look bad again, the crops will fail near all, and when are some of us getting home to help. . . . So I'm sick of this, so I'm getting out! I'm through with his schemes and his bloody devil of a god. . . . But Christ, how can I run out, they're all against him!

The lack had always been in him, old Brown saw. From the earliest days he could remember he had had no ease in human converse; even a deepest moment of compassion found him without power to console. Like the comforters of Job he could only stay by silent, lest in his miserable way he add to the grief of others. He had wept by young Austin's grave, and a mourning had been in his heart as the wagon bore the remains toward Kansas. Then he placed the box before his son and the child's mother, and as the two, stricken anew by their loss, lamented, he had only words for them heavy as stones and as comfortless: "He's gone, leave off weeping. He's in other hands."

And there was the night of his departure from the bleak Elba place. His son Watson had stood before him, very pale, yet resolute. He was eighteen and now he would be keeper of the family; he would have to face alone the dread Adirondack winter. The two scared little girls watched from a corner; Annie who was ten, and thin, and like a flame; gentle Sarah, slow after the mother, and an angel of patience. The babe slept in the hewn crib by the hearth. Mary Brown, pallid still from the confinement which had come hard, waited as he rolled up some small things in a bag. Leaving this white drawn lad to face the bitter season in the leaky unplastered house, with the grain low almost to nothing, leaving the lorn young girls and the defenseless droplet of life in the crib, that would rend him to his heart; but hardest it would be to meet Mary Brown's slow faithful eyes.

"Good-bye," he said. "Look out for them, Watson. . . . Good-bye, Mary. It's hard for you. But there's work outside bigger than any of us. I've got to help. Good-bye." He rode off into the cold mountain night and his face was stony. When he sent letters from Kansas to Mary he tried to tell her a little of his inner feeling, but always he had a starved ebbing sense, as of deep failure. . . .

("Dear Wife and Children, Every One . . . and I feel with you in all the hardships and discouragements you have to meet; but you are not alone in having trials. We found everyone here more or less unwell, without any sort of place, only tents, where even a stout man couldn't protect himself from the cutting cold winds and storms, which prevail more than in any place we have ever lived, even in your miserable Frosty region; and no crops of hay or anything had been taken care of; with corn wasting by cattle and horses, without fences; and Jason and Oliver and Wealthy are yet feeble with ague. We have made but little progress, but we have made a little. We have got a shanty three logs high, chinked and mudded, and a chimney so far advanced that we can keep a fire in it for the young ones. We have got a little crop of beans secured, which together with mush and milk and squashes makes our fare. We took up little Austin and took him on here; and Salmon has caught a prairie wolf in the steel trap. We continue to have rains with severe winds, and forming into ice as they fall, and the ground freezes in the cold night. Still God has not forsaken us and we get day by day our dayly bread, & I wish we had a great deal more gratitude to mingle with our undeserved blessings. Since Watson wrote I have felt a great deal troubled about your prospects of a cold house to winter in, and I have thought of a cheap ready way to help it much. Take any common straight-edged boards and run them from the ground up to the eaves, barn-fashion; not driving the nails in so far but that they may be easily drawn, covering all but doors and windows in that way, and breaking joints if need be. This can be done by anyone, even the weakest, and in any weather not very severe, and the boards may be afterwards mostly saved, for fires and planking. I think much too of your widowed state, and I sometimes allow myself to dream a little of sometimes again enjoying the comforts of home; but I do not dare to dream much. I have agreed, Mary, to buy the line-backed cow of Henry, so if she lives you can calculate on the use of her. We have received two newspapers you sent up, which were indeed a great treat, shut away as we are. We hear that Frank Pierce plans in Washington against us, that he means to crush the men of Kansas. Well, let the time come. Only blood can wash out all this vast dark sin. I trust you all to the care of Him who feeds the young ravens when they cry. I think Watson, when next spring comes, can gather a little money, shearing sheep in the valleys. Enough now. Your husband & Father John Brown.")

. . . a starved ebbing sense as of deep failure. And what, in "the work bigger than any" had he to show for his sacrifice of them? The hands of all men were raised against him, even those whom at the price of peace and very life he sought to help. Among his own band there was not one who believed inwardly and with passion his belief. He was not deceived. Owen went blindly, a hound for faithfulness; Frederick like a child. Wiener had slain through savagery; Bondi was vengeful; Salmon and Henry were wild boys. His youngest, who alone possessed the zeal that could burn for some high desperate faith, saw evil in all his striving (". . . you'll stain yourself, father . . . you hate sin more than you cherish mercy . . . there was a man named Christ . . . God is a god of love"). The old man shivered a little, his bony hand pressed the Book in his pocket. Was there a smallest chance then than he might be wrong? Was all this vanity, did he pursue a shadow while his loved ones perished with his absence, and here were destroyed by his touch? He groaned, desperately he sought in himself for strength.

*　　*　　*　　*　　*

"I'm getting old," he had said to the boys when the Ohio drought came and there was news of Kansas' richness. "I've got plans. I'm returning East." He had gone to the mountain place, he must dwell with himself, gather up the threads of his life; long enough it had been idle, mean with baubles, and ridden by lusts of gain. Now, before the last waning overtook him, he must see his way clear to a share in the great harvest. So day after day he sat in the farmhouse, alone in the midst of many; lay in the shadow of rocks; pondering the secrets of the Old Testament and the wrongs of a race; while the winter sun strode across the sky, and there were tempests and snow-storms, and the wind beat up and down the valley.

So I returned and considered all the oppressions that are done under the sun: and behold the tears of such as were oppressed, and they had no comforter. . . .

Spring stole in, sap of life rose and flowed, and there was a green peace and a tenderness upon the hills; but no rest for him, never a peace for him. Summer bloomed; and on a last day of July a newspaper came, weeks old. Brown read, then his hands trembled and a shining passion came in his eyes. Garrison had burned the Constitution!

The summer throbbed on. The old man went about withdrawn from all, haunting the deep still places of the mountain. A sense of some large fate, beyond the common life, grew in him; and fires mounted in his heart, consuming the baser self. Garrison had strengthened his resolve: there was a work to do in the world. But Lord God of hosts, he would go on beyond Garrison! White men had to be stirred from a slumber that was death, white men had to be torn from their own spiritual bondage before the Negro could throw off his chains and rise from the grovelling of beasts to the divine image. But not, he brooded, poring again and again over the yellowing news-paper sheets, but not with words, words, not with Garrison's sword of the spirit: ("In the kingdom of God's dear Son, love is the only magistracy. It has no spears, for they are beaten into plough-shares, no military academy, for the saints cannot learn war, no gibbet, for life is regarded as inviolate. . . . And that kingdom of the Son is to be established upon the earth, for the time is predicted when the kingdoms of this world will become the kingdom of our Lord and of His Christ.") No, not thus; the truth lay deep in the dark flaming older Testament: through the violent deed shall come understanding! It lay in the God of Gideon who took ten men and cast down the altar of Baal; in Joshua; and David who ordered all the enemies of his people slaughtered, women and children, flocks and herds, everything that breathed! For the Lord will plead his cause, the afflicted in the gate, *the Lord will spoil the soul of those that spoiled him!*

But still he waited in the mountains. He needed a last sign. Where should he strike, how should he descend into the heat and blood? Should it be Kansas where the men of his family were helping in the struggle? Or—a secret fierce joy swept him—was this the moment to realize the dream which had been for twenty years besetting him? He needed a sign. Gideon had seen fire rise up out of a rock and shrivel the flesh of a kid. He waited; and those about him watched with growing dread, so lost did he seem to their life.

Then the letter came. The letter was from his son John in Kansas: Send us guns, we need them more than bread! That night the old man went alone from the kitchen, swiftly down the hill-path to the great sloped crag, a stress of early autumn wind whipping raw at his body. The moon hung sharp white in the sky. Tahawus peak was a gleaming witch's hood and to the east Marcy loomed, dark, brooding, like a face of God's. He stood by the crag, putting forth his hand to feel it inexorable; a midge in a vastness. And now there was no question, no doubt; there was only time poised and hushed, and a call flaming in from the great night. Now he was undivided, he was a fever, a will incarnate. Tomorrow he would go, bringing guns. It was appointed. He would lead the men of his tribe. There came a rushing in his blood. Ah, more, he would lash the sins of the generation, scourge them with nettles and scorpions! In the slave markets of America he would light such a fire that the evil thing should be consumed as stubble in a pure white flame!

"Good-bye, all. . . . Look out for them, Watson. . . . I've got to help, Mary. . . . Good-bye."

*　　*　　*　　*　　*

Slowly, sitting there alone on a jagged slope of rock, deep in the Kansas timber, he raised his head from his hands. His mouth was tightened from a slack of melancholy to its bitter wonted slit: the slavers had burned Lawrence, in their hearts and in deed they had murdered, they had been closed all in evil to that compassion and that truth which cried aloud, did not He that made me in the womb make him, did not One fashion us in the womb? Encircling the old man was the full

≡*57*≡

throbbing solitude. The sun at its fierce height burned down; the rock was sharp against his back. His senses began to come live with awareness; he began to press hard against the jag, tearing cruelly through to his flesh; by his side the long nervous fingers writhed into gnarls of bone. Aye, these were no shadow —rock and pain and aloneness! These, he thought, now leaping up, these were the truth of his fibre, he had stronger drives than tears! He began to go fiercely back and forth before the rock, moving with his springing stride, the right shoulder thrust forward.

Later, in the waning day, he went quietly toward the camp. Oliver had said to him, "I would not have your conscience for riches"; but now he could face Oliver. For he had faced himself. The doubt, the moral ambiguity that had beset him was resolved into one great glowing peace. All was beyond him, in another's hands; like Moses falling in wrath upon the Egyptian flaying the Hebrew slave, had he not struck to kill, he had not been tested. Now he could answer Oliver:

Let a man be satisfied that his God demands thus and so, and he is forever free of the torment of divided counsels. I am but an humble follower.

CHAPTER IX

Hush, Mahala, Hush

THE BOY stood just within the doorway, looking out at the dim Paola lane, with its further white fence like a creeping wraith, and the black whispering mass of the trees. His lank body was outlined sharply against the light of the table-lamp behind. Now he drew a quick frantic pattern on the floor with his shoe, now his right hand gripped the jamb till the knuckles showed white. He could hear the rocker going steadily on the dark porch outside. Slowly, slowly, for a long spell. Creak . . . creak . . . creak . . .

Suddenly it ceased; a silence fell. He listened, straining.

Rock, ye damn rocker, rock! Silence. He felt he would scream in an instant. Then came the scraping, the creaking again. He let out a gasp, he turned and paced as in a fever the rude drab room.

But soon he stole again to the door, and listened, all constricted as before. Creak . . . creak . . . creak. . . .

What should he say? she would not hear. He could not leave her, he could not bear to watch her close. If only she would weep as in the beginning, wail and beat her head. Then he could hush her, hold her shoulders. From where he stood he was not able to see his mother, but she was a brand of grief in his mind, a heavy huddled figure, rocking, rocking, shrouded in the night's darkness, looking out with lost eyes. Creak . . . creak . . . creak . . . slow tortured rhythm, sound of her living anguish.

Oh, leave 'im be, for God's mercy! . . . get to your room, William . . . hush, Mahala, hush!

Christ, if they were delivered into his hands! He'd burn out their eyes with white irons, he'd cut their bodies alive, inch by inch! Christ, listen, listen, Ma rocking, oh Davy hacked in the road, oh the bleeding eyes of Ben!

Creak . . . creak . . . creak. . . .

He sprang out suddenly to the porch, past bearing it.

"Ma."

There was no answer, there was only her slow black moving.

"Ma, don't you want nothin'?"

She did not speak.

"Then I'm goin' for a spell. Just a turn into town, Ma. I gotta buy . . . stuff."

He went fast up the dark lane. His mouth was a cleft of hate.

"Rip his throat!"

"Give him mercy like old Brown did!"

"Kill the 'bolitionist scum!"

"Swing him up!"

"To the holler, hang 'im in the holler!"

"Let the coyotes eat him down!"

"To the holler! Hang the bitch in the holler!"

Back through the darkness the boy ran like a fury, half-weeping. "They got him!" he sobbed as he streaked along. "Ma, they got him, they got one of the god-damn murderers! To the holler, Ma, they're goin' to hang him in the holler!"

"Swing him up!"
In the deep small circle of the woods flaring with torches they howled for the life of the son of Brown. A short man stood rugged and set as a boulder by the side of Jason. He had a black beard and a neck thick as a bull's; his voice had a leashed low strength:
"Give him a chance for his life! Give him a straight deal!"
"We don't want your talk, Jakob! Hand the bastard over!"
They were as wolves kept from their prey by the gleam of a fire, yet ever circling closer; his shaggy eye and the sharp fierce words kept them at bay, but they were snarling and drawing the lustful ring tighter, and the venom slavered in their hearts. He could not hold them much longer. Let one take the lead and leap, and the pack was let loose for its blood.
"Are you men of the South? Or are you dogs?"
"He murdered five!"
"If he murdered he'll hang! But you've got no proof!"
"He's old Brown's son!"
Old Brown's son, old Brown's son, quivered up in Jason's mind, gentle Jason swaying in the flare of the brands, bound and stripped to the waist, half-dead; old Brown's son! sounding in his dimming senses like a wild cry of doom in a dream.
"Men!" the small bearded man called. "I'm a judge. I'm a man of law. But if I was sure this fellow helped at Potawatomie I'd put a bullet in him myself, so help me God! But I don't know, you all don't know! So give him his chance in a trial, give him a deal for his life like you'd want yourself!"
"He's old Brown's son!"
"Swing the bitch up!"
It was the end. They closed in, screaming with lust. Jakob crumpled with a gun-butt smash from behind. They tore at Jason, flung him ahead toward a great gnarled oak, beating him about the face and shoulders with their revolvers, kicking at him savagely as he stumbled. Preacher White, grinning like a skull, dangled a rope from a thick bough. They crashed Jason back against the tree; White fastened the noose about his neck.
"Say your prayers, nigger-stealer!"

The pale bleeding man moaned, "I've never hurt a soul!"

Dimly sounding beneath the feverish roar in his ears he heard White's voice. Others, older and more real, swam hugely to his mind and throbbed there: a new start Elly a new start altogether *boys Judge Jakob asked for a trial* the Territory's up that way Austin do you see shining there like candles and lamps *so we'll give him a trial* it's the rule of the river ye bury him tonight or he goes overboard *he's old Brown's son old Brown's son* only remember that not your peach trees *in cold blood five men on Potawatomie* you've no guts for a man's work, get back to your homes everything is quiet again *does he hang boys* oh you'll go for them you'll keep them safe Uncle Adair!

"Swing him up!"

Preacher White tightened the noose. The torches were flickering low. There was a deathly silence, only their eyes spoke their hate. Then White's voice sounded up shrill:

"May your soul burn in hell! May all enemies of——!"

"Yez can't do it."

She came in from the shadows, a heavy mournful woman in black. She moved close to Preacher White. She peered at the anguished face, the closed eyes of the son of Brown.

"Yez can't do it!"

"What the hell do you want?"

"He warn't there, he warn't one."

"And who the hell are you?"

"Mahala Doyle. I'm Mahala Doyle."

CHAPTER X

With Zeal as a Cloak

THE OLD man stirred the potted quail with the iron fork; then he bent to test the coarse flour baking in the skillets. Redpath, the newspaper correspondent whom Bondi had brought into camp, watched the gimlet-eyes, the quick brusque movements, even as he answered the eager questions of the dark boy by his side.

"The food is done," the old man called. The men came in from the shadows; took places, haunching about the blaze. The huge wild-eyed fellow kept staring at the newcomer; a chill quivered along Redpath's spine. Suddenly the old man stood up before the fire, tall yet a little bowed, wiping his hands upon his mud-caked trousers, the rest going all still and listening; and in the falling dark, the old man said:

"Grace to you and peace from God the Father, and our Lord Jesus Christ: who gave himself for our sins, that he might deliver us out of the present evil world, according to our God and Father: to whom be the glory for ever and ever. Amen."

Oh wonderful, went in Redpath's mind, what a picture for Eastern eyes, I'll burn up the wires, an old man dirty and ragged with toes sticking out of his boots, leaning over a pot with a greasy iron fork, a gray old patriarch cutthroat, copy for pious backbay minds, a killer praying to Jesus Christ in the dark!

"It must be a fine feeling," the boy was eagerly whispering to Redpath, "to know that your stuff, the words you write, can stir up people far away."

"Yes, it is . . . but tell me, what was it like that night?"

"I . . . can't talk about that." Oliver felt the old man's eyes on him. ". . . How . . . how did you get to know Bondi in Haiti?"

The old man called harshly, "Oliver, get off a little! Mr. Redpath and me will talk alone. All of you, get through. Move off a little, leave us to be alone."

Oliver got up sullenly. The others muttered among themselves across the fire. The old man sat down by Redpath's side.

"All respectfully," he said, looking sharply at the other, "I forbid any conversation about Potawatomie. And I must ask you, Mr. Redpath, if you desire any information of this company in relation to our conduct or intentions, to get it from me. I as captain of this company will answer for them whatever it is proper to communicate."

"Yes, of course. I want only to aid you, Captain Brown. I want to get your story before friends in the East."

"Good, sir." For all the restraint of the old man's way, Redpath sensed him eager. "I'll not stay in Kansas always. This is only a beginning. There are men in the East who can give me great help."

"What help do you mean?"

"Strength to go on. Money, arms, bullets. This is only a beginning. They will hear from me in the South. I will carry the war into Africa."

"What is your plan?"

"Sir, I am not ready to say. Its success depends on secrecy . . . I can only say this now. Let someone take men of good principles, God-fearing men, men who respect themselves. Take them into the hills, into the deep narrow defiles. They could defy all the armies of the South. I say this from observation, sir, not idly. I have studied tactics, I have studied fortifications and the movements of armies, here and in Europe. When the time comes I shall be ready. God has given the strength of mountains to freedom. Through mountains I shall strike . . ." But the old man had seen the excitement leap in Redpath's eyes. He caught himself, he became silent.

"Why then do you stay here in Kansas?" pressed Redpath eagerly. "What do you expect to achieve here?"

"A man can plan in his mind for distant things, yet handle what's under his nose. Kansas must come in free. There will be no settlement through peace. Peaceful agitations have failed. I shall force a settlement of the question by coming to close quarters with the slavers, by bringing both sections into armed conflict. A little fighting saves a deal of quarreling. There have been too many windy battles. The fight has been too long carried on by talkers, by politicians who don't care a penny about the true interest of the people, white or black. . . . We grope for the wall like the blind . . . we stumble at noonday as in the night, and we are in desolate places as dead men. . . . Aye, sir, bold deeds are wanted. Not a prophet giving laws, Mr. Redpath. Not Jeremiah with lamentations. But men not afraid to pull down unholy temples upon themselves, even if they go to their own end."

"I see," Redpath said, "that you are ready to give up much for your belief." (Sanctimonious old hypocrite, he thought.)

"There is nothing I will not give up . . . We are hunted here . . . I have a family living in great want in the East . . . This very moment I am waiting for my son Owen to return, to bring news whether his brothers and their families still live."

≡ * 63 * ≡

"There are few who would be willing to sacrifice so."

"I take no pride to myself. I am lower than dust in my own right. In my own right I am powerless and naked. But in each generation God makes His will known in advance to certain chosen ones. They perform it, sometimes unconsciously, sometimes beknown to themselves. He puts on them garments of vengeance for clothing, they are clad with zeal as a cloak."

Redpath stared at the old man. Damn me, he thought, look at him, look at his eyes! Damn me, he believes it, why, he believes it!

It was full night. In the outer timber, perched on a bough of the thick cedar, squat young Hen Thompson was trying to fight off sleep. From time to time his head dropped in sheer weariness. Then faint fading dreams would mingle with his sense for duty: a russet-haired girl walking in a field, or maybe his brothers close about the kitchen-table, jolly, jibing, their faces shining clean in the lamp glow; swift gleams darkening out into the still huntedness of the present. Then his head would come up in a jerk, he would listen all taut. He would curse, tear at another chunk of tobacco plug, and continue the vigil.

Old Brown lying in the midst of his sleeping men raised his head, listened. A few seconds hung still. The sound came again, a muted twisted call, drawn out. The old man sat up, his heart quickened.

Then a form shadowed in. The old man moved to meet Owen.

"John's taken," came the whisper.

"Does he live?"

"Yes."

"And Jason?"

"There's no word."

"Where is John?"

"Iverson's patrol. On the far Ottawa side."

"What are the chances?"

"A trap. There's almost a hundred. They'll finish him if we try."

The old man stood there. Owen waited. Then the father said, "There's some food in my bag." He dropped to the ground by the dead fire. Owen came and squatted by his side, chewing ravenously on some crusts. He whispered: "Had no food since sun-up. Had a tight run. West of Adair's a party sighted me. I took 'em about ten miles before I lost 'em in the bush. My horse was winded, near gone." He gulped some water from a canteen. "Iverson's close on us, we'll have to watch careful."

They stretched out on the ground. There were not many hours till dawn. Minutes went by. Owen put forth his hand to the other's back. The father did not move; Owen knew he was awake. Brokenly the man with the withered left arm whispered:

"Father . . . listen . . . I didn't tell you . . . Mrs. Kilbourne told me . . . Her boy was hiding John, but Iverson's patrol got 'em both . . . She said John's . . . John's mind is gone. Father, he's wild . . . like once when he was a boy."

The old man did not turn, did not move.

Wild, he thought, his insides shrinking, wild like when he was a boy! Nothing these long hunted hours had moved him to fear. Now he was moved, now he knew a terrible fear. As he lay there all sickened and clammy a ghost rose swiftly by his side, touching his heart with icy fingers. Another rose and yet another—a small woman in a wilderness home, Ruth his mother, lovely as night and early dead; wild lost Ann, his white sister forever asleep on the hill; Dianthe the faithful, the bewildered, Dianthe the fecund, doomed in lineage. Now in the blackness with bereft mournful eyes they hovered about him. Swiftly! they called, he is fated with us, go swiftly! Oh wild, clutched the old man's heart, oh wild like when he was a boy! Suddenly the old man imagined himself leaping up, half-screaming, "We ride, we ride for John!" and the others staring at him as if he were gone mad; felt himself running toward the mounts, his men following, snatching at their weapons, moving through the obscurity in a startled body.

Owen lay there, his eyes wide open, watching the back of the motionless old man. Soon the first light stole up the eastern sky, and the trees rose cold, sharp dark against the paleness.

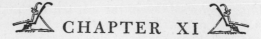

CHAPTER XI

This Is My Brother!

"YOU'LL BE safe here for a time," the black-bearded man said harshly. "They'll be cautious about breaking into my house."

"You saved my life, Mr. Jakob. I'll never forget it."

"I don't want your thanks. I've no love for you. I only want justice done, I'm a man of law. You're under arrest, don't forget it, and I'm going to turn you over to the regulars. They'll take you for trial to Leavenworth. If there's evidence against you you'll get the penalty, full to the hilt."

Jason put his hand weakly to his bandaged head. "They're all so bitter against me."

"You're an enemy of the South. We hate every last one of you. Your people want our heart's blood."

"I only want to live quiet. I only want to be let alone."

"Your father slaughtered five . . ." Something cruel crept into the man's eyes. "So don't thank me, Brown. Jim Doyle's wife saved you. Thank Jim Doyle's wife."

"No. No. I wouldn't be able to face her, I couldn't look in her eyes."

"Well, you'll have to. She's staying here with me, she's going to give evidence in Leavenworth with her boy. Tonight you'll eat at the same table."

When it grew dark, stoop-shouldered Cato the marshal opened the door of the upstairs room in which Jason sat, and said, "Come on down. It's time to eat."

"I . . . can't eat. I don't want to go down."

"Come on, hurry up. I'm hungry an' I've got to keep ye where I kin have my eye on ye. Anyway the Judge said fer ye to come down. Come on, now, git the hell down."

The night was hot and the small fire threw a bad fitful light about the kitchen. A lank raw girl was serving a hulk of meat to Jakob. Potatoes in a big bowl were steaming up. Mahala Doyle was sitting at Jakob's left, her head bent, her hands folded beneath the pine table. Will Doyle was next to her, hunched over.

Trembling, Jason sat down; the seat left for him was opposite Mahala Doyle and her last son. He gave her a swift shrinking look; the still figure in mourning cut to his heart, guilt swept him as though a finger of accusation were levelled. She said nothing all during the meal, kept her eyes low; the thin boy's smoldered with hate. Save for an occasional terse word between Jakob and Cato and the dull sound of earthenware and tin clinking, there was a silence. Jason could not eat, the food stuck in his throat. He kept thinking of the relentless one who had done all this, to himself and to the woman in black, to this boy who might have been his own, dead Austin grown; and his whole heart loathed the remembrance. When the ghastly meal was at an end and they rose, Mahala Doyle lifted her eyes to his for a briefest eternal instant. He could not stand it, he rushed from the room. All night the abysmal glance preyed upon him. It was like the hurt bewildered soul he had seen fading out in a shepherd dog's eyes, the eyes of Judah bleeding in the snow.

On the third night, very late, Jason was shaken roughly from a troubled sleep. It was skinny Cato, bending over him like a hawk. clawing at him. "We've got to git away!" the marshal whispered hoarsely. "They're plannin' to pull ye out an' string ye! Quick or ye'r gone!" With nerveless hands Jason got his clothes on. The two crept down the stairs, back through the dark house to the kitchen. The short bearded man was standing silently in the shadows by the open door, watching the back road. He was smoking a long slender cigar; he had a derringer in his hand.

"They're after you, Brown," he said in a low, casual voice. "They'll be along any minute now. Cat's going to try to sneak you south. Regulars are south near Ottawa water. If they corner you Cat'll give you a gun. Use it on yourself, Brown, it's better than hanging. There's a bad moon out, Cat. You'll have to go like hell."

All night they rode, pursued. They were up on two wild steely mustangs, and Cato was cunning as a hunted weasel. Before day came they had lost the Paola men in the timberlands; soon in a distance they could hear the Army camp-bugles sounding with the sun.

"We'll get you all, we'll get your old man, your whole cut-

throat family!" Major Iverson bound Jason's wrists behind, and
his upper arms; pulling the thin stiff rope savagely and tight-
ening it with his teeth. He was a burly man, with short arms,
and a bald head narrow like a red jug. His riders were beating
the bush for the Brown gang. "Bring 'em in," were his orders;
"it don't matter if they're dead." They were the Governor's
orders too; some even said a cold stern word had flashed from
Pierce in faraway Washington. Well, this was another one of
them, went in Iverson's tiny brutal mind. He knew how to
handle murderers. And there was a promotion waiting if he
make a good bloody sweep.

"And if your old man tries to get you loose, if your brothers
make a single move against us I'll put a bullet in your head!"
raged Iverson, raising both his short ugly arms above Jason, his
eyes greening with gall. A note had come in the night before:
I am aware that you hold my son—John Brown.

They prodded Jason ahead, flung him into the midst of
some dozen bound haggard prisoners. He lay where he fell, face
down in the rough sedge, exhausted and hopeless. Vaguely
he heard the others muttering about him, a bitterness in the
sound; but he had not the strength to care. After a while someone pulled at his shoulder, and whispered, "Brown." It was
a slight fair fellow, scarce more than a boy; young Kilbourne of
Osawatomie, whose father, a Kentuckian, had been shot to death
last year for voting Free-State.

"Kilbourne," Jason said weakly, "what are you doing here?"

"The same as you. They suspect we was in the killin's."

"Oh," groaned Jason. "He's ruined the peace of all."

"I wish't to hell I'd helped!" the lad whispered savagely.
"If I ever get outa this I'm joinin' up with your old man."

"Are you mad, boy?"

"I been speakin' to some. We're tired of actin' meek, of
bein' abused. Your old man's a fighter, he's the kind we need to
follow."

"You fool boy," Jason groaned again. "Will you go to your
death?"

"My pa went. They plugged my pa."

"Listen now, Kilbourne," Jason whispered. "You stay away
from my old man, do you hear? He'll bring you to evil!"

"They didn't give good to me. Then I'll give back evil."

"Kilbourne, for Christ's sake, stay away!"

"Aah, I know my job now. Even my lone ma can tell you

what it is—even her, kinder than any. . . . And why the hell are you so soft for 'em? I seen your brother, I seen what they did to him."

"John? Have they got John?"

"Yeah, they got John. That's how they got me. I met him wanderin' in the timber. I tried to hide him but they got us both. He's daft, loon daft. And they been beatin' him near to death."

"Oh . . . oh. . . . Where is he now?"

"Back of us, down a slope. They have to keep him close, he's ravin' that bad."

Jason tried to struggle to his knees, but the boy furtively watching the guard by the mottled sycamore held him down with his tied hands. "Look out," he whispered. "They're like butchers. They'll beat the life outa you for half a nothin'. Wait till later. They take us down to the mess tent near the creek for lousy slops. You'll get a chanc't to see him. We go by."

The prisoners shambled down the hill, two troopers leading them. It was high noon, a great glaring sun beat on them. "Behind the big rock," whispered Kilbourne. Jason trembled as they got close. Then he saw his brother. Oh, he shuddered, oh John, rent his heart. There the eldest son of Brown lay; bound; chained by each ankle to a stump; groaning; his face wasted and caked with filth. A welt, as from a whip, ran raw from his left temple to the right corner of his mouth. Blood matted his beard and hair, his sunken eyes were staring mad.

Jason, pierced, lurched from the captive-line, forward to the boulder. He kneeled by the other, his helpless hands quivering with a will to succor.

"John." There was no tiniest flicker of recognition; he seemed beyond recall, deep in a stark lost world of his own. "John, it's me! It's me!"

"Ye bitch! What are ye doin' here?" One of the guards was upon them, snarling with anger. "Who let ye leave the line?"

"He's my brother!"

"Get the hell up, or I'll bash your head in!"

"This is my brother, I tell you! For Christ's s——"

The trooper lashed out with a terrific blow to Jason's jaw. He sagged, and fell face down. Then a shriek writhed up through the bivouac. The violence had stirred the brother from his stupor. Now he leaped up and down, casting himself about in a frenzy, tearing at the chains. He began to call military orders; he was leader of the camp, he was again captain of the Osawatomies. The trooper, with cruel hanging jaws, yet fearful, circled about him, watching for a chance to slip in from behind and lay the maniac low. He had his heavy six-shooter out, the butt poised for a blow. Suddenly he darted in, the stock gleamed swiftly in an arc. There was a fearful thud. The maniac did not drop under it, he staggered crazily, his eyes rolling. Again, again the steel smashed down. Then he slumped, and lay still in a twisted heap.

Now he was a devil on a black stallion, they said, clattering the trails at night; now he rode a swift bay, fading in the gloom of swamps. He had been cornered near Lawrence and shot dead; he and his gang had raided a post outside Lecompton. Old Brown had been here, he had been seen there; this hour near the cabin of 'Taway Jones, the same hour forty miles south on Cygnes water. And Iverson would order out his troopers, lead them himself in furious prairie rides; or the blue-coats would spend themselves hunting along the river-bottoms, through the mud and the dense prickly tangles. Northward too, clear to the Missouri border, pro-slavers were beating the bush. And in the dim clearing by the fallen oak, so close to the cavalry encampment that night and morning he could hear the clear call of the bugles and draw his water from a common spring, an old man brooded upon the mystery of his days, the mystery of love and violence that gave him no rest and his highest joy.

CHAPTER XII

Chronicle for the East

"Kansas Territory, June 20, 1856.
Special to *The* ————— *Gazette*.

"THE POTAWATOMIE crime, in short, has had a consequence equivalent to civil war; it sowed a whirlwind; we are witnessing the harvest. . . . Thousands of peaceful Free-Staters will of necessity meet with indiscriminate reprisals, and the settlers in the immediate neighborhood of Osawatomie will undoubtedly have a special vengeance wreaked upon them. . . .

". . . From the welter a considerable irony emerges: Old Brown has become the recognized Free-State champion; he is now looked upon as the one man who can protect them against the very terror he evoked. Only a few days ago a messenger from Prairie City found his way into the outlaw's secret camp and asked for help against a large force of Missourians camping near the Black Jack spring. Brown commanded a small allied band. He made a night ride and a surprise attack at dawn; the Missourians under a Federal deputy-marshal Pate were routed. It was Brown's vindication. Now his name is cleared among his own people. He has pitched a camp on a small island of Middle Creek, and fortified it by earthworks. He commands a force of a hundred and fifty men and hourly recruits are crowding in. Just how long the old man will be able to work thus in the clear is open to conjecture. The news of the Black Jack battle has flashed over the Territory. Whitfield of Missouri is said to be marching down with a large force, and it is definitely known that Regulars are on the move to break up the lawless gangs of both factions. Brown says he will not be taken alive.

". . . and he seems fair to be assuming the proportions of a legend, both among his own people and his enemies. He is a presence in all Kansas. They raise him from every prairie and thicket; there is no smallest raid but he is the leader of it. At Franklin a pro-slaver meeting broke up in the greatest haste when it was suddenly reported that old Brown was riding to 'take out' some men; and the creek over which he was expected to attack was heavily guarded all night. It is known that only the deep fear of his vengeance has kept the slavery men from executing his two sons, who are held in the Leavenworth prison. Since Potawatomie he has moved much in secret, rarely seen, yet the idea of his being grows darkly. Recently, when a large party of Missourians were returning north and the rear ranks called out by way of jest, 'Old Brown's coming!' the van cut the mules from the traces and rode for their lives. He is the most dreaded man in the Territory."

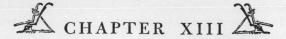

CHAPTER XIII

The Sons of Brown Quit

THE RIDERS thudded down the plain toward the creek, fifty dragoons in a streaming bluish line. Their rifles gleamed in the sun. Across the low swift water, on the island, the Free-Staters waited. They were drawn up behind earthworks. They were almost two hundred.

"We could beat them off," said the old man, astride a glistening black stallion.

"Quit that, Brown!" said dark Harley Williams, half-angered, half-pleading. "We'll not resist regulars."

"No," said Otis Carpenter, the second Free-State leader. "Let them come in. We've nothing to fear." Damned old loon, he thought, we've driven the slavers out, here's our first chance for a little peace, and he says, we could beat them off.

"Then get terms. We have two hundred."

"The only terms we want is to know there'll be some quiet here again, to get home."

Wiener came riding up to Brown. "Mebbe they have warrants," he whispered. "We could get away back creek. These won't help us."

"We'll wait here."

Cowards, thought the old man bitterly, when trouble came they called on us, but now they forget, this is their gratitude. But we won't run. They won't take us alive.

The first dragoons came up sharp into the shallows with a great guggle and clatter upon the wet stones and a white spume flying. They began to move swishing across the low water; a trooper held a tattered red regimental pennant high. On the island the old man wheeled the black stallion a little off to a side. A horseman quickly left the earthworks, clomped back to him; another, another . . . men of the Potawatomie night; Bondi and the Kilbourne boy, and a reckless young fellow, Ham Hyatt . . . nine men waiting in a body around John Brown, arms to hand, watching taut, watching darkly the incoming dragoons.

≡ ＊ 72 ＊ ≡

"I'm Shriver." The officer spoke in a cold voice, immaculately. He sat bent and skinny on his horse; his reddish moustaches drooped. He was a West Pointer, had recently been ordered to the Territory from the Kearney garrison. He had earned a name as a fighter in the Sioux uprisings. "You've got to break up this camp."

"We're protecting our homes," said Harley Williams.

"I have my orders. Armed bodies have to disband. You're assembled without authority."

"We're assembled to keep from being murdered."

"The Missouri men have been dispersed. You can return again to your homes."

Shriver's young aide was watching the old man sitting there on the black stallion. He would remember the lined bitter face, J. E. B. Stuart would remember the face. He saw the four young giants close by him; one fearful with his wild eyes and the long yellow mane; another, a mere boy for all his size, deathly white beneath his bloody head shroud; he saw the man with the stony brutish snarl and the gleaming bowie. By god, the young Southerner thought, it's him, it's him and his gang! Jeb Stuart's scalp suddenly went tight and tingling. In that instant the old man reined his stallion ahead a few steps, called harshly:

"If we break up we want terms."

"Terms? Who are you?"

"I'm a leader here. We want an exchange for our prisoners."

"My orders are to break up armed gangs. I'm not here to treat with hawkers and——"

"Sir, don't deem it beneath yourself." The old man's left hand gripped the reins in a white gnarl of anger. "I am known in this Territory."

"I don't care if you're known in Washington. I'll give your men half an hour to——" Suddenly something happened in the officer's level gray eyes, a startled understanding leaped there. Then a swift hot gleam, a very devil of challenge.

"Preston!" he called, his teeth showing, the word cutting the air.

A man rode out slowly from the massed troopers. He had a beefy face beneath a curling black hat. He was a deputy United States marshal. Nine riders pressed closer about old Brown.

"Preston. Look these men over. . . . Do you recognize any of them?"

The marshal with the warrant in his pocket stared into the eyes of the Potawatomie assassin. For a full minute they held. Then hoarsely the marshal said:

"I don't recognize none. There's none here I got warrants for."

Oliver Brown suddenly saw a dog slinking from a room before the sheer gaze of a silent gaunt man; felt himself, a small boy, shivering by a blazing hearth.

The camp on the island was deserted. The Free-Staters scattered to their homes throughout the region. They had fought off the slavers, they could be easier for a while; there was this man Shriver patrolling the country with his dragoons to break up armed gangs.

But the Brown men rode for the wild timber. They had no homes. Their cabins were ashes, their claims lay desolate. Though they did not need to fear now their own people, there were still a host seeking their lives; again the meagre existence of hidden camps and foraging and night rides would be theirs. Salmon Brown had come out of the Black Jack battle with a terrible head gash; he was faint and bloodless white. Owen had been struck near the spine by a partially spent ball; was half paralyzed. So this would be a time for resting, for nursing the wounded. Once more the secrecy of the older hunted days enveloped them.

But they could see that the old man was planning further. Some days he would sit for hours under the beating sun, and speak never a word; one night he suddenly rode his stallion out into a furious black rain, and was gone till day gleamed in the east. And Oliver, penetrating a little the secret fearsome mind, grew sickened and desperate: there would be more blood. The old man, he saw, would not rest here, he was not satisfied that a kind of peace had been won. His motive on the Potawatomie had never been merely to end the slaver outrages by showing Missourians that Free-State men would stand for their rights. No, from the very beginning he had sought deliberately to set men at each other's throats: *Without the shedding of blood there is no remission of sin.* And the boy, remembering the horror into which the old man's relentlessness had plunged them all, shrank in his soul:

I must get out. I must get out. Before it is too late. He can't

≡＊74＊≡

keep me, I won't be a tool for his murdering. My life is poisoned already, what can I go back to now, what peace will I find? I must get away, I have to think. Oh, I want to help in this fight for slaves, but I've got to know what I'm doing, to understand things. I'll do anything, I'll make sacrifices. But not this killing. Christ, not this killing!

The summer throbbed on; still Oliver stayed with the little band in the secret camp. Again and again; now facing the old man across the fire, now by his side on some furtive ride; the hate and rebellion trembled upon his lips, but he could not speak them. If only he were able to meet the man in some sudden flaring difference, come hard to grips with him, then he might tear free. But the gray bitter face, the silence, always the impenetrable silence, froze the very heart in the boy. Finally, one night, preyed upon unendurably by guilt and revulsion he cried to himself that he would make an end. They had been out that afternoon on a petty raid; Wiener, Frederick, Hen, and Ham Hyatt. They were in rags; at dusk they slipped back, and their mounts were laden with spoil. They had rifled a slavery man's store near Franklin; they had a dozen new outfits—palm leaf hats, check-shirts, linen coats, bandannas. The old man came in a little later from some obscure errand. He said nothing, but his eyes gleamed with approval: let the godless keep the servants of justice in good repair. Oliver watched the men trying on the stuff around the fire; watched Frederick fumbling with a gaudy bandanna, fascinated as a child with some new brightness; the dark prostrate figure of Owen lying in rigid pain beyond the circle of light. What am I doing here, thought the boy in a sudden clutching fright, is this my life? Soon Wiener, squatting, began at his slavering, his ugly mouth glistened wet over a piece of meat. Oliver felt that in another instant he must leap up, that something was cracking in his brain; he would let out a scream: god damn you all! But instead, as he sat, an iciness came over him, and he thought, tonight I will go. He felt no joy, no eagerness. He could not stand it longer, tonight he would go. When they were asleep he would take the mustang and steal off. By morning he would be fifty miles out on the trail to the East and sanity. It was his night for the watch, the way would be clear.

He sat at his post in the outer timber. A blanket was over his shoulders, the rifle across his knees. There was an oppressive

≡＊75＊≡

silence, innumerable sounds in a great black silence. The hours crept, crept. Midnight came. He waited the hour past midnight. Then he stole back through the brush, halting every few steps to listen. Nothing. Only the night sounds. He came creeping to the edge of the thicket where the mounts were tethered. His apathy was gone, now again he was in a desperate stir; if the men roused he knew he would not dissemble, he would leap on and ride like a fury. But the hush endured; Ned Scarlet, sensing his presence, whinnied once, but very softly; and he was not betrayed. He needed only to lead the mustang along the narrow trail which wound out toward the clearer country. Then he would ride hard.

But he did not lead the mustang along the trail. He stood there, holding the bridle. A slight trembling passed over him, like a quick wave. He looked back. His hand slipped from the bridle. He turned, leaving the mount in the trail, and crept again to the edge of the clearing. With nerveless fingers he bent aside a thick tangle of boughs and peered through. The last embers, like sullen scarlet eyes, were smoldering out in the obscurity. The dim figures lay huddled about. That great twisted heap beneath the white birch would be Fred. Salmon was over there, he could see the paleness of his head shroud. And that one, close by the dying gleams, was the old——

The boy began to tremble violently. He stood rooted in the vast moonless night; and knew that he was lost. He had been on the trail with the mustang—and had looked back, and in that instant was lost. A wetness sprang in his eyes. He hardly knew that he was dropping weakly to his knees; he did not know how long he knelt there, head bowed. He had no clear thought, no inner voice bidding him: stay, it will be treachery, these are the men of your family, you would feel the scorn of his eyes forever. He only knew that now he could not go. He got up and walked blindly back to the mustang. When morning came he was at his post in the timber.

He ate almost nothing; he did not speak. He took the old man's orders with a numb oblivious look in his eyes, as if he did not care what happened now. They all noticed it; even Fred noticed, and sometimes watched his youngest brother like a puzzled sorrowing mastiff. The very spirit seemed sucked from the dark boy.

Then it happened. At the lowest ebb of his hope, by the one

means he would not have dared even in a wildest dream, it struck swift and fierce.

Lucius Moles slipped into the camp one morning. He was Florilla Adair's cousin; a small, pathetic-looking man, prematurely gray, with timid importuning eyes. The old man had only scorn for Moles; the fellow would not fight, at the Black Jack battle he had been content to care for the wounded. Oliver liked him, felt sorry whenever he saw him: what is he doing in this hell? he ought to be tending flocks back in Ohio. This Lucius Moles came into camp.

"Florilla asked to see how the boys are doing," he said apologetically, answering the old man's harsh impatient look.

"Tell her they'll live to fight some more."

Though sudden clawing pains would leave him whitened and dazed, Salmon was much better, the head gash was slowly healing. But Owen was in a bad way; the spine wound had the big fellow down on his belly, helpless to move, and for lack of steady care the rawness had begun to fester and spread. He lay rigid beneath the dog-tent, gnawed. And always in the hot primitive quarters there were the clouds of stinging flies, like a scourge.

Unbidden, Lucius Moles slipped quietly to the tent. With gentle quick fingers he eased the suffering fellow a little; he washed the wound and changed the bandage. Three days he came in thus; and on the fourth, the Sabbath, he came to stay. He said nothing, simply laid his bundle down beneath the oak; and Brown suffered him to stay. The old man could himself be deft and soft as a woman with a sick person, but something was brewing in his mind, he had no eyes for common duty. He was away for days at a time, and none of the others was easy at the nursing or skillful. So Lucius Moles stayed.

He had been there a fortnight. Owen was getting worse; his bones were beginning to show through, and the canker was hideous. Moles confronted the old man:

"You'd best get him out. He'll go if he stays here longer. You ought to get him to a doctor and a clean comfortable place."

"I'll do as it seems fit."

The old harpy, thought the little man with mingled fear and wrath as Brown strode away; his son is near to death yet he must have his own way, his evil schemes come first. But in a few minutes Brown came back to Lucius Moles, and said:

≡＊77＊≡

"We'll move him. . . . I'll pay you to watch over him. See that he gets care."

"I'll do it, I'll keep him at my cabin. But not for pay."

"Good. I'll depend on you. There's other things I have to look out for." Aye, he had his plans. Tomorrow they were breaking camp, by nightfall they would be riding north. The Free-State convention would be held soon at Topeka. There might be trouble; he was going to be in the neighborhood of that town with his men. Moles was right, Owen would be a drag on the fighting men.

The next day he gave the order: pack up, we leave at sundown. Bondi and young Kilbourne rode westward toward Osawatomie: bring back some kind of a carrier, a wagon, an ox-cart, anything; Owen has to be hauled. The men began to gather their things together. Lucius Moles sat by the stricken fellow's side:

"You'll be sleeping in a real bed tonight, Owen. Florilla will be around tomorrow with some honest cooked food, maybe a good broth. And I'll go in to the settlement for Doc Kingsley. He'll have you up in no time."

The big fellow lay with his face down in the litter, silent. Then he twisted his head around a little, his face screwing up in pain. The cheeks were sunken and yellowed beneath the ragged beard, the eyes feverish. "What are they planning to do?" he asked in a whisper. Later he kept groaning, "And me down, and me down."

Moles rose and started with a pail toward the spring for some fresh water for Owen. He passed by Oliver. The boy was laying his few things out on a blanket. "How does he look, Lucius?" he asked. They were the first friendly words he had spoken to Moles since the little man's coming. Again and again, deep in the gnawing black mood, he had rebuffed Moles' shy advances; once so brutally that the other recoiled in bewildered hurt. But all the time Oliver had seen the man's simple tenderness for his brother, and was moved. Now he asked "How does he look, Lucius?" and the little man, sensing the contrition, halted, flushed with sudden childlike pleasure; and the two began to talk in low voices. Then Oliver bent impulsively to the blanket and picked up a large silver-handled revolver.

"Here, Lucius," he said. "I've got two others."

"Why . . . I . . . never use . . . I don't . . ."

"Take it. I got it for boot at the Black Jack fight."

The little man understood the spirit of this; he took the revolver. He thrust it awkwardly under his belt. Then with his hatchet-face shining with warmth he said, "Owen wants water," and went off. In a moment he returned, lugging the big pail, spilling the water at every step. He passed alongside Brown who was crouching to fix a fire. The old man glanced up; rose swiftly.

"Moles. Whose gun is that?"

"It's Oliver's. . . . That is, it's mine. Oliver gave it to me."

"Hand it over."

"Why, it was a . . . He gave it to me."

"Hand it over. You'll never use it."

The little man took the revolver from his belt. He handed it to Brown. In that instant the boy was upon them, black with anger.

"I'll take it," he said, quivering.

The old man gave the boy the gun. "Keep it," he said.

"I'll do as I want. The gun's mine."

"Keep it, I say. We've no arms to waste in Kansas."

"Here, Lucius. Take this, it's yours, I give it to you."

The old man snatched the weapon. The boy lunged for it, fiercely. The old man's left hand whipped out open to the boy's face, thwack! thwack! "You will?" he cried. The boy stood dazed, his cheek flaming. Then with a strange fearful joy, he laughed, he made for the other. Brown dropped the revolver, his gnarled leathery fist lashed out, caught the boy flush between the eyes; but he came in laughing, tossing the long black hair from his sight. "Stay off!" called the old man, livid; "stay off, or I'll kill you!" But he came in laughing. Brown struck again, full force; again; the boy's nose began to run blood. But he did not strike back, he took the blows, advancing, advancing with arms opened, like a huge young bear. Brown was swift and cunning; he retreated, he darted in, his fists beating, he twisted away, he was an old wolf. (The men closed around in a panting weaving circle. Ham Hyatt leaped up and down, screeching; Wiener's pig-eyes gleamed; the Brown boys, swaying with the blows, panting with short savage grunts, watched fascinated, frightened.) The boy came in relentlessly, the blood dripping; now he was close upon him, laughing. "I'll kill you!" the old man cried, and made a leap for the other, high and cat-like. The boy caught the scrabbling clawing form against his breast. His great arms wrapped around the old knotted torso, crushed inward. The old man's fists beat like flails upon his son's head but he was gone now, the arms were bands of steel. The boy lifted the old man a foot off the ground, he just held him there, crushing inward, laughing coldly, wildly. The old man's face twisted with pain, he began to cough, to choke, his eyes popped like frantic coals. Then suddenly a hoarse moaning cry heaved up from the tent. Owen had wrenched himself to his knees, his eyes burning with mingled fury and horror. Oliver heard the cry. The cold mad joy died on his face. He held the old man higher for an instant; then with a terrible look of hatred and self-loathing he flung him, like a sack of meal, to the ground.

The hours passed. There was a deathly quiet as night darkened over the camp. The men sat there, waiting uneasy and silent. Over by the edge of the clearing the old man sat hunched up, his face a drawn white mask. I'll kill him, he thought desolately.

Oliver sat on a log, alone. His face was raw. He felt tired, yet eased. I waited five years, he thought with a vague, almost impersonal sadness.

Full night descended. Bondi and young Kilbourne jolted in from the timber in a wagon; Wiener called out hoarsely, "The stuff's cooked!" They came about the blaze, slowly, one by one; they ate in a chill silence. Then Oliver said to the old man:

"I'm going East. I'm leaving."

The fire crackled, sparks leaped to the darkness. There was no other sound, save the crunching of jaws.

They stayed in the camp that night; the old man gave no word to move. One by one they dropped off around the embers, Oliver among the first, strangely gone in a deep drowned sleep, a dreamless sleep. The old man just sat there; and Hen and Salmon sat too, watching him like hawks. The three were the last unsleeping. Midnight came; he lay down. Hen and Salmon lay down—between him and Oliver. In the hushed early hours he silently rose. They watched him like hawks. But he turned away, faded into the outer blackness. They lay there taut, listening for his return. They knew something of what was going on in that fearful strait mind. Oliver's death or life lay in that mind; and they would be helpless. Just before the first grayness crept up the eastern trees, he came in. They gathered themselves, quivering;

but they would be helpless. He lay down by the side of his youngest son, Oliver in a dreamless sleep, dark Oliver who had his mother's life again. They could not see the tears in the old man's eyes.

The next morning he called them together. He tried to speak calmly, as if nothing had happened (off on a side Oliver was tying his bundle to Ned Scarlet), but he was visibly shaken.

"We're going to Topeka," he said; "there's bound to be trouble at the convention. Then we're coming back to watch Osawatomie. They'll be down again, Atchinson will be sure to try to sweep us before snow falls and the country is locked. Osawatomic has— "

"You better not count on me, Brown." Wiener wiped his beast-mouth with a red pudgy hand.

"What's that?"

"I been meanin' to tell you. I got business South. I'm goin' to N'Orleans."

Brown stared at the Austrian. Then the old proud scorn fired his eyes, and he answered, "Quit when you're ready, Wiener."

Salmon looked at Hen Thompson; gulped; wet his lips. Hen gazed hard at the ground.

"Me . . . me and Hen's goin' too. . . . We're sick of Kansas. . . . We want to get home again."

 CHAPTER XIV

Marching Men

THE END of the month found them on the road to the States. The four sons, Hen Thompson, Lucius Moles—and the old man. Wiener had slipped away with his graven leer to some obscure destiny of his own. Ham Hyatt and the Kilbourne boy had decided to throw in their lot with a gang of young jayhawkers. "I will be here when you come back," Bondi had said to Brown, as if he were sure that the old man would come back. Brown answered, "Keep informed about John and Jason. You'll hear from me." Now, as they plodded toward Nebraska, none in the small company knew what the old man was planning; he would tell them nothing. He sat up front, driving the wagon along the dun bitten country; Owen lay in the back. The others rode horses. It was a strange group; morose, withdrawn, torn by forces of bitterness and guilt and hope. Uneasily the younger men wondered, what is he doing, why is he with us? They could not see that he himself only dimly knew. When the time had come for the three young fellows to leave he said suddenly, "I'm heading that way too." Some bulwark had crumbled in him. It was as if he felt in his heart that he needed these young lives to draw upon for his strength; without them he would be helpless, the quiver would be empty of its arrows. Thus now he was driving the wagon, and they rode about him; through the chill autumn days, through prairie storms, slow and painfully over the barren swells endlessly dipping, endlessly rising out to the cold gray sky. And his spirit was darkened, once again he was divided in himself.

Go back. Kansas is waiting, the work of your life lies there, unfinished.

Aye. But these are the men of my family, my sinews, my strength.

They had been ten days out on the trail. The afternoon was drawing to a close; the first prairie shadows were lengthening, wheeling faint and vast across the dying land; nights fell swiftly now. Suddenly, growing from silence, a low insistent rhythm began to trouble the air. It grew louder, slowly louder; louder; it beat up into a dull dragging tramp. They looked back uneasily from time to time, but saw nothing: they knew many men were marching behind them. Then, a quarter-mile off, where the trail made the winding rise softly and full to the breast of the plain, they beheld the first of the line draw up upon the crest. Soon in a double file they came swinging down the long slope, some ninety riflemen; three riders led. They saw the Brown men. Two of the riders urged their mounts on, cantered up. They shouted a greeting; rode a little alongside the wagon. Then they wheeled and rode back toward the approaching column. They called out a name to the men in the vanguard. The men whispered it to one another, a sudden stir was among them. The name began to run like a current up through the moving line; it gathered a swelling strength to itself; then with suddenness sounded in a great mingled shout——

"Old Brown!"

——and instantly, all as if in obedience to a command the step quickened, the line broke into double-time, they came up hard toward the crawling wagon.

"Brown! John Brown!"

They streamed past on both sides, every eye sweeping the bent ragged figure; and the dusk sounded and echoed with the running feet and the clamorous unpremeditated cheers. The old man, enveloped in the shouting column, betrayed no pleasure; he glanced up from the team, nodding grimly, and his bony hand rose now and again in a swift imperious gesture. But the blood was surging in the Brown men. Oliver's throat swelled, his eyes gleamed with blinding pride. Frederick began wildly to cry aloud with the running kindled strangers.

Soon the little company was moving forward through a darkening silence; the last sounds of the force had died up the trail. These men were Free-Staters, going north to the Nebraska line. A caravan was waiting there, six hundred settlers from the East, ready to move into the Territory. It would have to pass down along the border of the bad Kickapoo region. The marching Free-Staters would be a guard against the Ruffians.

That night the Browns camped in a thicket. They ate their dry beef, and bread made from corn bruised between stones and baked in the ashes of the fire; and washed them down with tepid water from the wagon-cask.

The old man sat muffled in his blanket. The others lay about, smoking moodily, speaking in low snatches. Sometimes from the wagon a groan would come as Owen stirred.

The dark boy, the youngest, brooded: Tomorrow they would reach the Nebraskan line. The caravan would be there, ready to move down into the Territory. But the trail would turn toward Iowa and the East—and he would be taking it. He felt no happiness at the thought; his mind went back again and again to those running men. He could see them, swept hotly in a body, shouting suddenly from the heart; the old man, bent, haggard, raising his bony hand in the abrupt fierce gesture. That man was his father, known in all Kansas, a name quickening as a trumpet, a force in the minds of men! And the boy knew again the stirring of his blood, and it struggled with an old torment and old fears, and he was sick with irresolution.

Oh my God, thought John Brown, shivering; in visions I have been told what to do, then why do I falter now? Great Father, I am old, I am tired, give me will to go on.

The prairie silence grew deeper; the fire died. Stars glittered across the vast sweep of sky, cold, innumerable, terrifying. And below in the lonely night the little fevers beat on, and the travellers lay with their dreams and their sorrows.

 CHAPTER XV

The Roads

"WE KEEP on this way," the old man said harshly, pointing to the north. "You turn here." (Weakness is over. Though my own flesh rise up to deny me, I will go on. It has been said with truth that a man's foes are they of his own household; then I will go on with the strength of strangers. Those marching men believed in me. I live in their minds. And I saw many young men, bold young faces passing by. A great caravan is waiting, there will be young men, strong, eager, fighters for Kansas. I will lead them, aye, again I will be a scourge to evil. Weakness is over.)

"We keep on this way. You turn here."

Salmon and Hen Thompson rode a dozen paces out on the fork of the trail. Oliver wheeled close to Frederick. The yellow-haired giant was standing by the wagon-rear, agitated, biting at the nails and flesh of his thick fingers. Tears were in his eyes. Lucius Moles turned his head away, moved off a little.

"Fred!" the dark boy whispered. "For the last time I ask you! Come with us!"

"I can't! I can't!" the giant said. "I've got to live it out!"

For days, coming north, Oliver had pled with the great fellow. But it was no use, he only shook his head wildly and

≡ * 84 * ≡

cried, "I've got to go back to Kansas!" Deep in the dimness of that poor brain throbbed a memory: *Your boots, don't forget your boots against the cold, Allie!* it's nothing, he'll be back soon *Oh, what have you done to him?* father won't let me, but don't be afraid, it's nothing, it's nothing *Allie! Allie!*

"Good-bye, Fred."

The pale racked eyes looked up; and the giant said, "See what Effie Toombs is doing, Oliver."

"Effie To— ? Who is Effie . . . ? All right, Fred, I'll see." The boy held out his hand. The other gripped it with moist frantic fingers, crying:

"There were three pails, Oliver. I left 'em in the barn, they were new and shiny. Maybe you could use 'em."

"The farm's sold, Fred."

"The farm's sold? Sol-l- oh . . . maybe you could use . . . but see what Effie Toombs is doing, Oliver."

"I'll see what she's doing, Fred." Out on the fork Hen and Salmon were restlessly wheeling their mounts. The youngest brother touched Frederick's wild yellow head in a hopeless gesture of farewell; then reined Ned Scarlet up to the front of the wagon. A pain was cutting his heart, he thought: he'll be lost out here, he'll come to his end. The old man was sitting motionless, holding the lines.

"Good-bye, father."

"Good-bye."

"Don't . . . don't hold a grievance against me."

"I hold no grievance against you."

"I'll try to help . . . in my own way."

"Go. Ease your weakness. . . . But hear me now. . . . I do not release you. The work goes on, as long as I keep my life the work will go on. So be ready. I'll call on you again."

The boy's face was working. He longed to offer his hand. But the bluish burning eyes looked off beyond him.

"Be watchful of the young. Tell Annie her father bids her fear the Lord. . . . Say to your mother . . . we do not stop remembering her."

The boy wheeled swiftly away. In an instant the three young fellows were thudding out in a swirl of dust, eastward. The little company silently watched them. A mile distant the riders came to the height of a ridge. They halted, etched sharp against the cold morning sky. They waved; and were gone.

≡ * 85 * ≡

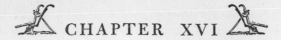

CHAPTER XVI

The Covenant:
Frederick "Lives It Out"

AND NOW there was a new gang along Cygnes water. The old man had forty riders. They were already a familiar fearful sight from Lawrence south to the Bourbon slaver country—fierce riders in a line of battle, with a gaunt man in a long white linen duster leading them astride a blooded bay. The older hunted days were dimmed; there was a Covenant, written in the balky painful peasant's hand, and now he was Captain John Brown:

"We whose names are found on these following pages do hereby enlist ourselves to serve in the Free-State cause under John Brown as Commander . . . and we severally pledge our word and sacred honor to said Commander that we will faithfully perform our duty as a regular volunteer force for the maintenance of the rights and liberties of the Free-State citizens in Kansas. . . .

". . . Signed: Noah Fraze. William Leeman. Luke Parsons. Boris Darrach (surgeon). Timothy Kelly . . . William Quick . . . Amos Alderman . . . Samuel Geer (commisary) . . . August Bondi . . . James . . . Cyrus. . . .

". . . Article 2nd: Every officer connected with this organization (except the commander already named) shall be elected by a majority of. . . .

". . . Article 9th: A disorderly retreat shall not be suffered at any time, and every officer and private, be, and fully is, empowered to prevent the same by force if need be & any attempt at leaving the ground, be, and during a fight, is hereby declared disorderly. . . .

". . . Article 12th: Keeping up fires or lights after dark or boisterous talking while in camp shall not be allowed, except fires and lights when necessary, and all uncivil, profane, vulgar talking shall be discountenanced. . . .

". . . No person after having first surrendered himself a prisoner shall be put to death without first having had the benefit of an impartial trial. . . ."

Captain John Brown had forty men; and he would guard Osawatomie.

Northward, across the Missouri border, eleven hundred slavers were bivouacked outside the town of New Santa Fé.

Jason Brown, released from the Leavenworth prison, found his wife and his boy at the Adair cabin; he had not seen them for four months.

"No, Jay," said the Reverend Adair firmly. "I can't keep you here."

"But where shall I go?" pleaded Jason. He was begrimed and his clothes were tattered; his face was pallid from confinement.

"Find your father. You'll be safest with him. And in the meantime I'll be getting things ready for you to leave for the East."

"I've been apart all these months, Uncle Adair! How can you tell me to go now?"

"Because you must think of Ellen and Tom. And I have to protect my own too. I've been let alone thus far, maybe my cloth has meant something. But if you stay here you may draw them. They haven't forgot Potawatomie."

". . . All right. I'll go . . . if it's best for them."

They went back into the other room. Florilla was urging solemn young Tom to finish the bowl of gruel. Ellen looked up from her darning with wide dreading eyes.

"I have to go, Elly."

"Oh!" White-faced, she clung to him. "You only just got back."

"It won't be for long," he said. He tried to smile. But he was so thin, and in his eyes there was something broken and old.

"Take us with you, Jay. Take us East, Jay."

"Soon," he said, holding her tight.

"Take us away from here, Jay."

"Soon, Elly, soon."

Later, he stood in the cold drizzle, and looked upon the ruins of his home. It was levelled to the ground, every last beam; it was a scarred wet mass. The small fields he had toiled over, won so painfully from the wasteland, were run wild again with weeds and prairie-grass. The corral-fence was down; no living thing was anywhere. Further along the plain he could see the ravage which once had been John's dwelling. Jason turned and went weakly toward the river timber.

Night came down as the raiders returned to the camp on the hill. It had been a good day, the cause of freedom was prospering: they had swept the Sugar Creek slaver settlement of two hundred head of cattle, and they had a rich plunder of clothing and provisions.

The men lay about, dog-tired. Below, in the dark valley, across the river, the few lights of the little town glimmered in the mist.

"Go on, Fred," said the old man. "You'll come down bad if you don't watch out."

The yellow-haired giant was sitting before the fire, visibly shivering. He was wrapped in a blanket against the wet wind. In the gleam his staring white-sick face was like a gargoyle's come to life. "Where'll I go?" he said.

"Anywhere. So long as you get indoors and find shelter. Florilla will keep you if she knows you're chilled. And if you can't do better, there are empty cabins along the Lawrence road."

"I don't want to sleep alone!" he cried.

"Go, now. I say for you to go."

Frederick Brown whimpered, and his eyes were piteous. Then, before the other's gaze, he rose; and shambled off, a mumbling hulk, toward the mounts. They were ready-saddled; he pulled himself up upon a white mare. They heard his hoarse wild cry as he clattered away into the darkness.

Near midnight, down on the prairie, a sentinel's challenge sounded. Soon they brought Jason Brown to his father. The old man embraced him. "My son, you are thinned," he said. Then, his voice faintly trembling, he asked, "Does your brother live?"

". . . and he was chained by each ankle. He kept screaming and casting himself about. Iverson said, keep that man still, or we'll do it for you. I tried to get him quiet, but he didn't have a glimmer of reason, he still didn't know me. He kept on yelling. Then Iverson sent three troopers into the tent. . . . They beat him worse than the first time. . . . They kneeled on his chest and pounded him. Once one of them stood off and kicked him full force in the back of the neck. And I had to watch, and I

≡ * 88 * ≡

couldn't do anything. I pleaded with them, don't kill a crazed man. No more crazy than you are, they said, we'll fetch it out of him. After that, John lay quiet for hours, like a log. He was unconscious and all bleeding. And I couldn't help him——" (Oh, the old man groaned in the dark) "——because they kept me tied. We stayed there about two weeks, and all the time they were hunting for you. They said they'd kill us if you tried to get us away. Then we were ordered to move again. They drove us on foot, chained two and two. I was chained to George Partridge. They drove us in a gang right up in front of Uncle Adair's house. Florilla came out and talked to Iverson. What does this mean, Florilla said, what does this mean in this land of the free, driving innocent men like cattle and slaves? She went on giving him a sharp cutting, but Iverson didn't say anything, he only laughed. Florilla gave us a little food. They began to drive us again. At Ottawa ford the Kilbourne boy dropped in a stroke. He got away a few days later, because they eased up watching him. . . . We went seventy miles chained like that. Then they threw us in the Leavenworth hole. We expected to be strung up any minute. But a man named Jakob acted like a friend. He got me released, he proved there was no charge against me. John is still held. He was active in Free-State politics, they say. Jakob promised to help him, he said he would get John out soon. . . . He's down to a shadow. Sometimes his mind is clear, but other times his mind is dark. . . ."

"My poor son," said the old man. "My poor John."

"When he comes back we must go East together."

The old man sat there silent for a moment. Then he said, "Aye, go East together."

"It's our last hope, father. We'd perish here."

"There will be only Fred left. Of all my sons there will be only the least."

"Father! Come with us, come home with us!"

"I long to. I hunger for home."

"Then for God's sake come! We've only known evil in Kansas."

"My work is here."

The first morning light was glimmering in the east as the four riders came over the crest of the Lawrence road. A hundred yards down, outside an abandoned cabin, the yellow-haired fellow stood watching his white mare nuzzle and crunch in the feed-bag; stood gazing with child-like pleasure. He heard the hoofbeats, and looked up. The riders came down fast upon him through the raw grayness. He did not stir, he gazed curiously at them. They reined up sharp, rifles athwart the saddle bows.

"Hullo!" the giant cried, dimly remembering the man with the black hat.

Preacher White fired. Frederick Brown slid to the ground, a bullet through his heart.

From the west, on the high ground above the town, two hundred slaver horsemen were swiftly approaching Osawatomie.

 CHAPTER XVII

Osawatomie Brown

"COME ON, MEN!" he called, and began running down the hill toward the river. They snatched at their weapons and followed him in a rush; but one fellow took a last hasty gulp of coffee. They could already hear the crackle of rifle-fire coming from the plain beyond the town. It was Ham Hyatt and his riders, detail watching over yesterday's cattle plunder; they had ridden out to engage the point of the advancing slavers.

"Parsons," said the old man as they ran swishing into the shallows; "were you ever under fire?"

The young fellow by his side was white-lipped, but he answered steadily, "No. But I will obey orders."

"Take more care to end life well than to live long."

Jason Brown was running close behind them, clutching the rifle his father had thrust into his hands; panting, dazed. The messenger's words beat in his brain, beat: they've killed Fred Brown, they've killed Fred Brown!

Now they were across, on the edge of the town. We can't make a stand within, thought the old man, there are the women and the young ones, we'll have to risk the river at our back. "Parsons!" he called. "Take ten men and hold that blockhouse!"

Then he headed swiftly for the fringe of timber along the Cygnes, his long white coat flying out behind him; and the rest followed hard. They scattered behind trees and rocks. The old man scurried from point to point, calling, "Make your shots count, make them count! Aim low! Be sure of your hind sight!" They could see a long double line of horsemen advancing from the west. The sun gleamed on a brass cannon. The cannon had been seen from the blockhouse too; the structure would be a deathtrap against the heavy shot; and in a moment Parsons and the others came running for the shelter of the timber. Three men crept in from Osawatomie, and took positions. Ham Hyatt's jayhawkers had retreated through the town, their ammunition exhausted, and one of their number dead. Old Brown had some forty men.

The Ruffians came sweeping down the open prairie. The Free-State rifles opened a sudden fire. There was a writhing and plunging among the attackers; four horses galloped away, empty-saddled. The rifles cracked again, the double line broke. But only for a moment; now they were dismounting, now they were advancing with a brisk fire upon the timber. Behind them the cannon was quickly unlimbered, and wheeled into position. There was a dull report; grapeshot whined about the Free-Staters, whipping the brush and snapping down boughs from the trees. The Missourians pressed closer behind a raking volley; they were two hundred. The Free-Staters gave way slowly (Noah Fraze lay twisted and lifeless in the sere grass); the stream was at their back, they would be trapped. The old man's eyes were blazing with a cold fighting fury, but he saw everything, his mind was like a blade for vigilance. they could stand at the bank to the last, or they could try the crossing and rally beyond. When they reached the old sawmill and the timber began to thin out he suddenly cried, "Get across! Get across!" They turned and ran for the river; they were lost if the Ruffians reached the bank before they were well across. They leaped in, began to strain through the deepening water. Charlie Kiyser, the Bohemian, was a lone figure on the bank; he kneeled behind some logs, firing (he could not swim, and did not know the deepest water at that point was only shoulder high). The Ruffians came rushing up. A dozen balls ploughed fatally the Bohemian's breast and head. Out on the stream the slugs were flicking up jets about the fleeing Free-Staters. The old man was a queer harried figure, with his broad straw hat and the two revolvers held high over his head and the coat-tails of the white duster floating outspread upon the water like wings. Young George Partridge and fat little Geer the "commisary" were straining forward among the last. Two riflemen suddenly appeared close on a jutting ledge upstream. The fat man dived, the bullets sprayed and slapped above him. Partridge halted, fired, and in that instant was pierced through the brain. He sank gently, staining the waters. On the further Cygnes bank the first of the fleeing "Covenanters" draggled up to safety. "Hold!" old Brown screamed as his men began to run for the cover of the eastern timber. "Hold!" But their powder was wet; across the stream were two hundred slavers. The fugitives scattered. Slowly the rifle-fire died behind them.

A white wisp of smoke curled up into the gray sky, a tongue of flame licked scarlet beneath it. Osawatomie was burning. The smoke blackened and billowed; it spread like a pall over the valley. High in the further Cygnes woods John Brown and Jason stood watching the flames. Tears were streaming down the old man's furrowed cheeks.

"God," he said; "see this evil. Let there be no peace in all this land till slavery is done for. . . . I have only a short time to live. I will die fighting them."

When night came the old man and Jason crept back across the river darkness to find the dead body of their son and brother.

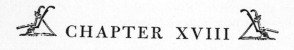

CHAPTER XVIII

Life Is Woven Wind

AFTER THE burning of Osawatomie, the old man, ill, and desolate with loss, found refuge at the cabin of 'Taway Jones. 'Taway was a Christian Indian who lived deep in the timber; Brown had once befriended him against Dutch Henry's gang. Soon the Ottawa said quietly, "They are after you again, they offer money for you." The old man went into a leashed rage. He strode unsteadily about the cellar, with the blanket trailing from his bowed shoulders to the ground, whispering fiercely, "They won't drive me out. I've got a right to walk free in Kansas. My children's blood has flowed for Kansas. . . . I'll stay, and I'll kill the first one who tries to take me, so help me God!"

All that afternoon the pride and bitterness kept storming in his heart; as always the imminence of peril served only to tighten the marrow of his defiance. But the ague-fever was mounting; when night came he was desperately ill, there was a consuming rage in his blood. For three days he lay chilled and parched and shivering. Then the fever died, and he was left weak, his limbs seemed drained yet heavy as stones. A rifle lay by his pallet, and two revolvers were in the belt on the floor; but they could have taken him like a child. The days went by, shortening with the oncoming winter; and he lay there, nursed by the Indian; and out on the obscure trails they hunted him, hunted him through the timber and the Swamp of the Swan.

Faintly his strength flowed back; the first time he tried to get up unaided he sagged down, he fell dizzy and trembling, and he wept for sheer impotence. But later a strange calm came upon him, and with it such a lucidity as he could not remember. It was as if the fever had seared away mists in his mind, as if false blinding lights had died there. He saw his way, he knew what he must do. Deep in the soul's wilderness, amid all the perplexity and the dark mortifications, there shone at last the great gleaming promise:

His work was done in Kansas. He had proved himself; he had made the sacrifice of blood before his God, and in suffering and in fire had been tested. Now he would go on . . . into the mountains! *Let someone take men of good principles, God-fearing men, men who respect themselves. Take them into the hills, into the deep narrow defiles. They could defy all the armies of the South. I say this from observation, sir, not idly. I have studied tactics, I have studied fortifications and the movements of armies, here and in Europe. When the time comes I shall be ready. God has given the strength of mountains to freedom.*

Lying prostrate in the cold dimness of the cellar, the thought possessed him like a vision. But now, as always, the mystical fabric of his mind was deeply threaded with vigor and a canny peasant sense. In his soul he could affirm the wisdom of the Master—was not Kansas but a link in the infinite chain of His purpose?—and cry aloud with bitter joy, He puts on me garments of vengeance, I am clad with zeal as a cloak; but he was not lost to the stress about him, the drive of the common life. The fire burned fiercely, but it was banked with vigilance; the heart might flood with the dream, yet the eyes watched lynx-like.

Winter was close, the vast driven blizzards would come howling down; then the thaw and the high impassable waters; and thus till spring would Kansas be held safe by the elements. Moreover, it was only a question of time before the ultimate triumph of the Free-State cause would be achieved. For without a rule of iron the slavers were helpless. Climate and soil fought against them, the slave crops could not live through the bleak seasons; and the wagon-trains kept rolling in from the East, like a tide. Kansas would come in free, brooded the old man, but for whom would there be freedom? The fight had been waged for soil, not for the souls of the blacks; the Free-State constitution excluded all Negroes from the Territory. He, John Brown, spat on so base a suffrage. There was no place for him here, he would leave them to their pottage. He had a sword to bear—*into Africa!*

*   *   *   *   *

The two brothers walked by the wagon as it jolted up the rough trail; the old surveying instruments rattled on the empty seat. The way was long, the horse had to be saved; so Jason guided her afoot and John plodded painfully alongside. (The elder brother's clothes hung loose from his body. Light had slowly crept back to his mind but something shattered and lost crouched still in his eyes, hung desperately on the edge of darkness.) They had been able to gather just enough money to send Ellen and Wealthy and the two boys eastward along the river-route; they themselves would ride and tie to Chicago. The old man was going into Iowa to seek Owen. Inside, now, he lay in the wagon-bottom, shivering and weak with the recurring ague, and the dysentery. He was covered with hay against the bitter winds that came cutting and swirling across the prairie. Those who had never seen him would not easily discern the dread "Osawatomie" in this feeble old rustic "surveyor." But beneath the hay his bony hands could quickly grasp the two revolvers.

". . . I am reporting from a camp near the Nebraska boundary. We got here yesterday, at noon. Just missed the arrest of the notorious Osawatomie outlaw, Brown. Learned that he had been seen at a deserted house near the Nawitch crossing with some of his gang. I ordered out a large detachment immediately. But they found only an old farmer and his two sons sheltering for the night. . . . Brown has already escaped into Nebraska. . . . Awaiting further orders. . . .

Lieut.Col. Thomas Bond, U. S. Army."

The stinging cold came down on the Kansas towns. The mud-churned streets froze like rock; and in the bleak draughty cabins the people shivered by the slow fires. Out on the prairie the wind lashed and howled, the wind was a fury; the gaunt creaking Cygnes cottonwoods harshly mourned above the shallow grave of Frederick Brown. Soon the great white shroud would descend upon it. Soon the whiteness would cover five unmarked mounds in the bitter valley of the Potawatomie.

They were camped for the night in a hollow, where the thrust of the wind was broken a little. The two sons huddled by the fire, beneath blankets, smoking their pipes. About them the night was a cold vastness; dark, without stars, without moon.

"Jason."

The old man was calling from the depths of the wagon. The son rose up slowly. He knocked his pipe clean upon his boot, and the tiny glowing coals whirled down and died. He thrust the cob into his pocket, sighing deeply, unknown to himself; and went to the wagon-flap. He pulled it aside and said:

"It's Jason, father."

"I wish to write home. Reach up here . . . the small bag, the one with my papers. . . . Now, Jason, light the lamp . . . and hang it here."

A little later the assassin sat motionless beneath the lamp that hung from the nail; with the soiled paper before him on a board, and a stub held tight in the long nervous fingers; with hay to his armpits and a shawl draped over his shoulders. He wore an old red wool hat, and the side pieces were turned down over his ears. In the wan light of the grimy lamp the face was deep-lined and sombre, like scarred slate; the mouth was a rigid twisted cleft. But from the cavernous eyes gleamed melancholy:

". . . and the idea of again visiting all you at Elba is so calculated to unman me that I do not allow my thoughts to dwell overmuch on it. May He give me to come home again & look upon the faces of my poor fatherless children, and Mary who bears with me for love of God. It must be, if ever, for only a shortest time; for as you know, I have another big brood of black chicks to scratch for. I trust you are all performing your service with patient spirit, *doing with your might.* I have had hard ague shakes of late; and John is uncertain in manifold ways. Watson, I want you to feed out the potatoes not too freely; and I want you to be exceeding carefull to have no straw wasted, but to use generous straw for bedding the cattle to keep them from lying in the mire. Again one of our number sleeps in the dust. It has been a bitter cup and we have drunk deeply, but still the Lord reigneth and blessed be His holy name for ever. *Faint, we are yet pursuing. . . ."*

The flap was pulled softly aside, and the gentle thin face of Jason peered in from the outside night.

"Do you need anything, father? I'm turning in."

"No. I need nothing."

"Will you be able to handle the lamp?"

"Yes, yes. . . . How does your brother do?"

"He's sleeping."

"God rest him."

"Father . . . tell them home, we wish to be remembered."

"I'll tell them."

"Good-night, father."

"Good-night, son."

When the old man had finished the letter he fumbled about the hay for the ancient leather bag. He thrust the paper into the bag. There were many letters in it; he saved religiously every commonest word. He was about to strain up toward the lamp when he saw that two letters had slipped from the bundle to the hay. He took them up, glancing at them almost heedlessly; he was tired. But the handwriting of one instantly caught at him, cut swiftly down to a slumbering depth of his mind. He held it closer before his eyes, dimmed badly of late by the ague; began to read:

"Dear Son John, I received yours of 13th on the 25th, and was very glad to larn that all your Famelys were so well, and that you had not been distourbed by the enemy. Your letters come very regular, and we look carfully after them. I have been faithful to answer them, not out of ambishon, but to keep one or more on the road all the time. My health at present is not so good; for three weeks past I am somewhat put to it to breathe, mostly nights, and sometimes feel as though death was at the dore. I feel as though God was very mersofull to keep such a great sinner on probation so long. My life has been of little worth, mostly filled up with vanitys, I have been the companion of fools. I ask all of you to pray more earnestly for the salvation of my soul than for the life of my body. . . . I am now at Edward's: it is rather a cold, stormy day. We have had a remarkable cold, snowe winter, and the snow is mostly on the ground now. I consider all of my children at Kansas as one Famely, and hope you will take turns in writeing. Your unfaithful parent, Oaken Brown."

The old man sat there very still for a long time. *John, get fires goin' when the sun goes down.* Then he placed the letters in the bag, reached up painfully for the lamp, and blew it out. He sank back into the hay faintly sweet with clover *Saviour, hear the children when they pray* and burrowed deeper into its warm dark embrace. Outside upon the still cold night rose the wild dogs' mourning, but the assassin did not know. He was lost in an older living time; he was a boy on a wilderness hill, setting fires at sundown; he was a boy at the bosom of his mother, Ruth Mills Brown, lovely as night, and doomed. The sands of his life were full again, he felt them pouring, pouring, pouring toward his destiny:

That it might be fulfilled which was spoken of the Lord by the prophet saying, Out of Egypt have I called My son.

INTERLUDE

INTERLUDE

Deep in the Remembering Blood

HE STOOD there barefooted in the hot black earth of the rows, holding the burning pine-knot—a boy in a torn cotton shirt and butternut jeans, supported by a single leather strap encircling his left shoulder—watching the sun as it crept low toward the forest with great spreading flames of blood and gold; to the east blue shadows were falling on the hills. The boy's sharp face was screwed up intently. He had no mind for the tiredness weighing heavy on his seven-year-old frame, his insides trembling for food; he had no eye for the maize yellow in the sunglow as old quince, nor the pewter plates hung on poles to frighten crows, gleaming with stabs of light. Pa had told him to get fires going at sundown. Tired or hungry, then, that was the thing, to get them going when the sun went down. For the wind had blown from the north and a little from the west two nights running. If on a third night it blew again, a summer frost would fall, and in the morning the grain would be dead. Last summer frosts caught them, and no corn got ripe; spring came along and there was no seed for planting. And see how hard it was with them now. No hot crusty pone, no rye-'n-injun melting soft in your mouth, only that hard sour bread Ma made from acorns baked in fire, acorns that fell from the red oaks and the white oaks. No johnny-cake, with molasses Ma said came across a wide water, across an ocean from the Indies; no sifted corn and kidney beans, all mixed and steaming and sweet. These days there was only cheese-clabber, and bean strips hung from the rafters. Old Christian Cackler, who was the first settler hereabout, he said it was the hardest year for provisions he knew in all his Ohio times (was that why Ma looked so hurt in her eyes, was that why he came on her crying?), Christian he said folks would always remember 1807 for fierce bitter want, those that lived through it.

But they could fight grain chill, and that was his job. The sun would be down in a minute—there! the wind was beginning to lull, it always lulled between the sun and coming of night.

He would kindle fires windward along the fields (is that why you were crying? but you were crying other times too)—

There! the rim hung just over the trees . . . now there was only sky, like blood. Swiftly he bent over the first pile of faggots and thrust the brand to them. The tinder caught flame, writhed up; the dry boughs took the fire with a leaping crackle. He loved the sharp fierce sound. There were five other stacks formed high at spaces of ten feet; he went fast in a stir across the row, kindling them. Then he set the phlox burning along the field's edge. The white flowers shrivelled to ash; the herb would go slowly, smolder and smoke.

The boy stood back, watching. It was his work. Pa had given him the job. The big man had come in last night from a week's surveying trip, caked with mud to the waist, his great shoulders drooping with weariness. It was just before the boy went up to bed. "Get fires goin' at sundown, John. The wind's come up nor'west twice runnin'." He gulped water from the noggin on the table; then in all his clothes—fringed hunting shirt of home-spun, baggy elk-skin trousers, moccasins—dropped to the bed-stead. He had been sleeping the night and the full day, twenty-four hours and still at it. "Get fires goin', John." Nothing else he had said, leaving the job to him. Well, he had done it, got them going. Now it was windless time and the smoke would stay low, over the ground slow slow it would creep, creeping and mixing with the evening vapors. Ma called them that. Evening vapors. You had, she said, to stay clear of them, because they brought fevers. Well, then all night the ground would be covered with smoke like a feather quilt, the grain would be hid from the chill till the sun came up the next morning to drive it away. He knew how that would look, vapors white as milk, vapors scudding, smoke drifting in the first cold sunlight. He was up early, he saw things stirring in the new day; in the sky, on the hills, in the waters of the creek. Well, then the corn would be saved.

The flames began to burn lower, from singing gold to fitful sombre flickers. Night was coming on; he could see hearthglow framed in the open doorway of the cabin across the wide clearing. Food, things cooking; sharply he felt his hunger. But he stood there, watching the flames. Pa had given him the job. . . . Fires at sundown, ran in his head. Fires at night. Fires burning. Like words in the Bible, the fierce words his dark soft ma would

≡ * 102 * ≡

read (why do you cry so often, do you have a pain, is it Ann's plaguing of you?) she would read about kings and warriors. Gideon had seen fire rise up out of a rock . . . maybe tonight she would read, but maybe it would be about Jesus our Saviour. Evening vapors, stay clear of them, son, they bring fevers. The boy looked uneasily about. Then he took a last proud look at his work. It was good, he could see smoke wheeling thick across the dark field. So he stepped quickly past the dying fires and went along the maize rows; went by the patch of scaly hops, and the pole beans high and ghostly over his head; and there was the sharp bitter smell of brimstone about. Rags had been dipped in sulphur and fixed in a row on short sticks. That kept crows off, and foxes. They knew the smell. It was like gun-shot.

He walked up the narrow path beaten down through a tangle of tall grass toward the house. It was a low log place with an attic where the boys slept; and there was a big shed jutting out behind for the beasts and the grain. Two years before when they came out to Ohio in the springtime Pa had put up the house. Neighbors had helped, coming in for the work from places all about. He remembered that like it was today; how the men cut down the trees for acres around, the toppling and the awful quivering crashes hour after hour; the sawing, and the teams of young steers, each with his head in a collar of hardwood, dragging the logs into heaps with chains, and the men with handspikes, heaving and cursing. Then the great fierce fires when night came on, with the sky all flaming and showers of sparks against the dark of it; the frightened bats flitting wildly in from the night, into the hot light, smashing against trees; and the bewildered owl that plunged straight to the heart of the flame. He remembered the food the neighbors had brought in, heaped on a pine-scaffold outside, everyone joining in to eat— bear meat and venison, squashes and butter-beans and melons, bowls of milk and peach cobbler, cider and cheese and apple-pie; then much drinking, and the young people in a rough wild dance to the measure of singing and beaten hands, and a great stir and laughter till the early hours. He remembered it all. Life was still and solemn, after.

Fires had cleared the ground about the cabin, but the forest was there. You felt it at night, heavy and mysterious, stretching out dark far far back, nobody knew just how far, nor just what was beyond. (Some said a great plain, all sky and straight silent

≡ * 103 * ≡

levels with seven-foot grass; some talked of an endless shining river.) Even in the daytime it was like a hood overhead, with the thick leaves whispering and shutting out the sun. Ma hated the forest and the dark hush. A sick gloaming, she said. But you could lay traps for badgers and coons, smash snakes, throw branches to get the wild pigeons whirring off in a scare. But at night it was different. You felt the forest then. A sick gloaming. There it was about him now, black and rustling. Wolves were in it, he had heard them howling on winter nights; and bears, deep in. An owl hooted as the boy came toward the cabin, and from the pond the bull-frogs were at their sullen croaking guggle.

The big room was a living and eating place in one; with a wide open-hearth made of sandstone slabs and heavy clay-covered timbers; with a clapboard table and rough hand-fashioned pine-chairs and three-legged stools. There were two makeshift bedsteads, formed with forked poles for end supports from which other poles extended into crevices in the walls, and split boards crossed widthwise to lie upon. The wall-logs had moss and mud squeezed hard into the chinks against the winds. They were bare now, it was August, but in winter they were hung with blankets, furs and deer-hides. Buck antlers thrust into joists held two flintlocks. There was a wooden ladder leading to the attic-loft where the boys slept. A draping of skins in patchwork hung from a beam in the far left corner, closing off a small alcove. Young Ann slept there. Roderick had his crib nearby.

His mother was bending over it now as the boy came in; tending the baby, soothing him with touches of her hands. Samuel, five and freckled and sturdy, was solemnly astride the big wooden shovel, shelling on its iron-shod edge the precious corn his father had brought back with him from the trip. Levi was stomach-down by the hearth, at his drawing. The boy went to his mother's side.

"Evenin', Ma."

She straightened up, a small frail woman in a blue woolsey dress, with black hair hanging in a thick double braid to her waist.

"Blessed evening, John."

She had a dark high-cheeked face, with lines that made her look older than thirty-two. Her eyes were bright, but as with a fever; there were shadows about the black lights of her eyes.

Her mouth was ashen, and in its peace seemed strangely at odds with the rest of her countenance; for she gave the sense of tensity, as if she were waiting always on the edge of some hovering fear.

"Get washed up nicely, John. I'll have your supper soon."

She spoke in a low voice, remembering her husband asleep on the bedstead across the room. But she spoke gently always.

John washed with water from the huge clay crock standing on the maple-chest; then rubbed his face hard with a piece of rough brown-crash till it began to shine like a bronze plate. He watched Levi through the towel. The older boy was belly-down on the puncheon floor (they had a floor now; last winter Ma was sick with the bitter cold knifing up from the pack-down dirt); Levi was drawing on a slate, with pieces of clay. His doe-like eyes were eager; from time to time he brushed back the rebellious brown hair from his face. He was twelve, hardly taller than John; when he was tired, which was often, he looked very delicate.

"There's good clay down to the hoss path," said John. "I'll bring 'em tomorrow."

Levi did not look up. "Ann and me found greens and blues today," he said. "Down to the creek, where the willow was split by the storm. Ma said they're soapstone. You find 'em in the beds of streams, she said."

John took three narrow strips of calfskin from his pocket. His bluish eyes held a faintest trace of scorn. "You make ox-whips with these," he said. "I'm goin' to make an ox-whip."

He stood proudly twisting the thongs in his strong young fingers. His bare legs planted wide apart glowed ruddy in the waves of heat from the fire. He had a tight jaw; there was an odd gravity in the lift of his small narrow head.

Now the mother came over to the hearth, bearing a large pot of uncooked bean porridge. She placed it with difficulty over the fire. "Levi," she said, breathing hard, "go up . . . and see if you can . . . get Ann to come down. She hasn't touched a snip . . . all day."

The boy rose at once, seeking her face with his hungry shining eyes; and went to the attic ladder. He loved her passionately. She was not his mother, though he did not know it. His own had died bearing him, back in Connecticut; his father had been stricken by a fever two months earlier; and the girl who had been his mother's friend during their maidenhood was rearing him. She loved the boy, remembering always his mother through him; and for himself also. He moved her with compassion; he was so different from her own grim John and sturdy young Samuel, he would be so helpless, she saw, against the thrust of life. And yet sometimes she was not sure of this. Sometimes he seemed strong. It was not anything he could do with his limbs or his body (his dry hollow cough worried her), but something happened in his eyes and then she felt he was strong. It was as if he could abide in a little inner world of his own, and it would be enough. And he had a power of understanding. Look how he was with Ann. Only Levi could help Ann, she herself could do almost nothing with the child. He would wander with her in the woods, and when they came back she would go about the house quietly. When night fell and often her restlessness became pitched almost to a paroxysm, it was only Levi who could still her. He just sat by, whispering to her from time to time. When she refused to eat and went for days without food, it was in the end Levi who got her, feverish and worn, to take a little of something. It was a strange power for quiet he had over the child. . . . Now he climbed the attic ladder to her. Maybe he could get her to eat.

The mother brought another kettle to the fire. "Coffee" was in it, a muddy liquid mingled of ground barley, parched rye, chestnuts and dandelion root. She hung it upon the cooking rod. John had gone unbidden to a corner of the room. He picked up a stool and placed it for her before the hearth. He said nothing, the young face immobile and stern as ever; yet as she sat down, smiling faintly, she knew how he was warm and moved for love of her. Then he took from the wall a long red-cherry shoot for stirring, and brought it to the mother. He waited, standing, hoping that she would need something else. She gave no sign, so he sat down on the floor by her side. All this, repeated each night, was done simply, yet with a kind of ceremoniousness in which both participated with subtle agreement, as though his bringing of a stool and a cherry shoot, and her smile for him, were the symbol of his love and her recognition of it.

Slowly she stirred the coffee with the shoot. Samuel came across the room to her side. She put her left arm about him, held him close.

"Are you very hungry, son? You're sleepy too. . . . Supper will be ready soon, then you can go up."

He burrowed the back of his tow-head into her bosom. She breathed in from him the smell of barn and loam and green boughs. She began slowly to rock with him. How like their father these boys were, she thought. She turned a little to look at him, lying in the makeshift. Except for the rise and fall of his back in breathing, he was still as a log. Last night he had come in bowed with fatigue and covered with drying mud. His gaunt furrowed face, ordinarily unbearded, was dark with a long ragged stubble. "Evenin', Ruth," he had said; and then to John, "Get fires goin' at sundown." He had gulped water from the noggin; then sagged to the bed. Nothing had stirred him since from his stupor, not the housework going on, the whimpering of the baby in the crib, the shouts of the boys outside, not the barking of the dogs.

That was like Owen Brown, to rag himself down to exhaustion. To spend your last ounce of strength in work was at once an enthusiasm and a dogma with him. "Go to," he would say to the boys at the outset of some task; "go to, and give your heart to it. No slackin' now, mind you, or you'll get fetched." They needed to strain every muscle in doing things, needed every energy for his satisfaction. They knew often the swipe of his great horned hands. Samuel's job was to bring in dry chips from the woodpile every afternoon, so the fire could be lit the next morning. If the chips were damp he had to dry them. Often in childish heedlessness he flopped them down on the floor, soggy, and left them so. The next morning the father before going out to feed the ox would find damp kindling; the fire would not burn. At about six o'clock of a bleak winter dawn the crack of doom would overtake Samuel lying drowned in sleep upstairs. His father would rouse him out, stand him shivering in his bare feet on the icy puncheon floor, and give it to him hard. "A man's best is often a poor skinny thing," he said even as the huge paw whacked the soft young rump, "but so long as it's his best I've nothin' to complain. It's your twistin' away from things you can do good that'll bring you a whoppin'."

Levi knew his judgment too. He was supposed to watch the leach-tubs out in the shed. He had to fill them through the

≡ * 107 * ≡

winter months with refuse grease from the cooking; then when the moon was in the spring quarter they could make soap. The bloated rancid smell of the grease sickened him; when he touched the clammy stuff his fingers writhed. But Levi was never whopped. Instead, Owen Brown would forbid him the use of the slate, or he might send him up to the loft just when the mother was beginning to read aloud from the Bible.

As for John, a blow from his father's hand was his deepest dread. It was not the smart he feared; he could take a hiding without a whimper. He could not bear the disgrace. It was the symbol of weakness, of his failing. He felt during such black moments his pride shamed before the family: he was no longer John who could do things, who could handle the horse and dig in the fields and burn fires at sundown; he was no longer his father's helper, he was a baby being whopped.

Most men who came out to hew destinies from this great Ohio wilderness went at their labors with varying degrees of fortitude, but for Owen Brown there was joy in the fight. Life was hard, but he liked it hard. "I was made for strugglin'," he would say. And so he was, a giant of a man in the prime of his strength at thirty-six, with shoulders formed for burdens, and limbs like steel, and courage fit to go with them. There was no hardship, no hazard to which he was not eager to measure himself. The backwoods community had come to know his stoutness, and it was his greatest pride that people called him "Oaken" Brown.

He was austere in his living. "A man's strong," he said often, "in the things he don't need." Thus he ate sparingly, though his appetite was gigantic. Mrs. Langford, an old woman who lived deeper in the forest with her two sons, remembered his restraint with amazement. She was a fat little person, clad always in a black tunic-like dress and a green poke-bonnet; with a monstrous goitre and large swimming eyes. She spoke in a gasping wire-like voice for the sounding of which all her strength seemed to be summoned: "He was passin' by hot and tired. He asked for a drink, so I fill up a good noggin of my best cider, cold 'n sharp as ever, and bring it out with a slab of apple pie fresh baked. And do you know what the queer one said? Think on it! He said, I'll drink nothin' but water, ma'am, thank you. Not pie neither, my meal time's not come. Think on it! Cider 'n apple, and him sayin' his meal time warn't come!"

He did not smoke, nor did he drink peachy and pig-'n-whistle, the home-fermented liquors the woodsmen used; revelling unrighteously all the while in his power to deny himself. Not that scruple held him. It was manlier, he thought, to abstain. He would have been the first to embrace the habits if he had been convinced of their needfulness. Whatever, in short, cultivated vigor was good; and he swore by the measures that did so to such a degree that he made of lustihood a fetish. In reality he was much like a boy, drunk with power, magnifying the importance of that which increased his own stature; a giant boy in whom consciousness of strength had bred up an alien arrogance. His fellows reckoned him magnificent and dangerous. His wife knew him to be magnificent and tender.

Only for her did he have forbearance. With his beasts, fellow men and children he was inflexible. "God made beasts to labor for men," he would say to John, lashing the stubborn ox Buck with the long whip. "Make 'em do your will. You only need feed 'em and give 'em shelter to be doin' your part." And to his wife: "No coddlin', Ruth. Get the best of your children in aid of yourself. They're bounden to help for the life you've given 'em, and the keep. We want to bring up men, and there's nothin' like work that brings sweat to make 'em so." Before the drive of this conviction he could rarely be tender with them, he could summon only an approximate justice. But with his wife it was different. He was all humble and awkwardly wistful. It would have been striking even in a gentle man.

They had met fourteen years before, back in Connecticut. He was a great raw young fellow then, a wanderer going from town to town, earning his way at odd jobs. One day he would help a farmer get in his crops, the next he would be twenty miles onward, an extra hand clipping sheep. He could tan leather and patch up shoes with skill, and sometimes would spend weeks in a town doing such work. Then he would become impatient to get on, and would go. Often he retraced his steps, hardly knowing what he sought; returning after an absence of many months to familiar places, so that in time people along the way began to know him. A strange kind of fellow, they thought, though none could say a word against his character. He worked prodigiously and kept to himself. If he never went to church, so too did he live abstemiously. If most did not like him, for he was blunt and uncompromising, all had respect for him: he needed only to find himself, to cease his rudderless existence, in order to make an honest mark. They thought his journeying the restlessness of youth. It was more than that.

His mother, left to widowhood at an early age with eight children, had spent the best of herself in a terrible struggle to keep life going for them. Brought up in a stern Puritanism which leashed affection and exorcized amenities, such tenderness as might still have flowed in her was stemmed and hardened by ceaseless drudgery into a residuum alternately impassible and bitter. Though sacrifice deepened the bed-rock of her maternal love, it was so harassing that it left little for understanding. There were no tender intimacies between mother and children. Where straitened circumstance might have caused a blossoming of feeling, nurtured by common hope and striving, and blown to fulness by a mutual sympathy, destitution destroyed it utterly, save at its meanest roots. The poor mother, hysterical with strain, else sodden with fatigue, aroused in her children only resentment or a grudging unspoken pity. The bickerings, the pettiness, the violent rages which were daily before Owen's eyes and into which he was often drawn, left him with a deep distaste for family life. At fifteen he had quit home, hiring out to a farmer a hundred miles away. Then, at a distance and in the midst of heedless strangers, he began to understand the pitifulness of his mother's estate. For the first time he saw in a true light her tremendous fortitude, he saw suddenly how blind and unconquerable her will to succor them had been, and that such a love had given those ugly gross years their single aspect of nobility. The realization saved him from bitterness, it softened the thrust of iron in his soul. He began to save, to send her every penny beyond his barest needs. He did not, however, return. He began his wandering, always living alone, as though only solitariness could redeem the botchery of his past life.

Thrown early into the company of rough hard men, he soon knew about women from their talk and, quick enough, from experience. Lust tore at his great body; he used the wenches he met during his journeyings, but contemptuously and often with self-loathing. For already an ideal of austerity, recoil from the sludge of his boy-years, was shaping itself in his mind. There had been nothing of beauty in the women of his family. The mother had given him his huge frame; she was a gaunt graceless

woman, with spirit blunted by the brutality of her life. His two
sisters, both older than he, were unlovely creatures, big-boned
heavy girls after the way of Brown children, with dull faces made
pallid by confinement and hands reddened with labor. They were
rough in speech; hard times had soured them so that they bick-
ered fiercely when they were not apathetic.

Thus when Owen Brown came to know Ruth Mills, he saw
her against the darkness of his experience. She shone against
it; was an image of beauty, an embodiment of all desirable things
he had not known in women. She was a slip of a girl, not quite
eighteen, dark and with deep brown eyes. She had soft ways.
Her talking was a miraculous thing to him. There were sweet
sounds in it, now a slow mounting of feeling, now a sudden fall
to shyness. It was in a low voice, about things commonplace
enough ordinarily, but transformed by her speaking them into
astonishing unknown matters. Often he listened for the sheer
pleasure of it, closed in his absorption to meaning.

She was the daughter of a Congregationalist minister, and
had been reared in the strictest formal atmosphere. And yet in
some way, despite the severity of her training and the long
years of religious forms minutely observed, she had kept a simple
faith, deep and child-like in its credulity. The whole tortuous
body of Calvinistic tenets by which her father set store, depravity,
regeneration, election, left her unmoved; she believed in God
and his son Jesus Christ who in love died for men, she believed
in the Bible and in an afterworld as a reward for goodness. She
professed to the creed of her father, lest she wound him, but
he sensed her defection and was fearful about her spiritual grace.
Her belief seemed to him now inadequate, now excessive; and
elements of mysticism in it filled him with dread—they were
Popish, he felt. But he never reproached her, something in her
would not let him. It was a fleeting withdrawn state that came
over her in the midst of some common labor or handiwork,
showing most in her eyes, in the dark dreaming shadows and
lights of her eyes. It was an obliviousness that was not vacancy,
as though with her outer self held in abeyance some momentous
issue were taking place within, an issue from which he was excluded, and might never know. He would pray desperately for
the salvation of her soul.

And the very thing the father dreaded drew Owen Brown
to the girl. His life had been down to a low level of existence;

≡ * 111 * ≡

coarse and without love and bare of solemnity. Now the faint sanctity he glimpsed in her, the frailty, mingling in a mysterious sense, fed his lack. He was untutored save in the rude wisdom come of hard living, and her modest learning filled him with a naive wonder. Sometimes she sang for him, as she loved to do, madrigals and songs that shepherds knew in older England; or spoke of God. This last she did with deep feeling; but he was unmoved, God was a name to him. Only her presence moved him. It weighed upon his heart, like an evensong heard suddenly by a pilgrim in a desert.

The chimney draught was unruly and sent smoke into the room. The mother's eyes began to smart. She moved Samuel a little from her and rubbed them with the back of her thin veined hand, making a smudge upon the paleness of her cheek. She felt a chill.

"The air's getting cold, John. You'd best shut the door."

The boy rose and went to it, a great heavy thing made of rough boards split from logs and built in upper and lower sections so that when a knock came or a call from without they could answer without offering easy entrance to an unwelcome visitor. In the beginning they had feared the Indians, tribes of Senecas and Ottawas, but now they did not. The savages were friendly, and for the most part kept deep in their forest hunting regions, northward toward the Lakes.

He pulled the door from its fastening, held it ajar for an instant, looking out. It was a clear night, with the moon sharp and low in the dark trees. Two owls hooted faintly deep in, one the mocking echo of the other. A wild pigeon whirred by just outside over his head, making a quick silver gleam. It's time to cut brush, thought the boy. Mrs. Langford's son Ez had said so yesterday. "You cut brush in the old of the August moon, Johnny, else it'll grow wild and cover all your place afore you know it." Now it was the old of the moon, old of the August moon he thought, the flow of the words one gentle after another pleasing him, and he'd have to remind Pa about the cutting. . . . He could do things about the place, he was the helper of his pa, and his ma too. He could do real work, not only in the kitchen like Levi. Levi couldn't tether Buck or get the crazy little ewe Bright in before dark came down. He couldn't whittle handles for spades and bill-hooks and pokes for the hogs, with the great Barlow jack-knife hanging behind the door. Pa never asked Levi to burn fires against the grain chill. He, John Brown, could do things. He closed the door in a glow, thinking again: you cut brush in the old of the August moon.

Levi came down from the loft and went to the little woman by the fire. "Ann won't come down," he said, mournful. She sighed and got up wearily from the stool. "Come then, boys, have your supper." They sat on high big chairs close to one another at a single side of the long table. She put before them bowls of bean porridge, the bitter three-day old acorn bread, and "coffee" in earthen mugs. By now they were famished; they waited, watching her. She stood across from them and they lowered their heads.

". . . and for the blessing of our daily bread. . . . Then grace to you and peace from God the Father and our Lord Jesus Christ who gave Himself for our sins that He might deliver us from evil. God our Father, keep my children in Thy ways. Bless them O Father, to whom be the glory for ever and ever. Amen."

"Amen," they echoed, raising their heads to the food.

She herself was not hungry; she would wait for Owen. She sat down again by the hearth, away from the smoke but near enough for light; this time in a large home-fashioned arm-chair. The family knew it to be "Ma's chair" and no one else used it. Owen had made it for her, with a cloth bag filled with dry leaves and grass to soften the seat, and a bearskin draped to ease the back. A worn Bible lay upon it always. She had had it since she was a little girl. Now she took it and held it in her hands unopened. She rested her head back against the skin and closed her eyes. Her breath came fast and shallow. Fatigue lay heavily upon her limbs.

People wondered about her and thought her a strange helpmate for Oaken Brown. He needed, they said, a real woman for his bed and board. Existence could be squeezed out here only in heartbreaking effort of tendon and sweat, and a man's work came to nothing without a fit partner. Her toiling had to match in degree, if not in kind, that of her husband; had often, indeed, in the necessity for patience and the demand upon ingenuity, to exceed it. Thus it was clear to them that the wife who had come out to Ohio with Brown through the Pennsylvania wilds, lying on her back in an oxcart, and had since, with scarcely a respite,

≡ * 113 * ≡

been down in illness, could not begin to measure up to the standards set by their stern mode of living and her husband's prodigiousness. It was well however not to voice the thought before him. Once in the beginning, a neighbor speaking in such a vein more in sympathy than malice, had been felled to the ground by a blow from Brown's huge fist. "Nobody can say it! I'm not fit to kneel afore her! The best of you ain't fit!"

When they had finished eating—hungry yet, they did not ask for more—the boys came quietly about her again. Samuel snuggled to her bosom, standing. John and Levi sat down upon the floor at her knees. They waited, looking up at her from time to time. She knew what they wanted; she smiled. She put her arms about Samuel; she began to sway with him slowly, her lips against his sandy hair. Then very low she sang.

> *Saviour, like a shepherd lead us,*
> *Much we need Thy tender care.*

They knew the hymn. Their lips began to move almost inaudibly together with hers.

> *In Thy pleasant pastures feed us,*
> *For our use Thy folds prepare,*
> *Blessed Jesus, Blessed Jesus,*
> *Thou hast bought us, Thine we are.*

She felt a warmth coming over her heart. The glow and the crackling, the singing and the boy held by her breast, lulled her senses. Her harassed eyes went a little quiet, the tightness in her eased.

> *. . . Blessed Jesus,*
> *Hear the children when they pray.*

They finished singing. She gazed into the fire, bemused. The boys were quiet and melted in a warm rich peace. The porridge gurgled in the caldron. A piece of pork, boiling succulently in the midst of ruddy beans, was giving off great blown gold-milky bubbles. The sparks from the fire, and the white flashings, the good fragrance of the cooking, the hymn echoing still, the feel of their mother close; all these mingled vaguely yet with power to move, like the substance of a gentle dream. And over her then stole a gladness stronger than the melancholy which was the set of her nature. She needed to live, ran a feeling; these young lives so twined into the fabric of her own, needed her love. In this wilderness, so it ran, in this far-out place barren of spirit she had to bring spirit. She had to bring these children to the God who was their Father. It was her burden of love, it was her duty to Him and them. Her life, thus fulfilled, would be good.

So they sat. It might have been a moment, perhaps it was a long time. They did not know. They only knew that suddenly the peace went from them. . . . Ann was in the room. Ann had come down silently from the loft and was standing in a corner watching them with her wild black eyes. The young girl resembled the mother strikingly; she had the same deep-hued hair, flowing in a cloud over her shoulders. Her scant woolsey dress showed very white skin at the throat and was tight against her ripening young breasts. She had a paleness that might have been beauty, but was not; for, setting off the strain of her jet harassed eyes, it took to itself the look of a pallor and a wasting.

"Come here, Ann," the mother called, whispering, and held forth a hand in a gesture of hopeless love. But she would not go, shaking her head and shrinking back deeper into the shadows. The little woman did not urge her, she knew it would not help, only make her more unquiet. The child was lost, the mother saw it, a sight that filled her days with mourning: this child of her flesh going about in a dereliction of soul—here she might tarry emptily, there be gone like a creature hunted; now in bed she might rise up, knowing no hour, even a darkest one of night, or at the height of the sun say evening prayer and slip from her clothes; for days on end abhor the sight of food, then in a moment glut herself to sickness. She was jealous of her brothers and full of distrust, yet would weep for sorrow when one of them ripped his hand on a nail, or sit grieving by the cradle when the babe was down with colic. She could lust for trifles which another possessed, like the rusty turkey-feather Samuel brought in, or the shining pin which held John's shirt; and no sooner got, tire of them. She had a madness for doing things three times. Thus, she would put on her buff bonnet before the small mirror hanging in the alcove, and go to the door. Then inevitably as if through some powerful compulsion she would return to the mirror and remove the bonnet; thrice repeating the whole action. These things the mother saw: child of her flesh going about in a doom.

The sin was hers ceaselessly throbbed in her mind; the lorn one was a visitation of God upon her. Never could she be free of a sense of guilt. Owen lying there, a great oak of a man, had no share in it. He had only grievance, not guilt. With another woman he would have cleft rich and true. The apple would have fallen near to the bough; there would have been children like unto him, sound and fit for living; not the poor wasted being sprung from her seed. True, he had for her no word of reproach, none ever, nor did his eyes hold even so faintly the accusation she dreaded to see in them. He took the child's failing as a sickness; a sickness far worse, to be sure, than measles or a broken limb, but always as simply an ill about which there was no question of blame. One was only gruffly tender, and saddened a little, never showing it; and philosophical. It was all in the struggle, it was a man's lot. He did not dream of right and wrong. Ann was Ann. She was their child, Owen's and Ruth's.

But his silence and his simple heart could not help her. It was a flaunt, she told herself, it was a flaunt to his wholesomeness. A great wrong had been done him. Because he spoke no bitterness, nor felt any, did that lessen her burden of guilt? Ann was a visitation of God upon her. She had been weak, she had yielded to evil.

That spring night long ago back in Connecticut, they were walking slowly along through the dim village streets. They were returning from church-meeting together, for now he went often to please her. The smell of wild crab-apple blossom was in the air and a warm yellow moon was riding low. It's simple, he thought. There she was by his side, he would tell her. So he spoke as they went and his plain face looked down upon her.

"I love you, Ruth."

"I love you, Owen."

They walked along.

Later they reached her home and stood together at the foot of the porch. . . . Owen put out his hand to her shoulder. "Good-night, Ruth." She too put out her hand, but could not reach his shoulder. She rested it upon his arm. He saw tears in her eyes. She's happy, he thought. Then with the heightened sensibility come of his love he was startled.

"Why, Ruth . . . you're half . . . cryin'."

She gripped his arm harder.

"Why, you're cryin'!"

He stood there bewildered.

"Are you mad at me then?"

"No. No."

"You'll marry me soon?"

"I can't marry you, Owen."

Soon he lowered his head and said, "Aye, it could not be. I'm not fit for you." He turned to go, but she caught at him convulsively.

"No, no . . . don't go, Owen! You're . . . too good . . . for me."

He turned his head this way and that, as though seeking help. "But you care, Ruth, you say you care. Then why can't you marry me?"

"Don't ask me, Owen. I can't, I mustn't."

"I'm not good enough for you, Ruth, I know I'm not. But I love you, God strike me I do . . . so I get sick thinkin' of bein' without you."

"God help me, Owen."

She would not say more, and he had no further words for pleading. He went quietly, saying, "You care, Ruth. I'll not let you be."

The next night Owen Brown went to see the Reverend Mills. . . .

After he had left, the minister continued to sit in his study; a little man with craggy brows, eyes like knives, and long white hands.

What is the right way, he thought; does God do this to test me? He slumped forward in the chair and buried his head in his arms upon the table. . . . Should he try to persuade her? He was her father and the desire for her happiness urged him that way. But he was a man of God too. Would this marriage be good in His eyes? Should he seek to further it, or turn these two young people from each other? He writhed inwardly, torn.

Ruth, he thought, saw the matter with tragic eyes. Her mother had died in madness. She had seen one sister buried after years of hopeless lunacy. Another had married; and had borne an idiot. Her brothers, both of them, had periods of ravening. She had escaped the taint; but the fear of it was in her, poisoning her life, making a horror of her memories, of her future a vast dread. Without his own persuasion he knew she would send Owen Brown away.

They had spoken together some time ago when it had become clear that Brown's intentions were serious. It was a burden of life, he had said to her then, which some had to bear. It was a way of God's not to be questioned. A common thing, showing here and there, in this family and that. Was it then a reason for embracing singleness, for defeating the express purpose of life? It was sinful, he said; and her despair was a sin. One had to trust God in these things.

But within himself his reasoning was less certain; his mind was a tragic arena.

He had spoken of God to her. "It is a way of His, not to be questioned." But was it? Was he consulting the will of *the* Father, or the compassion of *a* father, himself? He saw in this huge-bodied honest Brown one who would make a fine man for his girl. If she married him, if her blood mingled with his, the blemish might drown out, go forever. She might know sound motherhood, contentment, deliverance from dread. Single, loveless, with memories such as she knew rising up ceaselessly before her, her years would go in spectre-filled barrenness. Was it then such a fear and such a hope which were urging him to persuade her, or was it a true belief that the will of God lay there? How could he know? Even if he were strong enough to summon the dispassion to deny her the chance for happiness, how could he be sure that it was His will?

He groaned and rose from the chair. He walked about the room, back and forth. Faith of his fathers, where was it now? Why did it remain a poor helpless thing in his need? Why did it allow him to linger upon earthly considerations, when it was the soul that mattered, his daughter's and his own, and the soul of the unborn?

Later in the night, he went up to Ruth's room. It was lighted by a lamp. A breeze from the open window blew in fitfully, making the flame flicker and throw shapes upon the walls. Shadows crouched in the corners. She was sitting close by the window, rocking slowly. Some things she had been sewing lay on her lap. Her face was white and drawn, the eyes in a far restlessness. Tendrils of her dark hair blew about her cheek. The sight of her cut into his heart. He stood uneasily in the doorway, not knowing what to say; he had never been able to speak freely with her. She did not know he was there; continued to rock slowly, deep gone in thought.

"Are you busy, daughter?"

She turned her head quickly, startled.

"No, no! I'm not busy, father. I was just resting. Come in, father, please come in."

He moved to the center of the room with hesitant steps.

"How cool it is here. I didn't know it was so pleasant in your room."

He fumbled with the heavy gold chain hung in his waistcoat, cleared his throat and could say nothing. They remained thus for a moment in silence. Then she spoke as though he had been there for a long time and they were continuing a conversation.

"I saw him go, father. I saw him from the window as he went out. . . . What shall I do, father? Help me!"

Her words were uttered in a low trembling voice. He came to her side, putting out his hand, faltering; and began to stroke her head. She pressed her face against his coat. He continued to stroke her hair; felt all his compassion flowing to his finger-tips, speaking to her in the touch. Then he said, a thickness in his throat:

"Let us talk, daughter."

He sat down on the narrow bed, close by her chair, and took her hands in his, not looking at her. A message, oh Lord, he thought desperately, a message in my child's need. To her he said, looking now into her desolate eyes, "Ruth, listen to me . . . I know your unhappiness . . . and you know I want only your good. . . . You are wrong to feel as you do. I've said it to you many times, but now my conviction is strongest. He's a good man, Ruth. . . . Alone, each of you is wretched. Together, you will both be blessed. Try to see it that way, Ruth. You know I would not have you do wrong. You know I would not."

She gripped his hand tightly. "Oh, I want to see it that way, father. But I mustn't sin. I would ruin his life."

"You would make him happy, and yourself."

"But father . . . suppose there were . . . children? If there were children?"

"*Lo, children are an heritage of the Lord: and the fruit of the womb is His reward.* Trust in Him, Ruth. We're in His hands. It's a sin to question His ways. Rilla was troubled as you are, and see how happy she is, with a home and fine children. You too will——"

"And Emma? And Emma, father? She's my sister, too, she's my mother's daughter as well as Rilla. What if a home comes to be like hers? What if there are children like hers?"

She stared at him *(For I the Lord am a jealous God, visiting the iniquity of the fathers upon the children unto the third and fourth generation)* but he could find no words to answer. She began to sway from side to side, clasping her hands. . . . Then suddenly she slipped from the chair and rose to her small height. She threw her head back in supplication, closing her eyes.

"Oh my Lord, what must I do? Quicken me, lighten my eyes!"

He too now rose. There was a rushing of blood in him. Even as he spoke his words seemed strange, he had the feeling that he was listening to them himself to grasp their meaning:

"It will be well. What comes will be His will. Trust in Him, daughter. He has a place in life for us, there is His purpose in everything. . . . *Be fruitful and multiply.*"

The next month Owen Brown and Ruth Mills were married. Her father performed the ceremony. They moved into a small house on the outskirts of the town. A year passed; a child was born. Ann was born.

* * * * *

Life is woven wind . . . Upon the still winter night of the Kansas plain rises the wild dogs' mourning; and an old man wearing a red wool hat with the side pieces turned down over his ears sinks back into the wagon-hay faintly sweet with clover (Saviour, hear the children when they pray) *the assassin settles deeper into its warm dark embrace . . . Life is a dream and a mist. . . .*

And now it was another spring for the Browns in the wilderness, maples being run for sugar, while the last snow of surly treacherous March froze under the sharp night-skies and seeped dirty with the day-thawing. Soon the almanac would say it was time for soap, the moon was in the right quarter and the tides at the flood, and there would be leaching of grease in iron pots over a big fire out in the open. Then quick enough a steady gentleness of weather, and seed would be sown and all manner of care taken against bird-thievery—with brimstone smeared, and poles dressed for flapping in a breeze, and rye, poisoned with juice of witch root, strewn plentiful. Or now it was a hushed hot summer, and fevers bringing them low one by one, fevers creeping in, everybody said, from the wet dim bottom-lands south a distance. Or it was a busy anxious stretch; with gold-blue days and autumn husking, with cheer for full crops to pack the shed, but low spirits for scarcity, dread for the coming cold and hunger. Then would fall the white shroud of a deep stinging winter; some times shutting them in with desolation, others finding them with a bounty of food and thankful in their hearts.

And there was young John growing with the seasons, his days merged and moving in a deep steady flow with them. They gave his first truest instruction in living; tutors of the senses, engaging with stern lessons his sharp gray eyes and the fumbling child-fingers and his eager pliant frame. But if the slow cycle—winter gaunt on the heels of a flaming fall, sap of life stirring in the veins of the earth and swelling miraculously to ripeness; if hills and a wind coming down them and the great sound of storms struck first and deeply in the boy's dawning soul, other rhythms soon wrought even more incalculably. At nine he was tough as thong and grown broad in the chest, was driving cattle alone for fifty miles through the forest—and his mother was dead.

He had been working in the shed, chinking the walls with old rags and waste fleece from the last shearing, to soften the bite of the cold against the animals. Bright, the old ewe, was bleating weakly, making a lonely sound as the boy went out; the fowls, perched for a poor warmth on the backs of the gaunt-hipped cow and the big mare, blinked their cold glittering eyes. His numb hands fumbled with the door-catch; then after a last careful look about to see that all was shut and tight for the coming night, he snapped it, and walked around to the cabin. He noticed as he went the great turkeys silent on the utmost limbs of the highest trees, facing the north blast. How free they were, he thought, how strong and wild to sit in the sharp of the wind, to seek it out. Then as the swift darkness fell upon the bitter December day, Owen Brown lumbered out of the

≡ * 121 * ≡

front door, his gaunt face showing peaked and frightened. He was hatless and wore no outer clothes.

"John, be quick! Be quick as you can! Your ma's low! Get to Tulliger's on the mare, get Bess Tulliger here! Tell her Ruth's lost if she don't! Tell her the babe's come sudden on her and she's frightful in pain! Go hard, John, your ma's bad!"

In a few minutes the boy was riding like an Indian through the icy dimness, hanging taut upon the high white mare as she streaked clattering up the frozen road—three miles to the Tulliger homestead. Queer Saul Tulliger, white-haired at thirty and dumb as death, lived there with his aging sister Bess. He hated children; when they went by the house he cursed them with his fishy eyes. Bess, who treated him firmly and gently as she might a child, had a face like a homely man's, enormous hands that were a wonder for quickness and a heart soft for all things that lived. Few were born thereabout without her ministrations. "Thirty-eight young 'uns I brought already to the sight of this world," she would say, her near-sighted eyes bright and moist behind spectacles as she held up a new tiny bedraggled soul in some wretched cabin . . . and back at the Tulliger place mute Saul would be whining desperately, praying that the soul might sink back to the darkness from which it had come. To these Tulligers young John rode the tall white mare and called out fearfully his father's words; and in an hour Bess was helping Ruth Brown with her babe. For seven months it had lain close to the dark woman's heart and stirred with life and dreamed dimly; and now it came forth to light—and death.

"Y'er better so," thought Bess sadly, laying the tiny warped body in the crib Owen Brown had weeks ago fashioned for its coming. She covered the imbecilic face and its dead unopened eyes with a blanket, then turned again to the mother. She lay white and still. Owen Brown stood helplessly by the makeshift, looking down, his face working, his eyes pitiful.

"Do somethin' for her, Bess. Help her, Bess."

It was near midnight. Upstairs in the dark John was bending forward by the head of the attic ladder, listening, all scared and shivering. Levi crouched by him, his heart hammering to his throat. Samuel was asleep in his cot; Ann was moving restlessly back in the dim rear of the attic. It was very quiet in the room below, save for Bess creaking about or the ominous sound of a crock set down and the clinking of a spoon, or from time to time the hoarse whispering of Owen Brown. For the two boys straining there in the dark the minutes crept by with a weight of dread. Ma was sick. Ma was in danger. Ma, went in their young hearts, the sense of her filling them altogether. Ma, they pleaded in their hearts, Ma . . . Ma . . .

Downstairs the gentle ugly woman turned from the make-shift and said low: "There's no doin' anything, Brown. She's goin'."

"Don't leave me, Ruth."

"I'm tired, Owen."

"I'm nothin' without you."

"Look after the children."

"Oh, fight to stay, Ruth! I'm nothin' without you!"

"Forgive me . . . for . . . everything . . . Owen."

In a still dark hour of the morning, Ann, upstairs, suddenly began a low terrible wailing, chilling the blood in the two boys; and Ruth Brown was dead.

They buried her on the hillside rising beyond the house. Often on soft spring days she had rested there, warming her frail body in a good sun. Now four men-neighbors bore her to the grave—the babe again next to her heart—in a coffin slung on poles. Owen followed, walking alone, the tears running down his face. The three boys came dazed behind him. In the rear were Bess Tulliger carrying little Roderick in her arms, old Mrs. Langford with her black tunic, green poke-bonnet and goitered eyes, and wild tearless Ann. It was a raw day, a wind blew bitterly, and they lowered them into the earth of the frozen hill.

Ma . . . Ma . . . Ma . . .

But there were other rhythms than the flow of the seasons, and new lessons to be learned. At five John knew how to whittle ash; and he wept inconsolably over a lost red marble a Seneca lad had given him. At seven he could handle oxen; and he grieved in silence for months because the bob-tailed squirrel he had tamed suddenly sickened and died. Now at nine his mother was gone and faintly the seed of a coming wisdom was sown in him: The Father sees it best to take all the little things out of his hands which He has ever placed in them. And the boy began to wonder about God.

≡ * 123 * ≡

Pa, he had pleaded in his mind, the thought running ceaselessly as he crouched in the dark by the head of the attic stairs. You won't let Ma die! You won't let her, will you, Pa! Ah, he had thought, the great man in the room below who could lift a fallen tree between his arms; his father whom everyone called "Oaken" Brown, who spoke to them like thunder, and knew everything worth knowing, about fields and rain and the grip on an axe; the big awesome man who had put up this cabin and brought them food and was afraid of nothing; he would save their ma. All things he could do, this among them. You won't let her die, Pa!

And then in a deathly stillness the boy had heard a strange sound, beginning as a hoarse broken mumbling of words and ending with sobs that were terrible to hear. He listened, a chill quivering along his spine, and did not understand. Then suddenly he understood. His father was trying to pray. And now for the first time the boy sensed a new reality. There was a huge flash in his mind: Something bigger, stronger, more to be feared than Pa was in the world. Pa was weak before it, Pa who had never prayed was crying out now in prayer. The boy was terrified; he looked over his shoulder into the darkness; he was not conscious of Levi, not of Ann, only an immense *something* filling the room. God the Unseen, his ma had said often, and he, thinking a little about it, had wished for sharper eyes. You couldn't see the other side of mountains, he had thought, because they were too far away. You couldn't see God because he was at a great distance. If only your eyes were stronger or maybe if you knew where to look or if you turned your head sharply in one of His unguarded times, then you might be able to catch a glimpse of Him. But now in this blinding moment with his ma sinking and a great stern man crying by her bed the boy grew incalculably older; the senses were no longer all, suddenly there came a meaning into the things you could not hear or grasp with your hands. God was unseen, but He was near always.

And in the morning Ruth Brown was dead, and for the boy godhood had perished in Owen Brown and the Father had arisen in life.

The winter dragged out its raw dismal length; spring came

and the Browns had no heart for the freshness. It was all a lonely time for the family and a time of great mourning. Owen Brown went about crushed, the spirit sucked from him. For months after the death he did no work about the place, bestirring himself only to bring in a bit of food. He haunted the hillside; often was gone deep into the forest, the children not seeing him all day. If he stayed close, rare enough, it was only to brood by the hearth with dry sick eyes. He scarcely noticed them; when he did, it was with sudden glowering resentment as if they were intruders upon his remembrance; sometimes with such bitterness that one might have thought the young ones the cause of his loss. And burdens fell heavily upon John and his young face grew sterner. He milked and handled the beasts; got through in a poor way the spring sowing, Levi being more a hindrance than help; kept a fierce watch over Samuel and Ann. And all the while memory of his ma burned in him, giving him no peace or ease from pain. In the mornings he got the other young ones together and faltered through some lines of the Bible, twisting words and missing sense, but in the trembling boyish voice passing on to them a solemnity and an immediacy of love for the lost one. Levi could read more easily, but John would not let him. It was a way of speaking to her, it was like being with Ma a little. And before the wretched evening meal of stale bread and milk he would stand across from them sitting at the table and repeat the words fast and shining in his mind:

". . . and for the blessin' of our daily bread . . . Then grace to you and peace from God the Father 'n our Lord Jesus Christ who gave hisself for our sins . . . God our Father keep my children in Thy ways . . . Bless 'em, O Father, to who be the glory for ever 'n ever. Amen."

Summer came and it was very strange and still. Bess Tulliger had been riding over each day to look after the infant Roderick; but now she said she could not, there was her brother Saul who wanted tending.

"Brown," she said, "yer children need a mother. And y'er young too and need a woman. Ye ought to be lookin' to marry again, Brown."

He glared at her, then shouted in a fury: "You and your marryin' go to hell!"

"Don't ye be yellin' at me," she said gently. "I mean it good. May the Lord be kind to her soul, but ye can't live with the departed. Ye'd best think on it, Brown."

He rushed away toward the woods, shouting as he went: "Be gone, you damn witch!"

But she had done something to him with the words. The love of his simple heart might henceforth be with her alone whose grave was on the hill-meadow, but that one had said "Look after the children, Owen," and now he remembered, and it brought him back to the living. Feeling a guilt as of a trust betrayed he began to care for them; and in his gruff way showed them more tenderness than he had ever, so that it made them wonder. But his best was only a poor thing for the motherless ones; it was a bare hungered existence they led. When winter came on and Roderick was down badly with the whooping-cough, Owen Brown sent in desperation for Bess Tulliger.

"He'll go if ye ain't careful," she said.

"Stay and watch him, Bess. I'll pay you fer doin' it."

"Fer shame, Brown! Do ye think I come to help fer money? . . . But I can't stay. Saul's worse every day."

"Then what should I do, Bess?"

"Ye need a woman in yer house."

He had no harshness for her this time; his face only went sadder and thoughtful. "Mebbe . . . mebbe you're right . . . But the younker needs someone quick. I was dependin' on you, Bess."

"I can't come regular, and it's steady nursin' he needs." She thought troubledly of Saul, then in a sudden glow banished him from her mind. The moist angelic look in the ugly woman's eyes had a little of hungriness too. "He's wastin' here," she said eagerly. "Let me take him home, Brown. I'll bring him back to ye strong."

Now it was a December night again, with Christmas a week off and the white drifts high to the windows. The cold was fierce and in the snow-locked swept cabin the three boys huddled close together before the hearth, like freezing sheep. Ann with her lost eyes, Ann whiter than ever beneath her dark shroud of hair, haunted a corner. The wind was going like a fury outside. It sobbed icily through the log chinks and drove the smoke down the flue back into the dismal room.

"I wonder if Pa's out in the snow," said Samuel, shivering.

"He said it would be two or three days." Levi was very thin now, all shining eyes. His cough was deep and hollow.

"I wonder what he's goin' for."

John was sitting close to the big hewn arm-chair with the bear-skin drape. Ma's old Bible lay upon it. "It's freezin'," he said in a plain straight tone, "it's freezin' out in the night."

"The holiday's next week," reflected Levi, after a long silence.

"Let's get a tree in," said Samuel, brightening.

"Don't put up no tree!" John turned on them sharply.

"Pa'd let us."

"There's no sense. There's no use."

"It's fun doin' it."

"There's nothin' to hang."

"We have one every year."

"Not this year."

"Aw, John."

"Not this year."

"Come on over, Ann," called Levi, seeking to break another bleak silence. "It's warmer here. You'll get sniffles sittin' in the cold."

The young girl started from her corner, came from the dimness into the thrown light. She had not heard his words; she stood straining, her head cocked a little.

"She's listenin' for somethin'," whispered Levi.

"It must be Pa," said Samuel, gladdened.

John got up quickly and went to the door. "I hear speakin'," he said. In a moment there was a knock. The boys wondered, their hearts beating faster; their father would have hammered and roared: "Let's in! It's Oaken Brown!"

"Who's there?"

"It's me! Open up!" It was a woman's voice, and they did not recognize it. Feeling easier, John pulled back the creaky upper section of the puncheon door. An icy wind whistled through and stung the boy's face with sharp particles from the outside drifts; two coal eyes sparkled across at him. "Lor', open up! I won't eat ye! Open up, I'm nigh stiff!"

She came in, a big woman; stamping and blowing; shaking snow and ice from her mittens and rough heather coat and round black hat of wool; booming: "Lor' but it's fine to see a blaze again!" The young ones, watching her in amazement,

≡ *127*≡

had a quick startled sense of something bright and bursting and all alive. It grew in them as she whipped her hat off a great whorl of reddish hair, loosened the coat from her shoulders and swelling bosom, and strode to the hearth.

"Your father'll be right here," she said in a throaty voice, beating her hands hard upon her rump to get the blood going. Her eyes, strangely black beneath the red mass of her hair, sparkled at the young ones; curiously took them in one by one with a free friendly look. Then she gazed about the room, saying:

"It sure needs brightenin'! We'll have it so you won't know it soon. I can see what a starvin' lot you poor mites 'a been goin' through. I'll have you bloomin' so that none'll know you for the same! . . . You're Levi . . . You're John . . . Sure, your father's told me about each of you. I know you like long friends. You're Sam . . . and . . . you're Ann . . . Come now, don't be shy of me. I'm Sally Bool. I'm . . . well, your father'll be in in a minute."

The three boys had ranged themselves together by the door. Ann was shrunk tight against the wall. They stared at the unknown woman. Then John asked: "Where's my pa?"

"He's puttin' the team by, lad . . . You're John, ain't you? Your father said you're a real worker, half a man. He said you near kept the house from goin' to ruin."

The boy looked at her with hostile eyes. I hate her, he thought; I'll hate her if she stays. He said, "We're gettin' along all right."

Now there was Owen Brown's knocking and his call. He came in, his homespun clothes and black new-grown beard gleaming with hoar, and stood by the door, twisting his hat in his hands. The young ones watched him; he would not meet their eyes.

"She's Sally Bool. She's goin' to keep the house."

They looked from their father to her smiling uneasily, and back to him. They were silent and rooted with this new turn; John was white. Then Owen Brown angrily shouted:

"Well, say somethin', you fools! She's Sally Bool! Sally Brown! It's your new ma!"

Another instant the young ones stood transfixed, then suddenly John turned and went in a blind rush up the attic ladder. Like frightened mice Levi and Samuel scampered after him to the darkness above. Ann slipped along by the wall and faded behind the tattered draping of the alcove.

Quickly there were different days; warmth and a comfort about the house. It glowed with Sally Bool, Sally who was Chaw Bool's widow of a year, Chaw having been killed by a falling tree; Sally Bool Brown singing as she drew the hot batter cakes from the charcoal-bed, or tested the quince dumplings, or poured a gravy for the partridge all crisp and luscious. The blue muslin curtains were a new brightness; so too the pewter plates and basins standing proud in rows, and the polished brass warming-pan hung by the hearth. Whether Sally tramped with Samuel through the snow around to the shed for eggs, merry in speech and blowing breath-smoke upon the crackling air, or punched vigorously the back log of the fire with the slender iron-peel, wishing "May I have as many shillin's as sparks jump up!"; whatever she did, there was a buoyancy, a high strong energy astir.

I hate her, thought John, remembering other ways and a small gentle woman. I hate 'em all, he thought, seeing his pa and the two boys being won to Sally's side. And Owen Brown he could forgive least of any. He had brought her home to them, he had chosen another in Ma's place. John would never forget the first morning after she came. The boy had spent a tortured night, had tossed in a fury of resentment, and dreamed, and wept for loneliness. Long before the first glimmer of the dreary winter day showed, he was up. He dressed, fumbling, the icy wooden floor cutting into his bare feet. He shivered and it was more than physical pain; his young spirit was knowing a raw darkness too. He crept silently down the ladder; he must be clear of the house this day, he must get away from sight of the betrayal. The shed was better to be in, the frozen woods were better. He went on tip-toe across the room. And in the dimness he saw them sleeping close by each other. Her hair was flung like a net over the pillow—his ma's pillow, stuffed by her with soft white and black feathers from the eider-duck—and Owen Brown's hand lay limply upon her breast. The boy glared at them, a wave of blood rushed to his throat, his scalp tingled—and he could have struck them dead. Then he rushed out to the icy dawn and in a passion of hate and jealousy went floundering blindly through the snow-drifts.

Later, hungry and soaked to the skin, he made his way weakly back to the shed. There he tumbled to the hay in the fold, burrowed into its soft, full-smelling embrace and lay still and drowned in wretchedness. From time to time he heard footsteps close on the shed plankings, but he was not discovered; once there came faintly to his ears the "Hallo, John!" of Owen Brown calling in the woods. It was nightfall when the boy got up. His cheeks were raw and reddened from crying. His eyes were swollen, but there was a dry hard look in them. (It would be a long time before tears came to them again, he would be a man then, he would weep for his own young torn from life.) Now he stroked Mollie's throat, the white mare whinnying with pleasure. Bright began to bleat for his favor; the oxen's eyes were luminous in the dark. The boy was moved by a sudden warming love for these beasts and their slow mute devotion.

He went back to the cabin, drawn deeper to himself, his heart sheathed a little more against the touch of humans.

The old year went out. Levi brought Sally a muskrat bag. It gave a sweet smell and she was pleased with it. Samuel, finding life good with heaped platters of food and more freedom and the new brightness of everything, was Sally's small rough slave. John, savage with the treachery, scarcely spoke to the two boys. He exulted because the silent and mournful Ann shrunk away from Sally, shrunk into her far inner mist; exulted, thinking it was all for hatred of the big red-haired woman, forgetting that the poor girl had been so with his own mother.

The boy's implacability worked hardest upon Owen Brown. It gave the simple fellow a deepened sense of guilt, present from the very beginning of the new union; now enraging him, now making him in his thought strangely tender for the grim faithful boy. "Come back here, you brat!" he called once as John began to go up the ladder haughty and sullen past bearing: "I'll teach you to be high in your nose, I'll show you to be mucky with me!" Beyond himself, he snapped off his tough hide belt and began to lash the boy about the back and shoulders. His fury mounted as John stood straight and proud and took the blows without flinching. Then he was suddenly conscious of the white tightened face, the scorn in the boy's eyes, and his anger went. He dropped his hand. "Get out," he said, sickened. Indeed, the boy might have tortured him less. Sally could companion his bed, give his body ease; keep the house fit for living and children; even bring to his days something gay and lilting, unknown before; but the small bright flame of his heart burned steadily and alone for the other one dead.

And Sally felt his farness. I'm like a stranger in a home, she thought often, but never showed it with word or look. She gave her best, it was a bargain entered upon between honest people. All her life had been so; nobody, she knew, got it whole. You gave this up, you got that in return. She had loved Chaw, and he beat her and drank; Brown was a good man, but he lived with a ghost. Chaw hadn't given her a child; well, here were these without a mother. She would take them, easing herself.

But the fierce boy would give her no chance. If she sat in the hewn arm-chair his eyes would stab her, their light of fury would dart a message: Don't you sit in my ma's chair! Sometimes when he brushed by coldly as though she were not there and had not said a bright "Hallo, John!" or when suddenly he rose and went from the room, his face ashen with jealousy because Owen and she were close to each other merely for speech, then she almost hated him. But most often she thought, poor mite, he's lone. he's lost as a pup; and she was patient with him, urging Brown to be so too: "Let him go, he'll come around, he'll soften up." Reared in the easy heathenism of the wilderness, in its stern school of adversity, she believed in courage and a will-to-do and the strength of the body, not in God. But if she was a little amused by John's childlike faith, and skeptical of its object, and gently tolerant, she had only respect for the intensity which drove him. Each night when the boy got up at the table and solemnly uttered grace—Levi and Samuel being quick to lower their heads before his sharp sad gaze—she had a feeling of smallness. She wanted—just as she longed often to put her arm firmly about his shoulders, saying nothing—she wanted to bend her own to let him see she understood and was proud of his fealty; but she never did, she knew he would scorn it as deceit. Indeed, it was a strange unnatural sight for this boy to be standing and speaking so: ". . . keep my children in Thy ways . . . bless 'em, O Father, to who be the glory for ever 'n ever. Amen!"—and the two elders sitting there, quiet, upright, and hot a little with a vague shame.

The cold season was long this year, one fall of snow coming hard and deep upon another; they were shut close bound in the cabin, and the time moved tense with John's hostile ways and full of pain for all. The boy suffered most; at every turn he saw the violation of his memory, and his spirit was one raw thing. He moved restless about the place, like a young fox entrapped; longed for the break of the winter and the spring thaws. He chafed Owen Brown with his skulking and took a hiding often, more stubborn and proud than ever. Once, brooding aloft in the dark of the attic after a storm of temper and punishment, he resolved to run away. Where, he did not know, but when the first thaw came he would go. He nursed the scheme for weeks, giving no further fret to his father so that the huge man might be disarmed; and was drawn ever deeper to himself away from the stir and the life of the family.

February came, and the beginning of March; the snow packed dark and wet under the tread, and through the forest rose the vast faint sigh of its dissolution—and he knew the time was near. But now a new loneliness gripped the boy. He would be leaving the spot where the depth of his heart was given. There was a grave on a hill. A few minutes each day for many days— in the dim cold stillness before night descended, so that none might see him—he stood by the mound and held a council of grief. And in the end he knew he could not go. He walked down toward the cabin, all melted inside and knowing his first peace since the death. When spring came, he thought, choked and smiling a little to himself, he would put up palings to mark the place off. He might even sow kernels in half a circle; they would grow slowly to trees, great oaks or maybe cedar, casting a shade. Aye, when spring came he would set a fine height of clean white stones for her honor.

*   *   *   *   *

The assassin dreams in the hay faintly sweet with clover. The blood remembers . . .

Bess Tulliger came riding up the road to the Brown cabin on her little piebald, bearing the babe Roderick before her on the saddle. It was the first mildness after the lonely winter. The child's cough was gone, he was all plump and gabbling. John ran down from the hop patch to see his brother. He wanted also to speak to Bess. She had tended his mother. He would say something to her.

"He's got strong, Bess." He stood watching the child waddle about in the road. He gave a quick smile, pleased.

Bess peered at him from the saddle, her weak eyes searching. "And y'er awful thinned out, lad."

He felt warm for the homely aging woman. "I'll show him to ride soon," he bantered, strange for him.

"Now listen, ye better eat more, John."

The door opened and Sally Bool brightened through. "Hallo Bess Tulliger!" The boy turned instantly and went tightened up to the patch. Though the communion by the mound had given him a strength to endure, he was not softened any to Sally. He knelt in the red earth of the rows, jerking at the weeds with savage fingers. But he wanted badly to speak more with the other, so he kept an eye on the cabin; when Bess plodded away on the piebald he would cut quick across the fields and meet her where the trail made the sharp winding. She came out soon and he saw her trudge up the rise toward him; he squatted deeper and kept his head low, as if he did not care.

"My wind's poor . . . these days." She puffed and held her side.

He said harshly, "It ain't much of a hill." Within he was sorry for her, seeing her gray face, the under lip trembling.

"Huh! When I was yer years . . . I could . . . scoot up . . . like a jack!"

A mixed feeling was in him, longing and a dark pride. He moved a little way from her, to a new scatter of weeds. She followed closer.

"Ye might a' come down once to ast about yer brother."

"Askin' don't do no good."

"Ye could a' helped plenty times. It was a hard winter."

"We had it hard too."

"Ye oughtn't a'. Yer new ma's a wonder to keep a house."

At a kneel in the earth, he stiffened; a huge hate filled all of him, taking in Bess and the weeds and the red-haired woman down below:

"I've got no new ma! She's never my ma!"

"She is. Y'er sayin' an evil thing."

He leaped up, shaking a dead stalk in her face: "I'll say it a hundred times! I hate Sally Bool!"

"Fer shame!"

"I'll always hate her!"

"John, listen to me. Ye——"

"Go on down! I don't want to listen!"

"John, ye know I'm yer friend——"

"You're not my friend! Go down!"

"John."

"I've got work to do!"

"I was Ruth Brown's friend. I got a right to speak."

Now, still trembling with passion, he was silent. He stood before her, looking down hard, his hands clenched by his sides.

"I'm speakin' so because she would a' wanted me to, she'd a' been ashamed fer ye . . . I'll go, John. I'll go right away, I only got a few words to say . . . Listen, John . . . I know y'er holdin' her fast in yer heart. All yer life ye'll hold her fast. But ye got to be a man, John. There's pain in the world and there's all kind of sufferin'. Some get it worse 'n others. But all get it. Ye got pain now, missin' her. Sure, don't I know, John, how ye feel? But yer ma used to say it always, ye know she did. She used to tell ye of the ways of God. Well, God took her, he had a reason. He ended yer ma's work, she's restin' easy now. But the work's there to go on . . . don't ye see, John? There's yer ma's house standin', needin' someone to keep it goin', there's yer brothers and sick Ann to be watched. So Sally Bool came to watch over 'em and tend the house. Sally Bool came to carry on yer ma's work . . . Look, John. It's like yerself was called away seedin' time, and Samuel or Levi took up the bag and sowed . . . Then who are ye to be questionin' so? Who are ye but a fool and a wicked whimperin' brat if ye go on in yer bad ways? . . . So listen to me, John. Be fair to Sally. She's a good woman tryin' her best . . . Aw, John, I know, I know. But ye keep it in yer heart, lad, ye keep everythin' deep in, and ye trust to yer wise livin' God, and ye act up always like a man, the best ye know how."

He stood white and weakened, and she could have held him close for comfort. Then, "It's gettin' late," he choked. "I got kindlin' to do yet."

"I was goin', John. Come by when ye ain't so busy, huh? I'll cook ye something good."

He turned quickly from her, so she would not see his face. She watched him go toward the western woods. The sun was dying there, and he was a small thin figure against the glow.

There was a change in him. He still went silent about the house, distant from all, but he was no longer hostile and so bitter. It made living easier for Sally, she had his tolerance. His own days held less pain, for the urgency of his loss was dimming. And soon she had won his respect.

One day of the early summer Owen Brown came running up to the cabin, drenched in a cold sweat, calling: "I'm bit, Sally! Put the poke in the fire!" John hurried around from the shed; last year Sam Baird had come close to dying after the green asp flicked him. John watched Owen Brown hold his long knife-blade in the flame for purity, then sizzle it cool in the noggin-water. He saw his father, white as clay but calm, cut deep into the flesh around a tiny angry spot in the calf of his right leg. He helped the huge man stanch the blood with a small pine-bough twisting muslin. All the while Sally was holding the iron in the fire. When she had it a fierce red she pulled it out and came over to Owen Brown.

"It's ready," she said. "Get to your stomach on the shift."

"I'll do it myself, Sally, if you can't."

"No. Turn over. John, get some lard ready. The softest you can find."

Owen lay on the makeshift, gripping the sides. John stood by holding the lard and a fresh muslin strip. Sally was pale, but her hand was steady. "All right, Owen," she said. "It's comin'." He stiffened. She thrust the iron hard against the wound. There was a bubbling hiss. He gave a gasp and a mighty shiver, his knuckles whitened out hugely and the veins in his arms came up like thick cords; but he did not cry aloud. John felt a wave of nausea, he sickened with the cruelty of the pain, the smell of the crisping flesh, the great figure like steel convulsed. Then Sally ripped the iron from the blackened wound. A trembling came on her. She could scarcely spread the lard for cooling, and bind the leg. Brown was limp, the makeshift cover was wet with his tears. By night he had a strong fever; the white-ash bark they laid on the wound seemed not to help. Two days later he was back at work again, girdling to keep shadow from the new corn patch, limping with his axe from tree to tree.

John thought of the scene for a long time. It was of a kind to impress him; he had been witness to courage, to pain endured with little fuss. He was used to his father's mettle; if Owen

Brown had acted otherwise that would have been reason for sur-prise. But it was Sally who now loomed higher in his regard. She had held the iron, had burned it into the raw bleeding wound. He felt how much harder it must have been to inflict the agony than to endure it. For the boy that had been Sally's test. He would never again with purpose do anything to trouble her; she had his respect.

And soon his feeling deepened beyond respect. For months vague word had been spreading down from the Lake border: there was trouble with England, there might be a war. By the middle of the summer there was a war; five hot young fellows of the region went north "to git into a fight." (Ez Langford was among them. He would sink in a swamp, shot through the brain, he would no more "cut brush in the old of the August moon.") In the fall months bands of ragged militia moved steadily through the settlement, up the trail past the Brown homestead. "I'll go if it gets serious," said Owen Brown. "My pa was in the old war. He was in Train Band Nine, the Connecticut fighters. He died in a barn, they told my ma, and put up a strong fight afore they ended him. I was a younker those days, I can't remember his face. I'll go if it gets serious." It got serious; news filtered through the wilderness, Hull had been beaten, Hull had surrendered to the English at Detroit. More men were needed, provisions were needed. Owen Brown took down his rifle from the joist. "Maybe it won't last long," he said. "Rufe Langford and me are goin' to drive cattle north. There's no food, I hear. Good-bye, Sally. Watch 'em close. There's grain to last the winter. Hold up your end, John. I'm dependin' on you. Good-bye, younkers. Good-bye."

It was a winter that tried them to the last fibre. The snow began to fall in November, renewing itself steadily, and lying deep till March. There came days of cold that often seemed past bearing. Rolphe Muhlberg was gone to the fighting, his little mill was closed and the nearest one to the Browns was six miles off. So Levi helped Sally to pound the corn in the cabin, and the bread was soggy and bitter. Levi couldn't do much; he was al-most seventeen now, yet scarce taller than John twelve; he was narrow-chested and had thin limbs and his cough racked him worse and worse. After he forgot to lock the shed-door and the two hogs wandered and froze dead in the drifts, they let him do only the smallest tasks about the house. Most often he stayed close by the hearth, a hectic flush in his drawn face and his eyes shining larger than ever; reading a tattered copy of *Pilgrim's Progress* or the fables of Aesop. And he drew on the big new slate John had made for him, and Christian the pilgrim, shaped with soapstone colors, looked much like Levi; and so the boy went on dreaming life, and the fires within him burned too high, and his lungs consumed themselves.

Samuel was ten and strong, his young girth fashioned after Oaken Brown's; now he could help John with the hard work. When John felled the smaller trees, and wood could not be pulled in through the drifts by the oxen, the two brothers, going on snowshoes, would beat a path to the cabin, then drag up the split logs on a hand-sled: It was work to rend their limbs.

Samuel could help, but he was not beyond shirking, and the burdens were heaviest upon his brother. John did not complain, it was not even faintly in his thought. He exulted only; his father was away, he was doing a man's part. If he clouted Samuel often, it was not because of the extra work thrown upon himself; it was for the good of the other's soul. He came in at night, his hands stiff and blue, his growing body anguished with fatigue; but the grim spirit of willingness never abated. At the icy dawn he was up; when the day's final hour darkened he was still giving the last ounce of himself. Sally saw all this, saw it as a high fine sight, this boy and his sense for duty, the fierce naked energy he brought to its service; and yet she felt something pathetic in it too; a quality of waste, blighting the virtue. It was a kind of desolate splendor: a boy who would not know boyhood, a child weighed down early by the gloom of life, a stranger to ease and laughter. And Sally, remembering her own days, loved the boy, a pity mingling.

She was sprung from Scotch-Irish emigrants, brave, rugged, and fervidly emotional, settlers who had filtered in from the Carolinas to the fertile Cumberland country. Her childhood had been spent on the furthest frontier, by the Green River of Kentucky, a settlement open to wild beasts and the mad cunning thrust of the red tribes. Existence was perilous, the end might be sudden; they were cut loose from the restraints of the seaboard civilization; a rabble breed, shiftless, cruel, and criminal, had swarmed like locusts over the trail, mingling with the soldier element; hence life, under these pressures, became a huge sensual appetite, a passion unleashed. Sally remembered her great dark mother, Nancy Higgins, who smoked a pipe and had lovers casually, who could sing to bring tears and lash out with her fists like a border tough; her "paw," Sog Higgins, a squat red barrel of a trapper, forever drunk, and joyous. If the Higgins brood, with such a mother and sired so, knew a full share of squalor and the brutality of a godless spot, there was much also of flame and color and a wild heedless joy in living. This day they might be starved and beaten, tomorrow might bring a flowing feast and prodigality of love. If they saw much lechery they saw also brave things, deeds of swift courage and sacrifice; if they were exposed to sin and lowness, there was also before their eyes and soon enough in their lives the rich deep impulse to song, and the passionate tread of the dance, ancient as tribes, and the loins' hunger. All these Sally remembered, and felt vaguely how by the side of them the boy's life was impoverished. He had a wealth of faith, there was a beautiful bitter depth to him, but what, went dimly in her thought, what of joy, where was the ounce of joy that leavened life and was its reason and therefore the right of each? He would never possess it she saw, and grieved for him.

She tried to win his friendship and by the turn of the cold season it was done. Slowly, beyond his power to resist, he was drawn to her. They had now, with Owen Brown away, a common interest; they strove to keep life going for the family, their efforts jibed and twined, and the strength of one was the strength of the other. He felt a new pleasure when she set food for him; or they talked gravely of matters: of the shed floor that needed a plank, or the two old geese they might exchange with neighbor Ross for a winding of wool. Now he was sorrowful when he saw Ann a thorn to Sally's ease, when he saw the girl more frantic each day and swiftly wasting with wildness; a shame burned up in him because once he had rejoiced that it was so. "I fear she can't be livin' long," Sally said to him one night. After that he watched Ann with wonder and fear; and envied Levi because the older boy could get into her mind a little and sway her. Sometimes in a rare moment of stillness, sitting on a stool, white and worn and with her black hair clouding her fragile shoulders, she was his mother risen again, and his heart wept for both, wept for pity and loss. When she died at the bleak height of the winter, not ravening but quietly, as though she too were tired, they buried her on the swept hill close by

Ruth Brown. The house was hushed for a long time, but they did not mourn. Even the lads knew that now she would have her peace.

Spring stole in softly, gladdening them; but there was no word from Owen.

Then the wounded and sick began to return from the fighting at the North, and the travel was much through the wilderness settlement. The soldiers dragging back their wasted torn bodies had brought news from the front—and disease. A strange unknown fever began a desolation, far and wide families felt the touch of death. Saul Tulliger went his mute whining way and Bess was solitary. Wonderful old Christian Cackler, who had lived almost a century and was still a hunter and the presiding spirit at huskings and festivals, waned quickly, fighting to the end and berating fate for having cheated him of his due of years. The Deaumonts, who had a cabin on the hill called the "dandelion rise," lost the boy of their small twins and barely saved the other. Sally, seeing these things and hearing worse besides, kept the children close and watched them fearfully; Owen had left them to her care. One soft June day, all blue and fresh and with white clouds shining, she felt a strangeness stealing in her blood. By night-time she had a raging fever; the end of a week found her close to death. She drew to the utmost upon her deep store of vitality; only a tremendous will to live kept the light in her eyes. The neighbors fled from the sight of the Brown cabin. But the woman of mercy came, Bess Tulliger came. The crisis passed.

Sally was haggard and weak for months. Her now pitiful dependence upon John drew the boy's last lingering bitterness, drew it like a faint barb from the flesh. When he came in to Sally each day, silent and tight after his fashion, bearing a jug of rich foaming milk from the fresh yield; or sent Samuel to her with large white eggs to be drunk warm for building-up, he felt a glow of comradeship. He was her friend, always now he would be true, he would serve her. But one thing could not be changed. The boy was Sally's friend; but she could not penetrate to the true deepness of his heart, and he could not adopt her there. Only one being might have tempered his stern stubborn nature, and she lay on the hillside. Ay, Sally would think, I can't help him none; he'll go through his days with a devil of pride.

In October Owen Brown returned. He came limping up the trail and stopped by the field where John was deep in work, all unheeding.

"Hallo, John."

The boy looked up. His eyes leaped. Then he ran toward the huge man with a short glad cry. "Hallo, Pa!"

"Hallo, John."

They did not embrace; but their eyes did.

The look of him's good, Owen Brown thought. He's come up, he's got a strength. He's my son. I'm glad to be home.

The boy was trembling with joy, his knees were buckling beneath him.

"Is everything all right, John?"

"Sally's been sick . . . I got the corn in good . . ."

"I trusted you, John . . ."

They were embarrassed, they felt a little like strangers.

"Is the fightin' over, Pa?"

"No. Nobody knows when . . . But I got tired of fightin'. I couldn't see what it was all for, I couldn't see why we was all dyin'. My time was up, so I come home . . . I was hurt bad too, most in my head . . . But it's nothin'."

John saw how pallid his face was, how the lines were deeper.

"Well, finish up, John. Don't have me breakin' into your job. I'll go down to see the rest."

". . . Ann's dead . . . She died this winter."

The great fellow stared and gulped. Then a veil came over his eyes, and again he said, "I'll go down to see the rest." He limped off toward the house, and the boy's heart went with him step for step.

The winter could come now. The corn was in; they were all together.

*　　*　　*　　*　　*

The ancient leather bag lay in the hay near the sleeping assassin's breast.

"Dear Son John . . . and was very glad to larn that all your Famelys were so well, and that you had not been distourbed by the enemy . . . My health at present is not so good; for three weeks past I am somewhat put to it to breathe, mostly nights, and sometimes feel as though death was at the dore . . . I consider all of my children at Kansas as one Famely, and hope you

will take turns in writeing. Your unfaithful parent, Oaken Brown."

Out on the prairie the wind lashed and howled, the wind was a fury; the gaunt creaking Cygnes cottonwoods harshly mourned above the shallow grave of Frederick Brown. Soon the great white shroud would descend upon it. Soon the whiteness would cover five unmarked mounds in the bitter valley of the Potawatomie.

Though Faint,
Yet Pursuing

THE
SECOND PART

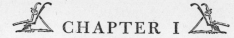

CHAPTER I

The Clansmen—1856

UP AT the Adirondack farm in Elba, they had begun to feel the bleak touch of the early northern winter. October was in its wane; the days were shortening, with swift sudden nightfalls; the sun when it shone had no warmth for them. Winds from the up-country bit sharp through the valley, sweeping the ridges barer of their leaves. Mother Brown, beginning her toil about the cheerless house with the first gleams of day, felt the cut of the cold through the unplastered walls; and watched with anxious eyes the tiny girl who coughed from the crib. Nell was two; Mother Brown had already buried seven young ones.

Ruth, heavy with Hen Thompson's child, shivered in the draughty kitchen, brooding over its coming. Heedlessly doing little tasks, from time to time she left off, and went to the uncertain fire giving off smoke into the room. It seemed not to warm her; she pulled the black wool shawl tighter about her thinned shoulders. Her first had died in a cold season. Three years back it was, in these mountains.

Picking the last berries in the bushy low places of the valley, her sisters, Annie who was thirteen and Sarah just come ten, were whipped too by the cold. Annie was a small white creature, with long corn-silk hair and snapping jet eyes. She could be gay and bright as a bird, but that was least her way; there were times when she was so stilled that none knew her and her face took on a lost look as though she had found something out. She was that way now, dreaming as she bent in the bushes, careless of the thorns. Sarah, large for her years, and slow after the mother, with patient eyes and warm coloring, shook the pail up, reckoning its tittle; and said gravely:

"It's not fillin', Annie. Look harder. We can sell 'em if we get more. We can get stamps to answer father."

The other, as though she had not heard, with an absorbed fierceness said, "Ruth's gettin' a child." She moved deeper into the brambles.

Sarah reflected, "I saw a cow get a calf once, Annie."

Along the fields from which the deep autumn stains had fled, leaving them dun, the two girls searched, chilled.

Up on the patch behind the house, Watson and Salmon were digging potatoes, hard at it. Watson rose to rest. He had the feel of a wind, coldest yet from the north, upon his cheek. "Smells snow," he said, sniffing. He had come up tall during the last years, his face taken on character. His blue eyes were without guile; a short fair beard made him look older than twenty-one.

"Yeah." Salmon, younger by a year, scraped a potato free of loam and threw it into the bag. He was haggard, not yet recovered from his Kansas wounds. "Cone Sanders said to watch for a heavy one."

Westward, with the sun just down, the peaks in the cold glow were colored up sharp blue and gold; but from the east of the ring, gray clouds in a mass were spreading. Even Marcy, vaster than any, whose hoar face glistening had been visible earlier, was now obscured.

"I wouldn't think nothin' if we get it tonight," said Watson, bending again.

"Yeah. Nuts have been plenty all summer, Cone said, and there's bound to be a high fall."

"I saw the boraura flamin' for a week in August. It'll be stiff."

They went at a good clip down the line, spading the furrows.

"You know, Watson, it's kind of good gettin' dirt on my hands again. I mean like this, diggin'. Back in Kansas when we were hidin' out, every once in a moon I'd get a hankerin', I'd feel like I wanted to . . . oh . . . run a maple to sugar, or cut kindle for Ma. It's funny, because I always used to want to get away from it."

"You can't. It's your life, you come up in it."

"Yeah . . . But look at the old man. He's come up in the life too. Ain't he clear? He's got heart for nothin' but his plans to free niggers."

Both had stopped digging. Bent over, their heads were close.

"I know," said Watson slowly. "I know. But the old man's different."

"Can't see it, Watson. I went through it down in Kansas, same as he did. Was hurt worse."

"I know. But look, Salmon." His face went eager. "I been

≡ *146* ≡

thinkin' about things, and here's the way I figure them. You wanted excitement, see, you wanted fightin'. Well, you got it, see? And now what? Now you're back, sick of it, wantin' a rest. You had a stir, but when you felt hankerin' for an axe, or mebbe sheep smell, you quit and you came back to it, you . . ."

"Yeah, but——"

"Now wait! Now just a minute! You see, Salmon, the old man . . . well, he can't come back like you could. He's got ideas. Ideas . . . And no matter how much he hankers for old ways of livin', he won't let go his ideas. They're biggest, see?"

Salmon blew his nose thoughtfully. "Yeah. I see your way a little. Sure, I see it. And I got this to say. It ain't right, lettin' your ideas be biggest. You got other things to look out for. There's people belongin' to you. There's others dependin' on you. That's bigger than ideas. Look at Ma slavin'. She's worth buryin' his ideas."

"Ma's had it bad. Sure, don't I know, watchin' by her all the time?" He scratched in the earth with his spade, thinking. "But I've got a feelin' about the old man. There's something big in the way he's goin'. The night he left here with the guns for Kansas, that was the first time I felt it. He shook my hand, he said, 'Look out for things, Watson. Look out for your Mother, look out for the young.' Then he kissed Ma. 'You been a wife, Mary,' he said. 'It's been hard for you. But there's work outside bigger than any of us all. I've got to help, Mary.' You know, my throat squeezed then. I had a great respect for him. It came from inside, like his heart was real heavy with ideas. I had a great respect for him."

"Yeah . . . I used to get the feelin' too . . . But now I ain't sure . . . since Kansas. I ain't sure . . . There was black work down there——"

"You see, we haven't got ideas," the other went on eagerly, scarce hearing. "With you it was to get some fightin'. You could leave off any time. You did leave off, you're back diggin' potatoes. But the old man'll leave off when he's dead."

They were silent for a moment.

"You know, Salmon . . . if I had ideas about something, I'd hang on to 'em too . . . I've always wanted to stick by home, raisin' things. So I'm doin' it. But if I had ideas and figured they were good, I'd hang on too." He laughed uneasily. "But I'm a home body."

≡ * 147 * ≡

"Yeah, always was. We got to dig. Dark's comin'."

They went at it hard again. When the snow lay heavy, and the valley was in deep white shroud, shut from coming and going, they would need potatoes. Potatoes; and bread from the corn, little enough, mowed in the cellar; and milk, if the cow, fed in scanty times on dried buds of hemlock and birch, stood up well. These would keep life in the family during the bitter cold days, until the thaw came and the liberating spring.

It was chill steely dusk now, time ordinarily to stop. But they were near the end of the furrow, so tacitly they kept at it. Watson dreamed as his quick strong hands delved for treasure in the crumby earth. Strange, it came to him, how when you married it changed things. You lay by her at night and for a while you were all burning, then you slept close, just warm, and peaceful as babes. Fellows he knew stayed with girls in houses down the valley, but he'd bet they didn't have his feeling. Salmon here said it was all the same, in houses down the valley and with your own. But Salmon didn't know. Married, there he was like old yet not like old, and it was only a month. Why, he saw things softer than ever, like the other day when he felt choked watching a lapwing ripped by a hawk. He'd begun to know things more than he used to about what other folks were thinking like last night when he saw Ruth looking into the fire kind of sad and he put his hand on her shoulder. He worked like blazes all day because when he came in at nightfall Bell was waiting with warm eyes and food hot for him and speaking in low words meaning more than they said. He was all quick and glad and——

"Hey, fellers!" There was old Bill Stemm with his white beard like a wraith in the dimness, calling to them in his cracked voice from the edge of the field. "Got a letter fer ye! Frum Kansas!"

Salmon got up in a hurry. "Finish 'em, will you, Wat? There ain't much. I'll milk. I want to get into light and read it. I been waitin' for this one long." He cut eagerly across the field to old Stemm and together the two went down toward the house. Watson, remembering that the cow was milking badly, shouted after his brother:

"Hey, Salmon, salt her, will you?"

Some time after, the digging finished, he slung the heavy

sack over his right shoulder and clumped down the slope. It was full night now, with the sky ashy and giving off a faintest redness. The air had warmed and there was no wind. He made unsteadily for the small barn, his shoulder aching; felt a flake brush his neck, another tickle his nose. A few drifted, he saw, across the segment of light slanting pale through the barn door. He went in, lowering the sack to the floor by the threshold.

"She's comin', Salmon, slow as feathers."

The other, his back to Watson, was on a stool, milking the cow by bad light from a grimed lamp. A rusting carriage body was a vague hulk back in the dark of the barn. The four stalls were empty; there were no fowls about. The two upper lofts were bare; a small lower one was half-filled with coarse browse for the single beast.

"Powder her, Salmon?"

The brother did not answer, kept his hands in a jerk, drawing the dugs.

"Better, Salmon, afore you go in. She's been fidgety. Her tongue's been hangin'." The brother remained silent and Watson thought: he's in a mood, I guess; won't bother him. He hitched up his belt, spat on his hands and hoisted the sack to his shoulders again. "See you in," he heaved; and started toward the door. Then, remembering old Bill Stemm, he halted, and strained his head around beneath the burden.

"Say, what'd the letter tell, Salmon? How's everything?"

The warm swish of the milk into the pail stopped. He saw the other sitting still.

"Hey, Salmon, what's bitin' you? I asked you a question."

Salmon rose from the stool and slowly walked up to Watson. His face was strange; he pulled a letter from his shirt pocket.

"Here, this'll tell you."

"Tell me what?"

"Fred's dead."

Watson stared; the sack slipped from his hands to the loose planking with a thud, some potatoes rolling out.

"Dead?"

"Yeah. He's buried in Kansas. The worms been at him for a month now."

Watson moved back and leaned up weak against the wall, his hand over his eyes. He was not crying. Salmon went back and lifted the milk pail.

≡＊149＊≡

"I'm goin' to Kansas tomorrow," he said. "I'm goin' to kill the bastard who got Fred." He walked to the door. "Come on, Watson. Gettin' late."

They trudged around to the back of the house, neither speaking. The snow was coming thick now; already a white mantle was faint on the ground. They stopped outside the kitchen door. Someone within cast a moving shadow upon the low curtained window.

"You got to tell Ma," said Watson.

"You got to do it."

"How'll I begin?"

"Soft as you can."

"She cherished him."

"We all did."

They stood, remembering him; his pitiful frantic face. Then Watson felt his grief quicken, felt a heartburning.

"How'd Fred die?" he asked, trembling.

"A feller named White. Martin White. He's a preacher."

"How'd he die?"

"Foul. No regular fight. Fred greeted him friendly. The bastard shot him through his heart."

Watson groaned; beat his head suddenly with his clenched fist. "Damn his soul!" Tears started in his eyes. "What'd the boys do?"

"The old man don't say. Only that White's been braggin'. I'm goin' to kill him."

The kitchen door was opened suddenly and young Annie caught them standing there taut in the thrown light.

"There you are! Was just goin' to hunt you up, it's so late. Ma's waitin' with supper." Her eyes were sharp on them. "You're funny standin' like that in the dark. It's snowin'. Ain't you hungry?"

They went by her, trying to guard their faces from her gaze. She's got hair like Fred's, thought Watson, with a stab.

"Evenin', Ma."

"Evenin', Ma."

"Evenin', sons. Waitin' for you."

She was a raw-boned woman with heavy limbs. Forty were her years, but long ago, with the bearing of many children and a hard life, the bloom had fled from her so that now she was old in look. Her sheenless brick-colored hair, fretted with gray, swung low over the brows and came in a huge coil above. The face was tired, her eyes steady and patient. She was the imperishable stuff from which the strong common life came.

"Bella's over to Thompson's, Watson," she said, lifting the kettle from the hearth hook. "The old woman's took down bad and needs watchin'. Mebbe, Bella said to tell you, she'll stay the night."

"She won't keep long," he said, waiting behind Salmon as the other splashed his face and neck with water from a basin. "Saw her yesterday like a dead skinny bundle. She won't let go, but her blood's runnin' cold. She's seventy-seven now. Where's Ruth?"

"Ruth's layin' down," said Sarah. "She gets tired quick."

"Hen ought to be gettin' back," said the mother wearily. "It'll be on her soon."

Annie, quiet in a corner, thought fiercely: I hope she stays the night! I hope the old lady gets bad, so she'll stay a long time! I hope she never comes back! When Watson stood, blinded with suds, groping for the towel, she made a rush across the room and gave it to him. He took it without a word; she flushed high. With the others she was cold and moody; she loved him. When he was in good spirits he delighted to tease her, and she would fight back like a pale young cat, exulting, excited by his rough tumbling hands. Then of a sudden, making him wonder, her thin face would warm up strangely and she would leave off with abruptness, going from him; and in a corner she would sit, devouring him with her eyes. When he brought Bella to live in the house, the young sister became sick with jealousy. It troubled the girl-wife; she was a little afraid of Annie's bitter eyes. She resents me, I feel like an intruder, she thought; and tried hard and often to win her over. But it was no use; the child was haughty and distrustful, nursing her hurt like an Indian.

"Bill Stemm was in for somethin' hot afore. You got a letter, he said."

Mother Brown spoke without hope or fear. Suffering down the long years had dried in her the quick easy well of feeling. Far back, when Brown and she were young, when he was away from home and she was low with sickness, in a single week three of her young ones had died. She had lived through that and kept her heart. You went on, always on, where you did not know, a force without law, big and blind as life itself, urging you to it. Brown spoke always of the will of God, but of that she was not sure. Only this she knew: you bowed your head to take the blows.

"Nothin' much, Ma," said Watson with a beating in his throat. "Things are quiet, Pa writes."

After she had fed them a plain meal, they remained at the table while she ate, because it pleased her, giving her a faint warm feeling. The boys smoked their pipes. Sarah, sleepy and plump, cherished with vague movements and little murmurings the raggy doll of her own making. Annie, sharp as a blade, swept them with her eyes, losing nothing.

"How's the young 'uns, Tommy and Johnny, does he say?"

Always Mary Brown asked about the children first. Ah, the grown hung on somehow; it was the young that counted. She had seen them, helpless as chicks, go from life. People worried about the old dying; but look at Agatha Thompson, seventy-seven, and fighting still; and Ruth's first dead; and poor Jay's Austin, rotting at four in Kansas; and her own, seven of them, strewn in graveyards from Vermont to Ohio.

"They're doin' all right, Ma."

"Read it, son, there ain't been one in a long time."

Watson looked at his brother. "You . . . you got it, ain't you, Salmon?"

Salmon took the letter from his pocket. He fumbled with it, then handed it to Watson, rising. "I'm goin' down to the cellar. The kid's coughin' worse. She needs some lard for drawin' her neck."

"It don't help none, son. God knows with the cold on us how we'll keep her . . . When you're down, Salmon, bring up some sage and dill for flavorin'. I got it strung. Some tansy too, if there's any left."

"Oh, yeah, I found out a new one," said Watson eagerly, slipping the paper slyly to his lap beneath the table. "Ma Buxton told me to tell you. You roast figs just till they begin to curl, then you stuff 'em with ginger. It helped her'n." .

"I been tryin' slippery elm in a raw onion poultice. But nothin' helps. She just cuts herself double. It makes me afraid, thinkin'."

Salmon had slowly drawn back to the table. He put his hand to her shoulder, patted it awkwardly. "It'll be good, Ma. Quit worryin'."

The gesture was unusual for him. She looked up, surprised, the homely lined face going softer.

"I heard a funny one, Ma," said Watson desperately. "Will Stultz was down to——"

"You was readin' Pa's letter," said Annie. "It tells somethin'! I seen you two talkin' outside!"

"You're a brat!" scolded Salmon, sickened, moving again toward the cellar door. "Why do you go puttin' ideas in Ma's head? You're a brat!"

He went stumbling down the steps in the dark passage.

"You got bad manners, Annie," said Watson, trying to smile. "I was tellin' you, Ma——"

"If there's somethin' I got to know, you better tell me, son."

"There's nothing, Ma! Honest!"

"Then read it."

"Sure, I'll read it! Here! There's nothing!" With hands he could not keep from trembling he smoothed the letter out on the table. "Lawrence, Kansas Territory," he began casually. Mother Brown heard the little choke in his throat and her eyes fastened upon his face. "Dear Wife and Children, every one, I have one moment to write to you, to say that I am yet alive, that Jason and family, John and family, were well yesterday——"

He stopped here as though he found it difficult to cipher the writing. "It's thin scrawlin'," he said; and his eyes were wet.

"You better tell me, son."

A tear went slowly down his cheek.

"You better tell me, son."

"Ma . . . it's Fred . . . Fred's dead, Ma."

She did not weep. She put down the fork slowly; then closed her eyes, holding her rough reddened hands tight before her. Annie began to whimper. Sarah was asleep with her head resting on the table near the mother's plate. From the bed-room came the baby's dry racked coughing. Mother Brown stared out. Watson could not bear it; he rose, upsetting his chair, and rushed to the cellar door. Then, with a single look back at the still figure, he went, half-groaning, down the steps in a blind lurch, bruising his shoulders against the sharp stone walls.

Later, the two brothers came up together. Mother Brown was washing the dishes; Annie was wiping. Sarah was still dead asleep. Watson sat down near her, his head low. Salmon, with his hands deep in his pockets, kept moving across the room, back

≡ * 153 * ≡

and forth, his eyes seeking Mother Brown. She worked; she did not look up. Once he stopped behind her, hesitating. Then he moved on again; and his face was bloodless. Inside, once more the coughing began, rasping the still gloom.

"Did you get lard?" Mother Brown spoke dully, going on with the work.

"No, Ma. I forgot, Ma." It was unlike his voice, choked with feeling. He came behind her again, desperately drew patterns with his muddy shoe upon the puncheon floor. Inside him he was crying out: Damn it! It's always you gettin' hit, Ma! It's always you gettin' beat! Here's some more hurt for you, Ma, god damn White! To her he said:

"I'm goin' tomorrow, Ma. To Kansas."

She turned, letting the rag slip from her hands to the basin.

"Ain't there any kind of peace for me, son?"

"I got to go, Ma."

"You only just come back."

"Yeah, but I got to go."

"You said you had enough of fightin'."

"Yeah, Ma, I said it. But this is different."

"Leave bad alone, son. Your brother went down."

"Yeah, that's why I got to go, Ma."

"I got the right to keep some of mine! I ought to have some stayin' by me!"

Watson moved suddenly from the table, coming to them.

"We'll be back, Ma," he said. "We'll be back soon."

They stared at him, mother and brother and Annie.

"We got to square Fred," he said, his eyes shining. She uttered a little sound as though he had struck her a blow.

"You fool!" cried Salmon. "What are you babblin'?"

"Tomorrow I'm goin'."

"The hell you're goin'!"

"I'm goin'. Fred's my brother, just like he's yours."

"You fool! Here's Ma you got to look after!"

She moved to a chair, and sat down weak, the life ebbing from her face.

"I could clout you one!" cried Salmon.

"My mind's fixed on it."

"You fool! One's enough! Ma needs a man!"

Watson looked his mother's way; the shining stayed fast in his eyes.

"Don't try to soft me," he said. "You can stay or you can go. My mind's fixed on it."

Young Annie, clutching the pewter plate she was drying, whispered, none hearing her, "Don't you be goin', Watson! Don't you do it, Watson!"

"I got an idea," he said low and warm. "I'm pickin' up where Fred left off. It's owin' to him. It's my idea."

"You got ideas, huh?" raged Salmon. "You got Ma too! You got Bella! What are you goin' to tell her?"

The words caught Watson hard. He turned, wavering they could see; and went near the fire. They watched him as he fought it out; Salmon impatient and fearful for the mother; Annie, torn yet almost glad for his going, in her a tide running strong beyond her understanding; Annie, caught fluttering in the net of her love like a small pale bird, so young to know already imprisonment.

Bell! thought the bearded boy, searching the flames. How could he leave Bell, how could he even tell her, it being only a month and he rich in love with her? He could leave his ma, and feel sorry to tears. He could leave her, because going, he would know a gladness too; it was like doing some hard generous thing that gave a warm hurt as you did it. He had felt it so watching her sink in spirit as he told her; he had pain with her pain, yet at the same time a wide free sense, like an escape. It was like staying inside for a long stretch during the cold time. He hugged the fire, wanting it warm; he had dreams in the glow, drowsy as Ludlam's dog. Then quick a day came, when, with the sharp of the cold still holding, maybe even more bitter, he longed to get out in it, and he went out in it, into the raw blowing, and the jog over the frozen hill, and the jagged way through the woods bare as poverty; and all the time, numb, and bit, and breathing like an icy cut in his lungs, he gloried in it, because it swept him clean fresh and gave a high sense. His ma was like that to the bearded boy, warm like the hearth with a glow and a comfort; but quick a day came when you left, knowing yourself a man, to get the wide proud sense, the freedom. You could leave your ma, yourself feeling sorry to tears.

But Bell! How could he go from Bell? He needed no freedom from her. He wanted their two lives melting to one, all the days of both in a knit together; he wanted to know what was deep in her, giving back his own deepness. To go from Bell, at the end of a month! To quit her bed, not to hear her speak, to lose her touch! How could he go from Bell?

"You got to stay, can't you see, Wat?" It was Salmon, impatient, seeking to weigh his brother home with scruples. "You're Bella's man, she needs you."

How could he go from Bell? How could he go from Bell?

"I know your feelin'," said Salmon. "But I'll get White."

In a stabbing leap it came back to Watson—a great yellow-haired fellow with a racked face and the mind of a little boy, dropping in the dust, shot through his bewildered heart by a preacher named White. Dropping dead in the dust because he had an idea. Ah, that was how he could go, go from Bell! You could leave because outside away there was something right to be done! You could leave because you had an idea crying! He turned, blood flowing hard in him to them waiting.

"I'm goin' over to get Bella," he said. "I'll be back."

"You mean . . . ?"

"I'm leavin' tomorrow."

Salmon glared. Then he turned furiously upon Annie. "Get on to sleep, you brat!" He shook Sarah up roughly. "Both of you, get inside, get on to sleep!" He drove them into the room off the kitchen where Ruth was lying and shut the door on them. Then he rushed up the stairs to the attic, shouting as he went:

"You fool! Stick with Ma! I'll get Bella!"

He came down again soon in boots and a rough coat. He kept his eyes from them; his face was working. By the kitchen door he slammed his old hat on, and with his back to them, growled: "Goin' for Bella." He went out, snow and the wind gusting in through the opened door.

"You never been from me, Watson."

"It'll be only a short time, Ma."

He stood by her chair, the lost bleeding eyes drawing his heart.

"He took the rest, it oughtn't be you too."

"Pa's got nothin' to do with this. I'm goin' for Fred."

"I'd never a kick for hard livin', but it's too much now."

"I been always by you, Ma."

"You been more than all, son."

He looked away to the wall; he gulped.

"You been father to the young 'uns; you been like a man for me."

Her words worked upon him, calling up the whole strong fused feeling of his life by her side. Pictures—he, Watson, by a fierce fire inside a house, helping Ma with the candle-dipping, the wax gurgling and all asuck in the caldron, the bay-berries giving off a clean green smell; Watson searching the woods for balsam and sweet-flag to freshen Ma's kitchen, because she loved it fresh; both together, dyeing-time, boiling red poke-berry and creeping ivy to get strong black and indigo with juice of golden-rod blossom for a rich green shade; Watson alone with Ma of a night in summer, trying to teach her who had never danced, try-ing to teach her flushed and shy as a maiden and quick to give up the hoe-down; Watson, now doing this for his Ma, now being that to her, the days slipping into nights and growing to light again, time spreading into years and time all one, he and she to-gether always, speaking little and knowing each other much, and the richness of it growing on them—pictures like these went be-fore him swift in a dream-row, fading.

"Don't you go, Watson!"

Her rough hand fumbled for his; she looked up seeking his eyes, he giving them. Full over the raised lined face he saw now her love spreading, he saw it as a shining, born in the heart, a shining like a wave beautifully warm in a flow from her to him.

"Annie told me about Fred." It was Ruth who had come in quiet from the bed-room, speaking in her low clipped way. He let his mother's hand go from his.

"You never asked how Fred died, Ma," he said, with a sud-den harshness new to his speech with her.

"I don't need askin' to know," she answered hopelessly, again seeing him shut against her pleading. "Bad men were mixed in it and wildness. Only harm's come from Kansas since they been there, only black news for me. And now you'd be goin' there."

He was all dogged now, blind sick, and he said nothing, lost to her ache and her way of seeing things.

"It's only quiet I'm askin' for," said Mother Brown, "and to have my men folk stayin' by me home." Her inwards felt a torn raw thing. She had no ease for her pain, for she could not weep, as if she had forgotten how.

"It's cold in here," said Ruth, going to the hearth. "You need more heaping. . . . Annie said you're leaving, Watson. You're going to Kansas."

She made a tall figure drooped slightly in her thinness; the black wool shawl hung long from her shoulders. Her face was plain, very pale now and shadowed, swollen too, a little, from the child she was bearing; a face with strong jaw and a wide straight mouth like a man's. The eyes were fine, they were old Brown's eyes, the same gray fire in them. And her hair, not red, but deeper than gold, like a turned leaf, was a rich coiled crown giving off lights, shedding a grace on her hardness. Now with her back to the fire, nursing her hands for warmth, she stood up gaunt and misshapen, black and sharp white beneath her hair aflame.

"It's time you went," she said.

"I'm goin'."

"You've been home too long."

"I ain't stayin' home. I'm goin' with the sun."

Mother Brown got up from her chair and walked slowly to the high dresser, rough-hewn from cedar. She fumbled, though it was in plain sight among other things, for the wickerwork basket holding her darning. She came back with a heavy lifeless tread, saying:

"You can give me no help, Ruth, can you, you can only be sendin' him." Then: "Move it for light, Watson. You and Salmon goin' 'll need fixed things."

Deep in a thought, he lifted her chair close to the fire, while Ruth said:

"Men have to go, Ma, we have to stand it."

"What do we get, but the pain?"

"Pa needs 'em all for the work."

"It's easy for you to tell 'em to go."

"I sent Hen. I sent my man."

"What are you believin' in so strong?"

"My pa."

"God keep him in life."

"God's driving him."

"Sometime I feel it. Sometime I ain't sure."

"I'm sure, Ma. He's letting it all go. Letting things and easy days go. You and home-living and his boys. He's letting all his life go, so that mebbe there'll be life for other folks, for black folks. We have to help, Ma."

"The hull of my days, Ruth, I been helpin'. You know I never hung back."

"You oughtn't, Ma. Not now, either. I see it holy, Ma, I feel it holy!"

Watson, his eyes lighted, and breathing hard, turned to Mother Brown: "Don't you see it, Ma? I never seen it till now! I see it like Ruth says!"

She looked at him full, then after a length of sad, musing silence, said slowly: "When I was a girl my pa took me a little south. I seen a small brown boy whopped red by a slaver in a field for makin' a young 'un's mistake. I seen all over afeard eyes and a slinkin' air. From then on I have a hate for it. Only —only—you got to live your own self, you want your own ones livin'. You give a lot glad, but you want your boys."

"Then you see I got to go, Ma?"

She began to work again quickly, bending her head over the sewing; and said, so low that they could hardly hear:

"I only see you're goin'. I only see mebbe it'll be the last of you."

CHAPTER II

Not from Vengeance

AT DAWN of the next day the two Brown boys went forth, into a swirling snowstorm. It had been going all night; the steep lonely mountain-roads were piled with drifts. Westport, the nearest railroad point, was thirty miles distant. It took them two days to reach the hamlet; a farmer's lumber-sled gave them a six-mile lift. They were blue and stiffened with cold, weak with the steady gruelling snowshoe tramp, but a few hours after their arrival, when the train churned out through the white banks, they were aboard it.

They travelled fast, westward. Their money ran low, and at Rochester they sought out their father's friend, Frederick Douglass. The Negro asked no questions, he gave them money. They reached Chicago. A wagon-train, they learned, bearing

Free-State supplies and arms, was about to leave for the Territory. The two Brown boys went to the office of the National Kansas Committee. Yes, said the agent, they were glad to get new settlers. He gave them each a glistening Sharpe's rifle. The covered freight-wagons began the long overland journey. They crawled westward toward Iowa, along the barren winter plain; and Salmon Brown lusted, lusted, and Watson burned with the strange new fire.

In Tabor, Iowa, their brother Owen read a letter: "Dear Son, I arrived in Chicago . . . and I am to see Theodore Parker . . . and I have hopes of prevailing on the Committee to grant me the two hundred rifles. If I can carry this through, it will be the first step, and much will grow . . . I learn that my sons Watson and Salmon Brown accompany the rifle-train, and passed me on the trail. I am filled with joy, my own house shall yet uphold me. Bid them halt in Tabor till my return. I have plans for them . . . Do you get the common news from home? Is your back improved? *Do* in earnest, *do* in earnest, there is a harvest to reap . . ."

It was a tiny prairie town of some thirty homesteads—and the most important "underground" station on the farthest frontier. Slavers called it "that buzzards' nest" cursing it perditionward; to hundreds of black men, on their desperate furtive way to Canada and freedom, Tabor had been as a north star in the gloom of night. It was a hotbed of abolitionism, but its people sought freedom for themselves too. They were two hundred settlers, Ohioans stemming from New England stocks, in whom a stern puritan austerity had been tempered by the free tolerant aura of the plains; they were in protest against the darker dogma, the doom of hyper-Calvinism ("what, shall a fiftieth part of mankind be saved, do what they will of evil, and others doing what they can in love and charity be damned? will you not see that God is beneficent and there is excellence in man?"). And because they had a fierce need themselves to go self-appointed ways they fiercely fought the enslavement of others: Tabor was a single straggling hostelry for Free-State fighters. Before the "pilgrimage" they got ready there, drawing from its cached sources of arms and lead; after it there was succor for the sick and the dying. To this town Owen Brown had come with Lucius Moles, to rest his torn wasted body; to Tabor old "Osawatomie," fever-ridden, had journeyed in the ox-cart, to brood, to plan, to gather his strength for the last, the supreme struggle against the Sin.

A sharp blue day glowed out; night fell. A winter moon rose over the still, naked prairie, rose up chaste, unbearably white; and in the pale darkness the wagon-train bearing the rifles for Kansas strained into the "buzzards' nest." The big wheels creaked along the frozen rutted lane, and the whips cracked. With joyous anger the town dogs came yelping and leaping, shattering the dark peace. All along the single rude street, lights flooded out from the cabin doors; the townsmen called greeting. The wagons halted in the "square"; and quickly the curious began to gather: for news of older remembered places, for sight of strangers, and the stir each caravan brought to the routine life.

Owen Brown hobbled up on his cane to the first of the wagons. His sunken eyes eagerly searched among the men un-hitching the horses, unloading. Brands were flaring; he peered into the flickering illumined faces. He moved on to the next wagon, dragging his legs stiffly, leaning rigid on the hickory staff; on to the next, hungrily peering. "Are two Brown fellows in this bunch?" he asked; and instantly saw Salmon. The younger brother was standing there, back turned; Owen knew him by the wide stub-born set of his legs, and the big round head, close-clipped and bared. Owen hobbled up behind him. He touched his shoulder with the staff. "Hullo, Salmon," he said in a weak voice, and his eyes were glad. Salmon swooped around. "Hullo!" he cried, and grabbed his brother's hand. Then they stood there, confused, un-easy. They had spoken no word to each other, either by mouth or pen, for many months. Salmon had once said to the old man "Me and Hen's goin' too, we're sick of Kansas" and Owen had remembered. It was the one thing he could not forgive: faithless-ness to the father. He never mentioned the name of Hen Thomp-son. His heart was shut against Oliver; that day in the Kansas camp, as he lay helpless and writhing beneath the dog-tent and Oliver was crushing the old man, he could have struck the dark boy dead. (You young devil! traitor! You'll have to come crawl-ing for your forgiveness, you'll have to do a mighty good act to wash that out! Traitor!) But here was Salmon, returning to the old man's side, seeing a light again.

≡ * 161 * ≡

"I'm sure glad to have you, Salmon. . . . Where's Watson?"

The warmth died in the younger brother's eyes; they went bitter and hostile. He was a different being, he stood fierce and darkly silent. Then Watson came leaping down from the wagon, crying "Owen!" and the two embraced. Christ, but he's been sick, thought the bearded boy, wincing, feeling the wasted body beneath his arms. And in Owen, clasping the other with his withered left arm, ran a deep vague mingled feeling: he is grown, he is strong, I love this boy, I must not let anything happen to him, but he must help in the work, father will need his strength, his zeal.

"Come on," said Salmon, stabbing Owen with his eyes. "I'm hungry. Tired." (Oh damn you, damn you, wasn't one enough? Not him, I tell you, not him!)

That night the two struggled for the heart of their brother. He listened in rapt silence, gazing from one to the other.

"But you can't go. The old man says for you to wait here."

"I don't care what he says. We're movin' on tomorrow."

"You're running out again, eh?"

"We're goin' down for White. To finish up what you and the old man didn't have the guts to finish."

"You bragging young fool. Do you think me or him was scared? When you were hiding in Elba the old man was fighting down there alone." Owen turned to Watson, beseeching. "He's got big plans, Wat! He needs us all."

"Plans," said Salmon in a desperate ugly voice. "Plans. I was in a plan once. The Doyles were in it, too. Mebbe. . . ."

"Keep still, Salmon," said Owen.

"I'm goin' to talk! You won't drag Wat into this. I been through it, I know what kind of plans the old man has . . . Listen, Wat, I never told you. . . ."

"Keep still, Salmon," said Owen.

But the savage voice went on; and Watson listened with startled eyes:

Writhe to the grass, Townsend, die bleeding with slugs in you . . . hush, Mahala, hush . . . five men dead on the Potawatomie. . . .

"Stay clear, Wat, for Christ's sake, stay clear!"

Then Owen, faint and white, passionately pleaded: it was war, life for life, the old man is driven, he is appointed to free the slaves of this land. . . . "Fred's dead, you can't bring him back! And the old man needs us all! Come in with us, Wat! It's a holy work! Come in with us!"

"It's murder, Wat! Hen saw it and broke free, Oliver broke free! Go back to Bella! Live your days through, peaceful!"

In the morning Salmon Brown rode out on the trail to Kansas—alone.

Three days later John Brown returned. He confronted the two sons; and Watson was shocked, he felt a sudden flooding sorrow. Hardly two years had gone since he had last seen his father, but it might have been ten, so aged did he seem. The long springing stride was gone; he walked a little stiffly and his shoulders were bowed. The gray face was thin and tired, and his throat was beginning to show withered; Kansas had taken a deep toll. He shook Watson's hand; and his voice faintly trembled with joy, "I'm glad, son. We need you." They told him that Salmon had refused to join with him again. The old man's face fell; he said with weary bitterness, "Maybe I deserve it. Maybe I deserve no better than that my own shall fail me." They told him Salmon had gone to kill Preacher White. He grew sorrowful. "He's wrong. He shouldn't have gone down for that man. Aye, my sons have always mistaken my true objects. I would not hurt one hair of White's head, I tell you I would not go one inch to take his life. I don't hold feelings of revenge. I act from a principle. My object is to restore human rights. . . . He shouldn't have gone down."

The words sounded in Watson's mind with a startling inspiriting force. That night his brothers had turned fearfully to him: what are you going to do, Watson? And he had answered, "I'm stayin' by the old man. I'm goin' to help in the work. . . . It's owin' to Fred. . . . I've got an idea." And here now was his father speaking, "I don't hold feelings of revenge. I act from a principle. My object is to restore human rights." The words were like the very echo of his own groping thought, only returned clearer and more eloquent a thousandfold, and somehow beautiful with solemnity and the truth of the heart. Then, as the old man began to speak of his plans (". . . and he said to me, Yes, be sure to come to see me, I think we can help you; and he said, Captain Brown, we in the East have heard of you, we know of your services in this cause . . ."); as the bluish eyes took fire and the gaunt face kindled with dark zeal, there died in Watson the pitiful sense of age and decline he had initially felt. A force seemed to be rising in the old man, drawn from deepest reserves, charging with power his whole being, his eyes, his frame, the leashed metallic voice. And Watson was at once swept and frightened. He observed, almost as for the first time, the four jagged lines furrowing up from between the shaggy brows to the low forehead, the jaw- and lip-muscles bunched in pendulous knots— come of concentration through many years upon a fixed idea; he marked the cavernous eyes agleam with a kind of fanatic violence; the whole countenance rigidly burning, as though granite should be shaped to express a desperate living dream.

"I am ready. The plan is fully drawn. Twenty years it has been laying in my mind, and now I'll strike. I need only the backing of these wealthy Easterners and I'll begin to gather my men. My sons, in Virginia they'll feel the blow! And the South will learn that God is not dead!"

December came. Owen remained in Tabor, to keep in touch with certain Kansas jayhawkers, to prepare the ground for the secret force that would soon be assembling. The old man and Watson headed for the East, riding and tying across the plains on a big mule.

CHAPTER III

Remnant in Israel

"CAPTAIN BROWN, did you go out to fight slavery under the auspices of the Emigrant Aid Society?"

"No. I did not, sir. I went out to fight that rotten old whore under the auspices of John Brown."

Young Sanborn listened to the harsh voice with intense joy. He had luminous eyes, very black; a wide mobile mouth, softly formed, with fair silky moustaches and a wisp of an imperial; his hair swept back straight and long from a wide white forehead. It was clearly a face of impulse and ardor, a dreaming face too—and from these somehow it drew faintly a weakness as well as its strength. Frank Sanborn was but a year and a half out of Harvard. He had recently given up his teaching place in the Concord village school; there was a work to do in these grievous days, there was an anti-slavery cause. He was now a secretary of the Massachusetts State Kansas Committee; he had no doubts about the will of God: slavery would end *when it was slain*. And here was this old man come miraculously before him, his militant ideal risen in sinew and blood and flesh. His dealings thus far had been solely with those who preached for the cause, gave money, formed committees; but here was one who had actually come to grips with the evil force, had fought with rifle and knife on the plains and river-bottoms of Kansas.

"No. I went out to fight that rotten old whore under the auspices of John Brown."

By heaven, thought the young schoolmaster, *this* is the man to do the deed! Look at that face, the naked grandeur of it! See all that the wind and the prairie have shaped and swept in that glance; the man is so transparent that all may see him through. *Dei gratia*, this is he who was to come!

I must be careful, thought the old man, I must not reveal too much. The boy burns, I can hold him to my will. But the others will be wary, they are older, caution will nudge them. If I lay the plan openly before them they may deem it folly. I must gain their confidence in my courage, yet not frighten them off with any hint of rashness.

Young Sanborn had his hero: now followed letters, guarded meetings; the mansion doors of New England dignitaries—Theodore Parker, the famous Boston preacher; swarthy, bearded Higginson, the young Unitarian minister; Doctor Samuel Howe who on his Grand Tour had fought against the Turks in the Greek revolt, George Luther Stearns, deliberate, cautious chairman of the regional Kansas Committee ("I shall confer with my associates about . . . eh . . . lending the rifles. . . . I am anxious to further any plan that will make Kansas' admission as a free state more certain. . . . It must be understood, however, that we favor only *defensive measures*")—the doors opened to a gray gaunt man dressed in an old-fashioned woolen suit of kerseymere, a high patent leather throat stock, a long severe overcoat with a cape, and a black fur cap: the whole effect being that of a rural deacon gone militant.

Aye, defence, caution, bills of sale! thought old Brown.

Breath-bubbles for knocking down a stone wall! "I trust, sir," he said, "that my word will be warrant for my deeds. What my actions will be I cannot now foresee, but I aim to do nothing that will hinder the cause I labor in. As for your committee, sir, I hope they will give no promise they are unable to fulfill. I go a steep road. Empty words will weigh me down."

He is right, thought Gerrit Smith, rosy, stoutish old gentleman in the mountain manor at Peterboro, New York; we must cease looking to ballots. There was a time when slavery could have ended through political action, but that time has gone by —forever, I fear. I vainly flattered myself that some immanent justice would slowly and surely prevail. But I see now there is not virtue enough in the American people to bring slavery to a bloodless end. All that remains for them is to bring it to a violent one.

Thus reflected pure-in-heart Gerrit Smith, philanthropist—strong feelings for a gentle old fellow who would turn white and sick at the mere sight of blood. But "violence" is a word, and has nothing to do (especially when it springs to thought by the side of a glowing hearth in a baronial manor) with a bayonet-thrust through the guts or men stiffening, staring up ghastly with wide dead eyes.

And in the West there is a huge homely man, a politician with a wilderness air and a dark yellow face wrinkled and dry; his hacked-out frame holds up the too-wide clothes, the shiny frock-coat, his lank bony body rises endless on a prop of enormous shoes. He is a lawyer in Illinois; he likes horse-racing and cock-fights; he knows the Bible and loves Shakespeare—he is Abraham Lincoln. He has a shrill voice, a piping voice, but he speaks slowly in gnarled quiet words, and the people who listen sense the forces that went into his making: storms, and yellow sun-baked clay of earth, and waters running and the great solitudes—they recognize the heart that is their own, speaking the gnarled, the deep wise words. He sits now in his shabby Springfield office, with his spidery legs wound up on the scarred desk, clasping his knees. An hour before he made the crowd at the corner-store roar with laughter; he could make a cat laugh, they said of him. But now he is the lone man, now he broods:

Compromise, not bayonets. We live in a world of men—

frail, mortal, fallible. We must try to do what we can with the imperfect institutions devised by imperfect men; fight ahead, learn from our failings. *Let us do what we can with the law,* seeking slowly to change it. For the better impulses of men will prevail in the end. I believe in the essential justice of the plain people.

CHAPTER IV

The Wanderer: the Hopes;
the Grief

FEBRUARY WAS approaching; the old man fretted, he was making slow progress. Gerrit Smith had sent a thousand dollars. Theodore Parker was trying to gather money from his reluctant congregation; so too Higginson in his modest parish. But Howe could only lend attention, and young Sanborn contributed a large fund of enthusiasm. For the rest: words; promises; breath-bubbles. "Oh," the old man bitterly exclaimed once, "if I could but have the money for my work that is *smoked* away in Boston in a single day!" True, Stearns had prevailed upon the Committee to give him possession of two hundred rifles and four thousand cartridge balls, and they had voted him five hundred dollars; but the emphasis only gnawed at his patience. *For defensive purposes alone.* "Of course," Stearns had said, gazing at him pointedly, "of course, we have no fear that they will be put to service for other ends." The old man could only choke down his wrath and let silence continue the subtle deception. He had no self-delusions about his course: he was double-dealing. And yet he had no scruples. For did he not know in his heart the godly way? Aye, if need be he would break every law of the Decalogue to follow it. Oh timid souls, with your defensive measures! What are you defending? your free-soil dividends? Oh merchant-rabbits!

But soon young Sanborn came to him, radiant. His enthusiasm had borne fruit: he had arranged to have John Brown appear before the National Kansas Committee. That body was soon to meet in New York; he could make a strong plea for help. The old man said nervously, "I mistrust this. I am not an easy hand at speeches. I'd rather face twenty Ruffians." But when the meeting opened at the Astor House in New York, he was present. As delegate from Massachusetts, Sanborn presented a resolution; that five thousand dollars be contributed to Captain John Brown for service in Kansas. The motion was vehemently opposed by various delegates from the further West. They had heard about John Brown. While they acknowledged his services in the Territory, they felt that he was too radical and violent to be entrusted with such a sum; that he might, in short, use it in ways which the Committee could not sanction.

Discussion. . . .

Will Captain John Brown submit to brief questioning?

He stood up, pale, rustic, severe; felt the staring weight of two hundred eyes.

"Yes," the low cracked voice answered. "I aim to organize a company for service in the Territory. . . ."

"If you receive arms and money from this Committee, will you invade Missouri or any other slave territory?"

"I am no adventurer. You are acquainted with my history, you know what I have done in Kansas. I don't expose my plans. No one knows them but myself. I'll not be interrogated—if you wish to give me anything, give it freely. I have no other purpose but to serve the cause of liberty."

The Committee voted: ". . . in aid of Captain John Brown . . . twelve boxes of clothing, sufficient for sixty persons . . . twenty-five Colt's navy revolvers . . . five thousand dollars, to be used in any *defensive* measures that may become necessary."

February came. Again the old man made a public appearance. He spoke before the Joint Committee on Federal Relations of the Massachusetts Legislature. A bill was up for an appropriation to defend the interests of Massachusetts settlers in the Territory.

The bill was not passed.

That night the old man sank down to the bed in his small dingy hotel-room and turned his face blindly to the wall.

But the next morning he was off for Springfield. He would

raise funds, even if he had to go begging from town to town. He began to speak before small gatherings; in school-houses, churches, town-halls. Springfield gave him one hundred and fifty dollars; Hartford and its environs six hundred; Worcester a cannon and two rifles. He would read his short speech from a wrinkled sheet; the harsh whip-like voice spoke strange words for a "beggar":

"It is with no little sacrifice of personal feelings that I appear in this manner before the public. . . . But I am trying to raise from 20 to 25 thousand Dollars in the Free-States to enable me to continue my efforts in the cause of Freedom. . . . Will the people of Connecticut, *my Native state,* afford me some aid in this undertaking? I was told that the newspapers in a certain city were dressed in mourning on hearing that I was killed & scalped in Kansas. Much good that did me. In the same place I met a more cool reception than in any other place where I have stopped. If my friends will hold up my hands while I am yet alive: I will freely absolve them from any expense over me when I am dead. . . ."

He spoke in Canton, and Collinsville, at three meetings—and gathered eighty dollars. New Haven gave him a thousand dollars—in promises. He strode from the hall, crumpling the paper-pledges in his skinny hand, longing to fling them full into the cold polite mask-faces, to cry aloud "I'll not burden you further! I do not love to ride free horses till they fall down dead!" He walked alone for hours through the dark wet glistening streets, through a desolate night of wind and rain; and the wrath ebbed in him, and he became quieter, and humbler in his spirit. He *was* a beggar. He needed these people; it was not as if he were with his own band in the Kansas timber and could fling defiance in the teeth of those who opposed him. Aye, more, it went deeper than that. He had no right to be proud. For himself he could be proud and defiant, but for the work, no. For the work he must be willing to know every prostration, every denial of his selfhood. Crawl on his belly, and eat dung, and beg. And most of all, be patient. Twenty years you have waited, the small voice whispered as he faded through the wet night as in a dream; twenty years. You can wait still, you can wait still, the day will come!

So the wanderings continued, and his life was this one great hunger; a hunger fed, in some incalculable process of the soul, by every new loneliness and assailing grief, by all the littler hungers of the simple peasant heart, yearning for hearth and family and the feel of the earth. From the wretched winter-swept Elba farm, where Mary Brown toiled and uncomplainingly suffered, holding life together against the perpetual poverty, came Watson's letter:

". . . since I got back . . . and there has been a forty hour drive of snow, and there is now almost a four foot depth of it on the levels. Our corn reserves and wood have gone down very low. Salmon made a try sludging through to the Busby's for stuff. He's laid up. His feet are near froze off. Most are down with chills. Been trying bark squeezings and whiskey, but it helps little. Annie wonders if we'll ever smell crab-apple blossom again, & will the frogs ever live this one through to come shrilling up with the spring. . . . Father, it is almost 2 months since we are back east and you have not come yet to see our family. Father, will you try to see our family for a few days?

"I am also waiting exceeding anxious for directions. When do we begin *doing in earnest?* It lays on my mind, I think of it all day and night. Bella is sick with *inside pains,* and we don't know what to do. Is there a *Remedy* you know about?

"Hen and Oliver got back. They'd been hiring out, farming in Illinois, to get expenses. Salmon is back too. He says Preacher White is dead, but he didn't kill him. White was shot in a fight before Salmon got down. Oliver thinks to marry soon. He met her in Illinois and he is sending for her. She's Martha Brewster. Ruth will be down any day soon, bearing. . . . The boys say *they will not fight anymore.* I talk to them, I have a full heart for it, but they keep saying they will not. . . . Father almost 2 years went since you left Elba, so try hard to come to see our family. . . ."

But beneath the dirty flaring hotel-lamp the bony hand nervously moved in its tight scrawl:

". . . and I send you fourteen dollars . . . and I cannot say whether I shall be permitted to visit you or not this winter or spring. I long to see how that little company of sheep, my sorrowing children, look about this time, but I cannot now say. For this is not our rest, in this world we have no abiding place or continuing city. We must remember 'the poor who cry' and feel grateful that we are counted in the least possible degree worthy to suffer for truth. Be all of good cheer. I may yet see accomplished the work of my life, and be permitted to return: and 'rest at evening.' . . . Tell my sons despite they are set strong

≡ *170* ≡

against me *I do not release them*. . . . See to it to have the
ground on the east side of the stream got into grass this coming
season. . . . Be all of good cheer & may the God of my fathers
take you for his children. . . . Do not noise it about that John
Brown is in these parts. I want to hear how you are all supplied
with winter clothing, boots. I have little time to go further. I
leave tonight to see a man in Concord. His name is Thoreau,
and Sanborn tells me he is a friend of freedom. Henry David
Thoreau. . . ."

*   *   *   *   *

He is a small man; lean and narrow-chested; with a brown
beard; big ugly sardonic nose; and vigilant gray eyes, with sudden gleams of blue in them, like metal, eyes that probe you clean
through. Perhaps he is sitting this moment at a small table in an
attic room. He is dressed roughly, in moccasins and brown jeans,
stained by rambling and rain and usage the color of earth. In a
corner of the severe room is a pair of high boots, dry-caked with
mud of the Concord marshes. The shelves, the maple dresser,
the long wall-table, are covered with lichens, fungi, birds' eggs,
the nest of a hawk, arrow heads, a flute, books, manuscripts. The
little man has no pipe, no bottle by him, only a trencher of un-
shucked nuts. He is writing.

They meet. They sup together at Thoreau's. (The old man
is at home at the ascetic table, laid with cheese and brown-bread
and tea.) They talk—this New England Pan of the icy coat and
the quivering passionate senses, bleak little animal who can drift
for hours in a boat, playing wildly his flute, gazing into the
water's green shifting peace, listening to the thrush-song rap-
turous in the dark woods; and this rustic covenanter with the
face of twisted steel, and in the gaze a blue distant burning,
Hebraist with eyes otherworldly, fearing, save it be religious,
every music of this life as the snare of the devil—they talk, and
for all the difference, know themselves brothers. Strange brothers,
who live as in different lands, tempered by different suns and
storms and springs, with unlike hungers and windings of the
brain; yet in some deep inward flow, some grim common dia-
thetic core—brothers. There have been moments when the old
peasant has counseled younger men: take more care to end life
well than to live long; Thoreau has been known to say: in pro-

portion as death is more earnest than life, it is better than life. Aye, these two are like the obverse faces of a single truth—the one, pursuing the ideal with the same intensity as others might a body-pleasure, ready to give up his very life for it, but only as it touches the freedom of his own soul, unwilling actually, physically, to stir a finger to reform the world; the other, not stopping short with the pure abstract idea, but fighting as a warrior in the heat and the din, eager to sacrifice for a vision his share of this agitated beautiful mortal-existence. Obverse faces . . . the thinker; the doer . . . the saturnine contemplative hatred of injustice; the dark bitter glory of action.

They talk the night away; of Kansas and slavery and hope for the future; and the metals ring out.

"I do not, Mr. Thoreau, attribute my little success to any star or magic. The reason larger numbers of the enemy buckled before me was because they *lacked a cause*. They had no armor against affliction. When the time came few men were willing to lay down their lives to defend what they knew to be wrong. They did not like that this should be their last act in this world."

(Look, is Thoreau's thought, how he does not overstate anything, how he speaks within bounds *those Ruffians had a perfect right to be hung* he does not give the least vent to his fire, he is a volcano with an ordinary chimney flue *I have had to skulk in swamps, with a price on my head and hundreds seeking me, but they could not take me, for it was perfectly well understood that I would not be taken* this talk is no mere gossip, it is not the foam that rises when a man's life has ceased to be inward and private *no little handful of men were willing to undertake it, and a large body could not be got together in season.*)

". . . The law will never make men free, Captain Brown. It is men who have got to make the law free. They are the lovers of law and order who observe the law when the government breaks it. . . . Nor does it matter how small the beginning may seem to be: what is once well done is done forever. . . . And even suppose blood should flow. Is there not a sort of blood shed when the conscience is wounded? Through this wound a man's real manhood and immortality flow out, and he bleeds to an everlasting death. I see this blood flowing now."

They part. There has been no material exchange, no written contract duly sealed, no donation to a fund. They have only spoken and touched; and each by the other has been fed in his own lack. Their destinies swing apart in vastly removed directions. But they will cross again, though not in the flesh. You, Thoreau, will read one of these days a piece of news about the old fellow, the hewn peasant fighter with the astonishing face— and with anguish and exulting you will be moved in the very depth of your soul.

 CHAPTER V

"Farewell: to the Plymouth Rocks; Bunker Hill, Monuments; Charter Oaks; and Uncle Toms, Cabbins"

SPRING WAS close now; the New England benefactors impatiently asked: why does Captain Brown linger? The thaws would be opening the Territory anew to the invasion of the Border Ruffians. It was his place to be there, ready for resistance. They had given him money and arms; now let him be gone. Stearns, with the inevitable circumlocution, informed the old man of his Committee's desire. "Soon, soon," John Brown said. "I know my affairs. Tell them I am not yet ready." Aye, he knew what these comfortable caution-bound committeemen did not dream. They had given him arms and dollars for defence in Kansas, but those arms those dollars would *never enter Kansas.* For the Committee's purpose he was generously equipped; for his own desperate plan of aggression he was still at the very beginning of his resources. Fifty, a hundred men, recruited, quartered in some secret place, armed, drilled—all this would demand vastly more than he had as yet been able to squeeze, dollar by dollar, from New England pockets. "Soon, soon," he said; and again went, now with a kind of frantic bitterness, "begging" through the countryside. But shortly he was scrawling in his ragged notebook: "Must return West; & go back without securing my proper outfit. Go, having failed to secure even the means of equiping: to say nothing of feeding sufficient men. I had when I returned no more than I could peril; & could make no further sacrifice, except to go about in the attitude of a beggar: & that I have done humiliating as it is. Must return West to keep good will of committee. When I attack *Africa* greatly important to have such *Names* as sympathizers. Sad of heart. . . ."

But these days with each bleak entry his long nervous fingers would flip back the stained pages, and his eyes would fasten hungrily upon certain harsh rows (how strange and senseless they would stare up before another's eyes!) of words and numbers:

> Circassia: about 550,000. Switzerland, 2,032,030.
> Guerrilla warfare see Life of Lord Wellington page 71 to page 75 (Spanish guerrilla: Mina). See also page 102 *some valuable hints.*
> Page 196 important instructions to officers (discipline and cooking).
> See also same book 235 these words: Deep and narrow defiles 300 men suffice to check an *army.*
> Charleston. San Antonio. St. Louis. Augusta, Georgia. Little Rock. Harper's Ferry.

Aye, he had his grief—but the hope, the hope!

"All right," he sent word to George Luther Stearns; "I am ready to return." There were fighters in the West, he thought; money or no money, he would begin to gather his men.

He made a quick trip to Rochester, to Frederick Douglass. The Negro leader listened to the old man; and answered with fired eyes, "I'm with you, Brown." Now from Pennsylvania to Ohio, from New York to Canada, on to a thousand smoldering hearts, a word would begin to move in slow secret lines among black men of the North.

Then quickly old Brown was back in the small Connecticut town of Collinsville. There he had lectured in February; he had had a talk with one Blair, a forge-master; had drawn from his boot-top a long two-edged dirk, and, turning it reflectively in his gnarled hand, had remarked: "You know, Mr. Blair, if I had a lot of these things fastened to poles about six feet long they would make a capital thing for the settlers in Kansas. They could keep them in their log-cabins to defend themselves against a sudden attack. Why, even women could handle them easily. . . . What could you make such things for, Mr. Blair? Say . . . five hundred . . . or a thousand?"

"Well . . . let's see. . . . I could make five hundred, I suppose, for about a dollar and a quarter apiece. Or if you want a thousand, for a dollar apiece."

"I expect I'll want them made, Mr. Blair."

Now on this April day John Brown was back in Collinsville. In the blacksmith shop Blair and the old man drew up a contract for a thousand pikes. Blair signed with a glow of righteousness: it was a nice job and he would be doing his bit for the good cause in Kansas. He could see Free-State women holding bloodthirsty Ruffians off at the point of his dirks. But in the other mind a different image flamed: a horde of black men, slaves unaccustomed to the feel of rifles were rallying, running wildly from the plantations, bearing pikes.

There was still another action that needed doing before he departed westward. There was a man in New York he had been told about; who must be seen, and sounded, and joined if possible to his side. Old Brown left for New York, fervently hoping.

For Hugh Fordes—the dark military-slender Englishman, with a great curling mass of hair, slightly graying; with worldly impeccable talk and run-down heels (giving the effect of improvident *chevalerie*); with eyes glittering and magnetic, and dilated ever so faintly yet unmistakably—for Hugh Fordes life was an opportunity to be grasped. "With cunning and ruthlessness" he was enamored of saying. And who more than he (so he would often interrogate himself), he with his exceptional talents, his brilliance and perspicacity, his deep instinct for leadership over men, was fit to grasp it? True, the opportunity in some unaccountable fashion had thus far perversely eluded him. Instead of the dominance over circumstance (which, it was plain to behold, was his by every right and attribute of a superior nature) he had achieved only the shabbiest kind of existence. From the day he was stiffly bowed out of Cambridge for neglect and profligacy (who was he to be burrowing like a worm in the fusty fecal soil of law), to the time he had written the letter to Sylvia his betrothed, russet-haired virginal Sussex maid, bidding her a florid good-bye, and had run off to Bordeaux with Eda Gue (the slut! thus he always recalled her, venomously; the lying lecherous slut!), Eda whom he had known a week and who had lovely olive breasts and the small dark round eyes of an animal; through the greedy marriage with dull Sarah Rochemont, heiress to the huge fortune of her apoplectic wine-merchant father, heiress speedily and irrevocably disinherited; through the shady disastrous venture as a silk-merchant in Sienna; and the brief unprincipled participation as a conspirator in the unsuccessful Garibaldian revolution (from which he emerged, self-titled, a "colonel") of 1848—each of his steps had pointed prophetically (save in his own mind where a maggot of delusion grubbed and sucked and bloated itself upon the ever-diminishing core of his lucidity) each had pointed in the direction of the hungered threadbare days which were his present destiny, the destiny of an adventurer, distraught and moonstruck and ceaselessly obscure.

But his fortune would change, he was far too profound a mind to be bogged forever; yes, he needed only a break in the dark run of his luck. In the meantime, he was living from hand to mouth, giving occasional fencing lessons, and doing odd jobs for the *Tribune,* translating articles from the French and Italian; and he was continuing to send weekly letters to his destitute family in Paris—poor bewildered Sarah Rochemont Fordes, once stupid and rich, now poor and stupider; and the two young daughters, Jane thirteen and Simone ten, dark and slim both, trusting, gentle as flowers—long grandiose epistles telling of his brilliant projects hanging fire, and how any day now fortune would descend upon them, only they must have patience, and faith in his power. Yes, he but needed a break in the black run of his luck.

One day in April old John Brown took the train for New York, fervently hoping, seeking a man who must be sounded, and joined, if possible, to his side; a military man, a "Colonel" Hugh Fordes.

By nightfall of the next day the bargain was entered upon. They shook hands warmly across the lamp-lighted table in the dingy lodging-house room; there was no written agreement, the code of honorable men would bind them. He, Captain John Brown, engaged Colonel Hugh Fordes as drill-master of the volunteer-regular company which was being organized for service against slavery. The salary would be one hundred dollars a month. He, Colonel Hugh Fordes, would, until such time as the said company was assembled, busy himself with the preparation of a manual of guerrilla warfare, to be called "The Manual of the Patriotic Volunteer."

Thus the secret which John Brown had kept in his heart's depth, guarded from all save the most tried and trusted, was unbosomed now in its least detail to this stranger of five hours' acquaintanceship. John Brown had long ago scrawled in his notebook the harsh rows of words and numbers: "Guerrilla warfare . . . important instructions to officers . . . deep and narrow defiles. . . ." These were theories painfully drawn from books; here was a man who had campaigned with the great Garibaldi ("So, Colonel Fordes, you fought under Garibaldi?"—"Sir, I was among his most trusted aides!") in the Italian passes. Brown's revelation, coming from so inward a being, was incredible—yet withal, inevitable. The old man only needed to hear, as in a joyous daze, the Englishman talk glibly of tactics, of how "by using the interior or shorter lines of communication it is possible to concentrate the greater part of scattered bodies and put forces into the field to meet separately those larger ones moving against them"—of how "it is imperative, sir, when a force is encumbered by almost as many prisoners as there are soldiers, to discover the strength and direction of all hostile movements, however insignificant." The old man was forgetting the fierce hunted Kansas days; the wisdom the swamps had soaked into his very blood and grain; the dearly-purchased knowledge of night-rides and hidings and the swift thrust. Now he could only think: by the great Jehovah! this was the man to ensure the victory! Between them they would be invincible, one the complement of the other, forming a perfect military unit—a leader with iron and a dream, a lieutenant with technique.

That very night Fordes hurriedly wrote to his family of three in Paris. The opportunity had come! Now they would see (they would not quite see, they would read his words mournfully and wonder how all this would help pay, when the landlord made his rounds, next week's rent). After these many weary months his ruthless and cunning stratagems had at last achieved their profound end. He had some of the wealthiest men in the North numbered among his staunch adherents; he had behind him, loyal and heedful of his smallest commands, a military organization composed of thousands of the most valorous fighters,

≡＊177＊≡

with ramifications cunningly reaching out through the whole length of the land. Why, there were no limits to the conquest he would effect, he might yet be the very Garibaldi of a revolution against slavery!

John Brown headed for Boston, quickened again by a rising strength. Action, action! He was up, he was doing; life was no longer a torment of abeyance, it was a striding toward the dreamed goal. He had his pikes, Frederick Douglass was working underground among the black comrades, he had this trained soldier Fordes enlisted in his ranks. Now he could go west to gather his fighters. Aye, God was smoothing his way.

But in Boston, a letter awaited him. It was from his son, Jason, timidly living in an Ohio village with Ellen and Tommy. It told the old man what he had been guilty for a moment of forgetting: his was not the smooth way, God was the great Tester, he must expect to endure nothing but hardness.

". . . a deputy United States marshal passed yesterday through Cleveland. I learn he has a warrant for your arrest, for doings in Kansas. Father, be on your guard. . . ."

The old man went suddenly faint, he felt a tiny unaccustomed panic in his vitals. He could not be taken now! he was on the very threshold of. . . . He went to young Sanborn. Sanborn reflected, disappeared for a few hours, reappeared. He had arranged it. Captain Brown must fade away until the danger passed. There was a plain house on a retired Boston street. Judge Thomas Russell lived there. The Judge was inconspicuous in the Abolitionist ranks (so that he might be more serviceable to the cause in quiet ways); no one would dream that John Brown was hiding there.

So the old man kept under cover; and spring came in a soft flood; and he sickened with fret and foreboding.

At night, before going up to bed, he would take out his two revolvers and repeater, to make sure of their loads. The family looked on, awed and a little frightened. "Here are eighteen lives," he would say grimly. Mrs. Russell he often advised, "If you hear a noise at night, madam, be sure to put the baby under the pillow." Once, after she had brought to him upstairs a bite to eat, and he about to barricade the room for the night, he called through the door, "I should hate to spoil your carpet, Mrs. Russell, and you must forgive me if I do. But you know I cannot be taken alive." Sometimes, in the sunny back-parlor, armed heavily, he would play with the little two-year-old Russell girl, tossing her up high and gently in his knotted hands, as he had loved to do with his own in rare moments of impulse, and then he would gravely tell her, "When I am hung for treason, little one, you can say that you used to stand on Captain Brown's hand."

As the days crept by, the faint panic persisted strangely. In some vague way he associated his present distress with the hopes, high and airy and false, which had immediately preceded it. He had been building castles, so he rebuked himself, when he ought to have been hauling bricks and beams; he had made his geese into swans. Then the brooding upon his own weak folly turned his mind bitterly again to the defection of others. One evening he came downstairs to Judge and Mrs. Russell, with a sheet of paper in his hand, and his face harsh and coldly tense. Might he read to them a little something he had scribbled out? He was, he realized, no scholar, he knew no more of grammar than a farmer's calf; but this in his hand was a judgment he had long wished to speak, yet had not been able to, he was so lame with his tongue. But now let them bear with the rude talk of a humble soldier; his only excuse was a full heart. He drew himself up, his head twitching nervously; and scorn mingled with desolation in his voice:

"Old Browns *Farewell* to the Plymouth Rocks; Bunker Hill, Monuments; Charter Oaks; and Uncle Toms, Cabbins.

"Has left for Kansas. Was trying since he came out of the territory to secure an outfit: or in other words the *means of arming and equiping thoroughly;* his regular minuet men: who are mixed up with the *people of Kansas:* and he *leaves the States;* with a Deep Feeling Of Sadness: that after having exhausted *his own small means:* and with his *family and his* brave men: suffered hunger, nakedness, cold, sickness, (and some of them) imprisonment, with most barbarous, and cruel treatment: *wounds, and death:* that after lying on the ground for Months; in the most unwholesome and sickly; as well as uncomfortable *places:* with sick and wounded destitute of any shelter a part of the time; dependent (in part) on the care, and hospitality of the Indians: and hunted like Wolves: that after all this: in order to sustain a cause, which *every Citizen* of this 'Glorious Republic' is under equal Moral obligation to do: *(and for the neglect of which* HE WILL *be held accountable* To GOD:) in which *every*

≡*179*≡

Man, Woman, and Child of the entire human family; has a *deep and awful interest:* that when *no wages are asked, or expected:* he canot secure (amidst all the wealth, luxury, and extravagance of this *'Heaven exalted'* people;) even the necessary supplies, for a common soldier. HOW ARE THE MIGHTY FALLEN? Boston, April, 1857

John Brown."

Now these days a green fire was wavering through the world. Outside the old man's captive-window the great elms were swelling with it, burgeoning; and the wind, deeply murmuring, bosoming the pure bird-voices, the sweet sunlit smells, the cries of street-hawkers and the faint distant joy of children, was restless with life. John Brown had no quick easy sense of beauty; he knew that to savor consciously the joy of the senses was to pay hostage to one's burden of sin: the eyes must seek the beauty of another world (in the Concord woods this moment a little goat-like man, up long before dawn, returns from watching the awakening of the water-lilies; perhaps later, on a silent hill, as the spring moon rises, he will listen raptly to the twilight sounds); but for all his bleak vision, somewhere faint in his blood, old Brown had the inescapable feeling of this spring, this green renewing fire, this restlessness of life.

Defiance rose in him, like sap; hunger for action. In his small upper-story room he would go striding back and forth, back and forth; his hide boots groaning; his hands, rigid as talons, clasped behind him; his right shoulder thrust forward, gaunt. Then one night at April's end, he feverishly wrote in his notebook: "U. S. Hounds on my track; & I have kept myself hid to let my track get cold. Will shoot dead any man who tries to take me"—and in the small hours slipped from the Russell house. He had been hunted before, the work must go on; he would turn westward "with Irons *in* rather than *uppon* my hands."

He headed for North Elba. Perhaps in this life he would never see them again.

* * * * *

He reached the Adirondack hamlet, Keene; hired a big sorrel, and rode over the mountain, along the wild winding trail. There was a murmuring of the spring freshets in the ravines; he drank in the cool healing air laden with balsam and hemlock, yielded his tired spirit to it, as to a benediction. Tall white clouds were sunstruck and gleaming adrift in the pure sky.

The half-circling eastward peaks were lighted up; vast Tahawus wine-colored; McIntyre blue, with mists; ancient White Face lividly gazing. What peace, he thought, his heart moved with love of all this; oh to rest again at evening! But here was the Indian Pass gorge, with its two overhanging cliff walls, black, sombre, rising up sheer thirteen hundred feet. Through it; and then beyond would be the abandoned moldering sawmill; then further along, the still deep pool beneath the white summit—and then the home, and the loved faces.

The trail wound out past the spruce ridge, into the clearing; and he could see, up a distance on the slow rise, the small dwelling squatted gray and stained against the sky. Faintly a cow-bell was clinking. White garments on a line were darting and billowing in the inconstant April wind. A young golden-haired girl, carrying a pail, was moving slowly toward the farmhouse. He came up the rise, the sorrel clumping. Suddenly, she stopped, stood for many seconds fixed and peering like a bird, like a startled yellowhammer. Then she dropped the pail; and came flying down swiftly toward him. He pulled in the sorrel, sat waiting; a warm lump was in his throat.

"Father!" she quivered in a high voice, clinging frantically to his stirruped boot, looking up.

He swung down from the horse. "Annie," he said; and held her hard to himself.

"I knew you'd come!" she whispered fiercely. He held her off a little, examined her with moist grave eyes. Her white face was burning with two small round spots in her cheeks, like young wild-apples. She had scarcely grown since he had last seen her, but there were new lights in her gray eyes, and for all her thinness, something womanly new in the swing of her body. And the sharp intense face was his own. "Aye, Annie," he only said, and kissed her hair. Then; she clutching his waist with her skinny arm; he leading the sorrel, stooping a little to reach her, his gnarled arm about her shoulder; they walked up toward the house.

"Oh John, you've returned."

"I come to rest awhile, Mary."

"Father!"

"Aye, lamb, aye. And have you been a good daughter? Have you been faithful, Sarah?"

Soon dusk descended, and the sons came in weary from the fields and the hills, and they met the old man with quick hard embraces, and their eyes shone. Then it was meal-time, of corn-bread and honey and bowls of milk; he stood familiarly again at the head of the clapboard table, leaning forward a little, his knuckles showing knobbed white on the back of the pine chair; and he said the evening grace. Later, when full darkness profoundly held the house, they sat about, with a great hearth roaring—John Brown and Mary Brown, Annie and Sarah, Watson and his Bella, Oliver and Salmon and small Nell, Ruth and Hen Thompson—and there was a deep patriarchal peace, as of old. The old man took Nell on his knee, Nell of three years, afraid, unused to him, but quickly lulled ("I sung all my children to sleep, and now I will sing to you"); and he began to intone in a low, cracked, off-pitch voice, Isaac Watts' old hymn *"Blow ye the trumpet, blow!"* Annie joined in shyly, then Ruth and Watson; and soon the bare room was transfigured with fervor and a unison of hearts; and melancholy was a presence too: *"Why should we start and fear to die!" "Ah lovely appearance of death!"*

But the peace could not last. A week went by, he was restless as a wildcat. Though he hungered for it, he was spoiled for this living.

Before he left he had words for them all. He sought them out gravely; this one alone, these two together, or perhaps they were three. He was without goods, he could only leave as legacy the counsels, the little wisdom his heart, from struggle and sin and prayer, had so bitterly garnered.

"I cannot stay, my wife. . . . If anything should occur to shorten my life, friends will help you. Amos Lawrence, a merchant in Springfield, has pledged a thousand dollars to buy this house and land for you, if I fall. . . . Be patient longer, be patient with me, Mary. These afflictions are but for a moment. They'll work out for us a far more exceeding and eternal weight of glory. . . ."

"Little sheep . . . be good girls, be faithful. Try to be more still, you especially, Nell, and never fret your mother. . . . Do whatever you do in the very best possible manner. . . . Attend regular to reading of your Bibles. Remember them that are in bonds as bound with you."

"Ruth . . . may you bear it easy and in health. May it grow up strong, a God-fearing one. . . . Reason calmly with your children when they've done wrong, Ruth. Spare the rod, never punish them if they tell the truth about it. If I had my life to live again, I'd do very different with my own. I meant to do right, but I can see now where I was wrong, and failed. . . ."

"My sons, I know you are set against practicing war. I do not wish to flatter any man into such work. I feel no more liking of the business than you do. But still I think there may be possibly in your day that which is more to be dreaded. . . . The cup of iniquity is almost full. Soon the time will come. Then you will get my call. *I do not release you."*

He had one last counsel on the afternoon he left the mountain home.

"When I was in Canton last month, I went to see cousin Charles. Canton, you know, is where my father was raised. I saw near Charles' house an old tombstone leaning against a stone wall by the road. I examined it. It was my grandfather John's. He died, you know, in the Revolution, fighting for his country's liberties. . . . Cousin Charles said I might have it, and he is sending it on here. Now, I want that old granite monument to be faced in Frederick's memory. I want it to be inscribed for our poor Frederick, who sleeps in Kansas. More, I want it to be, in the end, my own. If I should not return, I want the same plain monument that tells the death of my grandfather and my son, to tell mine. I want a short story, like those on it, to be told of John Brown the fifth. I think I have several good reasons for this. I would be glad that my posterity should not only remember their parentage, but also the cause they labored in."

Good-bye. Good-bye.

CHAPTER VI

The Fascination

It was winter. Whitman, the Kansas agent for the Massachusetts Committee, wrote his monthly report:

". . . and he was here but two weeks. I turned over to him

five hundred dollars, tents, bedding, cartridges. Then he left suddenly, declining to tell me or anyone where he was going or where he could be found, pledging himself, however, that if difficulties should occur, he would be on hand, and pledging his life to redeem Kansas from slavery. Since then nothing has been heard of him, and I know of no one, not even his most intimate friends, who knows where he is. In the meantime he has been much wanted, and very great dissatisfaction has been expressed at his course. . . . Captain Brown has simply disappeared from the Territory. . . ."

After leaving his family at Elba, the old man had driven his team westward. The wagon loaded with arms and clothing had creaked down through Pennsylvania, slowly into Ohio. His auspices were not benign. One of the horses went lame, ten days were lost, and the old man brooded and galled himself. Then, again on the move, to avoid notice he kept to the obscure ways, living on dried herring and soda-crackers and sweetened cask-water, sleeping in the wagon in every weather bright or foul; and soon he was steadily being racked by ague-chills and a strange numb burning in the right side of his head. Day after weary day the team crawled along the dusty roads; June was almost here and Ohio was not yet crossed. The illness consumed his hope, so that Kansas and the recruiting of men seemed vastly remote; he went on, fevered, dogged. "Have not given up," he wrote to the family; "but am much confused in mind and cannot remember what I wish to write. May God abundantly bless you all." He had a letter from his son John, farming a little, the shattered mind knitting slowly together; and the undertone of it deepened his own foreboding: ". . . it seems as though if you return to Kansas this Spring I shall never see you again."

Then the old man reached Hudson, Ohio. There the days of his childhood had passed, the gaunt bereft childhood, with Ruth Mills Brown his dark mother too early asleep on the hill, and wild white Ann. There he had married; and had lived in the log house, and his first sons John and Jason had been born of Dianthe; then in the new proud boarded dwelling, with the garden and the abounding orchard and the brook which watered the tan-pits. There, before his family and his working-men he had prayed in the cold winter mornings; and the first portents of Dianthe's doomed mind had risen to shadow their existence.

Many days now the traveller stayed in Hudson, haunting the old familiar places . . . and life seemed a dream . . . life was woven wind. . . .

June passed, and most of blistering July; the hot summer trails, through Illinois, Indiana, Ohio, lay stretched wearily winding out behind. The old man drove the team across the unending Iowa plains, exhausted, feverish, a neuralgic deafness in his right ear. August came with a yet fiercer heat; he reached Tabor. Owen was there to meet him, faithful Owen.

For weeks John Brown lay prostrate in Tabor. There was no "action"; his body was sick, he seemed to have no will, no drive. There were only subdued talks between father and son; and letters in the peasant scrawl, incoherent faltering letters going out to Elba, to Sanborn, to Frederick Douglass; and daily entries in the tattered diary, apprehensive, despairing. Yet beneath all the weakness lay the old blind persisting last-ditch iron. The sick body slowly gathered strength to itself, the letters went out grimmer, more defiant:

". . . Much as I love to communicate with you it is a great burden to write when there is something to be active about. . . . Have been full of cares and feeble health, but though I still get shakes I shall soon be righting up. . . ."

". . . They have not fulfilled. I was flattered with the expectation of receiving 1000 dollars, but there is not even the scratch of a pen from those who need not forego a single hearty dinner by the efforts they are called upon to make. Well, let it be, that failing is not new. We shall get on, just as fast as Providence intends. . . . I pray you all, love the God of my fathers. . . ."

". . . and Fordes continues to lay grievous on my mind. Before I came out I gave him an order for an advance of six hundred dollars, to help provide for his family. He promised to finish off the Manual and join me. Four months have passed, I have not heard from him. But *about* him I have heard too much. He is gathering money for his own needs, he is using his connection with Captain John Brown to solicit funds from my sympathizers. This must stop. . . . Therefore I request you to deliver at once this message to him: Colonel Hugh Fordes; sir; if you have drawn on my account for six hundred dollars, or any part of that amount, and are not prepared to join me at once, you will please pay over to my agent 600 dollars. John Brown. . . ."

"*August 10.* Fordes arrived today. He has the Manual. Well done; with brilliant observations on the tactics of armies; just what the work needs. Am pleased, I see I have been unjust to him. Gave him tonight sixty of my last hundred dollars. Owen disapproved. . . ."

"*August 17.* Have done nothing as yet with Kansas men, that being much beyond my present strength; but soon, soon. In the meantime we are beginning to take lessons & have (I think) a very capable teacher. First drill today. Rifle-shooting at a target on Tabor outskirts. Studying of Fordes' Manual. Discussion of military tactics and *plans.* . . ."

"*September 21.* Stronger. But Fordes very restless. Says he was hired as drill-master, where are the men? Patience, patience, the day will come. . . ."

"*October 14.* Vexed. Worried. Fordes is ugly. Demands more money. But I have none to give. Is beginning also to openly criticize the *plan.* I told him he greatly mistakes John Brown if he supposes I will take it kindly in him, or in any living man, to instruct me how to conduct my affairs or my duty. . . . Owen says to get rid of the man, without ceremonies. But must go slow. I fear him. Have been a fool. . . ."

"*November 1.* Fordes is leaving for the East. Will tell nothing about his plans. Says he is still firm in with me, and to let him hear when the men are assembled. I am helpless, dare not risk an open break; else I should know how to treat him up to his proper deserts. I told him: I trust you to honor my faith. . . . Must get Frederick Douglass and other friends to watch him close. . . . Weary. How alone I feel. . . ."

In the first days of the early winter an old man rode down into Kansas. He went quietly to a house on the outskirts of Lawrence, to Whitman the Committee's agent. Five hundred dollars were ready for him, and a good supply of equipment. The Territory was fairly calm, Whitman said, the Free-Staters were slowly winning through, at the polls, in the fields, in all the slow conquering ways of settlement. There was no likelihood of hostilities until the spring. What, then, were Captain Brown's plans?

"I wish not to have any noise about me at present. For I don't mean to trouble Israel. I'll keep the guns ready, and if it turns out that there is no need to use them in actual service I'll restore them unharmed. But you must not flatter yourself on that score too soon, Mr. Whitman. . . . Meanwhile, let it be unknown so far as possible that I am in this Territory."

Two weeks passed. John Brown went about secretly. Sometimes he was away on night-rides. Once two young fellows, strangers in this neighborhood, came to the Whitman house. The old man took them into the small back-room; they talked briefly in low guarded voices; then the young fellows went away. Whitman wondered and was nettled at the secrecy. Then suddenly John Brown left. The winter came on bitterly cold; and the agent wrote his report: ". . . he left, declining to tell me where he was going . . . pledging his life, however, to redeem . . . since then nothing has been heard of him . . . in the meantime he has been much wanted, and very great dissatisfaction has been expressed at his course. . . ."

In New England the merchant-supporters were filled with anxiety and irritation. The old fellow had their arms and money. What could he be planning? Suppose he went beyond defense, and incriminated them! Suppose he actually dared to enter Missouri and steal slaves!

They camped out on the prairie, just beyond Topeka; the old man and the four young fellows. They sat huddled in their blankets about the fire, and the wind cut in raw from the still dark night. (One was Stevens, Aaron Stevens, a big fellow of twenty-five, with a shaggy black beard and eyes black and gleaming like coals. No one knew much about him, except that he could fight like a devil and sing around night campfires in a rich clear bass, if you tried to get an idea of what his life had been he would go instantly into a sullen dangerous silence. Then there was ragged Kagi, meagre framed and a little stooped, with cold hazel eyes in a pale face. He was twenty-one; knew law, Latin, and history; had a mind like a blade, and twenty wound-scars from Kansas warfare. The third was blond Charlie Moffet, twenty-two, with a face gentle as a girl's. Southward, in the Bourbon slave country, they feared him and his gang of jayhawkers as a scourge. And the last was John Cook, a dark slim fellow. He had a patrician face; he found time, in the midst of hawking and jails and blood, to be a gallant, the greatest breaker of virginities in the Territory.) The tight-lipped old man talked, and the four young fellows listened:

They were going to leave Kansas, they were going into Iowa to attend a military school. All their expenses would be paid. Eventually, and that would be soon, they would begin operations against the slave forces. The risks would be great, but the rewards greater. He could not now say more. They knew him, they knew what he had done and stood for. They were haters of slavery, they were fighters; that was why he had picked them from among hundreds. So only let them come in with him, and there would be work for true men, for fighters. . . . Well, what was their word? Were they in it?

Soon they lay down about the dying fire, wrapped in their blankets against the wind. Remotely they could hear the prairie dogs howling along the cold silent night. The young minds beat on, restless, unsleeping: skirmishes, cattle-lifting, hawking, slave-raids. Life was restlessness, hunger. . . . Yes, they were in it.

In the morning the five men saddled their mounts. They rode northward, steadily. Four days later they came into Tabor, Iowa. They found Owen Brown there, and five other men— young men; all known to Kansas violence, save the tall Negro with the jagged livid scar running from mouth to left temple, black Richardson, fugitive slave escaped from Missouri. Young men. Luke Parsons, twenty-three, who had fought beside old Brown at the ravaging of Osawatomie. The Leeman boy, nineteen, an imp who spoke succulent profanities with the air of a seraph. Squat ugly "Plum" Tidd, twenty-four, with a barrel-chest and beautiful long fingers; he was an artist with a knife, could whittle ash to exquisite forms and wing a man's heart at twenty paces. Rolfe, who was twenty-six and looked forty, Rolfe the Welshman, bald and haggard-eyed, with a nose like a hawk and a straggly reddish beard; who wrote verses on "Liberty" and carried always in his side pocket a black silk handkerchief; and some called him daft.

Ten "students," and the "master" with bluish burning eyes.

They stayed in Tabor a week, making preparations for the journey: they were going to school in a remote Iowa hamlet, Springdale. Beyond that the old man would reveal nothing. And all was not smooth. Blond Moffet, who had been a leader himself and knew the heady taste of it, asked disturbing questions and became sullen when he met a stony silence. Handsome young Cook began to talk too much among the townswomen; he was told sharply to hold his tongue. Rolfe mumbled vaguely and poetically in his thin red beard. The imp Leeman drew the old man's wrathful rebuke with his oaths; he smiled his seraphic smile, skulked, and wondered whether to skip. But soon one night John Brown ordered the men to carry up from the cellar the packing cases filled with Sharpe's rifles, ammunition and clothing. They loaded the stuff onto the two big wagons, working silently in the flare of torches. Then when this was finished the old man gathered the men together inside the small frame house. He had, he said, something to tell them.

He stood behind an oak-bench near the fireplace, and gripped its back hard with his bony hands. In the thrown fitful light his face seemed all rigid shadow and glittering eyes. The men stood before him in a bunch, shuffling uneasily. It was quiet, save for their breathing and the crackling faggots. They watched his face.

"Men. . . . We're setting off tomorrow. It's right that you should know certain matters before we start. . . ." The hands on the chair tightened harder, they knobbed out white. ". . . Men. . . . We are not going back to Kansas later. We are not going to operate in Missouri. . . . We are going into the South. *To fight slavery in Virginia!*"

They stared, uncomprehending for many seconds. Then their faces went incredulous; a terror leaped in the black man's, the whites of his eyes distended. They all stood in a rooted silence, staring at the gaunt possessed face, at the eyes blazing out of the shadows with a wild life. Then Leeman breathed "Christ!"—and the uproar followed.

"Ye tricked us!"

"Not me, you won't get me!"

"Damn it, Kansas is good enough!"

"Sure, there's plenty 'a hawkin' to do right here!"

"Christ! It's plain crazy!"

The old man stood motionless there, gripping the oak, his eyes unquenched. Kagi was in a corner of the room, watching with his cold gaze. Suddenly, in the midst of the hubbub, he moved to John Brown's side. His pale face was scornful; he began deliberately to measure the men with his scorn. They felt it; one by one the voices dropped. Again a silence prevailed.

"Hear him out," said Kagi; and slouched back to his corner.

". . . and so for twenty years this plan to free slaves has held me, like a passion. And now it is the time! . . . Tomorrow we take the first step along the way. I don't urge you further. You can come in or you can stay out. . . . But give me no rash promises. If you join me be prepared to fulfill. You know the nature of the work. It will be desperate, and it will be holy. For God has created me to be the deliverer of slaves, just as Moses was the deliverer of Israel. . . . I give you the night to reflect. We leave with the sun."

The next morning the two wagons creaked out of Tabor, into the bleak misty dawn of the winter prairie. And there were ten "scholars," and the old "master" with bluish eyes.

For almost four weeks they plodded across the Iowa plains. Merciless lashing winds beat against them, flurries of wet snow, portent of the dread western blizzard. Their food supply was meagre, game was wary or long since fled. At night they camped out in the bitter cold of the open, avoiding the far-scattered towns. The men were mostly silent and sullen. Owen in his letter for home told how ". . . progress is feeble . . . today, for teams, bought and carried hay on our backs two and a half miles . . . some of the men down in the mouth; father used harsh words keeping them in hand . . . fierce night. . . ." But sometimes, before they dropped off to the drowned icy sleep, the old man might suddenly say "Let us sing"; and they would all join in, black-bearded Stevens leading with his deep exquisite voice, clear like a trumpet; and upon the cold night *The Slave has seen the Northern Star* would mingle with the faint weird baying of the wolves.

Soon, entries in the tattered diary, scrawled with stiffened raw-bit fingers, were sounding a new note; entries pathetic and absurd save to the hungered mind conceiving them: ". . . cold, wet and snowy; hot discussion upon the Bible and war. . . . Talk about prejudices against color; question for proposed debate: greatest general, Washington or Napoleon?" Pathetic, absurd . . . they were ignorant boys, most of them. And yet, already a faint difference was coming over them: a new seriousness; and, for all the cold and the hunger and the skulking, a kind of exaltation stirring vaguely in their hearts, almost unknown to themselves. They were wild fellows who had eaten of a fatal root in Kansas; some of them had already seen their names in the newspapers, as men to be feared or admired, as notorieties; they were forever spoiled for the common quiet life. And now that their first anger at being tricked had passed, and with the long prairie hours to brood through, the splendor of the prospect which the old man held out before them grew in their minds. It was no longer a mad scheme; they needed only to remember his swift metallic voice and the Virginia thrust became a magnificent boldness, it became not merely possible, but inevitable, aye, passionately to be desired. In Concord a man who had eyes that probed you clean to your true essence, had looked into John Brown's face, had seen there some pure naked force, and had been strangely moved—Thoreau. And now upon these boys, upon this reckless drifting material the old man with the inescapable gaze and the harsh mystical talk exerted his fascination. Step by step; deeper, deeper. In the end, because they believed in him, in *John Brown,* some of them would be ready to offer up their very lives for his cause.

Christmas came; they spent the Saviour's night out on the plains, in a snowstorm. They baked the whole last of their corn-meal in the slow fire, to go with the wild chickens they had brought down. The old man said a special prayer, standing there in the night with head bared, bowed to the whip of the wind and the snow, his voice husky and sad: ". . . in Him was life, and the life was the light of men, and the light shineth in darkness. . . ." (The young fellows were haunched about the fire, very still. The Negro fugitive watched intently, with his dim bloodshot eyes; his bluish hanging beast-like lips faintly moved. Steven's coal eyes were fastened on the old man. Kagi looked on, cold, curious, apart. The others hungered with greedy gaze after the crisping dripping fowls.) ". . . denying ungodliness and worldly lusts . . . and our Saviour Jesus Christ; who gave of himself for us, that he might redeem us from all iniquity and purify unto himself a peculiar people, zealous of good works. These things speak and rebuke and exhort with all authority. And let no man despise Thee. . . ."

Three days later they reached the "school," the tiny Quaker settlement, Springdale. They went to the farmhouse of one William Maxson; months before, on his trip westward, old Brown had prepared the way. They would board there, each at a dollar and a half a week, "not including washing, nor extra lights." Maxson would take the teams and wagons off Brown's hands in partial payment. (The Quaker asked no questions: he loved peace, but he hated slavery; he knew the old man's name for

Kansas violence, but by looking away he could quiet his conscience. Once he said, "Friend, I cannot give thee money to buy powder and lead, but here's twenty dollars toward thy expenses.") It would be a strange martial life going on in the midst of these gentle people; and yet, old Brown reflected, it would be somehow fitting, for were they not also friends of the poor and the outcast of the world?

Quickly the "lessons" began. On fair days they drilled for hours in a wide field behind the farmhouse; there were marching-maneuvers, and the men carried rough-fashioned wooden swords. Often they went out to the prairie thicket-swells: the old man would gravely point out "natural fortifications" and how they might be taken or held; or he would explain how to dislodge an enemy force from a hill-top by means of "zigzag trenches." In rainy weather they sat inside the farmhouse and discussed warfare and politics, and studied the Manual. They formed a mock-legislature and late into the long winter nights drafted laws for a "Free State"; they debated bills and made amendments. And all this was very serious, and the young fellows were absorbed and intent. They were preparing, they felt, they were learning how to hold important places in the fascinating new life to come. They had wooden swords now, but later these would be murderous steel; later these bills and speeches would hold a rich meaning in the world of affairs. The old man wrote east to Sanborn: "I want to put into the hands of my flock copies of Plutarch's 'Lives,' Irving's 'Life of Washington,' the best written life of Napoleon, and other similar books, together with maps and statistics of States." And again: "Please get for me a quantity of whistles, such as are used by the boatswain on ships of war. They will be of great service, every ten leaders ought to have one, at least. Send also some little articles, as marks of distinction, like buttons or emblems or talisman keys."

And of all the men, only pale Kagi, the lawyer, the student, saw with cool ironic eyes the pathetic nature of all this—the wooden swords, the illiterate fumbling debates, the little articles of distinction. And yet he stayed on, and was one of them. Sometimes, during the mock-legislative sessions, in the midst of the wearying talk, he would slouch from a corner and stand before them, a thin bowed fellow, unbrushed, unshaven, with a stained shapeless black hat low over his eyes, with one leg of his ragged pantaloons tucked into his high boot-top, the other sloppily hanging; and soon there would be a new grip in the air, like a current, his voice would be rising through the farmhouse; and held beyond themselves, they would stare at him, for he was saying with cold ringing merciless passion what they could but dimly think and dream:

". . . and man is both rational and moral, he cannot be deprived by law or custom of the essential prerogatives of personality. The rights of men are in essence no other than the rights of personality—to exercise his reason, to seek the light of his conscience, to enjoy the fruit of his labor—in short, to be free to live as a *man*. To treat human beings as property is the grossest denial and violation of that which by nature is inviolable! . . ."

Thus the training continued. But as the winter drew on toward its end and the first excitement of the new life died down, the inevitable restlessness began to stir in the "scholars." Confinement in the small farmhouse irked them; they came to hate the hayfoot-strawfoot drills. They were unused to discipline, and the old man's rigid crusty demands worked unbearably upon them. There were black marks for misconduct, and trials by jury. "Trial given Leeman," reported the journal; "for writing down the name of a female in the neighborhood. Pleaded guilty." Then later again: "Cook severely censured for hugging girls during Legislative proceedings." Black-bearded Stevens, with his smoldering gravity, had been a source of strength to the old man; as drill-master he had held the young fellows firm even in their most unruly moments, for they feared and respected him. But now he began to snap and growl, to side with the malcontents; once, during a maneuver he flared up violently over a difference of opinion and gave the old man "merry hell." Immediately after he was sorry and began to drive the men with savage severity, but the harm had been done. Soon Tidd and golden Moffet came to Brown. When were they starting, when was this damned skulking going to end?—Patience, Moffet, young men have to be patient. Twenty years I've waited.—Hell, we're sick of this. We've got guns, if you won't start, then we'll go down ourselves.—In good time, Tidd, in good time. Do you think our God hurries?

But all these signs of unrest alarmed the old man. He knew he must act soon, or lose them. When he learned one day that Cook had been talking again to women in the village, boasting that they were on a desperate secret mission, that he had killed five slavers and would soon kill more, then Brown knew that he must act at once. And maybe it would be for the best, he reflected. True, his men needed more training; but spring would be a ripe time for the thrust; and then there was Fordes, it was wise to check up on him at once, personally. And . . . deep in himself he too felt the restlessness. Aye, it would be for the best.

So he spoke to his men: All right, he was ready to lead them down. But there was one last thing to be done. When they struck, there must be those in the North who would stand behind them, who would turn the nation's mind in favor of their deed. So he was going eastward again, this last time, to reveal the true plan to the men of influence, Stearns, Parker and the rest. It would be hard, for they were cautious men who had never dreamed his real purpose but he was sure of himself, he could win their consent. "In the meantime, keep ready. Keep firm, and quiet, quiet. I'll send you the word soon. It will be this: old miners will come at once! Wherever you are, whatever you're doing, when you get that word, come. *Old miners will come at once!*"

And even as John Brown was slowly making his way eastward, an Englishman with a graying mass of hair and eyes magnetic and dilated ever so faintly yet unmistakably, was sending out from his New York lodging-house rambling feverish denunciations, obsessed letters to Sanborn, Howe, Stearns:

". . . and Brown is a reckless man who will not keep his word, he is an unreliable man, an avaricious man, unworthy to carry out your plans. . . . He engaged me for a year, and I absolutely demand another six months' pay. . . . You do not like my tone, you say, and will throw further letters of mine in the fire—as if you thought yourself the Pope, or the autocrat of Austria, Japan, or China. . . . I have been grossly defrauded in the name of humanity and antislavery. I have for years labored in the antislavery cause without wanting or thinking of a recompense. . . . I consider therefore that the distress of my family ought cheerfully and effectually be alleviated by the antislavery men of every school. . . . If the money is not forthcoming to fulfill that solemn contract I shall *disclose your conspiracy*. . . ."

The Committeemen came uneasily to one another with these letters. Conspiracy? What was the man talking about? And who in the name of heaven was he? Why, the fellow must be a madman. Or else he was a common blackmailer, an impostor trying to work a bluff on their pocketbooks. Sanborn sent ten dollars to Fordes, and a cold note. He could excuse much, he said, to anyone who was so obviously anxious for a family in distress, and promised "that if I find you have any claim on me, either in law, justice, or humanity, I will discharge it to the uttermost."

When the Englishman received Howe's letter he went into a terrible rage. He stormed about the dingy room, whining, kicking at the furniture. After a few minutes of this, a weakness came over him. He dropped on his belly to the low bed, and big hot tears rolled down his cheeks upon the blanket. He lay so for a long while, very still. Then he got up, and walked slowly to the small cracked oval mirror hanging by the gas-jet. He combed back his tousled mass of hair; adjusted his soiled black cravat; smoothed out the long shiny threadbare coat with a few elegant dabs of his hands. Then, with his shoulders set back and a haughty swing to his step, he moved to the table, and sat down stiffly. He seemed quite calm, his hands did not tremble as he picked up the quill; but his eyes faintly glittered.

". . . and I refuse to be quieted, since my children are being killed by slow torture through the culpability of you, the Humanitarians. You are guilty of perfidy and cruelty, you are perpetrating an atrocious wrong, while I am struggling to save my family. I am the natural protector of my children, and my defending them against your barbarity shall be prevented by nothing but death. . . ."

CHAPTER VII

We Can Overcome a King

ON THE first days of the onswelling spring John Brown arrived at the house of Frederick Douglass, in Rochester, New York. The Negro leader beheld the old fighter with an eager trembling warmth that was at once reverence and love. He could never cease wondering at this man whose whole life had become an immolation, an unrelenting vision of freedom for another blood. They embraced.

"I wish to stay here for a time, Douglass."

"My home is yours, Captain Brown."

"But I will not stay unless you let me pay my board."

The Negro did not protest; he knew his man. The board would be three dollars a week.

"I wish to be thought in the Territory, Douglass. My name here is Hawkins. Nelson Hawkins."

They talked into the late hours. First, the old man asked about Fordes. The Negro replied: It had been hard to keep track of him, he was constantly on the move; but this much they knew, he had been molesting Brown's New England friends again. The old man's big skinny hands nervously opened and closed. He said:

"He has probably told them the truth. . . . Well, it doesn't matter now. I'm going to them myself with it."

Then Douglass showed the old man a paper with some twenty names written on it. These were the men, he said, he had been searching out for years, true bold men of his own race, scattered from Maryland to Canada. They were but waiting for the word.

"Good, good," said old Brown. He eagerly scanned the list. Then he began to talk of the plan, and quickly the inevitable change came over him—the very soul of him rushed to his eyes, crouched shining and vigilant there. (". . . and these forts will connect one with the other by secret passages, so that if one is carried another can be fallen back upon, and death will be dealt to the enemy at the very moment when he thinks himself victorious! . . .") Douglass listened with a rapt joy. For him there was something dreamlike in all this. Ten years before, in a bleak New England house, a tall hawk-faced man in a rough wool suit and cowhide boots had stood before him. The man's bony hand had slid over the wall-map, stopping at the red smear which was New York State; the long nervous finger had run southward down along the gray shadings of the mountains—New York, Pennsylvania, Maryland—down along the Alleghenies till it came to a pause on the blue of Virginia; and there was the voice crying in a whisper: "God has given the mountains to freedom!" Douglass had come a long way from that night. He no longer believed that time and white men's hearts would eventually free his people.

No, slavery must go out in blood, there was no other way. He was with this old man, in all his soul he was with him!

And yet, when John Brown, before they went up to bed, cautiously drew a sheaf of papers from his breast pocket and showed it to Douglass, the great Negro orator felt a sudden apprehension. The sheaf was titled "Provisional Constitution and Ordinances for the People of the United States." The old man had thus far spoken only of slave-running, but this crabbed script spoke other thoughts: the governing and education of the freedmen, the recognition of neutrals, the making of treaties, the election of officers! Douglass had long ago understood the old man's love of formality and small pomps; surely, he instantly thought now, this need not be taken seriously, he is only amusing himself, all this pleases him. So the Negro glanced through the ragged document; expressed his interest in vague non-committal terms, and affectionately maneuvered the old man to his room. But later the former fugitive lay awake thinking in the darkness of his bedroom, and the ominous sense again agitated him. This was a strange strait mind, he thought, one could not be sure of its deepest workings. (It had always been so. Even in their most intimate moments together, the Negro had felt some desperate secrecy separating him from the man.) And there *must* be no rashness, thought Douglass, or his race might lose whatever little gains they had already made. He was not deceived. The North would shut its eyes to petty slave-raids, these salved a little its conscience. But let a man do a deed that touched its pocket, and they would turn snarling upon him, just as they had turned upon Garrison and his tiny band of extremists and irreconcilables. Economic safety moved the North, avarice, pride. The pure ideal for which this old man Brown so terribly and beautifully stood could strike no chord in the great gross heart of the North. If John Brown dared to go beyond slave-running, if that strange sheaf was truly the frame of his serious thought, then the North would join with the South—together they would rend him.

But no! thought Douglass, it could not be. Brown was too canny for such a false step. Yes, he must trust that old man; it was the hour, long-delayed, the hour of blood. (But anyway, he thought as he drowsed off to sleep, he would question further, he must be sure.)

But Douglass would not question further. Apart from the

old man's side, the little doubts, the scruples, the apprehensions ate at the former slave's certainty; his mind prompted him, prudence held him earthward. But let him only be confronted again by those fired eyes, by that conviction, and he would know abandonment: some sense in him deep beyond conscious thought, mingled of hunger and lamentations and the racial anguish, would possess in a flood his heart and his brain.

Day after day the old guest sat in the attic, endlessly writing; plans, diagrams; letters to the New England supporters. He was out of Kansas now, he informed them, he had perfected arrangements for carrying out an important measure in which the world had a deep and awful interest. He lacked a thousand dollars for a secret service. Would his friends, this last time, supply a little "straw" if he would absolutely make "bricks"? It was the most important undertaking of his whole life. ". . . Hope this is my last effort in the begging line."

Excited, irritated, slightly acid returns came to the Douglass house for "Nelson Hawkins": What are you planning; where have you been; why so unreasonably silent; what has been done with the funds already supplied for the Kansas field? Who is this scoundrel Fordes, and what credence shall we place in his charges? Come to Boston at once, we wish to confer with you.

Stearns, Sanborn, Howe, Higginson, "Esquirs": It will not do for Nelson Hawkins to be seen in Boston streets. But he has a revelation to make. Thus will you be pleased to come to a conference in Peterboro, New York, at Gerrit Smith's home.

A brief note went out to the Elba farm: ". . . I am off to see good friends, who I hope will be ready to come in for a share in the whole trade. If they come in, my soul will magnify the Lord, I will seem to be almost marvellously helped. But however the outcome, the language of Providence to me utters *Try on.* . . . The anxiety I feel to see my wife and young, once more, I am unable to describe. The cries of my sorrowstricken children whoose 'tears on their cheeks' are ever in my Eye; & whose sighs are ever in my Ears; may however prevent the happiness I so much desire. But courage courage *Courage* the great work of my life (the unseen Hand that girded me; & who has indeed holden my right hand may hold it still: though I have not known Him; at all as I ought:) I may yet see accomplished; *(God helping;)* & be permitted to return, & rest at Evening. . . ."

John Brown made the journey to Peterboro, New York. It was dark when he got off the train at the hamlet station; a soft thick snow was falling, the last snow before the rising of spring. Gerrit Smith's man was waiting in a big sleigh; he drove Brown the two miles over the dim white-deepening hills to the rich manor dwelling. Gerrit Smith, expansive stoutish old gentleman, with his rosy face islanded in luxurious whiskers, and his faintly-squinting bespectacled eyes, loomed in the ante-room. "Ah, my noble friend, welcome, welcome!" He swept the old covenanter into the baronial hall, with its massive oak pilasters and trophies and mellow burnished hangings, and the great hearth crackling and roaring its saffron welcome.

"Where are the others?" asked Brown.

"Sanborn is waiting upstairs. He will speak for the friends, they were unable to come. Stearns is unwell, and Theodore Parker is held by—" He halted and gazed in sudden uneasy abstraction at the other. "Ah, Captain Brown, you've made us anxious lately, very anxious!" But he hastened to add, "Ah, but we trust you, implicitly, implicitly!"

"Sir, I hope it will be so," said the old man. "Tonight you will hear me out. I have grave matters." To the mild rosy squire he seemed at that moment imperious as a dark Scripture; but within John Brown was faint, his vitals quivered about a sinking burning emptiness, his heart throbbed not alone with hope, but apprehension too.

That night the old man, Gerrit Smith, and Frank Sanborn the young schoolmaster with the fair silky imperial, sat before a fire in an upper room of the mansion. John Brown was talking, swiftly, terribly earnest. Gerrit Smith sat huge and slack in his chair, plucking frantically at his massive gold watch-chain; his face was a sagging blood-drained moon of dismay. Young Sanborn stared, while the mouth like a sabre-cut whipped forth its tidings. He had come here prepared, under the instruction of his vexed and uneasy Committee-colleagues, to confront Brown with cold rebuke, to demand a halt, subject to their discretion, on whatever secret venture the old man was contriving. But Sanborn was young, he had luminous eyes, a face of impulse and ardor; and he hated slavery. Thus now he could only stare unbelieving, swept by consternation—and the intoxicating joy that young men can know before audacity and the high mad gesture.

". . . and when the first blow is struck the blacks will rise throughout the countryside! Men from the free states will come down to join, escaped blacks will come down from Canada. From the Carolinas and Georgia and Tennessee they'll flock to my help. I will take provisions and horses from the plantations by force. Money, plate, jewelry will constitute a working fund. . . . I have arms, bullets, knives. My riflemen will hold the mountain passes until we can construct defences of palisades and earthworks. I will arm even women and children, give them pikes to defend these fortifications. . . . There are natural defences too, I will search out secret mountain defiles which connect one with the other. Those attacks we cannot overcome we will evade by retreating. . . ."

("Great God in Heaven!" thought Sanborn, passing a trembling hand over his wide white forehead. What madness! shuddered Gerrit Smith.)

". . . and I will be able to maintain a guerrilla war. I'll prolong it; I haven't studied for nothing the ways of the Seminoles in the Florida swamps and the Negroes of Hayti. . . . I will succeed in all these matters. Then I'll gradually enlarge my activities. We'll go down and occupy the fertile valleys bordering the mountains, we'll occupy the lowlands. There we will colonize, govern the blacks, educate them, and maintain them in liberty. . . . We will exchange white hostages for slaves to liberate. We'll follow all laws of war, humanity will always be observed. We will stamp out immoral practices, and——"

"Captain Brown!" Sanborn leaped up from his chair. "Why this is all terribly hopeless! It's doomed to failure, we can't dream of——!"

"Wait, Mr. Sanborn! Wait till I've done with my matter!"

Sanborn sat down slowly, on the very edge of his chair, sat taut and poised. Gerrit Smith groaned. John Brown stood there before them, possessed, drawn up into a half-inhuman look, fierce, piercing. He was like a great hawk, with his hooded glittering eyes and nose-hood, an aging hawk ready for the last soar and plunging, the last fiery swiftness before the long decay.

"We can't dream of it, Mr. Sanborn? Aye, we can do more than dream!" He drew a sheaf of papers from his breast pocket. It was the "Provisional Constitution and Ordinances for the People of the United States." "Our revolt will succeed I say, and through the dictates of this document slavery will be forever dead!"

He began to read: ". . . Whereas, slavery throughout its entire existence is none other than a most barbarous, unprovoked and unjustifiable War of one portion of its citizens upon another portion; the only conditions of which are perpetual imprisonment and hopeless servitude . . . therefore, we citizens of the United States, and the oppressed people, who by a recent decision of the Supreme Court are declared to have no rights which the white man is bound to respect; together with all other people degraded by the laws thereof, do order and establish. . . ."

Past midnight the strange council broke up. Later, Gerrit Smith and Sanborn, each, lay unsleeping through the still hours, dumbfounded, sickened. Nothing they had been able to say had turned the old man a hair's width. To every imploring criticism, to every difficulty, to all the manifest hopelessness of undertaking so vast a project with such pitiful means, he had his answer.

"Give a slave a pike and you make a man."

"Woods and mountain sides can be held by resolute men against ten times their number. Nat Turner with fifty men held Virginia five weeks. The same number, well-organized and armed, can shake the system out of the state."

"A few men in the right, and knowing they are right, can overcome a king. Fifty such men operating in the Alleghenies can break slavery to pieces in two years."

"They cannot take us, Sanborn. I say they cannot."

"No, no, Mr. Smith. It will succeed. I say it *will*."

"Except the Lord keep the city, the watchman waketh but in vain."

The next day the discussion continued. During the night he had sat up drawing diagrams of fortifications. He showed them now to the other two. On one side of the sheet were his balky pencillings: "Woolen machinery invented by N. Hawkins." He leaned over the table to explain them, and a shred of a smile cracked the rigid countenance as he said, "You see, gentlemen, I've been most of my life in the wool business, and I am entering the trade again."

The day moved on; they could not prevail against him, one by one he beat down their fearful exceptions. Like granite the old peasant held; and to the others there was something incantatory and grandly antique in his repeated "If God be for us, who can stand against us?"

In the wane of the clear sharp afternoon Gerrit Smith and young Sanborn went out and walked together in the snowy fields. The cold sun was going down over the dark-gleaming hills, over the woods and fields which Gerrit Smith's father had long ago bought from the Indians. The two men went in an agitated silence. Only months before Gerrit Smith had affirmed in his mind: We must cease looking to ballots; there is not virtue enough in the American people to bring slavery to a bloodless end; all that remains for them is to bring it to a violent one. But now the stoutish old man, brought suddenly—not merely in reflection, but actually, in terms of blood and familiar living flesh—brought to the edge of the abyss, to the dark valley of violence and death; now he blanched. And yet, went in his mind, here was this lonely obscure man, offering up every tie and ease, offering up life, for the sake of a despised race and in his zeal for his country's ancient liberties. How then could he himself not be shamed by this selflessness, how could he follow prudence, when all that was asked was a paltry sum and the grip of his hand? Gerrit Smith's mind and gentle heart fought on as the two men walked the snow-covered fields.

And young Sanborn was thinking: What though it was not *reasonable?* The act might be folly, but the man himself was right! And what could they do? To hold back aid would only delay, not prevent him. To actively oppose his plans would betray him, and that was unthinkable. And they could not remain neutral, for that passionate unsleeping force forbade indifference. *In rebus arduis ac tenui spe,* flashed suddenly to the young schoolmaster, *fortissima quoque consilia sunt optima!* And how true it was of the desperate disease this old Puritan was fighting —what else save desperate remedies could in the end kill the black growth of slavery? Frank Sanborn was intensely religious. As a Harvard student in his first year he had inscribed on the fly-leaf of his Bible: "I shall guide my life by leadings and omens from that shrine whose oracles may destroy but never deceive." Now he heard echoing the exultant voice: "If God be for us, who can stand against us?"

Thus inwardly turned they tramped the fields for a long time, scarce speaking. They mounted the slow soft breast of a hill and reached its height. In the west the sun had just swiftly died, tracing the sky with fires, cold, sombre. The two men, aging and young, stood gazing out, held by the wintry hush. Then slowly they turned their heads, looked full at each other; and the same avowal shone from the eyes of both.

"Yes," said Gerrit Smith; "it must be. You see how it is. Our old friend has made up his mind to this course, and he cannot be turned from it. We cannot give him up to die alone, Sanborn; we must stand by him now. I will raise so many hundred dollars for him. And you must lay the case before your friends in Massachusetts."

Then, silent again, they walked back to the house through the descending night.

Late the next day Sanborn left in the sleigh for the railroad station. He would, he said solemnly, see the Massachusetts friends at once.

In the Peterboro mansion, after dinner, Gerrit Smith's young secretary, Edwin Morton, sat playing the spinet. John Brown, his host, and a burly graybeard guest, Stewart, an old captain under Wellington, were listening. Morton, with a clear boyish voice, began to sing, a German serenade. It was brief, melancholy; the slender tinkling voice of the strings stole forth . . . tenderly rose . . . then, fading, fading, died in the throat of silence. . . .

"That was a beautiful song," old Brown said. His eyes were wet. "I never remember hearing it before."

"It's Schubert's," the dark youth said, turning from the spinet. "Franz Schubert's *Serenade*. . . . He died very young."

"Aye, that was a beautiful song."

Later that night the old man sat at a desk in his bed-chamber. With trembling hand he gripped the pen-staff and scrawled down what his exalted heart all this day had been feeling but had left unsaid:

"F. B. Sanborn, My dear Friend—I greatly rejoice that you feel ½ inclined to make a common cause with me. . . . How very little can we possibly loose? Certainly the cause is enough to live for, if not to — for. I have only had this one opportunity in a life of nearly Sixty years, & could I be but continued Ten times as long again, I might not again have another equal opportunity. God has honored but comparatively a very small part of

mankind with any possible chance for such mighty & soul sat-
isfying rewards. But my dear friend if you should make up your
mind to do so I trust it will be wholly from the promptings of
your own Spirit; after having thoroughly counted the *Cost*. I
would flatter no man into such a measure if I could do it ever
so easily. I expect nothing but to *endure hardness:* but I expect
to effect a mighty conquest even though it be like the last victory of Samson. I felt for a number of years in earlier life: a
steady, strong, desire; to die; but since I saw any prospect of
becoming a 'reaper' in the great harvest I have not only felt
quite willing to *live:* but have enjoyed life much; and am now
rather anxious to live for a few years more. Your friend John
Brown."

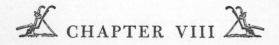

CHAPTER VIII

Let My People Go

A WEEK later the old man was writing to Elba: "Sanborn tells
me that the friends go the whole way in the speculation, *all
lengths!* To God be the praise!"

The die was cast. The Humanitarians had held a long
agitated meeting—they would support John Brown. Theodore
Parker sounded the temper of their participation:

"We must see dark hours before it is daylight—dark, and
bloody, I think. For nations don't settle their difficulties without
passion, and so without what comes of passion. . . . Frankly, I
doubt whether things of this kind can succeed. . . . But we shall
have to make a great many failures before we discover the right
way. *And this may as well be one of them!*"

Jubilant, wildly exultant, John Brown went swiftly about
gathering the last threads before he let loose his "shepherds."

He journeyed to Rochester, stayed there some days with
Douglass; three other Negroes came to join in a secret council.

Then the old man and the black orator crossed into Canada. They arrived at the town of St. Catherine's, a settlement of fugitives, former "freight" of the Underground Railroad; there Douglass had arranged for a meeting with a Negress. She was Harriet Tubman; huge, deepest ebon, muscled like a giant; with a small close-curled head and anguished animal eyes—she was wanted dead or alive, and ten thousand dollars would be paid for the body. Hundreds of slaves had been led by her to the north star and freedom. She went back and forth like a wild dark ghost, again and again; she had never lost a single soul on the desperate hunted flights. Among her own people she had become a legend: she was God-driven, they whispered. As a girl slave of sixteen on a Maryland plantation she had been struck in the temple with a heavy iron-weight. An enraged overseer had thrown it; brooding, she waited three years to kill him with a knife. Then she escaped; and a half-crazed sibylline creature began to haunt the slave-masters, stealing down in the nights and leading away through swamps and mountains her stricken people. This was the woman John Brown came to for help. . . . She would help, she said.

Then Brown and Douglass appeared in Philadelphia. They went to the Negro section of the city; met a little group of colored men at the house of one Henry Garnett, a preacher. The old man apologized for having urged that the meeting take place at once, on the Sabbath. "You see, we have a little ewe-lamb to pull out of a bog," he said; "and the Sabbath will be as good a day as any to do it. At all events, I trust that He will not reproach me." At this meeting was a small Negro with gentle brown liquid eyes. He was William Still, and some said he knew more about the "Underground" than any man in the land, that his head held a thousand obscure routes and stations. "You free them," he said softly to Brown. "I'll lead them out."

They parted, the Negroes and the old man; they shook hands with him, one by one, he standing there white alone among the dark alien blood; and their hearts swelled, and they could have sung for hope and passion, and a wild sad joy:

> Go down, Moses,
> 'Way down in Egypt land,
> Tell ole Pharaoh,
> To let my people go.

> *When Israel was in Egypt's land*
> *. . . Oppressed so hard they could not stand:*
> *Let my people go.*

*   *   *   *   *

Two days later a telegraphed message reached John Brown. "Return to Boston at once. Fordes has betrayed us."

CHAPTER IX

Give Up, Give Up

THE ENGLISHMAN, as week after week went by and only the frigid scornful silence answered his letters to the Humanitarians, had brooded, ever more vengeful and obsessed. Then suddenly, he left for Washington. There, in the corridors of the Senate, during a recess of that body, he forced his way to the side of Henry Wilson, buttonholed the Senator from Massachusetts. Hysterically he poured forth his grievances: his family must be saved, evil John Brown and his men must at once be intercepted. By nightfall of the next day the plan had also been revealed to William H. Seward, and Hale of New Hampshire. A letter went out from Senator Wilson to the Committee:

". . . and I write to warn you that you had better at once decide about a policy of getting those arms out of John Brown's hands. If they should be used for other purposes than defence in Kansas, *as rumor says they may,* it might be of disadvantage to the men who were induced to contribute to that very foolish movement. *Get the arms out of his control, and keep clear of him.*"

Room 129, said the desk-clerk at the American House in Boston. The old man went up. This time all the supporters were gathered, there were no pressing previous engagements. A heavy boding silence was in the room; he stood before them, terribly pale, and his eyes held a frantic sickness.

═ * 206 * ═

Well, he had heard, they said. This meant the indefinite postponement of the project.

"It need not be!" he cried, looking from one to the other with a fierce pleading. They could do it still, he said; the work once begun, all unfriendly plots would not avail against them. They must not overrate the difficulties, they must not be made timid by the first dark shadow that fell. A swift blow would——

No, it was impossible. In the face of what had happened it was sheer madness.

They were all ranged against him, he desperately saw. But then suddenly Higginson spoke, and the old man's eyes leaped with a last hope. "I'm with Captain Brown!" said the swarthy young clergyman. "I repeat what I said to you before—I protest utterly against any postponement. If the thing is postponed it is postponed for ever—because Fordes can do as much harm next year as this. I believe that we have gone too far to turn back now!"

"Aye!" cried the old man. They could do it! He had the means, he would not lose a day. As for Fordes, he would be handled properly. He had those who were thoroughly posted up to put on Fordes' track. Fordes would get what traitors receive——

Captain Brown! Enough of this folly. They could not listen to it.

"But my men will fall away! Everything that I have been building in my lifetime will come down to ruin!"

Captain Brown. We cannot listen. Our hands are still with you, but we have decided. . . . This is what you must do. You must go again to Kansas. Stay low there, let time pass. The alarm will die down, the suspicions. Then you will return and strike, and we shall be behind you. In the meantime tell us no more of your plans, do not burden us with details. We will trust you with our money, but we want no report save by action. . . . Go back to Kansas. Time must pass.

Stunned, he left them. He walked blindly through the streets; and his blood was water. The spirit of him sucked out, struck as with death.

But later, at night in his lodging-house room, the numbness went, and the full thought of what all this meant was like a jagged blade twisted in his entrails. He would lose his men, the Negroes would begin to doubt his courage and wisdom, they would fall away. Aye, it was the ruin of his plan, he was at the beginning again. And it was the last of his strength, he was old. He bowed his head to his breast. Then, as he sat thus, suddenly with great heaving gasps and tears like blood, he uncontrollably wept.

Give up. Give up. Every circumstance, all earthly things work against you. Give up.

Old Miners
Will Come at Once!

THE
THIRD PART

CHAPTER I

The Moon Besieged

ON THE Fourth of July, 1859, four men were going on foot along a mountain road in Maryland. It was hot in the strong sun, and the way went up at a steady rough rise; they stopped for a rest. Below them the Potomac moved in a warm summer flow, drawing rich clear color from the bright day; deep green by the edges where the woodland shadows slipped down; blue pale about the sand-threads and the tiny grass-isles, blue darker where the water went unfretted; and all of it from shore to shore in a gold and silver sparkle.

Martha'd like it here, thought Oliver Brown; she used to live by a river, we spent times along her river.

From the south the Shenandoah came, a slender restless thread losing itself in the larger body; and at the fluxion of the two, upon a tongue of land thus formed, lay Harper's Ferry, a small arsenal town with outlying houses climbing the rich carpet-slope behind.

"You could get full crops hereabout," said Jeremiah Anderson, wiping his gaunt red face with the sleeve of his rustic coat. He was twenty-six; had great gnarled hands. "You could get rich crops if you had a mind on it."

"Those mountains go south," said the white-bearded man, pointing out with a sweep the Blue Ridge hills. They went back unbroken far away, giving up their outline in a grayish haze. "Look at them. They're havens, they're full of natural forts. One man can stand out against a hundred in those passes. I believe God has given them for——"

"Someone's coming up the road," said Owen Brown, watchful.

"I'll talk if we need to," said the old man swiftly. "Remember your names."

It was a fat old Negro riding a mule. His round black face shone in the sun; he was all white of eye and tooth as he clumped past. They felt each a warmth as they thought of their secret. The day was the Fourth of July, and a man enslaved was going by them. Sky was pure, the Potomac water flowed beneath, a thrush was singing its heart out in the copse, and down the road on a mule went an old Negro.

From the Ferry a word was spreading, going out in slow searching lines to the north, to the west, to men in cities and lonely places:
The coal banks are open. Old miners will come at once.

In a dingy printing-shop of a Canadian town, Osborn Perry Anderson, a wizened Negro in his thirtieth year, who daily spat up blood from his half-consumed lungs and had more of it white in his veins than he knew of, took his foot slowly and for the last time from the treadle, and said to himself: I'll help my people. I haven't got long to go.

In the East somewhere a letter sought Richard Rolfe. But he, bald and haggard-eyed and with a straggly reddish beard, was wandering along the rocky harsh-blooming hills in Bardsey of his native Wales—the isle of the Saints. In the afternoon Richard Rolfe would write another of his bad poems on Liberty and Brotherhood; in the evening, three thousand miles from blacks ensnared, go to swill and wench at a low tavern.

". . . and the baby has just commenced to crawl. Oh, dear Dangerfield, come soon as possible, for if you don't get me somebody else will . . ."
Dangerfield Newby, freed-man, reading the words and remembering his poverty, felt a weakness in his magnificent body. Days later, reading others, he knew strength and a bitter hope. Southward, an anguished slave-woman prayed against sale, and tended, in moments snatched from toil, his seven young children.
In a small plain house on the outskirts of tiny Springdale, Iowa, the Coppoc boys, Edwin who was twenty-four years old, and Barclay who was five fewer, stood uneasily before their Quaker widow-mother. The younger said: "Ed and me are goin' East, Mother."
She, who in hatred of slavery had sown the seed in their minds, saw their eager young faces, and remembering a fierce old man who had stopped at the town with a band

of reckless boys, felt now a sudden fear like a cut in her.

"I believe you're going with that old man. You mustn't go. You'll come to bad."

"All your life, Mother, you've been bitter against the evil. We want to help do something."

"I'm bitter still. But there's a God, men have conscience. It will cease through that. Blood-letting is a sin bad as slavery. That old man will lead you to it."

The next day as they went down the front-steps of the house into the rain, she called to them in desperate hurt:

"When you get the halters around your necks, will you think of me?"

John Anthony Copeland; mulatto born free, and brown as bronze; closed his book beneath the light of a garret lamp in Oberlin, Ohio; and going downstairs, a twenty-five-year-old boy with slow passion and a proud straight lift to his head, said to his ebon mother in the kitchen:

"I'm not goin' to class tomorrow, Mam. I'm goin' to the old man I told you about once. The old man they call Osawatomie Brown."

In the same Ohio town, a hundred steps from Copeland's house, down a lane and up a turning, his kinsman Leary, no older and as brown, whose white grandfather had soldiered in 1776 under Nathanael Greene, stood in his saddle-shop, thinking: I'm free myself an' better off than I ever been. I got a reason for livin' on like now. I own a workin' place an' a honey-bab just born. Later, he put a lock on the front door of the shop, and went upstairs to his fuzzy little wife with her timid sloe eyes and the tawny babe at nurse, saying:

"I'm goin' on a trip, Julie. It's somethin' I can't tell you 'bout now, but it'll end good for all us. I'll be back befo' the summer turns."

By a fire set in a lonely night-black mesa, Luke Parsons, poncho drawn tight against the chill, read in the flame-gleam two letters; again and again. Just beyond the restless circle of light the tethered pony whinnied low, and from the far darkness came the wild-dogs' howling.

The coal banks are open. Old miners will come at once.

Parsons saw in memory by his side a bent gray man with

intense eyes, and a mile off a great body of hostile slavers coming on horses in a rush.

"Parsons, were you ever under fire?"

"No, Captain Brown. But I will obey orders."

"Take more care to end life well than to live long."

The young fellow by the fire saw a queer figure wading a river in the midst of bullets, with a broad straw hat and a white linen duster, the coat-tails floating outspread upon the water, and a revolver held high in each hand overhead. Parsons felt once again his own racked body being lifted slowly by Brown into a wagon; felt the old man's hands quick and sure as a woman's, tending his wound. Then, struggling—if you had a girl with black eyes and a slow smile, waiting, that made it hard too—he looked down again at his mother's letter:

". . . They are bad men. You have got away from them. Now keep away. . . ."

When morning came and the straight cliffs burned green and rust in the sun, Luke Parsons saddled the stallion and went off in a lope up the faint grass trail—westward toward Colorado.

Beneath a clear night sky, outside a farmhouse in the Canadian grain-fields, young Stewart Taylor, spiritualist, who earlier had read a letter, now read his stars:

For the most part if the Lights fall to the inclining of the Oriental Quadrants the travelling will happen to the east and the south. The Moon besieged between Saturn and Mars argues short life. The Lord of the First in a streaming Sign or infested of the Malevolents; and the depositer of the Light of Time being also in a violent sign and afflicted , , , violent Death portends.

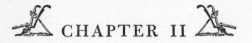 CHAPTER II

The Lark

ACROSS THE bridge leading from the Maryland side into Harper's Ferry, Owen Brown drove a buck-wagon with a heavy Suffolk stallion ahead. He went through the town slowly, not asking his way, and came after a troubled time to a small low house at the foot of Bolivar Heights. It was a poor wooden place with a weedy walk. Roses in a box smiled wanly from the glassless front window. Owen knocked on the post, the door being open. Within a man's voice answered in a shout:

"Come on in!"

Owen entered, and a tall slim fellow leaped up with a glad cry from a table cluttered with dishes.

"Brown! Owen Brown! Every day I've been expecting you!"

They shook hands, Owen feeling more warmth than he betrayed.

"My name's Smith," he said in a low disapproving voice. "You ought to know that. Kagi wrote it to you. My name's Owen Smith. I'm the son of Isaac Smith. You've got to remember that. Never use no other down here."

"I forgot, Owen . . . Owen Smith. I forgot, I was that glad to see you."

"We hear you're married, Cook. Is it true?"

"It's six months now," the young fellow said proudly; a faintest defensive note was in his voice. "She's better than I'm fit for, Owen."

"How could you do it, Cook?"

"She's—I couldn't stand letting her go, Owen."

"So you let us go."

"No, no! I'm in it strong!"

"The men are bitter against you."

"Damn 'em! It's my own affair!"

"It's our affair, Cook. You came here to spy out things. Instead you get tied up with a Southern woman."

"Damn 'em! Who said I'm quitting?"

"No one." Owen spoke in a cold low voice, reckoning his man and playing him well. "You don't quit, you never have. But the game's on, Cook. We've got a plan that needs a tight mouth, and you haven't got a tight mouth. We don't want things spoiling."

"Nobody's heard a breath from me!" the other said hotly.

"Don't let 'em." Owen looked about and pointed to the open door of the adjoining room. "Is anybody in there?"

"Nobody. She's in the garden."

"Close it. I've got to tell you things."

≡ * 215 * ≡

Speaking with a warmth that was not calculated but felt, he went on: "I know you, Cook. In Kansas I was together in fights with you. You get to know a man. I'd stake a lot on you."

"I know, Owen. . . . But what are you trying to say?"

"Don't throw us over with talk. Keep a tight mouth. We all have to keep a tight mouth. You know what it means to us. You know what we get if we lose. If we win——" Owen drew a long breath.

"Just tell me what you want me to do."

"What have you done?"

"I know the Ferry like this room. I know every road, every turn. I can draw you a plan. I know the lay of the arsenal."

"Good. . . . Now here's how things stand. We rented a house across on the Maryland side. Four miles along up the Boonsborough way. A place called Kennedy's farm. We're from New York State. Do you understand? We came down here because these late years bad frosts have been cutting off crops so we couldn't turn a penny. We aim to buy up fat cattle and drive them north. We expect to do a little mining, too. I'm Owen Smith. By brother's Oliver Smith. We're sons of Isaac Smith. You got it straight?"

"I've got it straight. . . . Oh, I've been waiting for this!"

Cook spoke in a vibrant voice. He was twenty-nine now, with exuberant eyes and a clean dark face touched with high color. "What's my share?" he asked again.

"Keep your eyes open and your mouth—— That's all. We'll let you know when we're going to spring it. . . . How'll you get away to us when the time comes?"

"I've been thinking how. I don't know yet."

"Do it this way. Tell your woman you're joining a mining crowd in Maryland. Tell her it'll only be for a few weeks. Maybe it'll sound strange, but by the time anyone can look into it, it'll be all over. By then, we'll be—we plan to work fast."

"What do we do after here?"

"I can't say, Cook. You know my father. . . . We'll go into the hills, I'm thinking."

"I've dreamed of this, Owen! Ever since I met your old man in Kansas I've dreamed of this!"

"Smith, I tell you. Smith."

"Smith. Owen Smith. . . . Are the boys in yet?"

"A few. They're coming in a little at a time, so nobody'll

get suspicious. They're all laying low up in the loft. There's Negroes coming from West and Canada."

"Suppose they're seen?"

"They won't be seen. We can't let 'em be seen. . . . Father's sent Oliver north again to bring some of my family women down here. It'll keep suspicion off if there's women about."

They heard sounds in the next room, a voice in low song.

"It's my lark," said Cook, his face lighting. "She's always singing."

"I'll go now," Owen said hurriedly. "I've got to get to Kagi. He's over the Pennsylvania line in Chambersburg. Guns and stuff are sent to him. I bring 'em down in the wagon, a little each trip."

He rose, thinking of her in the next room; and after a pause, said:

"Oliver's married a year now. His Martha'll be getting a baby. Watson's was born just before he left home for down here. And now . . . now you're married too, Cook. . . . I wish you all weren't . . . I wish you all come through."

Cook looked away through the window. Then he said slowly: "Other ones right along have been nothing. Just fooling. Just a man's throw. But this . . . Mary's for good. I'd like to come back to her."

"I hope you all come through."

"I met her the week after I got here. I got a job as a lock-tender on the canal, to cover my real business. Then I met her. We joined up."

"You should have waited, Cook."

"I couldn't, Owen. She's all the good I've been missing my whole life."

"You should have waited, Cook. It'll be a tight job."

"Did you want a man to stop living while he's waiting?" Cook asked in a sudden hotness. "Did you want a man to quit living?"

"Maybe that's how we'll end, Cook."

"Then we'll end! But while I'm living I want to live! Oh, I want to live!"

He raised his arms high over his head in a quick fierce thrust. A collie in the grass twists on its back ecstatically. A grazing colt in a field starts off suddenly into light low leaps, goes flush with motion, with flowing limbs in a curvet. . . . Cook

strained his arms hard; then called aloud in a hot proud voice:
"Mary!"

She came in, and Owen had a full sense of a presence all
cool and gleaming—like a man's dream. For an instant it was
so; then as she said, "Oh, I thought, John, you were alone"
and looked down without dismay at her earth-stained hands,
she sharpened for him into woman's form. He saw her golden
hair heavy-braided low to the waist; her young breasts in a
rich swell beneath the tight blue house-dress; the skin white
as new milk where the sun had not touched her, like honey
where she had known it——

"Mary, this is a good friend. Owen . . . Owen . . . Smith."

She moved to Owen, saying simply, "I'm glad to know
John's friends"; and smiled with her eyes. They were large, and
of a blue miraculously pure, yet the whites were shadowed
by a kind of faintest penumbra.

"I'm glad to know you," he said, awkward, and looking
down quickly.

Cook put his arms about her from behind, closed her tight
against himself.

"Isn't she a lark, Owen?"

"I guess I've got to go, Cook."

She struggled from the slender fellow, and said:

"I'm glad John has a friend here now. Will you come again
to see us?"

"We're working hard," said Owen. "To get a good start.
We're driving cattle and doing a little mining. I . . . I was
speaking to Cook here . . . about joining up with us. It'll pay
better."

"We don't live high now," she said. "But it's pleasant for
John at the canal. And then he doesn't have to be going away
from home for periods."

"I guess I'll be going," Owen said.

"Please come in soon, Mr. Smith. We'll both be glad." She
turned her deep eyes on Cook and brushed his hand with her
own. "You can help me to keep this bad fellow quiet."

"Good-bye, Miss. Good-bye, Cook."

Owen whipped up the stallion with a sad racing heart. Oh
what a gift for a man! he thought. Oh what a slake for a hot
wild boy! It'd mean Cook's life, that soft golden girl'd make his
life!

CHAPTER III

Does It Breathe Against
Your Heart at Night?

"ARE WE gettin' near?"

Annie Brown, with jet eyes darting and her blown hair bright in the sun, sitting by Owen up front on the buck-wagon as they went at a good pace along the mountain road, asked the question in a rising stir.

"A half hour, I'd figure," said Owen, flicking the chestnut with the whip.

Dark rich-bodied Martha, tight alongside Annie, turned her head to Oliver in the rear, who was being jounced hard on his rump by the loose narrow board; and said, "It's a grand country, Oliver. You feel it gentle in the air."

How are you? he formed with his lips, his eyes showing worry.

She gave him back a smile, and it was like a warm touch on the shoulder, comforting.

"Martha, will you go down there?" he had asked her up at the Elba place—his father had sent him north to bring back two of the family women.

(Mary Brown had already said him nay: "I wish your father well in his task, Oliver. I pray for his life, and the work to end like he wants it to end. But I got a home and youngish ones, Oliver. That's my work to carry on. So I'm not goin' South. I'm stayin' by home." Then from his mother he had turned to his sister, restless birdlike Annie. "I'll go," she said with a fierce joy.)

He had not dreamed of Martha going. But a day before the time to leave a sense of loss came like a crush upon his spirit. Maybe, he cried within; maybe I'll never see her again! Maybe I'll never see it born! He wrestled with himself. He cursed the thought as mad, yet sought to give it reason. And in the end —because his hope was small and his passion beyond prudence;

because she in her simplicity, in her deep calm nature like a mother's for understanding and comfort, was his other half, not better, not worse, but the half beautiful and placid, the haven for restlessness, the fulfillment of searching—in the end he yielded to himself, and came to Martha, fearfully.

"Martha, will you go with me South?"

She looked at him in quiet surprise; then said, "If you want me to go, Oliver."

"Will it be bad for . . . for . . ."

"It's long off yet. I can still work fine."

"Then come with me, Martha."

"When you say, Oliver."

And now in the buck-wagon she was giving him back a smile, like a warm touch on the shoulder, yet sadly. That was her special boon for him: beyond the need of his loins she fed him. Seventeen, in her dark round softness she was ripe as a woman; type eternal yet rare in the world, a mother of all living drawing passion of men. (The Goddess rising from foam, rising magic white and curved and with hint of flame, that one too held sadness in her eyes. *Look, I am the power over men for good and evil. I am the thorn in their hearts, the shape of their dream. I am the whore, I am the mother. I bring the anguish, the seed I bear. Look, I am the power over the lives of men.*)

They wheeled around a crook in the road, with great white oaks shadowing; and Owen said, "You'll see it now. We're there."

They drove up to an old gray two-story farmhouse, set well in off the road, with greenbrake thick around. The house was blistered with the elements; it had tumbled fences and no walk. A hen and her brood fled at their coming; silence met them. A black shade masking the open attic-window flowed silently in the wood-breath.

"My, but it's lonesome!" whispered Martha as they climbed down. "Is nobody in?"

"There's eight men in there," Owen said. "Six are hiding in that attic . . . not breathing because they heard wagon wheels."

Annie went swift before them up on the porch. A lank young fellow stepped into the doorway; and said: "You're his daughter. I'd know you anywhere, you're that alike. I'm Jeremiah Anderson." He rubbed a big raw hand on his trouser-front, then offered it stiffly. Annie took it in her own skinny one, letting it fall immediately as if it were a red-oak limb. "I'm glad you're helpin' my father," she said. The big farmer stood at a loss; then as the others came up from the wagon, he said, "Your father's cooked a pig in honor of you." Annie darted by him, led by the smell of crisping flesh; through a small bare room and to the door of another. There she saw him—a bent flinty figure, white-bearded, with coarse linen trousers tucked into high cowhide boots, with an unbleached cotton shirt open at his wrinkled throat, and a wide chip-straw hat. He was tending a pot over a stove.

During the summer and winter of 1858 there had been a new border chief in southeastern Kansas. He was known as Shubel Morgan—he had a flowing white beard, and a gang of young "devils." By the winter's end the blacks of the densest Missouri slave-settlements along a stretch of thirty miles had been frantically herded by their masters into Texas and Arkansas; there they were heavily guarded night and day. And throughout the West was posted a standing reward of three thousand dollars for Shubel Morgan's body. . . . The old year went out; two big emigrant wagons creaked northward along the barren plain. An old man drove one wagon, a black-bearded fellow the other; and a group of young hawkers rode alongside on horses. Huddled within the wagons were eleven black women and children—fugitives. Through mud and over frozen ground, through fierce driving snowstorms the wagons crawled. (A wire flashed from Washington; James Buchanan, President of the United States, offered a price for the capture of the slave-stealer.) Posses hunted the trails, regulars beat through the icy thickets. . . . The wagons came to the Nemaha River, the line between Kansas and Nebraska. The river-ice was strong enough to bear a man, but not a team. They took the wagons to pieces and slid them across. They laid poles on the ice and covered them with boughs and sticks, and led the blacks and horses over. They were half-starved, their limbs and fingers and ears were blue and numb with the below-zero cold. The old man, in his cotton trousers and broken boots, was torn by the ague, he had a gathering in the head which made him almost deaf; the journey continued. As they got farther north, into Nebraska, into Iowa, they no longer skirted the prairie towns; they entered the towns. The old man would glance at the big-lettered handbills—"REWARD"—would ask calmly for food; then they would be off again. Eighty days they crawled forward thus; they covered eleven hundred miles. . . . The end of March came. A boat wheezed out of the Detroit ferry-slip, headed slowly across the lake toward Canada. The Negro fugitives were aboard it; now there was a twelfth, a black baby two months old —they call it "John Brown."

Summer stole in softly. . . . The old man stood again before his family in the Elba mountain home. He was getting ready for the coming harvest, he told them; he had returned to say good-bye. He lingered a week; he carved the letters J.B. in the huge granite boulder by the house. "Put me here, Mary, when I come back," he said. Then on an early June night he left. His family stood watching from the doorway as he rode off into the long northern twilight. In the distance the great summits brooded dark and silent.

Mountains are inexorable; with reserves and secrets of endurance against erosion and the devouring elements. Into the making of the men and the women who live in the mountains go immense forces of silence, and a grain for abiding the changes of time . . . Loneliness whispers to loneliness, silence to silence. . . .

Annie, led by the smell of crisping flesh, saw him standing there, tending a pig by a stove—a flinty white-bearded figure with boots and a chip-straw hat. Something in the set of his body and bowed shoulders held her still, caught at her heart. Why! she thought, though she had seen him but a month ago; why! he is an old man, this man with the tired face is my father! He had always seemed to her ageless, unchanging, a stern man of whom she stood in awe, and loved; a being little seen but always felt as she went about her days, like a force or a gospel believed in; one who in his hands held her life and the power to shape it. And now she saw a bent old man by a stove. She went up behind him, quietly; and said:

"You asked for me to come, father."

He whirled upon her with leaping eyes; then they calmed, and his hands came forth to her shoulders.

"We need you, daughter. . . . Is your mother come?"

"Ma said to tell you her place is home."

"Your place is where your duty is . . . Is Martha come?"

"Yes, but maybe she oughtn't have. You know . . . she's carryin'."

"It'll be no harm. She'll do no work that she wouldn't do home. . . . I'm proud she's here, carrying. It'll get our feeling, Annie, it'll drink our hope. Where is she, I'll go to see her."

Annie stood there alone, in the kitchen bare save for a pile of dishes on a table and three unopened packing-cases. Carrying a babe! she thought; what a strange far thing! *(Did you ever hear it call, Martha? Does it breathe against your heart at night?)*

"Annie!"

She stood fixed, trembling; it was Watson's voice. Then he called her again. She turned, and saw him crouching half-way up on the garret stairs.

"I can't come down," he whispered. "It's orders. . . . How's things?"

"We come to help," she said, faint with his nearness. "Martha and me come to help."

"How's things home?"

"Ma's well. . . . The hay's took in. . . ."

"How's Bell and the boy?"

She felt her secret joy slag down to gall. "Everyone home's doin' all right . . . I'm goin' out to Pa." She turned like ice from him, felt a desolation; and remembered as she went her last moments with Bell.

"Your father takes 'em all. He ruins our peace."

They were together at Elba, out on a field near the orchard, drying apples for the coming winter.

"Don't you say it! Don't you speak against my father!"

They worked close together, spreading the apples, peeled the night before, on a low pine-bough scaffold where the sun and the bees and the sucking flies could get at their sweetness; and as they moved, their shoulders touching, they flung angry words at each other.

"He takes 'em all, he bleeds their youngness!"

"You lie if you say it! They go theirselves!"

"Everyone knows it! He had my brother Hen in Kansas, he took Hen from your sister Ruth. Now he's taken the young 'uns. They're only children, Dolph and Will."

"They ought to be proud to go. There's no work better they can do."

≡ ∗ 223 ∗ ≡

"They can keep livin', that's what they can do! They can live better than get killed! Oh, Annie, don't you see they're so young? Will and Dolph, and Oliver, and Wat?"

"I only see my father givin' everything to a holy fight. I see they all ought to help, down to the youngest."

"And what about us women, stayin' home? What about me with Watson gone?"

And Annie went into a jealous rage: "What about you with Watson gone? What about you? Ain't he my brother? Don't I love him too?"

"He's my babe's pa, Annie. My babe has a right to his pa."

Now suddenly they fell silent, both; smoothing out the moist stripped apples with their hands.

"Don't let's fight, Annie . . . I'd like to have you like a sister."

When the work was finished and the apples were beginning to brown in the air, they walked without speaking through the orchard, in and out of the bowed trees' shade.

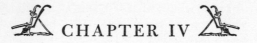 CHAPTER IV

The Vigil

"DAMN IT! I can't stand this waitin'!"

Up in the tight hot attic room young Hazlett stopped his sulky restless moving and dropped hard to a cot, making it creak. From another—there were five in a row, and two mattresses on the floor; rifles leaned against the walls—black-bearded Stevens called in low wrath:

"You fool! Hold your carcass still. They'll hear you down to the rivers."

"I tell you we've got to do something soon. I'm chokin' all over."

"Choke. Only do it quiet."

"Aah, I'm sick, I tell you, of sittin' on my behind! I want to get out with a gun, like I came for!"

Billy Leeman, imp-eyed, jeered from his mattress, "Why don't you debate, Hazlett? The old man wants us to debate in our spare time."

"Go to hell, Leeman. . . . Stevens, why are the Browns and Anderson roamin' around, and we stuck here, like pigs in a butcher's?"

"Oliver and Anderson are back in the yard washing your filthy shirts. Or maybe they're peeling potatoes. That's their roaming. . . . The old man and Owen are up to Chambersburg, to see Kagi about new men coming in, and to bring the guns down. . . . So quit your whining."

Hazlett sat up on the cot. He was twenty-two; big and powerful, but in a swift trim way, like a boxer or a sailor. In Kansas he had been one of Shubel Morgan's raiders. "Stevens, I ain't whinin'. I ain't backin' out. . . . But the old man don't tell us anything. Just tells us to wait, to wait. What's the game, just what are we headin' for? We've got a right to know."

"Did you think you came to shoot ducks? Listen, Hazlett, you stop whining, I tell you."

"I got to know what's ahead. I won't wait longer if I don't know. I'm askin' the old man tonight for open cards, see?"

"I think he's right," said stocky Will Thompson, looking up from his checker game with Watson. "I want to know too. We trust the old man, but we ought to be in on everything."

Stevens rose slowly from his pallet. "Listen, you fellows." His eyes burned fiercely. "I'm with the old man, do you hear?"

A silence held.

"My father's always been a secret man," said Watson . . .

"I'm powerful hungry." Tidd spoke, ugly as a toad with his bent legs beneath a barrel body, and his close-shaven bullet head. He was whittling ash with a long knife; it would be a woman's face. A half-hour before, Martha had come up bearing wild flowers in an earthen jug. "I'm powerful hungry."

"Why don't you do like Thompson," jeered Leeman. "Feed on your thoughts. . . . But you'd starve, Tidd."

Dauphin Thompson, stomach down on the pallet just beneath the open window with its drawn black shade moving faintly in the hot summer breath, looked up from his book; he had blue eyes. Sunlight slipping through between shade and casement fell on his golden head. He was Agatha Thompson's eighteenth child.

"It's a great book," the boy said, a little lost to them. "You all ought to read it."

"Is it good for our souls?" mocked Leeman.

"Channing wrote it. William Ellery Channing. . . . It's real beautiful. . . . It's what you think a little yourself, but you can't say it."

(". . . It is because I have learned the essential equality of men before the common Father that I cannot endure to see one man establishing his arbitrary will over another by fraud or force or rank. It is because the human being has moral powers, because he carries a law in his own breast and was made to govern himself that I cannot endure to see him taken out of his own hands and fashioned into a tool by another's avarice or pride. It is because I see in him vast capacities that I demand for him means of self-development, spheres of action; that I call society not to fetter but to aid his growth. . . .")

"I got hold of this book last year," said the golden-headed boy. "Oliver gave it to me. I've been reading it over and over since. I've been thinking about it. . . . He means . . . a respect for people. . . . That human beings are precious. . . . That's it! a respect for human beings."

"I'm powerful hungry," said Tidd. "Don't we ever get belly timber?"

"Shut up." Stevens leaned lower on his pallet toward Dauphin; his eyes were coals on the boy. "You know," he said slowly; "when you come to think of it . . . it's a little like us, isn't it? It's something like . . . what we're trying to do——"

"Get low! There's someone comin' down the road!"

It was young Annie, cutting in from the porch, flashing quick as a cat half-up the attic stairs, calling the words in a breathless scare. Instantly the men who were standing dropped to the floor, the others froze in their places. . . . Now they could hear the young girl stormily sweeping the porch; soon the sparking trudge of a horse going by, and a man's loud "Hallo!" Then the sound of hoofs on the stony road went lower, and died; and Annie was flitting up again with her shrill whisper, "All right! Now it's safe!"

Strange furtive days these were for Annie; she lived them as in a desperate dream. With the sun she was up, keen as a harrier; watching. "I can trust you, Annie, to do it right," the old man had said to her the first night. "I can trust you to keep it low that John Brown is here. Some say he's in Kansas, some say he's dead. Well, let him be dead . . . till he rises again. In the meantime let Isaac Smith live. That's your work, Annie. To keep Isaac Smith living before all these people hereabout. There's no one upstairs, mind you. We come to farm, we come to drive cattle north. You're the daughter of Isaac Smith. And watch, Annie. When you stop breathing then stop watching. For it's my life you watch —aye, infinite more than my little life. You watch the hope of the blacks, the seed God's put in my heart. So I'm placing my trust in you, Annie, I'm giving you a share in the work."

The porch became her domain. While Martha cooked and kept the house, Annie was two peering eyes. A faintest alien noise beyond the bend and there she was a streak on the stairs, calling her "Get low!" and there she was back again in a wink, sweeping or sewing or peeling potatoes with studied frantic ease; praying for her wits to be sharp.

Now as on her first day watching it was a small moustached man with silvered hair and a broad tan hat, riding up on a roan; a Mr. Unseld, all mildness, bowing with an open smile, from the saddle speaking: "Good morning, Miss. I have not seen you before." And she—her heart a furious buffet within as she answered, "I came a few days back"—felt her words a bad start, her way too sharp; and the beginning of panic was on her. Then as the mild little man, with no suspicion in the world, only curious after the rural manner, had question after question for her, and she floundered worse and deeper, suddenly from the kitchen came a sound of singing, Martha singing:

> When Christ-mas comes a-bout a-gain,
> Oh! then I shall have money;
> I'll hoard it up and box and all
> I'll give it to my honey!

The young voice in a lilt steadied Annie, gave a simple color to the moment, cloaking their guile in innocence; and the test, first of many, soon was over; he rode away, all unheeding.

Or now it was Mrs. Huffmaster, greatest danger of all, a fat little woman, malicious, with a glistening drop in her right eye and nostril. She would come waddling up from the house a little way in the woods, with her four barefooted young—like a duck and a brood.

"Two years ago I rented the garden you're usin' now. It's an interest I have in people workin' it. But you don't work it much, do you?"

"Your men folks has a right smart lot of shirts, Miss Smith. One, two . . . why ten I see, dryin' on the grass!"

"Down t'is always, that black shade. Have you got a corpse in the garret? Tee-hee!"

"Oh, is that why you have great ugly boxes in your rooms? Your ma's particular and asked you not to pack open the furniture till she's come?"

Annie's vigil did not cease with the end of day. For the men dusk fell like a dim blessed veil, they came down with it to devour the free time before sleep; in relays of three they slipped out to the garden behind the house. There, silently and with abandon they gave rein to their bodies; running, rolling in the grass, breathing hard the fresh dark air. But Annie kept her place on the porch, taut for danger; listened, straining, for something beyond the multitudinous woodland sounds—beyond the flutter of swallows with hollow trembling twit darting swift out from their roof-home in ever smaller circles against the deepening night; the low howl of farm-dogs off in a distance; the owl, ghost in the shadows, screaking away the pale hours, mocking.

Until late she would sit thus. Inside—round a lamp; the shades drawn—she could hear them speaking guardedly, now in a passion, again in boyish laughter. Sometimes a long silence would fall, and she would wonder why; sometimes in such a quiet a sense of fate strode in from the great darkness to her. It lay, she felt, upon them all, upon the house and each in it— "this you are, this you shall be, it is appointed"—and she could hear again her father speaking: "We are instruments in His hand. It was ordained from Eternity that my work should be this." The sense from out of the dark would be full over her; and she, a little creature, midge in a vastness, would forget her own vague pain as from a healing touch.

But then Stevens might go into a low song, a song for love to be sung round fires. Most of the boys would listen, pleased; a few would join in. And Annie, with the rich singing, would

≡＊228＊≡

suddenly feel again the urgency of her unrest, would feel it bitter, a young girl watching the dim stillness with dry hungered eyes.

Then the old man would come out to her, having finished a letter for home by the kitchen lamp.

"Are you tired, Annie?"

"I don't need you, Pa. Go in and sit with the boys."

"I'm better here. With me around they get stiff and shut."

They sat awhile, not speaking; like father the daughter, without easy words. The dismal owl was at its hooting still; about them the fireflies flicked the brush.

"You looked tired, Pa, when you got home tonight."

"It's only my body, Annie. My mind's live for the work."

"You looked worse than only tired, Pa. You looked worried."

"Your eyes are sharp, Annie. . . . Yes, I'm worried."

Inside again there was the silence. The dark drone of the woods filled the night.

"They're failing me, Annie."

"Tell me, Pa."

"They're failing me, those I placed trust in. . . . Annie, all my life I've been on a journey toward now. Now the time's ripe and I can't go ahead. Now when I need my men, and money, and all the help I can get, they don't come. I had fifty that said they were willing last year. There's only ten of us tonight. . . . I don't hear from Rolfe, I don't hear from Parsons. Hinton doesn't come, nor Moffet, nor Richardson. There's others. . . . My own boys see a different light. Salmon stays home, and Hen too."

"They're held up sure, Pa. They'll all be comin' in a bunch."

"My heart tells me no, Annie . . . I get a loneliness. . . . And our money's gone. I had to borrow today from Kagi to buy a barrel of eggs. . . . And how long can I keep the boys stuck upstairs? How long without being discovered? Hazlett came to me tonight. He said he was sick of waiting. If I didn't give him work soon, he'd find it himself. He had a gun, he said, he didn't need more. And there'd be others with him, he said. Wanted to know my plan. I told him to go. I told him if he had no trust in me, to go his way. The work would go on with one less. . . . He shut down then, said he didn't mean it so, said he'd stick. But I know, I can't hold them too long. They're boys and the blood's hot in them, they've been thinking on the idea too long now. I myself put it into them."

He brooded; she waited.

"And it's better so, Annie! It's better far they should be eager than slow with me. . . . Oh, we'll do it! And soon, soon!"

He bent over to her, vibrant now, half-whispering.

"Look, Annie! I've made no mention to you yet of my biggest hope, my biggest strength! Maybe it's too much to expect white men to risk their lives for blacks, maybe I've no right to be disappointed there. But the Negroes, the Negroes themselves! Listen! Tomorrow Frederick Douglass is coming down to Chambersburg. If I get him active in the plan, we win! We win, do you hear, Annie!"

"How do we win, Pa?"

"Look, you child! There's millions of slaves thirsting to be free. They know Douglass, they know his history; he's been a slave himself. They'll follow him, they'll follow his word, do you see? Annie, when we spring the trap and the word goes out to them they'll come in thousands, burning to get free. Then Douglass and me will lead them! We'll go south, always south, we'll sweep——"

He stopped quickly, catching himself; he straightened up, his voice went guarded: "I've said too much. It ends with you, Annie. . . . Remember. . . . None know my plans till I'm ready."

"I'll hold it, Pa."

Later, they began, Brown turning it so, to speak of older familiar things; of home and the land, of corn and the least child, of the quiet hard life on the Elba farm.

"How's Salmon's Abbie? Does she seem a good wife?"

"She's kind to Ma."

"When you get back home, Annie, watch your mother close. Help her all you can."

"I never slacked, Pa."

"Your mother's . . . had it hard always."

"I wonder if she'll ever have it better?"

"Don't question so, Annie. We're all in God's hands. Earth-living's only a tiny part of all. You go to a longer life, you get a real reward."

"Ma says she ain't sure. She says she only knows you got to do good. You don't think of reward and livin' after."

"Hush, Annie! You say wild things! You blaspheme!"

She shivered a little. Soon he spoke softer, and solemnly.

"You don't know better, Annie. You're young, you need to

learn. . . . Look, do you see fire-flies lighting the bushes? Do you know why, did you think it was for prettiness? . . . No, not for prettiness. It's God's hand you see there. . . . You see it in the smallest things. Some we're fit to understand, most is beyond our comprehending. But whether it's plain to you or not, you must always know it has a purpose; it has a place in the scheme of God."

"Seein' 'em light up, you wonder what it's for."

"The light's a scheme, Annie. It's for bringing new life."

"How do you mean, Pa, new life?"

"God makes them flame so, and it's a call for them to join. Then new life comes, Annie."

Did you ever hear it call, Martha, does it breathe against your heart at night?

"What's Martha doin', Pa?"

"Why . . . I got her to sleep, she needs it bad. . . ."

"Pa . . . will . . ." She trembled a little. "Will her'n come if Oliver's killed?"

"Annie!"

The flow that had been between them was suddenly stopped. Now they sat, a vast distance apart. Soon the old man rose; he said sharply: "I'm going in. The ague's on me again, and the kitchen's warm."

"Good-night, Pa."

"Good-night. . . . There's some things you don't question. You just take them as God's ways. You don't question them. It's evil."

"I wasn't meanin' evil."

"Fear God, Annie. Keep His commandments in your heart."

"I will, Pa."

"The men are up to sleep. Go in too. Sleep. The watch is over."

"I'll stay awhile. It's so fresh."

"Good-night, daughter."

"Good-night, Pa."

Soon the house went all quiet; and Annie sat there alone, with the night for company and the high bright stars.

Inside, by the kitchen lamp, old Brown turned the pages of his tattered Bible, seeking; then with a light and a gathering strength on his tired face, he read:

For these are the days of vengeance, that all things which

*are written may be fulfilled. Woe unto them that are with child
and to them that give suck these days! for there shall be great
distress upon the land and wrath unto this people. And they
shall fall by the edge of the sword, and shall be led captive into
all the nations.*

CHAPTER V

"I Go Wid De Ole Man"

THE TWO Negroes sat quietly in the last seat of the car; the train
was moving ahead at a good speed through gentle hill country.
When they spoke, which was seldom, it was in lowered voice,
though the passengers nearest them were well down the aisle.
The older one, dressed in neat black and a white starched collar,
had eyes set deep in a massive head. The other wore ragged
clothes; he was young, not much more than twenty, a full negroid
type, black and shiny, with wide swelling features; towering, as
he sat, hard and high and clean-limbed. "Mistah Douglass" he
would call the other with respect, groping for simple words like
a man seeking things in a dark place. Shields Green his own
name was; he could not have said why some called him "Emperor." Perhaps it was a slow deep dignity in his way of moving,
a dignity which they felt faint beneath the pained speech, the
ignorance, the rawness. "Emperor" some called him. Now as he
sat restless—the other so too, drawing a watch from time to time—
his dim brain traversed a tiny arc, with pain the beginning and
hope the end, and tumult in between.

When the train stopped at the next station, and they got
off, they would go to see an old man named Brown. He believed
in God, this old man, and he believed he could free all the nigger
slaves with guns and shooting. Well, he, Shields Green, "Emperor" Green, would go to this old man Brown, and he would
say to him: I am Shields Green. I want to help you. Give me a
gun, tell me what to do, and I will help. Because I have a pain
here, right here near my heart, it doesn't go 'way in the night, it

doesn't go 'way in the day, it is a pain in my heart always. It is a pain there because I want to see my son again. He is six years old now, and I think he is still on the plantation near Charleston in Caroline, I think maybe he's sold down South further. Wherever he is I want him, I want to see him. I gave him his name, Jeff I gave him. And I ran away from Jeff and left him. Left him to stay a nigger slave. It wasn't all my fault, but I left him. I left him to be a slave-boy and now my heart has a pain and I live black days. I see everything low and black. It came quick, everything came hot, blood was in my eyes, burning was in my head. He made Lil' dirty. That white nigger-boss, that bitch cotton-boss. . . . A preacher married us. He said we were married holy. He said Lil' was my wife, he said God was seeing it, and I was a man and Lil' was a wife before God. She could sing songs, soft honey songs, sometimes they had crying in them and you felt warm and hurt inside, and sometimes after singing I took Lil' soft and tight to me. . . . We lay in the canes . . . loved. . . . Then Jeff. . . . He's six years now. I gave him his name, Jeff I gave him and I want to see him. I looked for him that night. Couldn't find him. I looked for him, maybe he was playing out somewhere, but I couldn't find him. I looked for him but back in the house the cotton-boss . . . laying dead. He was blue dead, his tongue stuck out, I did it with my hands. He made Lil' dead. He dirtied her, that bitch drunk cotton-boss, he made her dead, I don't know how. But I saw her, and did it with my hands till he was choking dead. They would find the cotton-boss, they would kill me. Pull out my tongue, burn my eyes out. They would hang me to a tree and dogs would eat me. So I looked hard for Jeff. Dark . . . afraid to call . . . afraid to stay, they would kill me. I couldn't find him. I ran away. I got to Charleston. There were blood dogs after me. But I got to Charleston and hid in a boat in the water. In the morning it went far out on the water . . . an ocean . . . I got to the North. I was free, I wasn't a slave. I was in Canada and they couldn't get me back. . . . Jeff was three, now he's six. I got a pain here and I live black sick days. Low days. So I'm going back. Maybe they'll catch me. Maybe dogs will eat me from a tree. But when the train stops we will go to see an old man named Brown. This old man named Brown believes in God, and he believes he can free all nigger slaves with guns and shooting. I am Emperor Green. I have a slave boy. I gave him his name. Jeff.

*   *   *   *   *

"I knew you would come, Douglass! I knew you would not fail me!"

They met in an old abandoned quarry, well back in the hills behind Chambersburg—Douglass, Emperor Green; John Brown, Kagi. The two Negroes had got off the train; searched out a Henry Watson, black man and town-barber. Down in the cellar of his shop scores of fugitives on their way to freedom in Canada had cowered hidden in its secret places. Whispered words; and soon the two were climbing the steep way up to the stone works. They went cautiously; "Shubel Morgan," hunted by United States marshals, had a heavy price on his head, and a loaded gun in his belt. They went cautiously, and found him waiting restless among the jagged rocks; gray and sharp as the quarry itself, a stone-man with a heart, long beaten by storms. Kagi was there by his side, pale young Kagi who could read Latin and fight like a wounded cougar.

"I knew you would come, Douglass. I knew you would not fail me."

"I'm with you, Brown, in all my heart."

"God's strength be with you."

"What do we do? When do we start?"

"Listen!"

John Brown stood before them. Now for the first time he spoke aloud his final plan, began to reveal it in its fullness, in all its desperate intent—that which had smoldered in his mind for twenty years and was now a consuming flame:

A silent night-march into Virginia! The arsenal at Harper's Ferry captured! Arms from its huge store turned over to the blacks revolting through all the countryside! The mountain passes shut with bullets! Liberty spreading southward like a trail of fire!

"Do you see it, Douglass? Can you see it happening southward, southward?"

"Brown!"

"The nation roused?"

"Brown!"

"The chains dropping?"

A consternation flooded Douglass. In the name of God what was this fearful old man saying! What madness was this! A silent night-march into Virginia? The *arsenal* assaulted?

"Brown! It's mad! It's mad, I tell you!"

The words were like a sudden blow to the fevered old man. He stared unbelieving; then said harshly: "I do not understand, Douglass."

"I say it's mad, and you cannot do it!"

Brown stood frozen, save for his face which slowly went undone: the blood flowed down from it, the tight mouth trembled, a sickness rose in his eyes.

"It's a death trap, Brown!"

"You're . . . going to fail me, then. You too, Douglass . . . are going to fail me."

The Negro leaped up and went close to the old man.

"I'm not going to fail you, Brown! I came to help you! But you mustn't do this! It'll be your death! All of us!"

Scornfully the other said, "Is that why it's mad, Douglass? Because maybe we'll lose our lives?"

"If it would do good! If it would do good for my people, this minute I would die. I swear it, Brown! But we're worth more living!"

"Sometimes you're worth more dead. . . . Speak against my plan, Douglass. You called it mad."

He sat down upon a rock, looking bitterly into the dust at his feet. Kagi and the young Negro were tight still. Douglass began in pleading earnestness:

"Brown, you believe I'm your friend? You believe I want to do what's right?"

"I believe you, Douglass," the old man said, not looking up.

"Then listen to me, Brown! . . . Ten years ago you had a plan for running off slaves. I was against it then, because I believed in peace. Now I'm for it because I believe in blood. And I came here to see you, thinking the plan was the same, wanting to do my share. And I find you instead with another scheme, altogether different, fatal to all our hopes! God, Brown! Can't you realize what you'd be doing? You'd be attacking the United States Government! It would be treason! The whole country would turn against us! The whole movement would be set back fifty years!"

Now old Brown got up, dark as a cloud.

"Treason! Government! Words, only words! It's the kind of thing I've been hearing always, the kind of thing I'm sick to death of hearing! Treason, caution, government, laws! Blast them all to hell! I answer you back, Douglass! I answer you back with

≡ * 235 * ≡

humans, and right, and God! I answer you back there is a higher law than all!"

The Negro groaned in helplessness.

"Brown, you're living on earth! You're dealing with men!"

"I deal with God."

"Oh, I can't speak with you, Brown! I have no answers for such talk! Your way is wrong! It's wrong!"

The old man was calmer now. The first shock was over; he began to collect his wits for the struggle.

"I met a man last year in Concord," he said slowly. "His name was Henry Thoreau. . . . We talked. We agreed that justice is higher than law. And he said something I'll always remember. The law, he said . . . will never make men free. It is men . . . who have got to make the law free. He said . . . they are the lovers of law and order who observe the law . . . when the government breaks it."

Desperately the Negro thought: he will go on to do it; nothing I can say will shake him; it will be his death and his dishonor! To Brown he said, "You want to help the slaves. Why then do you think of doing the very thing that will harm them most? Why will you bring the nation's anger on them?"

"I'll rouse the nation. It needs rousing, it needs to be startled. When a man is near death and to hurt him will save him, then you hurt him. If you had to push a man down a twenty-foot fall because a rattler was about to spring, you'd push him. The nation needs to be roused. It's cursed, it's dying."

The Negro orator looked helplessly at Kagi and Emperor.

"It'll give courage to your people," Brown went on quickly, pressing. "It'll show them there's some willing to strike a blow for them, willing to do more than talk. It'll give them notice that the time's come to rally."

"I know Harper's Ferry, Brown. It will be a trap. Once in you'll never get out alive. They'll surround you, they'll hem you in!"

Kagi spoke up with his cool drawl: "We've been in Kansas with Captain Brown. They never took us. They won't get us here, either."

"We'll cut our way through!" cried Brown. "We'll get prisoners right off, we'll hold them as hostages. Even if they are close in on us, we can dictate our own terms of escape."

"Virginia will blow you and your hostages sky high, rather than let you hold the arsenal for an hour!"

"We'll win, Douglass, I tell you! Only come in with us, only give us your help! A Negro to lead Negroes! Don't you see how we need you?"

It did not end quickly. Through the hours they talked, neither giving ground. Late afternoon came, then the beginning of evening, and the four went silently back to Kagi's little room in the town; there the struggle began again.

"God is with us, who then can be against us?"

Midnight came; they would go on talking tomorrow. Settling himself for the night in a chair, Brown refused the single bed; Kagi and Douglass shared it. The young Negro stretched out on the floor. Soon they were sleeping; save Douglass.

He began to go over the plan again; perceived it even more clearly now as a sieve for flaws, perceived with renewed shock its madness certain. The old man was staking all on the belief that there would be an instant rising of the slaves in a mass, that they would throng to the arsenal, wild for freedom, to be led by himself and his white boys. But it would not happen so. He, Douglass, former slave, knew it would not. He had lived through days and knew his people. Men like Brown saw slavery as a vast moral evil, violating justice; believed the black men as restless under their chains as they themselves would have been. But they were like children, his poor people, fearful and bewildered. Brown would take life for his own liberty; that, in his eyes, would be right and the morality of an avenging God; the blacks, most of them, wanted hot yams and a roof and not to be beaten. Brown was a conscience incarnate; they were children needing love. He would wait for them, and they would not come.

The old man stirred in his chair; from sleep heaving in the dark a sound like a moan. Only the whiteness of his beard Douglass could see; yet in that moment the Negro was conscious, more than he had ever been, of John Brown, of an urgency filling the room like some strange terrible aura. Magnificent old man! he thought, pitiful old man; and shivered a little. Now at last he seemed to understand this man, whom once he had heard say to a son: Let the grand reason, that one course is right and another wrong, be kept continually before your mind. Now in a sudden almost unbearable insight the Negro seemed to behold the secret of John Brown's nature: the intolerance shutting off ease in life and its beauty, rejecting compromise and charitable allowance; the long far brooding over the wrongs of the world and the evil men do; the sense of ordination driving him always forward— "I have no choice; it is decreed by God." And Douglass felt like a smallest being, blind and dark-drifting, a mote whirled in a wind. Douglass wept.

They were up early the next morning. It was the Sabbath, a day of rain and wind. Kagi set up a pot of coffee. The old man made a short prayer, ending :"Grace to you and peace from God the Father and our Lord Jesus Christ: who gave himself for our sins, that he might deliver us out of the present evil world, according to the will of our God and Father: to Whom be the glory for ever and ever. Amen."

Then as the four took turns drinking coffee from the single cup, the talk began again; Brown for the Ferry assault, tight-lipped, iron; Douglass sickened, pleading for the original plan, the slow secret drawing off of slaves to the mountains. Finally, the old man, peaked and gray with chagrin, came close to the Negro; he put an arm about his shoulders.

"Douglass, come with me."

"I cannot."

"When I strike, the bees will begin to swarm. I'll need you to help me hive them."

"No."

"Douglass! I'll defend you with my life!"

The Negro looked full into the old man's eyes; then shook his head again. Brown turned away in bitterness.

"You've failed me, Douglass."

"You've changed your plan, Brown. The old one holds me, not the new one."

"You've failed your people."

"I'm living for my people. You're going to your death. I know it as we're standing here. I don't want to go to mine yet. I've got work to do."

He turned to the young Negro.

"Shields. The plan's changed. I'm going home. You've heard all we both had to say. If you want to, you can come back with me."

Emperor Green looked from one to the other, gulping; then he said:

"I b'lieve I go wid de ole man."

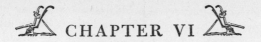

CHAPTER VI

The Invisibles

THE BAND of "invisibles" had grown. Kagi was down from Chambersburg, to stay; all the guns and pikes had already been moved to the farmhouse. Cook had left his "lark" back at the little village-house; with gay warm words for heartening her, and an emptiness in himself; scarce looking into her hurt eyes, he had left her—"to go on that mining trip." The Negroes—Dangerfield Newby who had a slave-wife and seven young ones south; Osborn Perry Anderson, consumptive; the two young Oberlin kinsmen, Copeland and Leary; Emperor Green whose boy was named Jeff—these had come. So too the Quaker Coppoc lads, and Stewart Taylor, from the Canadian grain-fields.

And with the fullness of summer heavy and hot over the mountains, the men in the packed garret knew fretted maddening days. To ease the tightness, the small cabin across the road was used for a sleeping place, five squeezing down upon the rotted floor and a sixth on watch during the night. It helped little; the farmhouse was filled with boys desperate for movement. Those who had been there longest were near the breaking point. Hazlett and Leeman quarreled and cursed from dawn to dark; Tidd was a brooding sullen bear, whittling, whittling with his deadly knife. Will Thompson was frayed to hysteria; his bright-haired brother could read no more. Bearded Stevens with his amber eyes lay still and savage, singing never. Watson Brown had a gnawing loneliness for a girl and a babe. All had begun to dread the light of each new day.

"You come to fight," snarled young Hazlett, glistening with beads of sweat, "and instead you stay stuck like stinkin' pigs! You get so you smell in your own nose!"

Cool wily Kagi saw how it was with them and tried to ease their restlessness, telling vaguely yet with crafty promise of a day soon to come which would repay them a thousandfold for their waiting. He tried to hold them hot for danger, yet just beneath rebellion. But they could not be held much longer, he saw. Soon too, the signs were showing him, they would all be caught, the plan revealed before it could be sprung. For Mrs. Huffmaster was a prying she-devil; with the Negroes in, it would only be a little while before she would ferret out their presence. And Cook had told Kagi that though as yet the townspeople were without suspicion, they were curious; they did not understand this farm which was never farmed, this mining company which dug no ore —the mode of living at the Kennedy place would eventually be questioned. And only the day before, Owen coming down from Chambersburg with Emperor, had been through the tightest kind of escape. Just over the Maryland line, keeping furtively to the backroads on foot, the two at sight of some men had hid in a thicket. Owen's coat had shown through and the Southerners, approaching and seeing one a Negro, had given chase; they suspected a runaway slave episode. Only at the point of his revolver had Brown's son kept them off. All the night in the mountains they travelled hard, with searching parties at their heels; in the morning they reached the farm run down to exhaustion. The signs were pointing to exposure; so Kagi went to the old man, and said:

"It's time to begin, Captain Brown."

"I'm not ready yet."

"They'll find us out."

"Not if each does his share."

"The men are going to blow. You can't keep them longer."

"Who wants to go, may go."

"If you don't give them work soon, they'll find it themselves."

"We need more men, we need more money. We'll wait. Young men must learn to wait."

"Begin soon, Captain Brown. It's my warning."

They talked farther. Kagi, before going from the old man, said: "Then give me leave to handle them. I can hold them longer if you give me rein, I know them and what they're thinking."

"I give you rein, Kagi. I can't watch everything, I've got many things to do. I give you rein."

So Kagi went about staving off discovery and unrest. First, he ordered the Negroes never to go downstairs, save at night; the white boys he allowed the kitchen in shifts of four, where they could talk with Martha cooking, and find a bit of ease and brightness. Jeremiah Anderson he had sitting well down the road on a log; "picking up from illness" he was to say to comers, first having sounded a warning on his jew's harp. That covered the Huffmaster danger too; often the men, meal-times, at the sounding harp and Annie's cry, had to whisk up the tablecloth, dishes and all, and slip—hungry fuming wraiths, blasting their nemesis perditionward—to the garret realm, and finish the food in a dead silence there.

When a sudden summer storm came breaking dark over the hills, Kagi told them all to go out into it, a liberty they had not dared before. Thus while others through the countryside fled to sheds and carts for shelter, the "invisibles" came tumbling down mad for cool, for wet. They howled against the big thunder, finding a wild relief in the free brute calls; they leaped with the jag of the lightning, and the furious streaming rain. They put out their tongues to drink the rain, they opened their shirts wide for the skin to feel it; fiercely they scuffled, pounding their fists upon one another, exulting in the shog and the bracing sting. Then, when a slit of blue showed far out along the sky and the sun broke through the storm with a startling golden shaft, glorying the hills, they would go back in; and they would know a kind of rest for that day.

Once Kagi saw a look in Leeman's eyes as Martha came up bearing drinks. The next night, very late, Kagi who had contempt himself for women and no lust, chose the more rebellious of the young fellows—Hazlett, Leeman, Tidd and Will Thompson—and they went, while the rest were asleep and Brown unaware, along the silent mountain roads to the edge of the town. They sought out a house, entered; and stayed. Hours later, with morning near, they crept back to the farm. For a while after, they had less need for raging.

But all these were only a shift against time. And soon again one morning, Kagi came to the old man; the old man harassed, with his plans one by one falling to failure, with money not coming in nor fighters; the old man sending out letters for help in his thin quavering scrawl, and finding it most in a sacred book, read in the early day and read in the night. And Kagi said:

"They're going to break, Captain Brown. Today I felt it coming."

"Do I have men with me, or fools?"

"Men. If you had fools it would be easy to hold them."

"I tell you I'm not ready yet!"

"Then you can only do one thing. Give them your real plan. Your reason for holding on. They think you're going to run off slaves into the mountains, like Douglass thought, and they can't see why you don't begin. Tell them the stakes are higher than that, and so's the danger and the trouble. Then they'll either break . . . or you'll hear no more from them until you're ready. It's a risk but it's your only chance."

"I'm ashamed of the men. Tonight I'll talk to them. Tell them that."

CHAPTER VII

"...And the Death-Dews Sleep on the Morass..."

THE TWO girls sat on the porch with light from the moon. The windows of the room within were shut despite the heat; and through them in a low vague murmur came voices, now a single one holding its way a good time, now many sounding angrily together.

"My pa's havin' it hard," whispered Annie nervously. She could see him in her inner sight, standing quivering gray before all the men gathered in the lower room, with the tallows burning and the blinds drawn; before all the men, white and Negro, twenty of them, telling his plan. Only a word here, a phrase there, came through plain to her, but she knew the note of his speaking and got its sense—now he was in straits, that curve in pitch meant pleading, that fall a lowness of hope; now his wrath was rising, because she heard a tightened pour of words and a silence following.

"I feel 'em contrary to my pa," she whispered again to Martha.

They listened, forgetting their duty as watchers. . . . Above a single cracked voice rose sullen mutters; they rose, they grew to a hubbub of defiance. Then suddenly at the height of it, these words plucked themselves isolate, took on a cutting edge, cleaving the clamor:

"You swine! Shut up, you swine!"

It was Kagi, calling his cold scorn, silencing them.

"You swine! Are you a gang of thieves? Or are you helpers to this man?"

Indistinguishable sounds came to the two girls; and Annie could not hold her patience. She got up swiftly from her chair, and whispering "Keep watch, will you, Martha?" slipped across the porch to the window. Sight within was shut off by the blind; the young girl held her head to the pane, listened hard.

"That's right!" she heard many saying together. "That's right! We want a reckoning!"

The voices trailed in Annie's hearing, faded to a long hum. She strained desperately to understand, wondered what her father was saying and doing; she did not hear him and thought proudly that he must be bringing his strength together. Then amid a silence, as though in answer to her thinking, so close within the window that it came sharply to her, his voice began:

"Men. . . .

"Men, I've got few words for you now. I feel sick for your failing. I feel sick hearing a host against me. I see Stevens rebellious. I see Tidd. I see my own sons rising to deny me. . . .

"You ask for a reckoning. I'll give you none. You heard my plan. You can come in it with me, or you can stay out. I don't order you in, I give you the privilege. . . .

"It's a high and painful work we're called to do. There'll be bloodshed in it. Friends will turn against us. We'll be cursed by men, as already I am; and there'll be a stain on our names. Maybe we'll die. . . . All these things I tell you in the midst of your protest, so those who come in with me will know the plain true nature of the task. I tell you all these things and ask you not to fear them. Because we're called to do it. . . . For myself, I feel God in it, like I've told some here a hundred times. . . . And I'll answer to Him, not to you. I'll give a reckoning to Him."

The voices went up:

"We can talk it over, can't we?"

"Aye, we can talk it over!"

"It's only right!"

"You never told us just what!"

"You tricked us into it, like once before!"

"The Ferry's a trap!"

"It's all wild as death!"

Annie whispered fiercely to herself, cried shame upon the

men, making Martha wonder: "Oh be still you all, why do you question him so?"

But now she recognized a voice, Oliver's, going on in fervor. She knew, without seeing him, just how her brother would be standing there; pale, flinging his head back to clear the long dark hair from his eyes.

". . . Captain Brown! You're wrong if you speak that way! If it's high and painful like you say it, if it means losing our good names and maybe our lives, then we've got the right to share in disposing of it! We've got the right of men to speak!"

And Annie answered, while the talk went on inside: "Oh for shame, Oliver! Why do you plague him, so unselfish? Don't you know that home he takes the smallest room? Don't you remember once he nursed a dyin' lamb? You ought to know he only thinks of others, he wants nothin' for himself!"

A boy's rough violent voice smote the vagueness. It was Hazlett raging: "You're all milk-livers! Sneakin' out now! You been cryin' for a fight and now when he's givin' it to you, you sneak out on your bellies! You're all bastard milk-livers!"

An angry confusion went over the room, the sound of bodies moving. There was an oath; then old Brown again spoke up in wrath, and——

"Annie!" Martha was up and by her side, alarmed. "I thought I heard noises in the trees downroad! It looked like someone moving!"

"Get by the door! Get ready to rouse 'em! I'll go to see!"

Annie darted from the porch, her eyes sharp for intrusion; she flashed across the moon-flooded road into the cover of the trees, and mousing forward without a sound was soon lost to the other's sight. Martha waited, trembling. In her strain she caught at the night-sounds and heard them fraught with danger. A minute went; two. She wondered whether she ought to call the men. Then a doughty little form was on the porch again, slipping in from somewhere like a shadow.

"It was someone, Martha!"

"Then I wasn't only thinking it!"

"I heard noises too, brushin' boughs! I followed but they got away! I think it was Huffmaster prowlin'!"

"Annie! Maybe it was someone worse! Maybe you'd better tell your father!"

"Maybe I'd better. . . . But he's grave in the midst of a matter. . . . But maybe I'd better."

She sneaked to the shut window and listened with her head close.

"I can't make nothin' out."

She stood in doubt, then went to the door and put her hand on the knob.

"Maybe I'd better. . . ."

Then as she hesitated the door was pulled inward from her grasp, and old Brown came through, giving her a glimpse beyond his shoulder of the guttering candles and the agitated faces of the men, all still as though in shock, and staring at his back as he went. He shut the door behind him, and stood a little bowed. Then, seeing Annie's tautness, he asked wearily:

"Why are you standing so?"

"I was about to call you, Pa. We heard noises, someone brushin' boughs."

His frame flashed a power of quickness, took on a sudden wakened mettle. In a bound he was at the porch steps, a derringer in his hand.

"Did you look into it, Annie? Was it down or up the road?"

"It was down! There was nothin' I could find."

He peered out, then said sharply as he went down the steps: "I'll take a look about. Anderson will have to stay a late watch tonight." They saw him stalk the pale road, the gun in a gleam, and disappear into the farther vagueness.

Her pa walking into the night with a gun, courting danger—that gave Annie no apprehension. He was a fighter, her pa; in Kansas they still trembled at his name. But she saw him now as he had come out of the room—an old man, a little bowed, speaking wearily. And that sight dismayed her. Was he beaten? Had he given up? She was consumed by a wish to know. . . . In an instant she had it.

"Keep watchin', Martha! I'll be out quick!"

She went to the door, her heart beating hard, and opened it cunningly; she faded in. Smoke and smell from bodies met her senses; she could scarcely see. She heard Stevens' booming voice:

"Tidd?"

"No! Against him!"

"Leeman?"

"No!"

"Oliver Brown?"

"No!"

"Kagi?"

"For him, you swine!"

"Emperor?"

"Wid de ole man!"

"Leary?"

"'Gainst him!"

A dead silence followed.

"Twelve against! Seven for!"

Kagi's voice throbbed up in scorn: "You swine. What will you do now? Who'll lead you now?"

Annie felt a hand grip her shoulder. Owen's face was close, inflamed.

"Annie Brown! Get the hell out! Quit your sneaking!"

She wrenched her arm from him, shrieking in a fury:

"I ain't sneakin'! I come to tell Jeremiah Anderson to keep a late watch! Do you hear, Jeremiah Anderson? My pa tells you to keep a late watch! And there's no use votin' him down! He'll fight you all! Do you hear? Jeremiah Anderson, you're to keep a late watch! My pa, your captain, tells you so!"

Flinging these words to their faces, she slammed out of the room.

The old man was sitting on the dark porch; Martha was gone.

"There was no one in sight," he said; "it must have been Huffmaster again." Then he added, "You had no business inside, Annie."

"Oh, do you know they're failin' you, Pa? Do you know they're votin' you down?"

"I know I need more strength than I feel."

"Oh, go in, Pa! Go in and fight 'em!"

"You're like a Brown. But you'd better hush, Annie. You don't know much."

"Oh, if I was a man!"

"Hush, I tell you. I'll think it through. . . . Did you believe because I was hard set, I was giving up? Let me be, I'll see a way."

He got up, began to walk to and fro; then he said: "I'm going into the kitchen. Martha's sewing there. I'll talk to her . . .

about plain things. It'll clear my head, I'll find a calm. By the morning I'll know my way. . . . Good-night, daughter. Stay till Anderson comes. Tell him to be extra watchful. . . ."

When everything was still, when the lights had been snuffed and the men were up to sleep, Jeremiah Anderson came out. He sat down on the top step before Annie's chair.

"I'm doin' like your pa said, Annie. Holdin' the late watch." She kept her head turned from him, giving off an iciness.

"Will you stay a little while, Annie?"

"I won't talk to you. I won't talk to any of you. I hate you all."

"Do you have a grief against me, Annie?"

"I heard you in that room! I heard you votin' down!"

"Then give up your grief. We're with your pa."

Joyfully she swung about to him.

"You mean you're in it still? And all the men?"

"Yeah. But I can't say more. I mustn't talk."

"Oh, nobody tells me things! You mustn't talk! Am I an enemy? Don't I help in the scheme like all?"

"You've been stout as a man, stouter than most. You're his daughter skin-through. . . . Don't say I told you, Annie, then I'll tell you this. . . . Your pa gave up bein' our leader. He resigned when he saw us shocked against the plan. Only Hazlett and Owen and Kagi spoke up with him. The rest saw a slaughter in it, the rest——"

"Did you, Jeremiah Anderson?"

"Me too. And your own brothers, even Watson. Most all we did. . . . Then your pa said, you live but once and you die but once, and maybe by goin' we'd do more for the cause than our lives would be worth any other way. But you're strong against me, he said, and I want to do nothing that may have a result of injury to the work. So here I'll resign. You'll choose a new leader and I'll obey. . . . Then your pa went out, speakin' no more. We voted and it was against him, twelve to a few. Then Kagi got up and said what'll you do now, who's your new leader? And all of us stared and had nothin' to say. . . . Then I don't know what happened. . . . You came in and flared at us. . . . That Dolph boy got up and spoke, he looked a girl. He spoke about havin' come to follow old Brown, about havin' respect for humans, and wantin' to make a sacrifice. And nobody was speakin' up against and I began to get a warm rushin' in me, and all sudden Stevens spoke for it, he been fiercest against it a minute before. He spoke something about bein' bigger than your own self, and did we have guts to stick through. Well . . . I don't know . . . something happened. We voted again quick . . . and it all ended by your brother Owen sittin' down at the table and writin'. . . . We all stood around to watch. . . . It was words for your pa, tellin' our trust. It said, Dear sir . . . we have all agreed . . . to . . . to sustain your decisions . . . till you have proved uncompetent . . . and we will sustain your decisions as long as you will. And Owen signed, your friend—Owen Smith. Your pa'll have it in the mornin'. . . . So you have no grief against us, Annie. . . . Will you stay, and sit out awhile?"

Upstairs in the dark room, Stewart Taylor lay on his floor-matting; his eyes were open. Tight about him the men were asleep, their breaths in rise and fall mingling for a great low sound.

I'm going to my death, the young Canadian thought calmly. The stars I read that night from the field were right. *The moon besieged between Saturn and Mars. . . . The Lord of the First in a streaming sign or infested of the Malevolents; and the depositer of the Light of Time being also in a violent Sign, and afflicted.* . . . I'm going to my death. . . . And I'm the only one of all the men who sees the end of this. I've studied history, I know about battles. . . . He has no definite place for us to retreat to, if we must. He has no definite hour to withdraw from the town. He places a river between us and our supplies and has no good force on the bank to make sure we can fall back to it. He disperses his men, dividing our strength. The mountains are pierced by roads from all sides, so that the enemy can easily get to us. We have no resources for food or defence or hiding. Sharpshooters can pick us off from the heights. . . . He has thought nothing out. He is driven forward blindly by an uncontrollable desire to do an act but how it shall be done best he does not know.

And these fellows sleeping here. They don't know what's happening. I could tell them. I know history. I know battles, I can read the stars. But I won't tell them. What is, is. What is to be, will be. . . . I'm the only one who sees the end. Tonight, faced with the thought of losing their lives, they fought the old man. Yet I knew when they gave in at the end what each was feeling. They were going into a death-hole, but death would come only for the others. Each would somehow escape. , , , It's strange how they cling to themselves. They cannot even begin to feel what it is to be dead; they apprehend fatality but cannot conceive it as their own share. It is because they have no belief. In their eyes dissolution is the end. Decay, they think, will set in upon them as it does upon a dog rotting in a field. Flesh into mould and that's all. If they felt as I, if they had talked with the living dead, heard their voices and their love, they would walk into this trap, recognizing that death is there waiting, but would have no fear, because life is beyond. They all have fear, because this living is all they know, and they cherish it desperately. Only Kagi isn't afraid, because there's something dead in him already, some ice in his heart. He has no hope in life, so he has no fear in death. And the old man! God and him! God and one man can overturn the universe! You don't know whether to laugh at him or weep when he speaks so. You don't know which to do, because you're not wise enough. You only follow him. . . . He'll bring us to death. The stars say it.

Across the road from the farmhouse, inside the little cabin, Watson Brown was writing a letter with a pencil stub by a failing candle:

"—and you can guess how I long to see you only by knowing how you wish to see me. I think of you all day and dream of you at night. I would gladly come home and stay with you always, but for the cause which brought me here—a desire to do something for others and not live wholly for my own happiness. I am in an old shack on the Kennedy farm where we keep some *things* and some of us sleep here. They are on the floor now, Kagi, and Tidd who is snoring, but it doesn't bother me, and your brother Dolph, laying gentle as a baby. Cook is outside. I can see him through the door. He's sitting on the grass, smoking. He has a gun in his lap, and the moon is on him. Cook has a wife too. I think he loves her very much. It is very late now and dark. I always wait till then to write, because then it is a little bit like being alone with you. I am alone now, but I have some good company, for I received your letter of August 30, and you may as well think I am glad to hear from you. You may kiss the baby a great many times a day for me. Oh, Bell, I am thinking of you and him all the time. . . ."

The garden behind the house was a place pale with light

from the midnight moon. Beneath a beech, well in from sight among the boughs hanging low about them, Oliver and Martha sat on a wooden bench, whispering.

". . . so we voted again, after Annie came in, this time to stay with my father! I tell you, Martha, we were swept sudden, all of us. We jumped up and everybody's face was shining, and when Stevens called—you know his eyes, how they shine when he's hard for something?—well, there he was with his hot eyes . . . he called, who's coming in with the old man, who's got guts to do it? And it went like a fire over us, and we said 'aye' in a body and the room rang. All of us said it, down to those bitter a minute before, and the niggers were all trembling, excited. . . . I felt in an eye-wink that everything was plain then. It put a meaning to things, to my being here, and for having to leave you soon. . . . It was funny, Martha! I thought of those lines, those Shelley lines! They began to run in my head, you know the ones. *If thine or theirs were treasures to be bought by blood or tears, have not the wise and free wept tears and blood like tears?* Oh, I was swept, Martha! All of us! *O Liberty! If such could be thy name——*"

"It's late, Oliver. Let's go in." She whispered desolately, making a move to rise. He held her by him.

"No, Martha! Stay, I tell you! I see you scarce at all! Stay, I tell you! Stay yet!"

"Then talk to me different. Not about your pa, and what the men said. Don't talk to me about the plan, Oliver."

"Why——"

"Tell me the lines we loved together. The other Shelley lines. Then I'll stay."

His face went softer. He moved very close; passed his arm about her full warm body, holding her tight; then kissed her cheek where the tendrils from her hair were wild.

"You're life to me."

"Say the Shelley."

"You're the sweet of it, light you bring me."

"Say it, Oliver, the lines we loved together. *"As dew beneath——"*

"As dew beneath the wind of morning,
Is my heart when thine is near it."

"We read that first by the river, Oliver. Do you remember? Just before a rain came up on a blue day?"

"And you had your hair up out of a braid, for your first time? And I tumbled it down to get you mad?"

She gave a little laugh, close to tears.

"I learned some new ones, Martha. I was on watch and I learned them. Listen. They go to your heart.

> *"Some say when nights are dry and clear,*
> *And the death-dews sleep on the morass,*
> *Sweet whispers are heard by the traveller,*
> *Which make night day;*
> *And a silver shape like his early love doth pass. . . ."*

"I don't like it. . . . It's too sad."

"It's beautiful, Martha. . . .

> *"And a silver shape like his early love doth pass*
> *Upborne by her wild and glittering hair,*
> *And when he awakes on the fragrant grass*
> *He finds——"*

"It's too late, Oliver, to stay here. You go up to sleep too. If you wake them late they'll be angry."

"Don't you go!" He tightened her against himself, knowing a warm rush through all his body. "I can never get to being with you. Everybody's around to watch. You'd think we weren't man and wife. . . . Stay, Martha, it's cool here. . . . Stay."

In the neglected garden; among the blue gentian pale with the night gleam, and the yellow roses, evening primrose, petals spread since dusk to the dark dews; Oliver and Martha remained together.

 CHAPTER VIII

Because the Day Is Coming

Now A kind of febrile calm was over the "invisibles." The strain of delay was no less racking, nor the fear of exposure; indeed these were rising in pitch as the summer crept on to its end. But beneath the fret and the quivering anxiety ran a current of high resignation. They had a goal now; the waiting, they felt, was no longer blind. They had made after the manner of free men their own choice; they had thrown a leader, and chosen one; they had rejected a plan, and said "aye" to its madness. Now they could wait. There was less raging among them, fewer quarrels and sudden uncontrollable outbursts of temper; a faint solemnity was settled over them. Down to the last wild boy they felt it: they were a single body, they were comrades, they were a body of sacrifice.

"No, Taylor. I don't know what I believe in."
Kagi was sitting on the attic steps with Stewart Taylor.
"Then why are you here, Kagi? You have no faith in God. That's why I'm here. . . . You said freedom for others leaves you cold. I'm here for that too. . . . You see the same flaws as I do in the plan, you know what the end of it must be. And yet you're here. Why?"
"I don't just know. I give myself a number of reasons, none of which I believe. . . . You see, Taylor . . . for me life is a monotony. To make it bearable I have to try to speed time, to cram an emptiness full. . . . I've never loved a soul in my life, Taylor. I don't know what love is. . . . I've turned to books and learning. I've studied magic, I've studied law. I've found nothing in books, only a veil or a despair. . . . So my cult is risk. Desperate living. Taking the chance in a thousand. . . . I'm spoiled for peace, you see? That's why I went to Kansas. Maybe that's why I'm here. . . ."
Taylor stayed silent, and something in the slow grave brown eyes of the Canadian drew Kagi on:
". . . Then too, when I hear the Thompson babe speaking of sacrifice and respect for humans, and the Coppocs about the holy right of every man to freedom, I know that doesn't touch me. Intellectually, yes . . . but my heart not at all. And men don't go to die with their minds, Taylor. They only go when their insides flame up. My insides flamed, never in all my life. . . ."
He smiled a cold old smile.
". . . Sometimes I think it's the old man. . . . I see something in him which I lack myself, which makes my emptiness. I don't know just what to call it. I can't put it easily into words. . . . It's building something by your own power. . . . I see the old man in a world of his own making. I see in his every move, his every breath, the spirit of a man creating—the eagerness, the isolation.

. . . You know, Taylor, I sometimes think that if tomorrow word came that all slaves had been set free without condition, the old fellow would go undone, he'd die in a month, of heartache. He could never see it settled peacefully now. He's worked so long with force, all his plans are so bound up with it, that if his object were to be gained now through peace his very motive for living would go. . . . Something creative, Taylor. . . . Why, look at these kids. They think they had a choice in keeping him as leader. They had no more choice than a seed has to grow in this field or that. If they had taken his resignation, in a week he'd have been giving advice, in two he'd be ordering, in the end have them tight in his hand again. . . . The man burns with something, Taylor! and he gives it to those around him! He wants to make the world over. God has told him to. He'll fail. . . . But he's winning all the time, don't you see? Because he's living in a world——Look at these fellows, every one of them different; he's touching them, making them feel and think and work as he does. . . . But he has no mind. And that's what I've got a curiosity about. I want to see what his blind drive can do. I want to see just how far faith without mind can succeed in making its own world."

Stewart Taylor sat silent. Then slowly he said, "Kagi. You're wrong, Kagi. . . . You said you never loved a soul. . . . You said you don't know what love is."

Down in the kitchen Cook was sitting on a packing-box, poised for flight, near Martha making a biscuit-batter. ". . . And people think," he was saying earnestly, "that I'm in this because I'm wild. Maybe I started that way. But it's not that now, it's not that at all. I'm in it because I believe in what we're doing."

"Oliver speaks so, too," she said sadly.

"They ought to see it can't be wildness." He lowered his voice a little, gazing hungrily at the dark girl. "Not when you've got a wife home it can't be for wildness."

They both went silent, Martha whipping the paste hard. After a while he said, "I wish sometimes you'd see her. She a lot like you, Martha. . . . Only she's all golden. I call her a lark. She's always singing."

"Oh, then why did you come here? Why did you leave her?"

Outside, sitting on a rock, Martha's boy-husband was writing a letter home:

≡ * 253 * ≡

"Dear Mother, Brother, and Sisters—Knowing that you all feel deeply interested in persons and matters here, I feel a wish to write all that is encouraging, feeling that we all need all the encouragement we can get while we are travelling through eternity, of which every day is a part. I can only say that we are all well, and that our work is going on slow, but we think satisfactory. I would here say that I think there is no good reason why any of us should be discouraged; for if we have done but one good act, life is not a failure. I think Martha and Annie will be getting home soon, because the day is coming, though our father stays silent. I hope you will all keep a stiff lip, a sound pluck, and believe that all will come out right in the end. Small Nell, I have not forgotten you, and I want you should remember me, and take care of your cough. Mother, please watch Martha when she gets home. You know how she is and you know a lot about such things. I will see you soon again, I think. Salmon, you may make any use of the sugar things you can next year. Please, all write. Believe me your affectionate son and brother, Oliver Smith."

Upstairs, in the loft crowded with men, Copeland the young mulatto student was reading aloud from a pamphlet:

" '. . . and a man held against his will as a slave has a natural right to kill every one who seeks to prevent his enjoyment of liberty. This has long been recognized as a self-evident proposition, coming directly from the primitive instincts of human nature.' " The young Negro continually sought, as he read, the faces of the other blacks: Osborn Perry, the consumptive; Emperor Green, groping in his tiny mind; Leary, yellow, withered, smoldering with the fearful suggestion; and, his slow animal eyes watching, Dangerfield Newby. Bright-haired Dolph Thompson was listening with a troubled heart. He whispered to Stevens who was lying silent on a mattress, "He oughtn't to speak that way, Stevens! It's a sin to preach blood that way!"

"I don't know, Dolph. I don't know anything. Let's hear him. He's got a right to speak."

" '. . . and the African race have but little desire for vengeance, the lowest form of the love of justice. In Santa Cruz, for example, if a slave excited others to run away, for the first offense his right leg was cut off, for the second offense his other leg. This mutilation was not done by a surgeon's hand. The wretch was laid down on a log and his legs chopped off with a plantation axe, and the stumps plunged into boiling pitch to staunch the blood; for the live torso of a slave might serve as a warning. From 1830 to 1846 it was common for owners to beat their victims with "tamarind" rods, six feet long and an inch in thickness, and set with ugly spikes. When that process was over, the lacerated back was washed with a decoction of the Manchineel, a poison tree, which made the wounds fester and long remain open. Then in 1846 the Negroes were in rebellion and took possession of the island; they were twenty-five thousand, the whites three thousand. But the blacks did not hurt the hair of a single white man's head. They got their freedom but they took no revenge. Suppose now, twenty-five thousand Americans, held in bondage by three thousand Algerines on a little island, should get their masters into their hands, how many of the three thousand would see the next sun go down? But there is a limit even to the Negro's forbearance. San Domingo is not a great way off. The revolution which changed its black inhabitants from tame slaves into wild men——' "

"I think you ought to stop, Copeland!" broke in Dolph Thompson suddenly, rising pale. "You're sowing hate! I think you ought to stop!"

The young Negro's eyes were flushed with blood. "Why should I stop? Am I telling too much truth?"

"You only tell a part of it! We didn't come to kill people!"

Leeman called up: "Say, Mollie, what'd you come for, to read Channing's sermons?"

"If you'd been in Kansas fightin' with us," growled Hazlett, "you'd speak different."

"I'll do my share, don't you all fear!" the boy quivered. "Only you're wrong to be——"

"Shut up, Dolph!" called his brother Will from across the room. "Shut up your whining! Don't the old man himself talk about blood? Go on, Copeland, say what you've got to!"

"This is a white man writing these words," said the young Negro bitterly. "Not me, a nigger. A white man. Theodore Parker. He's one of the great men in the North. He writes his sermons with a gun by him for protection. His people were in your Revolution, your fight for being free. . . . Not me, a nigger."

And his voice went on low and terrible with hate. . . .

≡ * 255 * ≡

Across the road, behind the little cabin, Watson and Tidd, breaking orders, lay hidden cool and deep in a copse, sucking at the dying autumn stems.

"So he's two months old, the runt codger?"

"Yeah. He was born just before I left for here. We called him Fred. . . . My brother's name was Fred. He was shot in Kansas."

"Your family's give a lot to this nigger business."

"Yeah. . . . Two months old. . . . I'd like to see it."

"Will you run your own farm when you get back?"

"Sure, I'd like to. I always wanted to feel I was bindin' my own stacks. Layin' up winter stores. . . . I always wanted to hear a bell ringin' in my own pasture. To fill a basket from ripe orchards, all mine."

"I like farmin', too. I'd like to settle down peaceful."

"Sure. You ought to be thinkin' of it when you get back north."

"But you need a good woman. You need someone helpin' you."

"Ain't there no girl you like?"

"Me? With my face?"

"Hell! There's someone for everyone, Tidd. You ain't so bad."

"Me? Aah, I oughta be called Toad, not Tidd. . . . But I'd like to settle down peaceful."

* * * * *

In Washington, John Floyd, the Secretary of War of the United States, was reading a letter:

"Sir: I have lately information of a movement of so great importance that I feel it my duty to impart it to you without delay. . . . I have discovered the existence of a secret association, having for its general object the liberation of the slaves of the South. The leader of the movement is "Old John Brown" late of Kansas. He has been in Canada during the winter, drilling the Negroes there, and they are only waiting his word to start for the South to assist the slaves. They have one of their leading men in an armory in Maryland. As soon as everything is ready they are to come in small companies to their rendezvous, which is in the mountains of Virginia. They will pass down through Pennsylvania and Maryland and enter Virginia at Harper's Ferry. Brown left the North about three weeks ago and will arm the Negroes and strike the blow in a few weeks; so that whatever is done must be done at once. . . . As I am not fully in their confidence, this is all the information I can give you. I dare not sign my name to this, but trust you will not disregard the warning on that account...."

CHAPTER IX

Augurs, Bearers of Holy Things

WHEN THE heat-storm was over, the men trooped upstairs again. They lay about, eased a little with the quick savage sally and the wetness; while outside the land lay fragrant and peaceful before the coming of night.

"... Take two cocks in a pit," Stewart Taylor was saying to Barclay Coppoc. "If you want to know the winner, beforehand, you get their colors and link them with the planets. ...Venus is white or purple. Scorpio is black with gray speckles. Mercury is sky-bluish. And so on. Now, the cock whose color is closest to the planet which is a superior planet, or has most essential dignities, or is most strongly fortified, this cock will be pointed out as the winning cock."

"The winning cock!" jeered Leeman. "Did you ever hear such fiddle-faddle in all your life?"

Taylor turned his slow brown eyes on the wild boy.

"The stars are the secret of life. ... I can see from your ignorance of true things that you know nothing about stars, Leeman. ... Read Lilly for your soul's sake. Read his opening page. 'The more your knowledge is enlarged by this comprehensive science the more should you magnify the power of God and strive to preserve yourself in His favor. Beware of pride and self-conceit, yet never forget your dignity. Consider your nobleness and that all created things both present and to come were for your sake created, for your sake even God became Man——' "

"Hell, Taylor! Don't worry about my soul! Tell us some more about cocks and planets! And oh! did you ever get to figuring out what my signs are, like I asked you to?"

"Yes, I figured them out."

"Wonderful! Let's hear them. But don't you bring in my soul again or I'll turn in to sleep!"

The men drew about, grinning, expectant.

"You are a native of the Moon. You will know those diseases under the spell of the Moon. . . . You will have coughs and frenzies, you will have worms and complaints of the bowels. You will have lunacy and crude humors."

The men hugged themselves with delight. The irrepressible Leeman looked faintly repressed.

"You may also be a native of Mars. Then you will have corruptions of the blood. You will have carbuncles and bloody-flux, Saint Anthony's fire and all disorders proceeding from abundance of heat."

"Say, where can I get this book?" grinned Leeman. "Does it have anything about Venus?"

"I haven't finished with you" said Taylor. ". . . Mars is your inclining planet. It is a malevolent planet, in nature hot, trumpeter of its own fame and consequence, lover of malicious quarrels and affrays, obscene, rashly inhuman. . . . A foul nasty slovenly knave, covetous and seldom rich."

While the men rocked with delight, Dangerfield Newby slipped out of the room to the head of the attic stairs. Each day as it grew late the huge Negro waited there with a pounding heart. Owen Brown would be in any minute, bearing mail. Maybe there would be a letter for Dangerfield Newby. Maybe the fierce young white girl would bring it up to him, as she did often for the others.

". . . Leo the noble lion rules both back and heart, Virgo the bashful virgin claims the belly part, Libra, the reins and loins. . . ."

"But all seriously, Taylor," broke in Stevens, impressed, "can this star reading help you to really know true important things?"

"The stars have the secret of life and dying. . . . 'You will daily converse with the heavens, your capacity for acquiring knowledge being unlimited by your Maker you will instruct your mind according to the image of Divinity and——' "

"But those are only words. That's vague. . . . Can you tell me something about us? About the work we're doing?"

Dangerfield Newby crept furtively down the stairs.

". . . and the old man under Saturn. . . . When Saturn gives testimony its children will take care of sacred animals, they will be weepers and sextons. . . . When Saturn gives testimony it will make sacrificers, rulers of men and women, augurs, bearers of holy things. They will be pipers at funerals, and conversant in mysteries, lamentations and blood."

A silence was now over the room, the men were uneasy; and Dangerfield Newby slunk in, all trembling. He went to Kagi, sleeping on a pallet in the corner; shook him frantically, whispered:

"Miss Annie want you! She said to you, come quick! Huffmaster see me!"

Kagi leaped up. "You swine! Didn't I tell you never to go down!" He slipped out to the stairs like a cat, while the men stood taut and hushed.

"You can't wait longer," Kagi calmly said later to the old man. "Huffmaster will spring it this time. If you delay we're trapped. We've got to start quickly while they're still only suspicious. . . . It's just the right time. Everything's our way for conditions. The crops have been good all over the countryside, all in and housed, perfect to use when we need food. The moon's just right. Slaves are more discontented in this season than any other. They'll rise now, if they ever will. . . . Another black hung himself down in Jessup's orchard yesterday. It must have aroused the others. It's a high time, Captain Brown."

"Yes, it's a high time. We'll begin, Kagi. We still need money, we need a greater force. But tell the men, Kagi. Tell them to get ready, in their hearts. We begin—Sunday."

That night, as though in answer to Brown's need, the great reason for delay was removed. Owen drove in from Chambersburg; a frail boy, about twenty, was with him. He had a nervous white face, without the sight of one eye; he had a small bag with him.

"They told me about you in Boston," he said in a high voice. "So I came down to find you and help. My uncle is Francis Jackson. He's an Abolitionist. I am too. My name is Merriam."

"How do you think to help?" the old man asked dubiously, sizing up the stripling.

"Like your other men. . . . I brought money too. I just came into my inheritance. Down in Haiti two years ago I made up my mind to give it all to help slaves to escape. I have half of it

≡ * 259 * ≡

here. They told me you were hard up." He opened the bag. There were six hundred dollars in gold.

"I can get more if you need it. I had my will drawn yesterday. If I die it goes to the Abolition cause."

The next day the two young girls left.

"Good-bye, boys," said Martha, trembling as she stood at the head of the attic stairs. "God keep you all safe."

"Good-bye, all," said Annie in her sad sharp way. "Good-bye, all."

"Good-bye, girls."

"So long, kids."

"Good-bye, Martha."

"And say hello to Bell for me."

"Good-bye!"

CHAPTER X

The Sabbath

JOHN BROWN slipped from the cot. It was still dark; the day would soon come. He dressed silently, with care; Owen, Oliver, and Jeremiah Anderson were asleep about him. He went into the kitchen, closing the door gently. He lit the lamp. Then he got the stove going with a wood fire; set up the huge kettle for coffee that the men would take, and a pot of water for his own tea. He shivered. The ague which had seeped into his body during the secret hunted days in the Kansas swamps, was still strong in his blood. He shivered with it, feeling a flush along his throat; and knew that the day coming boded rain.

He took his Bible from the chest, and went to the window. A dimmest gray began to show in the sky. The Sabbath is here, he thought; and it will be given to His work. It will be hallowed, but not rest from labor. And as he stood there with the book unopened in his hand, he felt a joy sweep over him:

I am not in a dream. I am John Brown here in the kitchen,

with a fire going and the smell of coffee in my nostrils. I am John Brown, a man doing the common duties of life, living in this world. But I am more than John Brown. I have no desires that are my own, because I have passed beyond all desires. I am not in a dream, I smell the coffee, but I am two. I am the clay, yet the self which is He. I exist, yet I do not, save in His will. I am not in a dream, the light breaks outside, I hear a crow. It is the Sabbath, the day of our labor.

And almost all things are by the law purged with blood; and without shedding of blood is no remission.

Rain clouded the window in a slow dismal fall; a wind shook it to a devil's tattoo. Owen Brown sat on the porch, with a rifle under his old coat. Inside the men thronged the room, very still. Stevens was reading solemnly in his deep vibrant voice: "Whereas, Slavery, throughout its entire existence in the United States is none other than a most barbarous, unprovoked and unjustifiable War of one portion of its citizens upon another portion; the only conditions of which are perpetual imprisonment and hopeless servitude or absolute extermination; in utter disregard and violation of those eternal and self-evident truths set forth . . . therefore, we citizens, and the oppressed people, do for the time being ordain and establish the following Provisional Constitution. . . . And Congress will be composed of not less than five or more than ten members . . . at no times shall there be swearing, filthy conversation, indecent exposure, intoxication or . . . and before any treaty of peace shall take full effect . . . the majority of the Supreme Court . . . the Commander-in-Chief of the Armies. . . ."

". . . And now, gentlemen," said the old man. "Let me press this one thing on your minds. You all know how dear life is to you, and how dear your lives are to your friends; and in remembering that, consider that the lives of others are dear to them as yours are to you. Do not, therefore, take the life of anyone if you can possibly avoid it. But if it is necessary to take life in order to save your own, then make sure work of it."

The hours moved slowly. The men oiled their rifles, tightened the iron pikes on the wood-shafts; then they waited. The old man sat in the gloom of the kitchen, writing a letter by the lamp-light.

Night came. They ate the meal which their Commander-in-Chief had prepared, the last meal they would eat in this farm-house; they had heard the old man say the last grace.

He took down a tattered old cap from the wall, the battle-torn Kansas cap.

"Men. Get your arms. We will proceed to the Ferry."

War into Africa

THE
FOURTH PART

For these are the days of vengeance, that all things which are written may be fulfilled. Woe unto them that are with child and to them that give suck in these days! For there shall be great distress upon the land and wrath unto this people. And they shall fall by the edge of the sword, and be led captive into all the nations.

CHAPTER I

If You Knew My Heart

AT 7:05 in the morning of Monday, October 16, 1859, the Baltimore & Ohio train bound from the West to Baltimore arrived at the small village of Monocacy, Maryland. Before it came to a full stop, Phelps the conductor leaped from the caboose and went scrambling up the runway to the telegraph office. At 7:07 the operator was furiously tapping out a message to the master of transportation at Baltimore:

"Train held up five hours at Harper's Ferry by insurrectionists. One hundred and fifty strong. Baggage-master killed. Say they have come to free slaves. Leader says this is last train to pass bridge east or west. If attempted will be at peril of lives. Telegraph wires cut east and west of Ferry. Notify authorities at once."

By 10:27 the head of the Baltimore & Ohio, John W. Garret, had telegraphed to President Buchanan of the United States; John Floyd, Secretary of War; Governor Wise of Virginia; and Major-General George Stewart, commanding the First Light Division, Maryland Volunteers. By noon three companies of artillery from Fort Monroe, a detachment of Marines from the Washington navy-yard, and the Fredericksburg militia were speeding toward the scene of the reported disturbance; Colonel Robert E. Lee of the Second United States Cavalry in command, Lieutenant J. E. B. Stuart second in command.

Floyd, Secretary of War, pale, pacing back and forth in his Washington office, remembered a letter which some weeks ago had come to him. He had swept it into the basket as the work of a crank, a madman. ("Sir: . . . information of a movement of so great importance that I feel it my duty to impart it to you without delay . . . having for its general object the liberation of slaves by insurrection . . . he has been in Canada during the winter, drilling the Negroes there. . . .") Floyd had been too busy with certain furtive affairs of his own to pay attention to such a fantastic letter. For who could know, perhaps some day soon the South would have great need for guns and powder and cannon. Floyd, the United States' War Secretary was in his heart more truly Floyd of Virginia. He was seeing to it well and secretly that huge supplies of military stores were being shifted from Northern arsenals to the South. Now, remembering the letter he cursed himself.

And in a thousand cities through the nation men were reading their newspapers with incredulous excitement:

". . . The statements are fully confirmed. Two hundred Negroes and one hundred whites are in revolt, all armed with Minnie rifles, spears and pistols. They have all the arsenal buildings in their possession and access to thousands of weapons. They expect, it is said, a reinforcement of twelve hundred slaves by morning. . . ."

". . . Every light in the town had been previously extinguished by the lawless mob. All the streets, every road and lane leading to the Ferry has been barricaded and guarded. . . ."

". . . He has refused to let anything pass. All the east-bound trains are lying west of the Ferry. Your correspondent has just seen a letter from a merchant of the town, which was carried by two boys over the mountain, and who had to swim the river in order to escape. The letter states that almost all the leading citizens have been imprisoned and many have been killed. Beckham the Mayor was shot twice by the gang, and died. They are said to be disguised, the whites being painted as blacks. . . ."

". . . The ringleader, who is said to be named Anderson, made his appearance at Harper's Ferry five or six days ago, and since that time has been driving around the place in an elegant barouche drawn by four horses. . . ."

". . . The captain of the outlaw band was an old man with a white beard. He was heard to say in addressing the conductor 'If you knew me and understood my motives as well as I and others understand them you would not blame me so much.' "

". . . The citizens were in a terrible state of consternation, most of them being shut up in their houses, and not a light to be seen in the streets or anywhere. It is difficult to describe the excitement throughout the entire section. Rumors of every sort are flying about. As yet it is impossible to divine the cause of this outbreak. Some are of the opinion it is a bold concerted scheme to rob the Government pay-house of funds deposited there on Saturday. We are informed by others that the leader of the rioters is a noted Abolitionist agent of the Underground Railroad. He is from Troy, New York, and has made frequent visits to the Ferry. His conduct toward the black people had been noticed on other occasions and involved him in suspicion. He is represented as a most desperate and dangerous man, and one who is likely to cause a great deal of trouble before he will yield. The marauder chief was heard to exclaim, 'If you knew my heart and history you would not blame me.' The Negroes rely upon him, and will implicitly obey his directions. There are said to be more than six hundred armed slaves and whites. . . ."

 CHAPTER II

The Night-March

THEY HAD buckled on their arms. They had thrown the long gray shawls over their shoulders (it is my winding-sheet, thought Stewart Taylor); and filed out to the cold wet darkness of the fall night, the Sabbath night. Owen had driven the horse and wagon to the door; it was filled with pikes, faggots, a sledgehammer, and a crow-bar. The old man clambered up. "Come, boys," he said. The wagon began to creak down the lane, the men swinging behind, two and two, hiding their rifles under the shawls. Watson as he moved by found Owen's hand; they gave a quick deep squeeze. Edwin Coppoc, in the last of the line, halted for an instant, embraced his young brother, their lips meeting. Then, to the three remaining behind at the farmhouse, Owen, frail Merriam, and Barclay Coppoc, their comrades became shadows fading in the damp lonely night.

A bad wind was blowing up from the river-gloom. The little fat man walked slowly across the bridge, swinging the lantern, pressing his coat tighter about himself. He yawned, shivering a little, thinking vaguely: twelve noon to twelve the middle of the night is a rotten long dull time to mind a bridge, nothing ever happens, the sleepiest job in the sleepiest town. For seventeen years Will Williams had been watching the Potomac train-crossing and having the same drowsy glum feeling as the night closed in. Lights changed from a color of danger to safety, trains went by in a slow hissing rumble, a hand might gleam waving from the white-red glow of the firing-cab, an unknown voice call in swift fading comradeship. You watched the bridge, making the way across every hour, swinging the lamp. At twelve, Pat Higgins, (but Pat was always a few minutes late), would come with his little growl; then the shift would be over, you would go home for something hot and a deep drowned sleep; then a new day would get around, with lights and trains and again slow time crawling. But it wasn't really bad except on raw nights like this one, with a drizzle seeping down and the wind like a knife, making the last hours hardest. Will Williams came to his tiny watch-coop at the Maryland entrance of the bridge. He settled inside on his bench with a sigh; he relaxed, nothing coming in till the 1:25 A.M. West-to-Baltimore. He carefully drew the stub of a cigar from his outer breast pocket. He put it into his mouth, rolled it luxuriously, bit on it. He lit a match, he——

"Come out of there!"

Will Williams' jaw hung. The match burned down to his fingers. A big man with a black beard and shining eyes stood in the coop door; Williams stared down the glistening barrel of a rifle.

"Come out, quick."

"Quit jokin'."

He came out, scared and incredulous. A lean young fellow was standing there too, with a rifle. "Quit jokin'," Williams kept saying. Then from the darkness a wagon came creaking onto the bridge and fat Williams saw a line of men. He saw their set hard faces, the shine of rifle-barrels; it was no joke. But it must be a joke. Why, there was Cook, John Cook the boy who tended the canal-lock. He knew the boy well, he'd married sweet Mary Turner, blessed luck. And there was that old gentleman sitting up on the seat, Mr. Smith, the new farmer at the Kennedy place, Isaac Smith who had a quick straight way and you respected him. Why, they were up to some joke! But Will Williams felt the rifle murderous against his paunch.

"Oliver Brown. Will Thompson. Newby. Guard the bridge. Await orders. The rest, follow me."

≡ * 268 * ≡

Now they were moving along the bridge. Now they were over, they were in Harper's Ferry. They went along the narrow street; passed the railroad station with its green flaring lights; passed the saloon, seeing no one and not being seen. The wet night was with them; folks were close by hearth-fires, not dreaming danger. The Ferry had known its last belligerent men during the Revolution, beyond the remembrance of living citizens. This October of 1859 they would as soon expect lava to rage up from the gentle Virginia hills as bloodshed in their streets, as eighteen men moving desperate in the night with guns, like ghosts risen from a grave. Suddenly ahead the whole village darkened, lights dotting the obscurity clean up the Bolivar heights suddenly snuffed out. Tidd was at work. In another instant the armory loomed black by the Potomac bank. Old Dan Whelan would be drowsing in the arsenal yard. Thousands of arms would come into their possession. Hazlett and Jeremiah Anderson crept forward to the gate.

Five miles south of the Ferry, in an upstairs room of his plantation, Colonel Lewis Washington, great-grandnephew of the First President, slept fitfully. Downstairs, hanging above the fireplace, were an old pistol and a sword. The pistol had been presented to George Washington by Lafayette; the sword was the gift of Frederick the Great.

A little after midnight Lewis Washington stirred in his bed, vague sounds threading his sleep. Then two loud knocks came upon the heavy oak door. He sat up, startled. "Open up!" a voice boomed. He slipped from the bed, thrust his feet hastily into slippers, and went in his night-shirt to the door. He pulled it open. Four men stood there with levelled rifles. One, a Negro, held a burning flambeau.

"You're our prisoner," said the black-bearded man. "Get into your clothes."

Washington stared. "Will you have the courtesy to tell me what this means?"

"Yes. You're coming with us. And your slaves too. Get dressed, quick."

He prodded the thunderstruck Washington with his rifle. The colonel dressed, as in a fantastic dream. "Where are you taking me?" he asked, trying to speak with dignity as he slipped on a boot.

"Osawatomie Brown wants to see you."

≡ * 269 * ≡

"And who, pray, is Osawatomie Brown?"

"Have you never heard of Kansas?"

They went downstairs. The colonel's sister, gray-haired, wrapped in a dressing gown, sat proud in an arm-chair. Her look was eloquent: Lewis, cowhide these ruffians out of the house. Old Bettina, the Negress, was glaring defiantly at two armed men. One was a mulatto, the other a slim dark fellow.

"Good evening, Colonel Washington," the dark fellow said.

"Mr. Cook! What does this outrage mean?"

"I've been trying to calm Miss Washington. You will come to no harm."

"What does it mean, I say?"

"We're freeing the slaves of the South. We're prepared to do it."

The black-bearded man broke in roughly, "Enough talk. You, Mr. Washington, take down that sword, and that pistol too. Quick. . . . Now hand the sword over to Emperor Green. . . . Now the pistol, to Leary."

The Southerner was pale with the indignity.

"It's Captain Brown's orders," said Cook, half-proud, half-ashamed. "He said we'd start the work with a symbol."

Tidd came in growling through the front door: "The wagon's ready."

"Sir, your carriage awaits you." Stevens bowed low in mockery.

They went out, leaving the two women behind in the darkness. In the driveway was the colonel's small phaeton. Behind it was a large four-horse farm wagon. Six slaves stood startled and bewildered by the wagon. "Come on and fight to get free," Tidd had told them. Now they looked fearfully at their master, cringing. Colonel Washington stepped up into the carriage with hauteur. He felt more like himself now that he was out of his nightshirt. Stevens got in beside him, taking the reins. The rest, whites and Negroes, climbed into the wagon. The first hostage was taken. The first bondmen were freed.

A little past twelve, Pat Higgins, night-watchman, walked out on the Maryland bridge to relieve Will Williams. A shameful night, he growled in his thought, may it go quick. He puffed on his pipe as he trudged along the trestle and cursed himself for not bringing his ancient outer coat.

"Halt!"

Three forms rose dark before him. Instantly, intuitively, Higgins turned and began to run. A rifle sounded, a bullet snipped a furrow in the Irishman's scalp. His leathery old body dodged from side to side up the trestle. He made the town entrance and leaped behind the wing of the station. He stood listening; there was only silence again.

At 1:25 the Baltimore & Ohio train drew in at the Ferry. ". . . but I didn't know what 'halt' mint any more than a hog knows about a holiday!" said Patrick Higgins in great excitement to the conductor, Phelps. "There's no sign anywhere of Will, and sure there's somethin' evil about!"

Phelps and the engineer, half-incredulous, walked up the tracks to investigate. Rifle-fire came from the bridge. Hastily the train was backed away out of danger. Phelps ran to the telegraph office. The wires had been cut.

Shephard Hayward, free Negro and baggage master at the Ferry, rolled his hand-truck down the platform as the train came in. It was a good job. He had held it for seven years now and they had been the happiest of his life. The little fund at the bank was growing; the whites all respected him, only yesterday old Mayor Beckham himself had inquired in a true friendly fashion about his family in the small new house at the foot of the Heights, was the boy better and how was the flower-bed coming along. It was a good deal for a "nigger" to have reached such a secure place in a Southern community, to have pulled himself up from the slime to a man's place. Shephard Hayward, not seeing the watchman about, not seeing the swing of Higgins' red lamp, walked around the corner of the hotel and on toward the bridge to look for him; Shephard Hayward walked crooning to himself. Dangerfield Newby, Negro with a wife and seven children enslaved, waiting with rifle poised over the railing, saw a man moving up in the dimness of the trestle. His finger trembled on the trigger. He called "Stop!" The man kept moving up, Newby's finger pulled in sharp. Shephard Hayward gave a little choked cry, he turned and staggered back along the bridge. Just over the end he dropped and lay moaning, with a bullet and agonized bewilderment in his heart. The first death-blow for the cause of blacks had been struck.

Back at the darkened farmhouse, Owen Brown, Merriam and the Coppoc boy were waiting through the slow fearful hours.

≡ * 271 * ≡

They could only wait. Their share would come later. The others would put the spark to the touchwood; these three would heap the fuel. When the first bullet cut to a soft living wall of flesh, making it dead; when the first oppressor sank lifeless before a black man's eyes, showing a way to freedom, the slaves would come in wild crowds to the Kennedy farm. These three would give them guns, old Brown had said; this was the point from which their strength would swell, would swirl. Now his son and the two boys waited throbbing, hoping.

And soon through the hills a boy of the South was streaking on a horse. By dawn he would be in Charlestown, eight miles away. By dawn the alarm bells would be ringing, tolling on— insurrection, civil war. The Jefferson Guards, men and boys with old muskets and squirrel-guns, would be falling into line before the court-house. In Martinsburg from bed or breakfast men would hurry armed to the town square. Bells ringing terror over the countryside, bells tolling, slaves rising bloody, the Shepherds-town troop forming, the Hamtramck Guards rushing, tighter tighter the net drawing about an old man and some boys.

CHAPTER III

Tell Kagi, Stand Firm

THE FIRST gray cold light came into the arsenal yard. The men were ranged about the gate with rifles, watching the still empty street. Across the town the bell of the Lutheran church had begun a steady ominous ringing. Close by the watch-house some of the prisoners paced, scared and hollow-eyed. Forty-two had been brought in during the night; now the rest were huddled inside. The handful of liberated slaves stood stupidly about, furtively trailing their pikes, ashamed to look full at the masters they were guarding. They were cold, they were hungry, the cabins on the plantations would be warm, food would be smelling good in the fires. But they were afraid of the old man with the fierce eyes. He kept moving about the yard, watching everything like a hawk. Now he strode over to Lewis Washington standing pale and outraged against the wall. The sword of Frederick was gripped in the old man's hand. He held it proudly, as if it were a true fit weapon for this leader. He began to speak to Washington, earnestly, his words were almost an appeal for justification: "I am very attentive to you, sir. I may get the worst of it in my first encounter, and if so, your life is worth as much as mine. I took you first for the moral effect it would give our cause having one of your name as prisoner." Or again turning to the prisoner of illustrious lineage: "You will find a fire in there, sir. It is quite cold this morning." But Washington would never answer, as if it were beneath him, and all the time his keen glance would take in the other—the gleaming bluish mettle of the eyes, the stiff whitening hair projecting close above on the low brow, the mouth like a sabre-thrust—and even as he hated the sight of the face he felt its awful unsmiling strength.

Just before daylight, in the flare of the torches, the old man had addressed the prisoners, "I came here from Kansas, and this is a slave state. I want to free all the slaves, and I have possession now of the armory. I hope that no harm will come to you. But if the citizens interfere I must only burn the town, and there will be blood. I am here in the name of the Great Jehovah."

As the first grayness was showing, the Baltimore & Ohio train began to pull up very slowly to the bridge entrance. At three o'clock Old Brown had sent word to the conductor by a Negro that the train might proceed; but Phelps would not trust the word; surely the arches or timbers were cut. The old man left the armory now and walked out on the trestle with Phelps to reassure him. The train drew across, took on speed, soon was lost wailing in the swell of the hills, in the direction of Monocacy. (Bend low over the keys, operator, tap tap frantic tap to Buchanan, to Lee, to Governor, tapping drawing the net tighter ever tighter!) Meanwhile Boerly the grocer stepped from his doorway a little beyond the arsenal to see what the unusual early noises were about, the church bells ringing so strangely, a train whistling through the town at such an hour. Boerly was broad and red-faced, he was the town's wit, the jolly-man. He could take two ends of a cider cask in his huge hands and hoist it up on the counter to be bunged, and he and his childless "old lady" would drink more of it than they sold. Now, in his blue cotton shirt, his face shining red with a fresh cold wash, he stepped out into the street, into the autumn air, the brisk living day. Three steps from the door a bullet ploughed his brain. He fell with his head twisted in the gutter, his bare white feet sticking up grotesquely above the walk, the blood oozing down the red shining cheek. Dauphin Thompson, white as the mists rising in the wooded heights, stared aghast; the smoking carbine quivered in his nerveless hands. His young vision had not connected the vague beautiful idea of Liberty with men stiffening in the streets.

Kagi, holding the rifleworks with Copeland and Leary, saw the train pull across the bridge, and smiled calm and bitter. The old fool, he thought, why did he let it pass. The news will spread hours before we want it to. We could have held these farmers off indefinitely, but this will mean the troops. Kagi felt the imploring harassed eyes of yellow Leary upon him, the proud fine eyes of Copeland the Oberlin student, and the same question was in each pair, what now, what now? Poor devils, thought Kagi, this does mean everything for you, this does mean your hope, your life. Instantly he took out a small note-book and pencil from his pocket:

"Get back over Maryland bridge to hills. Why do you linger? Your purpose accomplished, terror struck through country and blacks roused. Trapped here if stay. Kagi."

In the armory yard too the men were wondering, apprehensive. For a short time they had been stirred to vast hope, flushed with the incredible success of the plan. Everything had gone like clock-work, all the vital points were theirs: the Potomac bridge was under guard, Kagi held the rifleworks, Hazlett and Osborn Perry the arsenal, they themselves the armory. They had hostages. But now a fear began to grip them. Where were the hordes of slaves, where was Owen leading down thousands to their aid? From time to time they turned their heads from the gate to look back at the old man. They felt the golden minutes slipping; but he gave them no sign, only stood there with that cold-frenzied face. He seemed to be waiting, possessed of some deep invincible secret, and somehow, seeing him thus, blindly they had faith—save one. Look, thought Stewart Taylor, he is paralyzed, he does not know what to do now. He has thought nothing out further than this. He has the town, but what he shall do with it he does not know. Every minute of delay rouses the country more, and still we stand here guarding a yard. Kill, burn, escape, advance, die, only do something that will achieve a positive end. But no, behold God and one man overturning the universe!

Now Old Brown was portioning out to the prisoners the coffee and biscuits which he had ordered brought in from the Wager House (he would himself take nothing nor would he give his men any for fear the food had been poisoned). Now he was opening the gate to allow young Reason Cross to return home for a moment under guard. "My aunt will be frantic with worry," pleaded the lame boy with the long patrician face. "I have been out all night. She will think I am killed. She is very ill. I'll come back." Or Old Brown would be talking courteously to the huddled prisoners: "I think after a while, possibly, I shall be enabled to release you, but only on the condition of getting your friends to send in a stout Negro as a ransom, as a new member of the army of the Lord."

And Stewart Taylor beheld God and one man overturning the universe.

The sun rose up over the Bolivar Heights. The sun ran blazing cold golden down the stained autumn hills into the Ferry streets. The dawn swiftly sharply brightened blue, the Potomac caught rays, the Shenandoah, and there was a gleaming over the pure morning waters; but death in the town, panic in the town, and the Lutheran bell tolling, tolling. For years patrols had ridden and men had watched the night-roads; now the dreaded thing was upon them, slaves in revolt, slave-stealers murdering and pillaging. There must be thousands of the vengeful whites and blacks; only men with powerful numbers would dare to attack the slave border. And with the rise of the sun the whole populace was gathered upon the Bolivar hill, the women and young ones clustered in terror higher up, the townsmen running about, shouting, dazed. Some few had weapons, ancient flintlocks, axes, small rusty fowling-pieces. Starry, the young doctor, rode on his sorrel from group to stricken group, trying to calm them, to get them into some kind of organization. But far down the central street they could see a heap in the gutter, Boerly dead; they were doomed. In their apprehension they seemed not to observe the very slaves they dreaded shrinking in their midst, terror-struck equally with the masters.

"Tell Kagi, stand firm," the old man said, crumpling the paper in his hand. Stevens stood there, hesitating. "We could make it," he said, not meeting his leader's eyes, looking off to the gates. "We have the bridge."

"No."

"You owe the men a chance. We'll be hemmed in. There's no sight of Owen and the slaves."

"The slaves will come."

"Kagi's in danger."

"Yes. I know."

"Kagi's exposed, he's isolated."

"Tell Kagi, stand firm."

Stevens' hand came up in a half-salute. (He had once been in the Army, a soldier in the Mexican war under Taylor; had been tried for "mutiny, engaging in a drunken riot and assaulting Major Blake of First United States Dragoons"; he had escaped into Kansas.) Now his eyes gleamed with a proud fatal look as he strode quickly to the gates. Stand firm, throbbed in the old man's mind, the slaves will come, the slaves will come. Not back, we must not go back. It will mean the ruin of my plan, we will be at the beginning again. And I am old, it is the last of my strength. His eyes fastened hungrily upon the bridge entrance. They must come, the labor of his life hung on it. We will move into Africa, he thought fiercely, or we will die here. Let Kagi call, let Stevens plead, have we not sworn to a sacrifice? No, not back. Ahead, southward, down into the great Black Way, or let us die here.

Now among the townsmen the first paralyzing consternation was over; they saw that they had vastly overrated the number of the raiders, that the little band in the yard was receiving no reinforcement, that the separated detachments could be harassed and cut off. A boy came running up excited: he had discovered that one of the end workshops beyond the confines of the yard was open; it was filled with guns that had been placed there for protection against possible freshets at high water. There was a rush for the shop. Soon men were sniping from the houses nearby, and the rocks and trees of the lower hill. By ten o'clock a steady point-blank fire was being directed upon the armory and the yard. The bullets splintered and spattered about the prisoners shrinking in the flimsy watch-house.

A handkerchief on a rifle showed in the yard, a flag of truce. Joseph Brua, one of the hostages, slipped through the gates. In a silence, he called up, pleading: "For God's sake, stop shooting! You endanger the lives of your friends! The captain offers you a truce! Leave the armory in his possession and let the firing stop on both sides!" Brua ran back, the gates opened, he slipped in. Immediately the shooting began anew, heavier. Old Brown was fighting for time; but his parley had only succeeded in convincing the townsmen that the raiders were on the defensive. Soon the "miners" were being attacked at each point. A dozen men crossed the Potomac a short distance above the Ferry, sneaked down the tow-path of the canal and concealed themselves in the brush above the bridge entrance. Oliver Brown, Newby and Will Thompson were exposed on the trestle to a cunning, almost unanswerable fire. Another party crossed the Shenandoah and took a sheltered position opposite Kagi at the rifleworks. Hazlett and the consumptive Osborn Perry, across the street from the yard, alone had a fighting chance; they had the arsenal building at their backs, and then the Shenandoah.

It was a question of time. On one side the Jefferson Guards, speeding by train, the Shepherdstown troop, the Winchesters, the Hamtramck battalion, Lee, Stuart, the Marines; on the other an old man staring at the bridge entrance: they will come, they will come!

CHAPTER IV

The Deaths

IT WAS noon. The machinists, the workers of the arsenal would have been leaving the buildings; some to sit in the yard with their lunch boxes, out in the warming sun; others to walk home through the quiet streets for a hot meal. But now above the desultory cracking of the rifles a sudden murderous fusillade blazed in the direction of the bridge, then a great mingled sound rose, the running tramp of many feet, voices shouting. Old Brown leaped for the gate, his eyes taking on a wild life. At last! At last! The slaves were coming, Owen was leading down the slaves! Then even as the thought formed exultant, a man came running from the trestle entrance, two followed hard behind—Will, Newby, Oliver. They were fleeing toward the armory. The slaves had not come. The Jefferson Guards had come. A blackness crushed down upon the old man's heart. But swiftly he flung the gate open, calling with fierceness: "Cover them up!" and strode into the street. The raiders followed to a man, forming a desperate deadly line. The Jefferson Guards came in a ragged rush. The little band held. The old man cried "Let go on them!" There was a volley; the attackers halted, then scattered hastily, toward the Wager House. The guns behind had been silent, as if the townsmen were merely witness to the drama of the maneuver. But now as the detachment of three came panting up to the gates a sniper hidden in a house at the foot of the heights took quick savage aim; fired. Halfway up the street Newby staggered, Dangerfield Newby dropped with a ball through the arteries of his throat, instantly dead. Slave woman, slave mother of seven slave children, do not write again of Newby's babe "just commenced to crawl"; do not beg: "buy us soon, for if you don't get me somebody else will." Bow your head in the fields, in the darkness by the cabin croon your darkened heart out: "Oh dear Dangerfield, come this fall without fail, money or no money I want to see you so much, that is one bright hope I have before me."

The other half of the Charlestown men had meanwhile come down from Bolivar Heights and occupied the saloon on the Shenandoah side. A detachment had swarmed into the houses between the hill and the arsenal, from which they were sending a direct fire into the yard. Tighter tighter the net. Now there was no way of retreat into Maryland, no means of communication with the Kennedy farm, they were cut off from Kagi at the rifleworks, from Hazlett and Osborn Perry in the arsenal.

"Oliver. Was there no sign of your brother?"

"There was no sign."

The men heard, and the last hope died on their faces. Leeman's eyes desperately sought the rear gate. He was the youngest, only eighteen. But the Potomac lay there, a full half-mile across; a man swimming could never make it, he would be riddled by a hundred guns. Leeman's eyes hungered upon the river. He was the youngest. They were all so young, they might have been boys in a college—Dauphin twenty-one, Edwin Coppoc twenty-four, Barclay twenty, Hazlett twenty-two, Tidd twenty-five, so young Watson, Merriam, Copeland, Cook, Stewart Taylor twenty-two, Will Thompson twenty-six, Oliver twenty, oh so young and doom in their hearts, there was no sign of Owen.

And the old man with the flowing white beard and the sunken terrible eyes stood there, shooting, ordering, brooding defiantly: it was not over, he was not beaten. Time, only time, and they would yet come through; flaming in his mind was the thought of Owen. Aye, no surrender, the protection of night would surely bring them in; even now they must be lying on Maryland Heights, waiting for the darkness. Hold on, stand firm, this is the labor of my life. And the hostages, he thought, he still had them as an overpowering threat. Long ago a concerted attack could have wiped out his band, but in such a charge the prisoners would also go down, and these Southerners would never sacrifice their kindred. He, John Brown, would not hesitate thus; let there be a true just reason and he would offer up every life. But these men would not; and now John Brown went into the watch-house. He surveyed the forty-odd prisoners. "I want you, sir," he said, pointing at Lewis Washington. "Come, Mr. Brua. And you, sir. . . . And you. . . ." Eleven of them, the most prominent, were taken from the watch-room and crowded into the back part of the small engine-house. Then the old man ordered in the slaves he had armed, and posted the remnant of his men close about. The engine-house would be their last refuge. That, and the hostages.

"Gentlemen, you are the most influential." With stiff dignity he addressed the chosen prisoners, with solemnity as in a speech. "I have only to say now that you will share the same fate that your friends extend to my men."

The Shepherdstown troop was in, the Hamtramck Guards, three companies from Martinsburg; a thousand surrounded the town. But the struggle was not alone against the desperate odds of men. Time. Time. "Will Thompson!" called the old man.

Agatha Thompson's boy came up.

≡ * 279 * ≡

"Take the lame fellow with you into the street. Keep him ahead of you. Treat with them for a stop to the firing."

A moment later Will Thompson was a prisoner in the Wager House.

Time, time, night will bring them in, beat in the old man's head. "Stevens! Watson Brown!" The two came up, waited. "Put a handkerchief on your gun. Take Mr. Kitzmiller with you and negotiate so that we may leave the yard."

"Captain Brown," said Stevens. "You saw what happened to Thompson."

"You have my orders."

"Damn your——! Why don't you run things so we'll have a chance? . . . You have the prisoners! Put a bullet in one, throw him out of the gate! Send a nigger to say we'll kill 'em all if we can't get clear!"

"You have my orders. We will injure no unarmed men."

Stevens glared at Watson. The boy stood blanched, his eyes pleading: I have Bell, I want to live, the babe's just born. But no, there was the face like granite, unrelenting: let the grand reason that one course is right and another wrong be kept continually before your mind. The boy turned his face, hopeless, undone, toward the street, toward his fate. And into the black-bearded man's eyes again came the fiercely proud fatal look. His hand rose sharp in the habitual half-salute, and the man who once in the far West had been imprisoned for insubordination under a commuted sentence of death, now strode to the engine-house door.

"Kitzmiller!"

The two raiders and the prisoner walked slowly across the yard. Stevens was waving his rifle high; it was topped with a white handkerchief. The firing ceased, save at a distance where Kagi was trapped. Watson Brown opened the gate entrance. Kitzmiller went first, shrinking with fear. The three began to walk slowly up the street, toward the Wager House. Ten feet. Fifteen, the surrounding stillness deep. Twenty. Twenty-five, a rolling whining volley, rifles recoiling in the upper windows of the saloon. Stevens slumped, the white handkerchief dropping, slugs in his side and breast. Watson plunged to his knees, face agonized, his hand clutching his belly. Kitzmiller was clumping frantically toward the hotel. Watson Brown got to one knee.

Again the intense silence, with a devil's tattoo faint down the rifleworks. Watson Brown began to drag himself back up the street, dropping, writhing, rising, moaning, a hundred shamed staring eyes riveted. Watson Brown reached the gate, suddenly there was another rattle of firing, poured in from the hillside. But not at Watson. Leeman the imp-eyed was taking his chance for life.

He had seen his two comrades shot down. He went icy trembling cold, then like a madness the blood rushed in his head. Suddenly, swift as a hound he whipped for the rear gate. He sprang clawing, slipping, then fell back. The volley rattled, he sprang again, held, pulled up, leaped the seven-foot gate. He darted along the river edge. It ceased, it turned down sharp to the water. Leeman stood quivering still, his eyes moving like a cornered weasel's. The rifles were finding the range, bullets were crumbling the shale at his feet. Leeman slid down the bank to the water's edge. He pulled out his bowie, slashed at the accoutrements, the cartridge belt, the rifle-sling, flung his two revolvers away, tore off his boots; and ran into the river. He waded furiously a dozen steps, he cast himself upon the waters and began to swim. All about him the bullets were flicking up white jets. He made for the cover of a tiny green-rock islet fifty yards out. Now the militiamen were down to the water, now ten of them were wading out. Leeman draggled up on the islet, a bullet smashed his shoulder. He lay there, panting, at bay, watching the men wade closer closer through the shallows with guns uplifted. Leeman threw up his arms, gasped, "Don't shoot! I surrender!" But they came on, one eagerly savagely in the lead, bearing his rifle high. An instant later Billy Leeman was dead, half his head blown away. All afternoon the boy's body lying on the edge of the rock, hands dangling in the water, blood staining the water, would be a target for hundreds of marksmen. Later it would slide down somehow and float in slow ghastly eddies toward the bridge.

Joseph Brua said, "I will go." He walked past the old man, crossed the yard. As he went without fear down the street toward Stevens sprawled in the gutter, a shot flicked the walk. But it was the only one; he was recognized. Brua lifted huge Stevens to his back. He sagged under the burden, moving in a zig-zag toward the Wager House. He went up the steps, went in. He came out alone and walked back toward the yard. He took his place again among the prisoners in the engine-house.

"A doctor is looking after him," he said.

"Thank you, sir," said old Brown.

But Brua's act was like a briefest gleam in a mad black chaos—snuffed out by the beating drowning lust. Gentle old Fontaine Beckham, Mayor of the Ferry and chief agent for the railroad, nervously ventured out on the trestlework, despite warnings. His heart was sickened, oh this violence in his streets, poor dead Shephard Hayward his helper. He must do something. Maybe he could reason with these outlaws, stop the bloodshed.

Edwin Coppoc, crouching in the doorway of the engine-house, saw a man sneak behind the water tank near the bridge. The young Quaker levelled his rifle; you murderers, you filthy murderers, he cried inside himself, thinking of Watson Brown all torn in the engine-house. The man showed his head. Coppoc fired, missed. Behind him, Alstadt the slave-owner cried, "It's Beckham, it's old Mayor Beckham! Don't fire!" Young Terence Burns laughed hysterically, "For God's sake, don't fire!" Coppoc fired, the dark wings again brushed the little town, and Fontaine Beckham crumpled upon the timbers. *Peace, Quaker, peace, thou shalt not kill.* And in Will Book No. 16 page 142 Jefferson Court Records, Charlestown, a recent entry showed that Fontaine Beckham (he was the greatest friend of the black man in all the county) had provided for the liberation upon his death of one Isaac Gilbert, Negro, his slave-wife and three children. The Quaker boy's shot had liberated them.

The two men ran toward the Wager House, Chambers the saloon-keeper, and young Harry Hunter. "The bitches, the god-damned bitches!" Hunter was crying. "They murdered my uncle!" The two men rushed up the steps of the Hotel, burst savagely into the room where Will Thompson was being guarded. In another moment they were dragging him out by the throat. They headed for the trestle where Beckham had fallen, and the crowd mad for revenge followed howling. "I don't care!" Will Thompson kept crying blindly as they dragged him; "kill me, I don't care! Eighty million will rise up to free the slaves! I don't care!" Hunter and Chambers placed their revolvers against

Thompson's head. "Die, you bastard!" They fired, he twisted crazily, before he fell a dozen balls had ploughed his young body. They threw him through the opening in the trestle; he dropped forty feet to the river rocks. All day Will Thompson's carcass would be riddled, his white face ghastly with agony of death staring up.

And you, Kagi, look out! They're creeping up, they're closing in on you! Oh Kagi, quick, breathe in the last sweet shining air, oh drink the sun with your eyes! Bullets bullets close about thick as a tomb thick fatal shutting out light. Back, Kagi, back, Copeland and Leary, climb hard, desperate up on the Winchester tracks. Leap down, splash gasp swish into the ice of the waters Shenandoah. Storm of lead behind, Virginia guns opposite in a blazing wall of hate. Turn desperate, not back, not forward, turn with the downflow, east as the river flows to the sea, labor, wrench, the flat rock juts. Scream, Leary, flail screaming the stained waters, own no more the workin' place an' the honey-bab just born, cough gurge blood, nevermore be back befo' the summer turns. Oh Kagi, here it is, cease wondering, now you know the last darkness. Sink easily, move with the waters moving seaward, flow deep to the peace of the dark shining Sea the Father ancient before earth. Tremble, Copeland, alone alive. Be dragged back, a nigger living is sport. Knot the white handkerchiefs, townsmen tie them tight, lynch lynch nigger Copeland the student of Oberlin.

Now the rifleworks are empty. Now they are silent.

 CHAPTER V

Night

NIGHT IS down. They are hemmed in at the armory. The men from Martinsburg, trainmen chiefly, charged into the yard at dusk, many falling, and the raiders are hemmed in the engine-house. It will be their last stand. Night is down. There is no shooting. The militia are picketing the engine-house; their work is done, soon the Marines will be in, the majesty the power of Government. A thousand men surround the tiny stone-building. Inside are eleven prisoners, four trembling slaves, one dead boy, two dying boys, five living raiders—Edwin Coppoc, Jeremiah Anderson, Dauphin Thompson, Emperor Green, and the Commander-in-Chief of the "Provisional Army," John Brown. Loopholes have been knocked in the stone wall. The five men stand there, waiting in the obscurity, their rifles to hand.

The moon besieged between Saturn and Mars . . . the Lord of the First in a streaming Sign or infested of the Malevolents, and the depositer of the Light of Time being also in a violent Sign and afflicted. . . .

Stewart Taylor lies dead in the engine-house.

On the brick floor close by the Canadian, Oliver Brown is moaning, bleeding his life away.

Watson Brown lies breathing quietly, deeper deeper into the gathering Darkness.

A message comes in, under cover of truce: Surrender. The painful peasant hand writes:

"Captain John Brown answers—In consideration of all my men, whether living, or dead, or wounded, being soon safely in and delivered up to me at this point with all their arms and ammunition, we will then take our prisoners and cross the Potomac bridge, a little beyond which we will set them at liberty; after which we can negotiate about the Government property as may be best. Also we require the delivery of our horse and wagon at the hotel. John Brown."

We are lost, the old man thought. The words of the fat little slave beat sickeningly incredibly in his head. "Get to the wall with a gun," he had ordered them. Then the answer came, "No, mebbe we kill massa." They had cringed back with the prisoners. And as upon a black night a sudden piercing jag of lightning reveals to a traveller the ruin of a wasteland ahead, so did the old man glimpse a ruin. In his mind he staggered, in his mind he bent his head, stricken. Woe is mine, oh sackcloth, oh ashes! This then was the bottomless sand he had builded his hope upon!

These were the blind creatures for whom peace, family, life, had been lost!

Then the demand came: Surrender. And at the word his fibre stiffened, a vast scorn rose in his heart. They would not fight for their own liberty? Then still would he free them, or failing that, show them how free men could die for faith.

"Captain John Brown answers: In consideration of . . . ."

And when it was written and handed out the faint small voice that would not perish sounded in his brain again: Owen! Owen!

The torch flared in the yard, outlining a form. "Approach!" the old man called back. The man came close slowly. Old Brown opened the door a hand's breadth; he held the sword of Frederick. The other raiders with cocked carbines stared out into the darkness; they were ready for trickery.

"What do you want?"

"I want to speak to you under a truce. Let me in. It is for your own good."

The door opened a little wider. The man slipped through, bearing the torch. The doors shut.

"I am Sinn. Captain Sinn of the Fredericksburg company."

"Well, sir?"

The militiaman looked about the engine-house, saw the exhausted prisoners, the slaves, the prostrate boys, the four raiders by the loop-holes. God, what madness, he thought.

"Surrender," he said. "You have no chance."

"You have my terms."

"There can be no terms."

"You shot my men down like dogs under a flag of truce. And I, I had full possession of the town, I could have massacred every soul, burned it to ashes. These prisoners, they are not scratched, I have given them every courtesy. And you say no terms."

"Men who take up arms as outlaws must expect to be shot down like dogs."

"Sir, we knew what we would have to go through before coming here. I have weighed the responsibility. I will not shrink from it now."

"Sinn!" It was Brua. "For mercy's sake, let them leave! They've been punished enough. His two sons are dying here."

The militiaman said, "It can't be, Mr. Brua." He turned to

the old man again. "I wish to avoid danger to these citizens. I wish to save your men from further bloodshed. I beg you, surrender. I promise you protection from the crowds, a safe——"

"You have my terms. A free way to the mountains."

A groan came from Oliver Brown. Sinn looked down, watched the boy by the dim light of the torch; felt pity.

"You have no chance. For the last time, I beg you. Give in."

"We will die just here."

Sinn bowed, turned to the door. Old Brown opened it. Sinn looked back once again, his eyes lingered over the three forms lying on the brick floor. "I'll send in the company's doctor," he said; and went.

They stood there in the dark, in the silence, waiting, waiting.

"Father."

The old man went to the bearded boy.

"Father. I'm dying."

"The surgeon is coming. Have courage, Watson."

"Oh, I mustn't die. But I'm dying."

"I would help you, my son, if I could."

The old man walked back, took his place by the loop-hole again.

The surgeon came. "Good evening," he said. The old man held the torch as the Southerner kneeled by Oliver.

"He is my son," the old man said.

"Tell them to kill me," Mary Brown's youngest boy whispered. "I can't stand it."

The other's hands were swift and tender about his torn breast.

"Tell them to kill me. They won't kill me."

The doctor rose. His eyes met Old Brown's. He moved to Watson's form; kneeled.

"He is my son too."

Quickly again the doctor rose, gathered his things together with finality. He went to the door.

"Will my sons live?" asked the old man.

"No" the lips formed. "They will not live." The old man handed the torch back to the doctor who stood there an instant, thinking: I will always remember this. Strange, tragic. Men killing, conversing with one another, aiding the wounded, then killing again. "I will try to come again in the morning," he said, "good night"; and went.

The old man stood once more in his place, holding the still watch. Now he trembled and his eyes were unseeing:

"O Lord God of truth, my rock and my fortress, have mercy upon me, for I am afflicted! Mine eye is consumed with grief, yea, my soul and my flesh! I trust in Thee, I say: Thou art my Lord. For this God is our God for ever and ever, He will be our guide even unto death."

And twelve miles off in the chill darkness, sick with fatigue and hopelessness, five men lay in fitful dreading sleep beneath the pines of the Maryland Heights. Tidd, Barclay Coppoc, Merriam, Cook—and Owen Brown.

About them was the great mountain night; no slaves, no single slave, only the grief-laden night.

All morning Cook and Tidd had been moving the guns down from the Kennedy farm to the little schoolhouse near the canal lock. It was the old man's order; they were to help Owen arm and organize the slaves, the schoolhouse was to be a second rallying-point, and when all was going well in the Ferry and the command came, the whole body of men and arms was to move down. Twenty slaves had been gathered during the night-hours to the farm and the schoolhouse; their masters had been led to the old man in the armory yard.

"Go home, children," Cook had said to the puzzled young ones as they came trooping up the road. "I shall have to hold you a prisoner, Mr. Currie. You see, there will be no school this morning." He went on to tell the astonished young teacher that this was a war for liberty, his school was to have the honor of housing for a while the arms of the liberating forces, all the slaves in the country would soon be freed, do you understand, young Mr. Currie? No, Mr. Currie did not understand, and as the two sat there and the handful of dazed Negroes stood with their pikes, the sound of rifles firing came faintly to them; and Currie pleaded:

"Mr. Cook, what does it really mean?"

"Just this," said Cook easily. "It means that your people are resisting our men, and we are taking the town by force."

And back at the farmhouse Owen Brown looked again and again at the black men huddled on the porch, and was swept by a great apprehension. Twelve. Twelve slaves. Christ, only twelve. Where were they, why weren't they coming in eager

≡ * 287 * ≡

burning hordes, like his father had said they would come? His fingers trembled upon the battered silver watch. Eight o'clock. . . . Nine. . . . Eleven-thirty. . . . He looked at the black men. Twelve. Only twelve. Why, the fellows must have the town by this time, the whole countryside must be roused! Where were they then, where were the slaves? And then suddenly in a staggering flash the words of a thin fierce young girl cut through his mind. Annie! he groaned within. Christ, Annie!

"You've come to a wrong place. House-niggers are treated too good. Up in Elba old Lem Cawley used to tell me about hisself bein' a slave. House-niggers won't fight to get freed, Lem said. They live easy, he said, and some even get to love their owners. Only hungry niggers, beat in the fields, 'll fight to get freed."

There was Tidd driving up again with the empty wagon. One-eyed Merriam and young Coppoc, breaking with the strain, ran down to meet him. Owen all fearful and fighting to beat down the rising inner panic, stood still, waited for Tidd to come up.

"Tidd," he said evenly. "What's happening?"

The ugly fellow jumped down heavily, growled, "Shootin'. Don't like it neither. I'm takin' one more load back, then Cook's goin' to go down and spy out."

"Tidd. Any more blacks in?"

"Blacks hell! There's still eight, and you kin see they're itchin' to run!"

"Why don't we do something," cried Merriam, his eye frantic.

"Shut up, Merriam. . . . Tidd. Listen, now. Don't you get shaky. The old man's always counted hard on you. You got to stand by him now, Tidd."

"All right, all right! But I tell you this, Brown! It's time long ago to be doin' one o' two things! Run ahead or run back'ards! Cook's going to spy out. Then we'll know which to do. Ahead or back'ards!"

Owen, all sickened, watched Tidd drive off with the loaded wagon. He would obey orders: stay at the farm, hand out arms, come when I give you the word. But now a longing rose in Owen to take a rifle and go running down the mountain road. The old man was fighting down there, his brothers were fighting down there. Obey orders. Obey orders. But the hours were passing. One o'clock. . . . Two-twenty. . . . Five of four. . . . Deep in him the conviction formed, growing: no word would come. Twelve slaves. Only twelve. Their plan had failed, they were lost. Well, then they were lost, he thought savagely. He knew what to do. He had done it in Kansas. He would take a rifle and go down. He would fight by the old man's side.

Cook went hard scrambling up the slope. The angry rattle of the rifles was filling the sharp air, rolling echoing between the hills. Cook climbed the great oak, his heart pounding to his throat. He looked down. The Ferry lay open to his sight; small; held in the flowing embrace of the two shining rivers; straggling up the russet carpet-slope behind. It lay there etched and bright in the cold autumn glow—the slender bridge, the station, the gleaming tracks, the neat armory buildings with their clipped plots. But there was more. Small dark figures moving swiftly in the streets. Puffs of smoke rising in a jagged line about a small gray building, smoke drifting up from its walls. Cook's eyes picked out a body of men clustered on High Street, a half-mile off. They were pouring a fire in upon the engine-house. He cursed savagely, a blind pitiful impulse raised his rifle; he would draw their fire upon himself. He sighted; shot. Again, again. Again. He was seen. An answering volley splintered up against the oak. Again the dark fellow sighted. Again a dozen balls thudded about him, his slender supporting limb was cut, he fell crashing fifteen feet to the rocks of the incline below. He lay there stunned. Then groaning he rose, his face and legs lacerated, an intense pain tearing at his right shoulder. He was not wounded. He hobbled down the road; began to run painfully in the direction of the schoolhouse. He overtook a young boy who was just slipping in from the Ferry. "Hullo, Mr. Cook!" the MacDonald boy called in excitement. "Ha' ye seen what's happenin' at town?" No, Hugh, what was happening at the Ferry?

Then, in the dark before the porch, they stood about Cook, staring at him as he spoke the end of their wild dream: ". . . the engine-house. . . . Only seven left. . . . The rest are killed."

Owen took his rifle. "I'm going down," he said.

"You're mad!" cried Cook. "We can't help! They're gone!"

"Your brother's down there," said Owen to young Coppoc. "Coming?"

The Quaker boy stood trembling.

"Owen," said Cook. "He's dead. Your old man's dead. There's no use going."

≡ * 289 * ≡

Now, miles off in the darkness of the Delaware mountains, the five fugitives lay down on the cold earth to snatch a broken desolate sleep. Hours ago the last freed slave had slunk off through the timber back to the home of his master.

In the engine-house the raiders kept the vigil. "I will come again in the morning," the doctor had said. But he would not come, they knew it; their fate would come, storming the hold at dawn. It was bitterly cold, a chill as of death lay about the stone floors and walls. The outside night, cloudy, moonless, crept through the loop-holes, deepening the blackness within. The drunken shouts of the militiamen had ceased. They were resting from the heat of the day's valor; Dangerfield Newby's ears had been sliced from his head, the brutal indignities to his cold stiff body had been tired of; the poor white wretches from Loudon Heights had scavenged the dead; the riddled hulk of Will Thompson down in the trestle rocks was this hour being granted its first ghastly peace. A new sound was in the silence, the slow disciplined tread of the Marine guard, cordon about the engine-house. "Rest," said the old man; "we have till morning"; and the prisoners and the Negroes and the raiders lay unsleeping side by side on the stone floor. He was still at his place by the door, now forty hours without food, without sleep; calling from time to time in the stillness of the night: "Men, are you awake?" And always there was the moaning of the dying boys.

"Father!"

"I am here, Oliver."

"I can't stand it! Shoot me!"

"No, Oliver. Have patience."

"Please! please! Oh, Martha would do it for me!"

"No, my son. I think you will yet get well."

Then later in the grievous black silence: "Father!"

"If you must die, die like a man does."

And golden Dolph Thompson, his hair matted with grime and blood, sat by the side of Watson; held the carbine in one hand, with the other stroked the head of his sister's young husband; rocked, heartbroken, Oh Wat, Wat, as the doomed boy sobbed with anguish; and the words which Brua had spoken earlier mingled with his present grief for a single throbbing horror.

"You are committing treason," Brua had said; "treason against your government."

Dolph Thompson had stared. "No, that isn't true! Captain Brown! Is it true that we are committing treason against our government?"

"Yes, I think it is, Dauphin. I think it is true."

"Then I won't fight more! I came to free slaves! I won't fight more, I won't commit treason!"

But the old man was at a distance, in this desperate lost moment he was far in the dream which his life had been. Yes, gentlemen, ran in his mind, ran so incalculably that he would never know whether it was speech or thought, if you realized my past history, if you knew my heart, you would not blame me for being here. I went to Kansas and the pro-slavery people from Kentucky and Virginia hunted me down like a wild animal. I lost one of my sons there. Yes, gentlemen, we are Abolitionists from the North, we've come to take and release your slaves. Our organization is large, and must succeed. I suffered much in Kansas. I expect to suffer here, in the cause of human freedom. I have been well known as Old Brown of Kansas. I shed blood on Potawatomie. Slaveholders I regard as robbers and murderers, and I have sworn to abolish slavery and liberate my fellow men. And now I am here. . . . I have failed. . . . Two of my sons were killed here today.

"Oliver!" the old man called in the gloom.

No answer. Silence.

"I guess he's dead," Old Brown said.

CHAPTER VI

Dawn

WHITE RAVELLING mists drift down the morning hills. The rivers are gray and still. A vast murmur is rising from the thousands massed on the Loudon slope, the Bolivar heights, the railroad platform, the streets, the windows of houses. The Marines in their dark blue tunics, in their pale blue trousers and white belts, are deployed about the engine-house, fifty paces off. A little ahead two files stand, waiting, twelve to a file, facing the stronghold's front. The first twelve are holding sledges, the second fixed bayonets; there will be no shooting, the hostages must come out unharmed. Israel Green, Lieutenant U.S.M.C., will lead them. He is wearing a light dress-sword, hastily snatched up at the barracks; a light dress-sword (he does not dream what this will mean). Lieutenant-Colonel Lee, whitened, straight, gentle, is on a horse beneath a tree; he is in citizen clothes. Young Stuart, his aide, stands by, Jeb Stuart, cavalry-man, tall, robust, with a nut-brown flowing beard and wide moustaches. He is wearing a feathered hat. His order is: present the demand; no parleying, yes or no; if it is refusal, wave the hat. The Marines stand erect; the tumult of yesterday is gone; everything is precise, disciplined; a business is at hand.

Inside the stone house five men are waiting at the loop-holes. They have arranged their carbines and pistols; they have barricaded the double iron-bound doors of oak with the rusting fire-engine; the hose-cart is hard against the stone abutment between.

"Take more care to end life well than to live long."

Now Lee glances at his heavy gold watch. It is half-past six. He looks about; everything is ready. He hands the white sheet to Jeb Stuart. Stuart salutes sharply. The great hum fades, a silence is fast upon the town, upon the hills. Three thousand eyes watch the bearded plumed officer move in a long hard stride toward the stone house. He halts before the door on the right; calls. The door is pulled open a little. A flinty bent old fellow with a low brow and a long white beard stands blocking the crack with his body and a cocked carbine. His bluish blazing eyes cut like a gimlet into the younger's staunch fresh paler blue. They hold, gauge metal; a recognition wells into each, their minds in that deep instant o'erleap the instant; they are in Kansas.

"You are Osawatomie Brown. We had you prisoner once."

"Yes. But you could not keep me."

Stuart hands the paper to Osawatomie Brown. Slowly, deliberately, as though it were a lading bill of his far merchant days, the old man reads:

"HEADQUARTERS, HARPER'S FERRY.
October 18, 1859.

"Colonel Lee, United States Army, commanding the troops sent by the President of the United States to suppress the insurrection at this place, demands the surrender of the persons in the armory buildings.

"If they will peaceably surrender themselves and restore the pillaged property, they shall be kept in safety to await the orders of the President. Colonel Lee represents to them, in all frankness, that it is impossible for them to escape; that the armory is surrounded on all sides by troops; and that if he is compelled to take them by force he cannot answer for their safety.

R. E. Lee.
Colonel Commanding United States Troops."

"No. I prefer to die just here."

Instantly Jeb Stuart wheels back from the door. His hand goes up, the feathered hat flashes once, twice. And now the Marines come on the run, the first line hard, swaying with the sledges, the second, the bayoneteers, at a slower double. "Calm, men," the old man is calling. "Sell your life dear, sell it dear." The rush comes on, the inside carbines crack; the sledges begin to thunder upon the timbers. The powder smoke is seeping through the clefts, the prisoners and the Negroes huddle back against the wall. The sledges beat, thunder, unavailing. The raiders fire, load, fire blindly in the smoke and the din, the doors swaying. Then swift and sudden a silence; and young Dolph Thompson cries, "Captain Brown, I'm going to surrender!" The old man stands waiting, he will die just here; Emperor Green's eyes burn dark and desperate white. Brua shouts in the instant's quiet, "One surrenders! one surrenders!" but the instant is gone with a terrific crash. The doors buckle, splinter. The raiders fire, fire. Outside they are battering with a heavy ladder. Crash! crash! the right hand timbers rip in and upward, the opening is made. Israel Green plunges through low into the dense smoke, dress-blade in hand. He rises, miraculously untouched, and doubles around the engine. The old man is at a kneel, the white beard falling away from his face, he is pulling the carbine lever to reload; he has brought down the first two Marines to follow Green, Luke Quin is dead with a hole through his belly, the second is shot through the jaw. "That is Osawa-

≡ * 293 * ≡

tomie," says Lewis Washington to Israel Green, stepping forward calmly. Green springs at the kneeling old man, who looks up like a hawk toward the danger. Green lunges fiercely, giving an underthrust of the blade midway the other's body. The old man rises, falls to his knees. Green slashes and the bite is deep in the neck at the skull's base. Again the lunge and the light blade bends double on a chest bone. Green grips the weapon by the middle, now is smashing the hilt down, once, again, thrice, savage as though to reach the skull. The old man slides down, is still. And the Marines have come in like tigers over their fallen comrades. Jeremiah Anderson is bayoneted dead against the engine. Dauphin Thompson is pinned against the rear wall, pierced by steel clean to the heart. "Hold!" Israel Green is shouting. "Hold!" The assault is over. The war into Africa is done.

O   to Struggle!

THE
FIFTH PART

"O to struggle against great odds
To meet enemies undaunted
To be entirely alone with them
To find out how much one can stand!"
WALT WHITMAN.

CHAPTER I

The Talons

"ARE YOU Captain John Brown of Kansas?"

"I am sometimes called so."

"Are you Osawatomie Brown?"

"I tried to do my duty there."

The dead and wounded had been carried out and laid on the neat clipped armory-lawn. An immense cry went up: hang them! But the Marines were formed in a line bristling with bayonets; the crowds were held off. Lewis Washington had fastidiously drawn on his gloves over his unwashed hands and paid his respects to Lieutenant-Colonel Lee. Old Brown had been carried bleeding and insensible to the paymaster's office.

Now it was the afternoon; he lay on a pallet, his hair and beard clotted, his face all smeared with powder and blood. Stevens lay by the side of his leader; flat on his back, with his hands folded upon his breast; very still and white; his eyes were closed. A group of men stood above the two prisoners, looked down with cold curious hostility; men of the Virginia Commonwealth —Governor Wise, Senator Mason, Congressman Faulkner, Andrew Hunter, State's Attorney; and Senator Vallandigham of Ohio. A little withdrawn were Lee, Jeb Stuart, and a Doctor Biggs. Two reporters were hastily writing. The old man's eyes glittered up fiercely at his questioners; he was like a broken-winged hawk lying on its back, with talons curved for further fight.

"Mr. Brown, who sent you here?"

"No man sent me here. It was my own prompting and that of my Maker—or that of the devil, whichever you please to ascribe it to. I acknowledge no master in human form."

"What was your object in coming?"

"We came to free slaves."

"How many men did you have?"

"I came to Virginia with twenty-one men."

"What in the world did you think you could do in this state with only twenty-one men?"

"Sir, perhaps your ideas and mine on military subjects would differ materially."

Lee had been whispering to the doctor; now he stepped forward, broke in: "Mr. Brown, if this questioning is difficult for you, I will exclude all visitors from the room."

"Not at all. I am glad to make my motives clearly understood. . . . I am here a prisoner and wounded because I foolishly allowed myself to be so. You overrate your strength, gentlemen, in supposing I could have been taken if I had not allowed it. It is by my own folly I have been taken. I had the means to make myself secure. I could have gone away, but I had thirty odd prisoners whose women were in tears for their safety, and I felt for them. Besides I wanted to allay the fears of those who believed we came here to burn and kill. For that reason I allowed the train to cross the bridge. I did it to spare the feelings of those passengers and their families, and to allay the apprehensions that you had got here in your vicinity a band of men who had no regard for life and property."

"You killed unarmed citizens passing in the streets."

"Sir, if there was anything of that kind done, it was without my knowledge. Your citizens who were my prisoners will tell you that every possible means was taken to prevent it. I did not allow my men to fire when there was any danger of killing innocent persons, if I could help it. You, Major. . . ." The old man pointed at Jeb Stuart. "You entered first. I could have killed you, just as easy as I could kill a mosquito. But I spared you."

Jeb Stuart bowed. The old man said, "My son was killed carrying a truce." Governor Wise thought uneasily of the boy he had spoken to in the watch-house before coming here; the boy lying on a bench with a pair of overalls for a pillow; dying. "What is your name?" the Governor had asked.

"Watson Brown." He spoke gently, and the look in his eyes had touched the Southerner to the heart.

"Why are you here, my boy?" And then startlingly like the words of this old man the answer came: "Duty, sir."

The questioning went on in the paymaster's office, now one, now another directing it.

". . . but if you will tell us who provided money for your expedition, that would be information of some value."

"I cannot implicate others."

"How many were there engaged with you in this movement?"

≡ * 298 * ≡

"Any questions that I can honorably answer I will. Not otherwise. So far as I am myself concerned, I've told everything truthfully. I value my word, sir."

". . . and who was the secretary of your Provisional government?"

"That I would not tell if I recollected, but I don't recollect. I may answer incorrectly, but not intentionally. You see, my head is a little confused by wounds, and my memory is obscure on dates."

"Who lanced that woman's neck on the hill?" It was Doctor Biggs, curiously, hesitantly.

"I lanced it. I have sometimes practiced in surgery when I thought it a matter of humanity and necessity. But I haven't studied surgery."

"It was done very scientifically," Doctor Biggs said, turning to the others. ". . . They have been very clever with the neighbors, and we had no reason to suspect them, except that we could not understand their movements."

"I think, my friends," the old man said, "that you are guilty of a great wrong against God and humanity—I say it without wishing to be offensive—and they do right who interfere with you at any time and at all times."

"Oh! You consider this a religious movement?"

"It is, in my opinion, the greatest service man can render to God."

"Then you consider yourself an instrument in the hands of Providence?"

"I do so consider myself."

"All this bloodshed, then, this violence, how in heaven's name do you justify it?"

"Upon the Golden Rule, sir. I pity the poor in bondage that have none to help them. That's why I am here. Not to gratify any personal revenge or vindictive spirit. It's my sympathy with the oppressed and the wronged, that are as good as you and as precious in His sight. And I want you to understand, gentlemen"—here the old man raised himself a little—"I want you to understand that I respect the rights of the poorest and weakest of colored people oppressed by the slave system as much as I do those of the most wealthy and powerful. . . ."

"Mr. Brown," said the Governor sternly. He was angered by this calm strength, this bloody old man who weighed his words as if he were at home on his farm, righteously reproaching some uneasy rustic. Why, the man was speaking as if he were under no smallest conviction of guilt, entitled to all the respect of an honorable prisoner of war. Nettled, the Governor summoned his haughtiest, most crushing platform manner, and said: "Mr. Brown. The silver of your hair is reddened by the blood of crime. You should eschew these hard words and think upon eternity. You are suffering from wounds perhaps fatal, and should you escape death from these causes, you must submit to a trial which may involve death. Your confessions justify the presumption that you have committed a felony under the laws of Virginia. It is better therefore that you should turn your attention to your eternal future than be dealing in denunciations."

The answer came: "Sir, I have from all appearances not more than fifteen or twenty years the start of you in the journey to that eternity of which you so kindly warn me. Whether my time here shall be fifteen months, or fifteen days, or fifteen hours, I am equally prepared to go. There is an eternity behind and an eternity before. This little speck in the center, however long, is but comparatively a minute. The difference between your tenure and mine is trifling, and I therefore tell you to be prepared. You have a heavy responsibility. I am prepared."

They stared at him. He went on slowly: "Aye, let me say furthermore, that you had better, all you people at the South, prepare yourself for a settlement of that question. That must come up for settlement sooner than you are prepared for it. You may dispose of me very easily. I'm nearly disposed of now. But this question is still to be settled. This Negro question, I mean. The end of that is not yet."

So he lay to their sight, the hawk broken-winged, with talons curved for the last fight. But they did not see him as he lay hours later, weeping in the dead of night, a stricken bereft old man.

He had failed, the labor of his life was down in ashes. The great good for which he had agonized was now forever beyond his bleeding hands. They would hang him (oh that was nothing, come quick, come quick). But to go in emptiness, to go in the sorrow of this world's black deep sin! That was the death, he had effected no good. There would be no harvest, desolate would be the fields, the dark fields of ruin. Aye, he had offered up upon the altar tender flesh of the young, flesh of sweet savor, poured young blood for a sacrifice; and before his eyes it had turned to a shambles, and the unholy had bathed their fingers, they had devoured the offering made by fire unto God.

And the old man groaned, tossed upon the pallet in an anguish of defeat. Only Stevens, lying on his back in the darkness by his leader's side, still, hands folded, would ever fathom the deepness of the other's despair, the terrible moral bewilderment.

Some moments in the night's feverish procession a sense as of a dream would come upon the old man; such a dream as sharpens horror yet does not hold full sway, so that the dreamer thinks even as he yields: I need only will it and I am free. The black breathing terror of the engine-house, the growing knowledge of the slaves' failure, the assault, the cold triumph of the Virginians, the suffering of his two dead boys; all these mingled for a vast phantasmagoria; and the sense that it was only a dream which he could conquer at will came upon him. Then he stared wildly about the darkness, felt the silent presence of Stevens by his side and the rack of his wounds, heard the faint ribaldry of the drunken howling street-crowds; and the incredible truth was there again, piercing him.

Save me, oh God, for the dark waters are come into my soul! . . . Our soul is bowed down to the dust, yea, our belly cleaveth unto the earth. Lover and friends hast Thou put far from me, and mine acquaintance into darkness. Thou hast given us like sheep appointed for meat, and hast scattered us among the heathen. . . . Wherefore hidest Thou Thy face, my God my Father, and forgettest our affliction?

Yet our heart is not turned back. For Thou art my hope, Oh Lord God, Thou art my trust from my youth. By Thee have I been holden up from the womb, Thou art He that took me out of my mother's bowels. Then cast me not off in the time of old age, forsake me not when my strength faileth. For mine enemies speak against me, and they that lay wait for my soul take counsel together, they say: God hath forsaken him, persecute and take him, for there is none to deliver him. . . .

Oh God, be not far from me, make haste for my help. Oh spare me, that I may recover strength, before I go hence, and be no more.

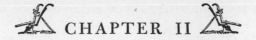

CHAPTER II

Friends and Enemies

THAT NIGHT Frederick Douglass was fleeing north to Canada. Before a week ended he would be on the seas; England would hold him safe. It was not the only flight. The Virginians had found an old carpet-bag at the Kennedy farm. Maps were in it, crude military plans, a Provisional Constitution—and hundreds of letters. Therefore turn tail, men in the north, Humanitarians. What does it matter that it was you who put money, pikes, rifles, into the old fellow's hands; you who said: we do not have much faith in your ideas, but we believe in John Brown, so tell us nothing of your plan, nor burden us with inconvenient knowledge; we want no report save by action (you see, we must consider our honor, and in this way we shall be technically innocent). Good heavens, your reputations are endangered, your very lives! You never dreamed that you could ever be so compromised in the eyes of the law by those secret dealings, "higher law" dealings of which you were so proud. But these are savage realities; this is treason, not petty slave-running in Missouri; this is a desperate drama which the whole nation will look upon. Suppose, you men of conscience, Governor Wise should stalk you, suppose the Commonwealth of Virginia should demand a requisition? Have you thought of that? No? Well, rush to your lawyers.

"Yes, you may suddenly and secretly be arrested and spirited away."

Do you see your danger now? Hurry, Sanborn, hurry to Canada; they can't touch a man there! Canada, Stearns! Follow them, Howe, destroy all your correspondence, go in a panic after Douglass, Sanborn, Stearns. And Gerrit Smith, kindly, weak, vaporous old man. For months your physician has suspected an impending breakdown. You have eaten and slept little, you have been exhausted without knowing it; the symptoms may well have been nervous exaltation, a first stage in insanity. Now you are reading the terrible reports in the newspapers, they will accuse you of treason to your country, it will be stark ruin. Therefore go mad, it is a proper time. Hide in the oblivion of the Utica asylum.

Canada. England. Utica. Safety. . . . But the small faint voice, will it not cease, will it give no rest? Beat it down then, casuistry will do wonders.

"I, Samuel Howe, hear that rumor has mingled my name with the event at Harper's Ferry. That event was unforeseen and unexpected by me; nor does all my previous knowledge of John Brown enable me to reconcile it with his characteristic prudence and his reluctance to shed blood or excite servile insurrection. It is still to me a mystery and a marvel. All my contributions have been given through a sympathy for the man and without cognizance of his purpose."

One would stand firm. Swarthy Higginson, the Worcester clergyman. (Theodore Parker was in Rome, burned out, pitifully seeking a brief stay to his days. Always he had been willing to perish with the using, to spend and be spent; and he would be dead before the year's end. He had never been afraid of men, could offend them because he cared nothing for their hate or esteem; now he would bear testimony, like the true one he was: Freedom is not bought with dust; Christianity cost something once, the Christianity of Christ. There are some statutes so wicked it is every man's duty to violate them. The American Republic is the child of rebellion, the national lullaby is "treason"; Hancock and Adams slept with a price on their heads. He, Theodore Parker, only regretted that he was not "at home again to use what poor remnant of power is left to me in defence of the true and the right.") The others had fled. Only Higginson would stand firm. Let him be brought to trial, to testimony; he would defend the old man before the country. Savagely he asked: is there no honor among confederates?

And that same night, while the old man lay crushed and Douglass the Negro had begun the exodus, Governor Wise and Andrew Hunter sat in a room of the Wager House. The candles on the table were guttering low above the black bag and the stack of letters. The two men were whispering, excited, bitter. Yes, an immediate trial. The tumult among the blacks and whites alike must be quieted. These men must go quickly to the gallows. They could do it, there was an old Virginia law: when an indictment is found against a person for felony, in a court wherein he may be tried, the accused, if in custody, shall, unless good cause be shown for a continuance, be arraigned and tried in the same term. The Grand Jury was now in session; already Judge Parker was presiding at Charlestown over the Circuit-Court. They would obey the law; else the traitors could not be tried till the next term, six months off; and for six months the state and the country would be in a huge ferment, the militia would have to be ceaselessly under arms. Yes, it was clear, they had the evidence, these men must go quickly to the gallows. They would observe all the judicial decencies—at double quick time.

Two nights later, in a cabin of a straggling town on the plains of Kansas, six men and a woman sat before a fire and talked in low stirred voices.

". . . an' get Montgomery."

"Pike Seamans'll come."

They were "jayhawkers," Free-State men. The woman was Mary Partridge. Her brother had died at Marais des Cygnes, fighting under a gray gaunt man in a linen duster.

". . . we got Doy free at St. Joseph."

"An' you can count on Silas Soulé."

They had him trapped in Virginia, the bastard slavers had old Osawatomie.

CHAPTER III

Thoreau Burns

FOR TWENTY years he had been letting newspapers go by, almost unnoticed. What should a living man have to do with gossip of the street, when the very morning and evening were full of news —the sun coming up, or tracks in the snow, or a lark disappearing behind a cloud. A ramble, with the senses vibrant and watching, told the true wealth of the day, not a column; a man attended best, not to the affairs of the market and the forum, but to the affairs in Massachusetts fields. Do not read the Times. Read the Eternities.

But for many days now Henry Thoreau had been devouring newspapers. He would not, for mere idle amusement, run round the corner to see the world blow up; but this was a convulsion which had magnificent character—an old fellow lay in the Charlestown jail. By Heaven, Thoreau exulted, he had actually done it, the land had at last bred a man! But it was not as simple as pure joy for Thoreau; a rage mingled with it and gripped his vitals. They were going to hang Old Brown. This act, this piece of absolute goodness, so rare that it was fit to leaven the whole foul inert lump which was the nation's guilt, was going to be rewarded by a gallows rope! They were calling it mad, the North was sending up a single vast cry, disavowal of John Brown. It was swelling from the press, running like burning grass before a wind, the whole gamut from nonresistant Abolitionists to the Republican politicians. Even Garrison had called it "misguided, wild, apparently insane." Insane! thought Thoreau; if he had gone with five thousand men, liberated a thousand slaves, killed a hundred slaveholders and had as many more killed on his own side, then these same editors would call it by a more respectable name. Fools, blind fools! Could they not see the sublimity? The mass of men were on a level with wood and stones; they served the state as machines, with no free exercise of the judgment or moral sense; commanded no more respect than lumps of dirt; yet they were esteemed good men. And here was one who served the state with his *conscience* and was scourged as an enemy by it! Because he had wisdom and would not leave right to the mercy of chance; nor, since there was but little virtue in the masses of men, wish it to prevail through the power of the majority; therefore they would crucify him. Ay, fools, cowards, did not any single man more right than his neighbors constitute already a majority of one?

Nothing in all his life had ever moved Thoreau so deeply. Other events past had sometimes disturbed his beautiful stoic calm; there had perhaps been some fallacy to expose, a blindness to pillory, some hypocrisy in the lives of his neighbors drawing his cold scorn; for, despite all his disdain of worldly matters, he had never been able to still the puritan conscience that owed instruction to the minds of men. But this burning at his vitals was more. It was friendship. What though he had seen that old man only a dozen hours altogether? He loved him, he loved the temper, the ideal. Perfect love did not need to admit the feeling of affection. To be true friends two persons needed to be something inhuman to each other; inhuman, like the elements, like rain and earth. So this furious storm-beaten old visionary was to him now; the principle for which he stood (oh beautiful madness!) made them brothers.

Thoreau did not know himself. The train of his thought would bear but a single burden. The very face of nature mourned. The blue mountain wall of Wachusset was ominous, it was a judge pronouncing a doom. That sunset, with the sky flaming full to the east and the soft clouds, rippled like sand, dripping light—there was no meaning of beauty in it. It faded down behind a dark gibbet. He stood by a pond and in agitation and sadness thought: what signifies the wonder of nature when men are base? We walk to lakes to see our serenity reflected in them; when we are not serene we go not to them. Two herons were flying northward, high up, silent in the last light before evening; Thoreau's bluish eyes followed the course of the birds as they faded out in the hushed sky. The eyes, as he went, lingered upon that giant oak, hued like a rose with the autumn death, scarlet against the dark evergreens. But if the unsleeping, the miraculously aware senses perceived, the mind was far withdrawn from the familiar mysteries of the solitude. So great a wrong as this coming fate implied overshadowed all loveliness in the world.

He went towards the village, striding furiously along the green cool of the pines, and through dark abandoned orchards; a little fellow, lean as a wolf, with a brown beard and an umbrella. Those great pockets of his, incredibly enough, were empty this nightfall. No little treasures—a handful of chestnuts, or a hawk-egg, not even a bit of moss or flint—were in them. And the inside of the old straw-hat was empty too, the herbarium wont to receive frail flowers and stems against crushing. Instead Thoreau bore within himself the inescapable image.

He walked through the still streets of the little village and was filled with a strange astonished rage that there should be peace here, that the old routine survived still. What, you sit by a table, and converse, you go about your affairs indifferent? Old Brown is on trial, do you hear? The arraignment began today, he will be hanged! What, you answer he deserves his fate, he was bloodthirsty, reckless of human life? Yankees, clay, stuff to stop a hole! Don't you know the man's a metal? You can only ask of the metals that they be tender to the fire that melts them! To naught else can they be tender!

Thoreau could not sleep. In the small hours of the morning he wrote down his thoughts of scorn and sorrow by the light of a lamp:

"Look not to legislatures and churches for your guidance, nor to any soulless incorporated bodies, but to *inspirited* or in spired ones."

He saw the old rebel lying on the arsenal floor, slashed, bleeding, calmly speaking in the midst of the inquisitors those miraculous words:

"No man sent me here. It was my own prompting and that of my Maker. I acknowledge no master in human form. . . ."

"I pity the poor in bondage that have none to help them. . . . It is my sympathy with the oppressed and the wronged that are as good as you, and as precious in the sight of God."

They did not know their testament when they saw it! And Thoreau felt rushing in him a current of new faith, like a re-newal—this man had appeared, the age could not be dead! Ay, nothing save the greatest verse could apply to the sacrifice of Old Brown! With hands quivering, beneath the lamp he swiftly, pas-sionately wrote:

"Only what is strong and true and solemnly earnest will recommend itself to our mood at this time. The sense of grand poetry, read by the light of this event, is brought out distinctly, like an invisible writing held to the fire."

But the crime against the State must be punished. The trial was on. There were the newspapers, coming daily to Concord; despised by Thoreau; yet devoured, so that every movement of the drama in the Virginia court-house was etched in his brain.

*   *   *   *   *

The crowds gape, jostle. A great excitement eddies in the open square, where only a week before boys and men with old guns, the Jefferson Guards, rushed into line. Suddenly the an-cient bell in the court-house dome clangs deep, jagged; instantly following and mingling unseen drums roll out upon the sharp autumn air. The great crowd-voice veers tenser, the heads are craning, every eye holds the door of the jail. It opens. Militiamen are beginning to file down the steps into the street. In column of twos they move raggedly up on either side of the short narrow path that leads to the court-house, a high building, pillared and venerable. They halt, face each other. The rear rank of each file swings to the right about. "Port arms!" The fixed bayonets gleam, a bristling avenue is formed. The crowds surge up close. From the ends of the square, cannon are trained upon the scene.

Now two men come out of the jail door, the county sheriff and Avis the keeper. Next, two armed guards. A hush, expectant, almost absolute, has fallen; faintly somewhere a child is crying, pigeons whir low and swiftly by. A black-bearded man appears on the threshold. His arm is heavy about the shoulders of a huge young Negro; his head is swathed in bandages. Together they go slowly down the three steps, the bearded man tottering. Another Negro follows, young too, straight and slender as a javelin. And last, the old man and the Quaker youth, manacled to each other.

The militiamen are standing set against the crowd, but from it, for all the hate, there is no hostile move, only a staring silence. Something about these five prisoners moving slowly and silently between the bayonet files, stifles the jeers; something like an aura, a single deep doomed pride, moves darkly with them. There too is Stevens faltering, pitifully faint, with his handsome face bloodless white above the black beard and his jet eyes gleaming and torn. He has three musket wounds in his head, two slugs in his right breast and a deep raw forehead gash. And the old man walking by the side of the boy. The old man with the blood-stained bandages about his head. The long white beard; and the face like slate, sabre-slashed. Eyes fierce, sunken, glittering. No, there are no jeers, no taunts; only the deep staring silence.

Down the court-room aisle they walk, through the restless sea of turned pitiless faces. Now as before there is the hush; they can feel the stabbing weight of five hundred eyes. The air is stifling, reeking with odor of human bodies and stale smoke. The prisoners are led to the bench. The morning light streams through the high dirty uncurtained windows and falls about the five in a wan pool. Smoke from the old pipe wood-stove is further polluting the air. The bare plank floor is strewn with chestnut shells and scraps of paper. The gavel sharply raps, and in this room of whitewashed walls stained with hand-smears, in this room where farmers and tradespeople come, and debts and acres and vagrants are given judgment, the old man and the four youths, white and black, look up at the cold sober countenances of the magistrates, eight in a row behind the table; face the power of the Virginia Commonwealth. The gavel has rapped, the trial is on.

"Do the prisoners have counsel?"

Harding, county-attorney, rises to put the question. He is a short man; heavy. He has a raw bloated face, a hooked nose and brutal eyes, the face of a wastrel. Some political stream threw him up on Jefferson County. He will get fifty dollars for trying this case. He is sober now; savagely his voice rasps out; every word, every gesture reveals his attitude: no frills, quick work and a hanging. "Do you have counsel, or do you want counsel to be assigned by the court?"

The four young prisoners, uncertain, look as one toward the old man. He presses his bony hand on Copeland's shoulder (the young doctor Starry who saved you from the lynching gave you a chance to go like a man, Copeland) and rises painfully from the bench. His angered eyes hold Harding's for an instant. Then he turns, and now is facing, not the prosecutor, not the bench, but the spectators. Yet the eyes are distant from them too; the hewn Hebraic face is raised high. Beyond this old court-house is a vastness, great cities, plains, the mountains, seas rushing, the millions, the poised vastness a nation. Speak, Brown of Osawatomie, hold the innumerable condemning eyes, speak in the profound silence, passionately to your countrymen:

"Virginians! I did not ask for quarter at the time I was taken! I did not ask to have my life spared. The Governor of the State of Virginia tendered me his assurance that I should have a fair trial. But under no circumstances whatever will I be able to have a fair trial. If you seek my blood, you can have it at any moment, without this mockery. I've had no counsel, I have not been able to advise with anyone. I know nothing about the feelings of my fellow prisoners, and I am utterly unable to attend in any way to my own defence. My memory don't serve me, my health is insufficient, though improving. There are mitigating circumstances that I would urge in our favor, if a fair trial is to be allowed us, but if we are to be forced with a mere form, a trial for execution, you might spare yourselves that trouble. I am ready for my fate. I don't ask a trial. I beg for no mockery of a trial, no insult, nothing but that which conscience gives or cowardice would drive you to practice. I ask again to be excused from the mockery of a trial. I do not even know what the special design of this examination is. I do not know what is to be the benefit of it to the Commonwealth. I have now little further to ask, other than that I may not be foolishly insulted only as cowardly barbarians insult those who fall into their power."

The silence endures. The old man is sinking back to the bench, breathing hard, and ashen with the strain.

The Court designates C. J. Faulkner and Lawson Botts as counsel for the defendants. Are the prisoners willing to accept?

"If I am to have nothing but the mockery of a trial I do not care anything about counsel." The old man does not rise, he speaks feebly now. "It is unnecessary to trouble any gentlemen with that duty."

Harding swells and bristles: "You are, sir, to have a fair trial."

"I have sent for counsel to the north. I am a stranger here. I do not know the disposition or character of the gentlemen named. I could have my own counsel if I am not to be hurried to execution before they can reach me."

"Answer the question, sir! Do you desire the aid of Messrs. Faulkner and Botts? Answer yes or no!"

"I cannot regard this as an examination under any circumstances. I would prefer that they exercise their own pleasure. I feel as if it were a matter of little account to me."

Mr. Faulkner rises instantly, speaks with indignation. He resents the prisoner's criticism of his and Mr. Botts's appointment. Moreover he helped in the fighting against the raiders, and has since then expressed strong opinions about their guilt. Also he has important professional engagements elsewhere. He wishes to be relieved of the assignment.

Will Mr. Green serve as counsel for the defendants?

The mayor of Charlestown stands up to a swift angular height; drawls, "I accept the honor."

Will Mr. Botts serve?

Yes, he too (a small thin-knit man) will serve. He feels it his duty, despite the graceless intimations of the prisoner, to carry on the case.

The heads are wagging throughout the room, the eyes relay the stir. Why, the prisoners have the two best lawyers in Jefferson County. No ordinary criminals ever get such able defence. But, the eyes are saying, the minds flashing, but it's no use, it's all a formality. These men have no chance. There's the evidence and the law. Let the witnesses be examined, let the statements be sworn to, the indictments will come in, they will be found true and binding. These men are doomed. Aye, and a just thing. Nigger-stealers. Traitors. Midnight assassins.

Now the witnesses are being called by Harding.

Lewis Washington. Yes, he was one of the engine-house hostages. Yes, the prisoners did . . . Yes . . . Yes . . . Mr. Brua . . . Mr. Kitzmiller . . . Yes . . . Yes . . . Yes . . . And the old man is sitting there with his eyes closed, as if he has no slightest interest in the proceedings. Later the minutes will read: "Sundry witnesses were examined, and the Court being unanimously of opinion that the Prisoners are guilty of the offence with which they stand charged, it is ordered and considered by the Court that they be sent on to the Circuit-Court for trial according to law."

*   *   *   *   *

And in New England, in the village of Concord, sorrow and rebellion were wildly flooding the spirit of Henry Thoreau. He felt the very rocks sweating anguish. The Virginians had placed the old man in prison, as if he were mere flesh and bone! They could not confront his belief, only his poor body. Would they not, could they not see that lock the iron door upon him as they might, the true life of the man would follow them out proudly without let or hindrance—and *that* was all to be feared? Half-witted State, timid as a lone woman with her silver spoons!

And these Concord men, going about righteously. Yankees! You with leanness in your souls! It does not surprise me that you speak of John Brown as an ordinary felon, for who are you? When a noble deed is done only those who are themselves noble are likely to appreciate it, and you have either much flesh, or much office, or much coarseness. This old fellow is flashing through the darkness in which we live like a meteor, nothing so miraculous in the country's history has ever happened, and you have nothing to say or feel save "felon"!

Oh, he must speak at once aloud, so these cowards would see

≡ * 311 * ≡

that he stood apart from them! As he loved his life, he must
speak, and side with the light, and let the dark earth roll from
under him!

CHAPTER IV

"...Being Moved and Seduced..."

IT WAS twenty-four hours after the first arraignment. The Court
was waiting; the prisoners had been ordered in to plead to the
indictments. (Outside, the town leaned forward, cocked its head.
Militia trod the narrow streets. Against the closed shops, the
startled familiar peace, waves of restlessness broke. Citizens went
about carrying rifles.) Again the room was tight-wedged with
spectators and newspaper men. Judge Parker sat in the presiding
chair. He was a smallish man, with a straight close mouth and a
strong jaw; the steady gray eyes were gentle. Now as he waited
he was thinking: this would be difficult, he was bound in duty
to judge men whose actions deep in his heart he execrated; the
traditions of his revered Virginia called powerfully upon his
sympathies. But he was a man of law, he reverenced his calling
even beyond those traditions; with every power, then, he could
summon, this trial would be conducted with judicial decency
and impartiality. The whole South was crying for the blood
of these men; he must make no smallest concession to the popu-
lar frenzy, he must be steel against the passion of the moment.
They would be denied no presumption, benefit, or right to
which they were entitled; the honor of the State of Virginia was
equally on trial before the judgment of the——

The prisoners were coming through the door, led by Avis
the jailer . . . Coppoc. Copeland. Emperor Green. Then Stevens,
borne on a mattress by four attendants. Finally, the old man.
They carried him in on a cot; he had been weakened by the
previous day's exertion.

The two wounded men lay within the counsel's railing, near

Botts and Mayor Green, and directly before the bench. In the silence Stevens' breathing sounded up like a rattle. He's dying, flashed through the crowd-mind, he'll die of his wounds if they don't hang him promptly. Andrew Hunter, special prosecutor for the Commonwealth, thought with anger: the old murderer, he can walk as well as I can, he's going to try to hold up the case, he's out to get every smallest delay. But he has me to face now, not Harding alone, he'll earn every delay, in ten days I'll have him on the gallows. The formal procedure had already begun; now, even as Hunter was thinking, the old man threw off the counterpane and struggled to his feet. He motioned for assistance. A bailiff came and stood by him. There was a stir in the room; the people remembered the defiant courage of the first day, the impassioned "Virginians!"—the room went very quiet. He began—a manacle hung from his right wrist; he wore loose black carpet-slippers—low and uncertain:

"Your Honor . . . I do not intend to detain the Court, but barely wish to say, as I have been promised a fair trial, that I am not now in circumstances that enable me to attend to a trial, owing to the state of my health. I have a severe wound in the back, or rather in one kidney, which enfeebles me very much. But I am doing well and only ask for a short delay of my trial, and I think I may be able to listen to it, and I merely ask this, that, as the saying is, the devil may have his dues, no more. I wish to say further that my hearing is impaired and rendered indistinct in consequence of wounds I have about my head. I cannot hear distinctly at all. I could not hear what the Court said this morning. I would be glad to hear what is said on my trial, and am now doing better than I could expect under the circumstances. A very short delay would be all I would ask. I don't presume to ask more than a very short delay, so that I may in some degree recover, and be able at least to listen to my trial, and hear what questions are asked of the citizens, and what their answers are. If that could be allowed me I should be very much obliged."

Judge Parker's gentle eyes rested upon some invisible point high above the rear door; and the voice mild but firm spoke slowly from the bench:

Before passing on the defendant's plea it was necessary for the indictments to be read. Would the prisoners stand in accordance with the dignity of the Court? Would the clerk of the Court read the indictments?

The three young fellows stood; Coppoc quivering a little, but, withal, resolute; Copeland proudly; Emperor Green huge, glistening black, dazed. Two attendants lifted white-faced Stevens, held him limp under the arms.

". . . John Brown, Aaron C. Stevens, Edwin Coppoc, white persons . . . Shields Green, John Copeland, Negroes . . . evil-minded and traitorous persons . . . not having the fear of God before their eyes, but being moved and seduced by the false and malignant counsel of other evil and traitorous persons and the instigation of the devil . . . are hereby charged with:

"One, confederating to make rebellion and levy war against the State of Virginia . . .

"Two, with conspiring to induce slaves to make rebellion and insurrection . . .

"Three, with committing murder upon Thomas Boerley, Fontaine Beckham, Luke Quin, white persons, and Shephard Heyward, a free Negro . . ."

The prisoners had heard the arraignment, said the Court. The plea was in order. Guilty or not guilty.

John Brown?

Not guilty.

Aaron C. Stevens?

Not guilty . . . not guilty . . . not guilty . . .

Mr. Botts rose: the prisoners had elected to be tried separately.

Quickly Andrew Hunter and Harding conferred; announced: It was the choice of the prosecution to try the commander of the Provisional Army first. They believed the immediate selection of the jurors was in order.

Mr. Green protested: He wished to urge the justice of Captain Brown's appeal for postponement before a jury was impanelled. They had had little opportunity for examining the indictment or preparing the defence. Moreover the client was ill. It was obvious to all eyes.

Mr. Hunter answered sharply. He opposed the motion for delay. The prisoner's wounds were at worst superficial. There must be no further subterfuges for gaining time. The trial must be swift, the efficiency of the Virginia law must be demonstrated.

"Dr. Mason," said Judge Parker. The court-physician stood up in the second row. "You have recently examined the prisoner. Is the nature of his wounds such as to justify a stay of his trial?"

"I believe the prisoner fit to stand the requirements of the trial, your Honor. Neither his hearing nor his mind is impaired by the injuries."

"The request for delay is denied. The impanelling will begin at once."

Richard Timberlake.

Are you a free-holder of this county? Have you expressed any opinion as to the guilt of the prisoner? This man will be hanged if you find him guilty. Do you have any conscientious scruples which will prevent you from finding him guilty because the death penalty may be his punishment? Do you . . . have you . . .

William Rightsdale . . . George W. Tapp . . . Isaac Dust. . . . The voices went on, rumbling, high-pitched, timid, drawling; and the old man lay there with his eyes closed, the counterpane drawn up to his white beard.

 CHAPTER V

Over Which an Ancient Spectre Hovers

IT HAPPENED with startling suddenness.

The procedure of the third day had just begun; the first formalities were being gotten through; the voice of Judge Parker was low and calm over the packed room, the sea of eyes. Harding was nodding off his last night's whiskey. Andrew Hunter, by his side, was glancing hurriedly over some notes, ignoring his colleague. The old man lay again on the pallet within the counsel's railing, alone this time; very still; his eyes smoldered upon Botts's face. The small wiry lawyer was leaning forward in his chair, his thin legs coiled around the supports. He was like a spring poised to leap out. Judge Parker's voice halted. Botts rose swiftly.

"Your Honor!"

In all urgency he wished to plead again for postponement. Counsel for the defence (Hunter stirred angrily: another evasion, another subterfuge) had in their hands new testimony of startling significance. It was a telegram (the old man's eyes were slits of fire) which had been received late last night. They wished, in consideration of its obvious and important bearing upon the defence, to reveal its purport to the Court.

Indeed, indeed, assented the Court.

Green slipped a paper from the table and handed it to Botts. The audience strained. The old man's body took on the hawklike rigidity. The thin lawyer began to read:

"Akron, Ohio, Thursday, October Twenty-seventh, Eighteen Fifty-nine. . . . To C. J. Faulkner and Lawson Botts. . . . John Brown, leader of the insurrection at Harper's Ferry, and several of his family, have resided in this county many years. Insanity is hereditary in that family. His mother's sister died with it, and a daughter of that sister has been two years in a lunatic asylum. A son and daughter of his mother's brother have also been confined in the lunatic asylum, and another son of that brother is now insane and under close restraint. These facts can be conclusively proven by witnesses residing here, who will doubtless attend the trial if desired. . . . A. H. Lewis."

Order! Silence in this room!

Slowly, at length, the excited whispering died; but a throbbing was in the court, like a great pulse. Botts went on quickly: he thought it only fair to state that the defendant had refused to avail himself of the plea of insanity (Hunter's lips curled) and that the movement had been undertaken without his approval or concurrence and was unknown to him until the receipt of the despatch——

"Your Honor!"

The old man was raising himself from the pallet. He stood up, swaying, holding the blanket to him. The haggard face blazed with scorn.

"I will add, if the Court will allow me, that I look upon it

≡ * 316 * ≡

as a miserable artifice and pretext of those who ought to take a different course in regard to me, if they took any at all, and I view it with contempt more than otherwise. As I remarked to Mr. Green, insane persons, so far as my experience goes, have but little ability to judge of their own sanity, and if I am insane, of course I should think I know more than all the rest of the world. But I do not think so. I am perfectly unconscious of insanity, and I reject, so far as I am capable, any attempt to interfere in my behalf on that score."

It was like a bolt from clear skies. The hush hung. Every eye followed him down to the mattress, beheld him kneel, trembling with faintness. Then the startled murmur broke, swelled higher, higher, drowning the gavel; hubbub ruled.

It was astounding! Andrew Hunter was staring; Judge Parker's discreet eyebrows had gone up perceptibly. Even the sodden Harding blinked from his dimness. The old scoundrel had been fighting for time every inch of the way, desperately "playing possum." Now here was the first real chance to hold up the trial indefinitely, even more, a chance for very life, and he was rejecting it utterly! Chagrin began to mingle with Hunter's perplexity; there was some cunning here and he did not know how to meet it. The Virginian's eyes bored into the wounded fanatic, as if he would penetrate to the very workings of the secret mind. Crazy old cutthroat!

Not this, God. Not this . . . Do not let the madhouse be the end of my search . . . For twenty years I have fought against slavery, according to your word . . . I have sinned, I know I have sinned. But have I not mingled the blood of my children with your despised poor? Oh God, let some good arise from this ruin . . . Israel Green snatched up a light dress-blade instead of a sabre; in the engine-house the blade thrust for my life, and did not find it. Oh let it be spared for a good death! Let this end of my time, in some way yet unknown and inscrutable, serve you.

Only not this. Not this, God.

". . . I look upon it as a miserable artifice and pretext of those who ought to take a different course in regard to me, and I view it with contempt more than otherwise. . . . I am perfectly unconscious of insanity and I reject so far as I am capable any attempt to interfere in my behalf on that score."

Botts looked helplessly at his associate. Green rose. (His face was tight, expressive: see what we are up against; the man thwarts us at every turn; but we are men of law, and though we detest all he stands for, we will do our duty by him.) "Your Honor. We confess extreme embarrassment in urgin' a defence which the client has publicly repudiated. But the course open to us is single, it's obvious. We plead adjournment; the existin' circumstances cry out for 'n investigation."

"I object," said Andrew Hunter. "There is no proper cause for postponement."

"The objection is sustained. In the absence of sworn testimony supporting the plea of insanity there is no true legal question before the Court. The trial will proceed."

The old man sank back upon the pallet. He drew the blanket about himself. He closed his eyes.

". . . and you sent the boy?" asked Higginson.

"He ought to be there tonight," said LeBarnes.

Outside, the narrow Boston street lay quiet and coldly dappled. The sun cut sharp through the elms. A bell chimed faint and clear, twice in the autumn distance.

"Bowditch was dubious. He said they'd suspect him."

"Damn Bowditch! He's against every plan I've broached. He can't see that it's no time for caution. Impossible, wild, hopeless! What does he think this is, a business deal? Why, the boy's very youth will throw them off. They'll think he's some impulsive fledgling lawyer who's rushed down to help the old man. They'll never suspect."

"They may. Does Massachusetts need a stripling to represent her in a trial of this importance? . . . Well, we can't lose much."

"I told him to watch everything closely. To see and talk with him, and get to us anything he may want to say. I told him to make a plan of the town. How many troops, and where they're placed. The site of the jail and exactly how it's guarded. The nature of the surrounding country. Do you see?"

"Yes . . . yes . . . it may help. . . . But let's get to these other matters. It's too slow, LeBarnes, the whole thing's going too slowly! He'll be gone before we stir."

Eagerly they talked. . . . The son in Ohio, the eldest . . . coming east with men . . . the German radicals, a hundred of them under a firebrand, Metternich, down from New York . . . Kansas jayhawkers . . . outside Charlestown, a swift dash on the town, the escape on the horses of the cavalry companies . . . Orsini bombs, hand-grenades. . . . The countryside paralyzed . . . .

Aye, and that other desperate scheme, all else failing: the Governor of the State of Virginia spirited away by night . . . out to sea in a fast tug, faster by many knots than the single gunboat off Richmond . . .

Henry Wise, hostage for Osawatomie Brown . . .

 CHAPTER VI

The Trial Draws to a Close

IT WAS the fourth morning. The frail beardless boy came into the court-room. Amid a profound astonishment he spoke:

"I am George Henry Hoyt. I am a member of the Massachusetts bar and I have come to assist in Captain Brown's defence."

The room was astir with derision and mistrust. Andrew Hunter instantly protested: "Mr. Hoyt is unknown to us. Let him prove his position under the Massachusetts bar, his right to practice in this court."

"We have no need of assistance," said Botts coldly.

"I do not know Mr. Hoyt," said the old man. "But I request his help, as one in sympathy with me."

"I regret that I have no formal proof at the moment," said the youth. "But I shall be willing to take no active part until my status is established."

Spy, thought Andrew Hunter, damned Yankee spy.

"I see no reason," said Judge Parker, "to object against additional counsel. I suggest that formal proof be dispensed with for the present. Let the oath be administered."

". . . so help me God. . . ." George Henry Hoyt entered within the counsel's railing; took a place beside the old man's pallet. The prosecution continued, Hunter addressing the Court:

". . . And the evidence shows without a shadow of a question that when the defendant went to Virginia and planted his feet at Harper's Ferry, he came there to reside, and to hold the place permanently. True, he occupied a farm four or five miles off in Maryland, but not for the legitimate purpose of establishing his domicile there. No, for the hellish purpose of rallying forces into the Commonwealth and establishing himself at the Ferry, as the starting point for a new government. Whatever it was, whether tragical, or farcical and ridiculous, as the learned counsel for the defence have just presented it, his conduct showed, if his declarations were insufficient, that his provisional government was a real thing and no debating society, and in holding office under it and exercising its functions, he was clearly guilty of treason. As to conspiring with slaves and rebels the law says the prisoner is equally guilty, whether insurrection is made or not. Advice may be given by actions as well as words. When you put pikes in the hands of slaves and have their masters captive, that is advice to rebel. It is punishable with death."

Now Harding began the examination of witnesses to support his colleague's denunciation. Lewis Washington . . . Joseph Brua. . . . And once again by these brief sober affirmations the whole mad Ferry thrust was evoked. Then Andrew Hunter rose. He drew some papers from the old black carpet-bag on the table. He began, without comment, to read:

"*Whereas, Slavery, throughout its existence . . . is none other than a most barbarous, unprovoked War of one portion of its citizens upon . . . Therefore we . . . and the oppressed people . . . do ordain and establish for ourselves the following Provisional Constitution . . .*"

Andrew Hunter moved to the pallet, handed down the sheets to old Brown.

"Do you recognize this writing?"

"It is mine."

Hunter moved back to the counsel's bench. He took up another paper; without a single word, began to read.

". . . It is mine."

". . . Yes, I held such a belief. I hold it now."

". . . Yes . . . Yes . . ."

By noon the prosecution rested: treason, insurrection, murder.

". . . and I ask that the penalty be visited on the prisoner, whom the law denounces, whom reason denounces, the penalty which our safety requires and which the laws of God and man approve."

During the midday recess young Hoyt was closeted with John Brown.

A half hour before the session was again to open, Botts and Green entered the jail. The young fellow had a startled incredulous look upon his face; the eyes of the wounded prisoner shone with a proud fervent yet strangely softened light. The two were not speaking; they were sitting silent, as if between them worlds lay.

"We begin the defence this afternoon," said Botts, frigidly pointed.

"I do not know the Virginia law," said the boy. "I have nothing as yet to suggest."

"How did you expect to help?"

". . . I was not sure. . . . But I felt I might help . . . in some way. Even if it was only to bring to Captain Brown the knowledge that we in the North had not forgotten him."

"Undoubtedly." Botts turned to the old man. "You still insist that we go on with the defence as you have suggested?"

"Yes, I think it is best so."

"Very well then. But the responsibility is yours. You are insisting that we concentrate the defence upon details that the Court will inevitably consider irrelevant. Your case is desperate even with the best kind of a defence, yet——"

"Here," said the old man. "I have written down these points for you to follow."

Botts read the paper; then silently handed it to Green. The angular man's eyes moved swiftly, a flush began to redden up his leathery neck.

"Damn me," he drawled. "What fool stuff'll you have us workin' upon? Thar's no use, don't you see it? All's been brought out over'n over again."

"Yes. But I wish it so."

"Damn me. Thar, see this for a rock-hard defence." Green in a helpless anger flipped the paper into young Hoyt's lap:

We gave to numerous prisoners perfect liberty—get all their names. We allowed other prisoners to visit their families, to quiet their fears—get all their names. We treated all our prisoners with the utmost kindness and humanity—get all their names, so far as may be. Our orders from the first and throughout were that no unarmed person should be injured, under any circumstances whatever—prove that by all the prisoners. We committed no destruction or waste of property—prove that.

"Thar, see this for a rock-hard defence."

Aye, what do you know of my dream?

In the afternoon the defence began.

". . . My name is John Dangerfield . . . I am a clerk in the armory . . . yes, I was there . . .

". . . At night the firing stopped. You see, it was pitch black in the engine-house and we couldn't see anything. I talked a lot with Mr. Brown that night. I found him a very brave man, and I found him sensible on all subjects except slavery. He believed it was his duty to free slaves, even if he lost his own life. . . . During a sharp fight one of his sons was killed. He fell, then he tried to raise himself, and he said, it is all over with me. Brown did not leave his post at the porthole, but when the fighting was over he walked to his son's body. He stretched out the limbs and took off the dead fellow's trappings. Then he said to me, this is the third son I have lost in this cause. Another son had been shot in the morning and was then moaning so you could hardly bear to listen. They brought him in from the street, all ripped with slugs. He was dying. But when his men wanted to fire on someone passing, Mr. Brown would stop them, saying, don't shoot, that man is unarmed . . ."

"You are a Virginian, are you not, Mr. Dangerfield? . . . And you, of course, have no slightest sympathy in principle with the prisoner? . . . And yet you are testifying in his favor?"

"Yes, I feel it's my duty. He made me a prisoner, he had me and other men in his full power and could have killed us. But he spared our lives. When his sons were shot down beside him, almost any other man would have taken life for life . . ."

"Your Honor!" said Andrew Hunter. "I object strenuously to the introduction of such testimony at this time! There is nothing in these facts which the jury can consider. What difference will it make if a thousand witnesses should testify to the defendant's kindness, or his merciful instructions to his men? Mr. Brown's so-called humanity has already been brought out again and again, and as to the nobility of his motives, that has even less relevance in a court of law. The point in question is the prisoner's guilt under the charges of the indictment. Treason, insurrection, murder! This entire testimony is a sheer waste of time! It has no more bearing on the case than the dead languages!"

Objection overruled . . .

"My name is David Sinn. . . . I was in command of the Fredericksburg militia during the raid . . .

". . . and I have never seen any man show more courage and forebearance than John Brown showed that night under those terrible circumstances. . . . Besides my admiration for the man, I am testifying for Captain Brown so Northern men will have no opportunity to say that Southern men were not willing to appear as witnesses in behalf of one whose ideas they hated . . ."

". . . My name's Benjamin Mills. Most people call me Ben . . . I'm the master-armorer. I been that for six years now. Before that I was twenty years doin' . . . eh? . . .

". . . Well, then one of the old man's boys went out with a handkerchief for a truce. He was shot down. Then he came crawlin' in——

(Oh stilled young hearts!)

"—to the gates. I gave him some water, tried to ease him, but there wasn't no use. . . . The old man didn't seem to hold no grudge, he only said kind of choked that our citizens had done it like . . . like barbarians. . . . He was expectin' reinforcements all along. When his men got to losin' hope he would say, it'll soon be night, and he kept sayin', Owen, Owen. He said to shoot no one save they was bearin' arms, and if they do let them have it. . . . It kind of seemed to me he wanted to make terms more for our sake than to be safe his own self . . ."

". . . and nothing but the truth, so help. . . . I am Harry Hunter . . . Fontaine Beckham was my uncle. . . . He was shot down on the trestle. . . . Chambers and I ran to the hotel. The Thompson fellow was tied up there. We were going to shoot him but Miss Foukes got in front of him and shielded him. I guess she was afraid we'd spoil her carpet. So we dragged him up to the railroad bridge, right to the spot where they'd killed my uncle. We gave it to him, dropped his body——" (as the prosecutor's son calmly drawled on there was no sound of sympathy or horror in all the court-room, save on the pallet the old man suddenly groaning aloud) "—to the rocks in the river. I don't regret it. They killed my uncle. He was the best friend I ever had. I'd have killed anyone I could get my hands on . . . Sir? . . . Yes, I'd have killed them all, truce or no truce."

Thomas Osbourne?

Silence.

Joseph Wiltshire?

Silence.

(Scoff, call all this irrelevant—what do you know of my dream? I cherish no illusion, the sands of my time have run out, long ago my body's life was forfeit. But the dream—Almighty Father! speak through me, speak through me to the hearts of men. Grant me a little time more to reach them. Not Virginia, not men of a jury. But the North, the South, my land, my country!)

Reason Cross?

Silence.

Abraham Avey?

Silence.

The old man suddenly struggled to his feet:

"May it please the Court! I discover that notwithstanding all the assurances I have received of a fair trial, nothing like a fair trial is to be given me! I gave the names, as soon as I could get them, of the persons I wished to have called as witnesses, and was assured that they would be subpoenaed. I wrote down a memorandum to that effect, saying where those parties were, but it appears that they have not been subpoenaed as far as I can learn, and now I ask, if I am to have anything at all deserving the name and shadow of a fair trial, that this proceeding be deferred until tomorrow morning, for I have no counsel, as I before stated, in whom I feel that I can rely; but I am in hopes counsel may arrive who will attend to seeing that I get the witnesses who are necessary for my defence. I am myself unable to attend to it. I have given all the attention I possibly could to it, but am unable to see or know about them, and can't even find out their names, and I have nobody to do any errands, for my money was all taken when I was sacked and stabbed, and I have not a dime. I had two hundred and fifty or sixty dollars in gold and silver taken from my pocket, and now I have no possible means of getting anybody to go my errands for me, and I have not had all the witnesses subpoenaed. They are not within reach, and are not here. I ask at least until tomorrow morning to have something done, if anything is designed. If not, I am ready for anything that may come up."

Green sprang up furious: Mr. Brown had openly charged them with bad faith, had cast reflections upon their professional conduct! They could no longer go on with the case! They had represented the prisoner to the very best of their ability, they had faithfully followed his instructions, even against their own judgment, had performed every duty which law and honor committed them to! Now, since their motives were questioned and a lack of confidence in them expressed in open court, they would resign and leave the case in the hands of the gentleman from Massachusetts!

Blanched, stunned, in the midst of the stir and the hostile derisive eyes, young Hoyt sat. Then he rose, his thin hands frantically clutching the back of his chair, and said:

"I have just come from Boston. I have travelled night and day. I have had no time to read the indictment, and I know nothing of the criminal code of Virginia. . . . Other counsel from the North are due in Charlestown tonight. I beg in fairness to Captain Brown that the case be postponed until their arrival!"

"Exception!" cried Hunter violently. "These delays arc making a farce of the trial!"

"I second Mr. Hoyt's appeal," said Botts. "His difficulties demand consideration. Mr. Green and myself can no longer act in behalf of the prisoner, but if the Court will grant a postponement we will devote every spare moment to prepare him for his duties. We will put our notes and knowledge at Mr. Hoyt's command."

"The trial is adjourned until tomorrow morning."

The light in Bott's office burned steadily far into the early hours. The thin lawyer and the boy sat talking, talking, the great books and the papers cluttered before them. At four in the morning the boy's eyes closed, with sheer exhaustion his head slipped to the table; he was dead asleep. Botts quietly rose, turned out the light. He walked home through the dark silent lanes. He felt a sorrow in his heart, he felt it in the night, a sorrow vast and moving, yet impersonal.

(Trampled bloodwet fields of Manassas, oh brothers locked in anguish falling to the long bleached sleep!

"Lawson Botts: Colonel, Second Regiment Virginia Volunteers, Army of the Confederacy. 1823–1862.")

At ten o'clock the next morning the Court resumed session. There were two new faces; eminent lawyers from the North, Samuel Chilton of Washington, and Hiram Griswold of Cleveland. Immediately they requested a delay of a few hours: the case was curiously confused; Mr. Griswold was unacquainted with the Virginia law.

"The request is denied. The prisoner has had able counsel. He has had the fullest opportunities for defence. He has chosen to make a change, the responsibility is his alone. I should at once accede to the request, however, if this were the only case on the calendar. But the end of the term is near; in fairness to the other defendants and to the State the action must be undelayed. The trial will proceed."

The end was nearing. Young Hoyt, peaked and shaken, continued the defence along the lines the old man had laid down to Green and Botts: summoning of the engine-house hostages to establish his humanity to them. In the afternoon Chilton, seeking time, submitted a motion that the State elect one count of the indictment and abandon the other two. It was, he said, gravely difficult for the prisoner to defend himself against the three distinct charges at once. No, ruled Judge Parker, the trial had begun under the complete indictment; it must continue under it. The most that could be granted was a motion for arrest of judgment at the conclusion of the trial. He ordered the prosecution to begin the summing up. Late that afternoon the Court adjourned. There would be a respite of a single day, the Sabbath.

On Monday morning, Andrew Hunter, addressing the jury, concluded the case for the Commonwealth of Virginia:

". . . Administer justice according to your law. Acquit the prisoner if you can. But if justice requires you by your verdict to take his life, stand by it uprightly. Let retributive justice, if he is guilty, send him before that Maker who will settle the question forever and forever."

*   *   *   *   *

"Gentlemen of the Jury what say you? Is the prisoner at the bar—John Brown—guilty or not guilty?"

"*Guilty*."

"Guilty of treason, guilty of conspiring with slaves to rebel, guilty of murder in the first degree?"

"*Guilty.*"

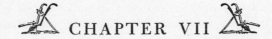

CHAPTER VII

O North, South, My Land, My Country!

"DOES THE prisoner have anything to say why sentence should not be pronounced on him?"

The gas-lit room is packed with people. They are filling every square inch from the counsel's railing out to the wide hall, out to the corridors and the entrance steps. Just as last night to hear the verdict they stood silent and moved, agitated by one hope and dreadful expectancy, so now spreading out into the dusk of the streets do they strain to witness, to hear the last of the doomed old man. He is sitting on the bench beside the pale boy counsel, gazing fixedly at the Judge. In a flat quivering voice the clerk asks the question, the question quivers into the rapt silence: does the prisoner have anything to say why sentence should not be pronounced on him? John Brown turns his head to stare at the clerk; then sits unmoving, as if stunned. Hoyt whispers hurriedly to him. The old man shakes his head twice. A moment goes by; now slowly he is rising to his feet. He grips the table before him, leans over it a little, his face working with consternation. Oh, is his thought, I am not ready, I am not ready. He stands unsteadily so for many minutes, bent over a little, gaunt and tragic in the green flickering light; the deep silence endures. Then slowly, haltingly, he speaks:

"I have, may it please the Court, a few words to say. . . .

"It is unjust that I should suffer such a penalty. Had I interfered in the manner which I admit, and which I admit has been fairly proved—for I admire the truthfulness and candor of the greater portion of the witnesses who have testified in this case—had I so interfered in behalf of the rich, the powerful, the intelligent, the so-called great, or in behalf of any of their friends, either father, mother, brother, sister, wife or children, or any of that class, and suffered and sacrificed what I have in this interference, it would have been all right. Every man in this Court would have deemed it an act worthy of reward rather than punishment. . . .

"This Court acknowledges too, as I suppose, the validity of the law of God. I see a book kissed, which I suppose to be the Bible, or at least the New Testament, which teaches me that all things whatsoever I would that men should do to me, I should do even so to them. It teaches me, further, to remember them that are in bonds as bound with them. I endeavored to act up to that instruction. I say I am yet too young to understand that God is any respecter of persons. I believe that to have interfered as I have done, as I have always freely admitted I have done, in behalf of His despised poor, I did no wrong, but right. Now, if it is deemed necessary that I should forfeit my life for the furtherance of the ends of justice, and mingle my blood further with the blood of my children and with the blood of millions in this slave country whose rights are disregarded by wicked, cruel, and unjust enactments, I say, let it be done. . . ."

"... I pronounce the sentence of death ... Friday, the Second of December . . . hanged by the neck till dead . . . dead . . . dead . . ."

We Shall Walk through the Valley in Peace

THE
LAST PART

". . . Thou hast left behind
Powers that will work for thee—air,
* earth, and skies.*
There's not a breathing of the common
* wind*
That will forget thee; thou hast great
* allies:*
Thy friends are exultations, agonies,
And Love, and man's unconquerable
* mind."*
*   WORDSWORTH.*

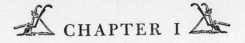

CHAPTER I

If I Am to See the Ruin of My House

THE TRAIN wound northward through the stubborn swirling rain, moaned into the foothills of the winter Adirondacks. Higginson, with distressed eyes gazing from the misted window at the bleak dripping country, brooded:

What a fatal power he has over young men; they were all so young. And now here is this one speaking so—oh, it is something that even I, a clergyman, have never really known, a spiritual rapture so intense that it can touch men of the most diverse natures, and move them to think and feel as he does. He wanted to make the world over, and those wild irreligious boys believed in him, and died. Wild boys—did *we* not believe in him too? . . . How weak I feel before all this, how helpless, how small. What am I doing, have I a right to interfere?

In the dark clergyman's breast-pocket young Hoyt's letter lay; live, eloquent, seeming to stir against his heart:

". . . and he has positively refused his consent to any such plan. Nothing I have been able to say has moved him from his determination. He answers that he would not walk out if the jail door were left wide open. I do not understand him sometimes, he is astonishing. I only know that he moves me in some profound way, so that I have almost come to believe that he, a prisoner in the midst of his enemies and under sentence of death, can answer more wisely than any as to his next step. All other men seem beside themselves. You cannot imagine the excitement here; the country all around is guarded by mounted patrols, and large bodies of troops are constantly under arms. He alone is calm. . . . The people about here are determined to have him die for his offences, but even they applaud the honor and the supreme bravery of the man. . . . Yes, I believe it best to give up hope of rescuing our old friend. For he wants to hang! Heaven save his soul, the old man *wants* to hang!"

No, Higginson had groaned when the letter came; we must save him, he must be made to change his mind. That night he spoke to his wife, a woman with lucid eyes.

"What shall I do? We can't let him go this way!"

"Does it depend now only on his consent, Tom?"

"Yes! The Germans are ready. Yesterday LeBarnes got word to them that I personally pledge the hundred dollars for each man, up to a hundred men. Montgomery is on his way, with the Kansans. And Redpath is working with the eldest son in Ohio. We only need his consent and we'll do it!"

"Thomas. . . . Promise to be careful. . . . It sounds so desperate."

"We can't fail him now."

"Yes, I know. You . . . you were in it together." They sat silent. Then she said, "Tom. I know what you must do."

"Yes, my dear!"

"Go to his family, at once. If he can be swayed at all, only one of them can do it. Speak to Mary Brown. Let her go south. Let her plead with him."

In the early afternoon the train pulled into the mountain hamlet, Westport. Higginson got off, carrying a small bag. He walked nervously along the rude platform; it was drizzling. Higginson saw a man sitting on a buckboard. He was young and bearded, he had a big ragged coat on and a soaked cloth hat.

"Tell me, my man, do you know Salmon Brown?"

"I'm Salmon Brown."

"Oh . . . I'm . . . I'm Higginson, Thomas Higginson."

"Been waitin' for you."

The clergyman made a half-gesture, as if to offer his hand, but the other was looking straight out; Higginson dropped his hand. He clambered up to the other's side, and his heart was pounding. Salmon Brown started up the mare, the wagon creaked forward. Higginson from the corner of his eyes watched the brown-bearded face; it was set in hard bitter lines. This must be her last son, Higginson thought; he blames me, what shall I say to him? "I hope your mother is well," he said gently.

"She's doin' all right."

Salmon Brown savagely flicked the mare's mottled haunch. Damn you, he thought, you and your pity, god damn you, why do you have to be coming up here, can't you leave us alone now?

He had been on the Elba hill, the afternoon the letter came, spading with his big hard hands against the coming time of snow and hunger. Nothing was changed: there he was bending as of old in the furrows, and the raw tangy feel of the new season was in the air, and the peaks brooded vast about, lonely in the great sky. But he, the speck on the hill, had Abbie now, and Watson and Oliver were gone down into some dark fate ("Oh Bell, cannot come home while such things are done here"—"I will see you all soon again. Salmon, you can make any use of the sugar things you can next fall"); aye, there was a great change.

Then, as he was kneeling there in the earth, Lumpy Hoag brought the letter to him. "Bill Stemm said to be sure to git it to you. None else, to be sure, he said."

Virginia . . . the thin balky peasant scrawl.

The hands of the son of Brown trembled with the paper. The hulk of a boy stood staring at him, his eyes vacant and round, like small sick-green buttons.

"Well, what are you standin' for, Lumpy? I got it, ain't I? Get off, you block, get off!"

The poor dullard, alarmed, shambled down the hill, mumbling; he turned his head every few steps to look back in dim reproach. Salmon Brown waited, his breath was a throbbing cut in this throat. Not till the boy had disappeared among the hill-bottom trees did he open the letter.

When dusk came on Salmon Brown raised the bulging sack to his shoulders and clumped down the slope toward the glow which was the farm, the home. His body this night was not blessed weary with the rich disburdened ache that simple men know who have done the long hours' toil with tendon and sweat, and homeward are renewal, warmth, the known faces. Instead, he felt weak in his limbs and his chest held a dark numb spot. *On Sunday, this Sabbath night coming, we start.* It was already Tuesday. They had done it—or they were dead.

"Go to your bed, child," his mother said later to the solemn drowsy little girl, Nell. Mary Brown was changed only a little; there was more gray in the huge sheenless coil of hair, but the same sad patience was in her face, in her tired eyes. So, during the last years, the pine walls of the home might have changed; grayer, scarred, more beaten, but staunch yet against the storms. The other faces about the table spoke more truly the passage of time—fierce Annie with her hair up; like a young rose, Sarah, blooming upon a crag miraculously; Bella, mother of Watson's babe, Will Thompson's and Dauphin's sister, Bella lorn and wasting with some fateful inward malady; homely Abbie, sweet and clean as a nut, recently come here to be woman to Salmon; and Martha, heavy now and slow-eyed, cleft of Oliver, astir with his pulse.

"Go in, my Nell," said Mary Brown. "Go to your bed."

"Leave her be," said Salmon. "Leave her be awhile."

They looked at him, as one. Annie's eyes searched him. He could never be withdrawn and secret with her, she could lay him bare with a look. "Tell us," she said.

"Oh, is it something?" Bella weakly cried.

"It's nothin'," he said. "It's only a quiet letter from father."

He took the paper from his pocket, slid the table-lamp to himself. "Come here close, Nell," he said. The child with the sharp grave face came and stood by him. Mother Brown who had been listening by the stove put down the skillet and came behind Martha's chair. Their eyes hung upon him; he began to read:

"Parts Unknown; Dear Wife and Children all . . . and perhaps you can keep your animals in good condition through the winter on potatoes mostly, much cheaper than on any other feed. I have encouragement of having fifty dollars sent you soon, to help you get through the winter; and I shall certainly do all in my power for you, and try to commend you always to the God of my fathers. . . . On Sunday, this Sabbath night coming we start. . . ."

Now they understood why Salmon had wanted Nell "to be awhile"; now they understood the vague deep spirit that moved the rough fellow. He did not know how to pray, and they must pray together. Aye, in Elba, there must be this night a service.

". . . Read the *Tribune* carefully. It may not always be certainly true, however. Begin early to take good care of all your animals, and pinch them at the close of the winter, if you must at all. . . . I have sent along four pairs blankets, with directions for Martha to have the first choice, and for Bella, Abbie, and Annie to cast lots for a choice in the three other pairs. My reason is I think Martha fairly entitled to *particular* notice. To my other daughters I can only send my blessing just now. Save this letter to remember your father by. . . ." (The voice broke, the heads were low, a hush like mourning was in the room.) ". . . Everything will come out all right. *He* will be with us. God Almighty bless and save you all. Your husband and father John Brown."

So they sat bowed in a silence save for Bella's low sobbing. Aye, let small Nell be awhile, let her too hear the last word. Mary Brown, standing above the circle of the younger stricken life, asked:

"Where . . . where are they now? What are they at, Salmon?"

He could not answer, kept his head down. Annie, dry-eyed, answered, fiercely answered, "It was writ Thursday, Ma. They're in it now."

"Then we ought to know soon."

"When the paper comes."

Oh God, Mary Brown silently prayed, keep 'em in life, they're but boys, God. We trust in your mercy. Keep a watch over 'em, oh God.

Salmon Brown drove Higginson in the buckboard through the wet falling darkness, over the lonely Keene Mountain road that wound its steep way among the crags and the spruce and birch of the vast unbroken forest. The two men sat silent; for hours they had been so. They had come thirty miles, and after the first few Higginson had given up trying to break through the other's bitter unspoken hostility. The clergyman was shivering with the damp and chill. But long ago during the dismal ride his irritation with the other had died (who could reproach this boy for churlishness? the flesh of his brothers lay mouldering in the valley of the Shenandoah, a gallows must darken his sleep); and Higginson, shivering, felt a compassion in his very bowels.

Soon Salmon Brown was guiding the spent horse up along a dark wheeltrack narrow between rows of gaunt spruce. They creaked past a still black pool under a cliff, it gleamed for an instant in the light from the wagon lamp. Then for many minutes Higginson was aware of nothing save deep obscurity and a rustle and whispering among the dripping trees. But suddenly he had the sense of a clearing—and they were there. Lights from a low dwelling blinked through the night mist.

Mary Brown greeted the clergyman in the bare little parlor. She was ashen pale and her eyes were tragic and dark-circled; but she was calm as she spoke. "Does it seem as if freedom is to gain or lose by this?" she asked. Oh, thought Higginson as she led him into the kitchen, she *would* be this way! She bade him take the wet outer clothing off; brought a pair of old slippers; filled a basin for freshening up. Then she set hot food before him and

≡ * 335 * ≡

her son, on the big pine table with its starched threadbare white cloth. Annie and Sarah were doing the dishes, Abbie was darning by the hearth, Ruth sat quietly by. The first uncontrollable grief of the Brown women had passed, the lamenting. They were settled now into the deeper devouring anguish of silence. Upstairs, Oliver's young widow Martha lay with a black death in her heart, and in her womb the new life stirring. Higginson as he ate could hear the low lost quaver of Bella singing her fatherless babe to slumber. He choked upon his food; yes, these were the old man's people, they could be no different. Soon, pale and visibly moved, he told Mary Brown why he had come:

Everything was ready for the rescue; would she go to Charlestown to plead with her husband; she alone could save his life.

"Yes," she said. "I'll go to John."

The clergyman longed to grasp her hand, to say words of comfort, of hope, but he could not, there was something so terribly alone and final in her sad slow dignity.

"You mustn't go, Ma," said Annie suddenly.

"What are you sayin', Annie?"

"If Pa says no, then you mustn't try."

Higginson was staring startled at the young girl. "It's your father's life, Annie," he said.

"My father knows best. If he won't be saved, you mustn't try to save him."

Salmon Brown had been listening, an intensity had been deepening fiercely in his bitter face. Now he gave a low cry. "Go down, Ma! Speak to him!"

She knew that cry, the clansman's; she had heard it before, like a doom. "Not you, Salmon," she said. "You're not in this. Don't you be thinkin' on it."

"I'll speak to Hen," he said, not listening, turning to the clergyman. "There's fellers in this valley that'd help!"

Swarthy Higginson felt the fire of him, his own blood rushed to meet it. But there was Mary Brown sitting before him, still and white. He said quietly, "I know how you feel, Brown. But your mother's right. . . . They need you here . . . now."

The passion died in Salmon's eyes. He rose heavily and went from the room.

That night Mary Brown sat up very late, sewing. There were some socks she had been going to send down to the old man in the Charlestown jail, some woolen underclothes; now she would bring them herself.

Early the next morning Salmon Brown drove his mother and Higginson back over the Keene trail, down through the highland valley with its towering summits blue and frosty rose in the great gleaming distance. They rode all the day in the buckboard, and Higginson talked with Mary Brown, and he loved her.

"I always prayed," she said to him, "that he might be killed fightin', and not fall into the hands of the slavers. But I can't regret it now, when I remember the noble words of freedom John uttered at his trial. . . ."

". . . I have had thirteen children, Mr. Higginson. Now that Watson and Oliver died, only four are left. . . . But if I am to see the ruin of my house, I can only hope that God'll bring out of it some benefit to the poor slaves. . . ."

 CHAPTER II

These Light Afflictions

"I UNDERSTAND, Mr. Avis, that I am to be allowed to communicate freely with my friends."

He stood by the barred opening of the prison room, looking through at the jailer beyond in the corridor. The old man's hair was brushed back neatly from the low forehead, his full beard lay fresh and white upon the bosom of the loose ragged black coat. The gashes across his face were yet unhealed and raw; long chains were fastened to his ankles from an iron base in the center of the floor. His eyes were bright and calm.

"Yes, Captain Brown," the jailer answered. He was a big round-shouldered man, with uneven white teeth and level eyes. He had been among the leaders of the townsmen in the fighting. "Write whenever you wish. But I have orders to examine all your letters."

"There is nothing I'll write that all may not read. . . . You are kind, Mr. Avis, and I thank you. You show as much kindness in treating me as you did courage in fighting me."

"Well . . ." the jailer said haltingly, looking down. ". . . This is all . . . too bad." He raised his head. Their eyes dawned into each other, the eyes met in a grip.

Later as the cold darkness of the early winter night descended, Avis returned, bearing a lighted candle. He unlocked the heavy iron door and entered. (Two guards stood at either end of the short hall, they had orders to kill the prisoner at the first suspicion of escape; twenty armed men were an unsleeping cordon about the outside yard.)

"I have finished my letter," the old man said. He handed it to the jailer. "When you direct it, Mr. Avis, may I ask that you direct it to Mrs. John Brown? You see, there are some other widow Browns, and this letter is meant for Mary, my wife."

"My dear Wife & Children, EveryOne, I suppose you have learned before this by the newspapers that two weeks ago today we were fighting for our lives at Harpers ferry; that during the fight Watson was mortally wounded; Oliver killed, Wm Thompson killed & Dauphin killed. That on the following day I received Sabre-cuts in my head; & Bayonet stabs in my body. Watson died of his wound on Wednesday the 2d or on Thursday the 3d day after I was taken. . . . I have since been tried and found guilty of treason; and of murder in the first degree. . . . Under all these terrible calamities; I feel quite cheerful in the assurance that God reigns; and will overrule all for his glory; & the best possible good. I feel *no* consciousness of *guilt* in the matter; nor even mortification on account of my imprisonment; & irons; & I feel perfectly sure that very soon no member of my family will feel any possible disposition to *blush on my account.* When and in what form death may come is but of small moment. I feel just as content to die for God's eternal truth and for suffering humanity on the scaffold as in any other way; and I do not say this to *brave it out.* No; I would readily own my wrong were I in the least convinced of it. I have been confined, with a good opportunity to look the whole thing as 'fair in the face' as I am capable of doing; and I now feel it most grateful that I am counted in the least possible degree worthy to suffer for the truth. . . . Finally, my dearly beloved, be all of good comfort. This life is intended as a season of training, chastisement, temptation, and trial. These light afflictions which are but for a moment shall work out for us a far more exceeding & *Eternal* weight of Glory. I hope to be able to write to you again. My wounds are doing well. Copy this, Ruth, and send it to your sorrow stricken brothers John and Jason, to comfort them. Say to my poor boys never to grieve for one moment on my account; and should they live to see the time when they will not be ashamed to own their relation to Old John Brown, it will not be more strange than many things that have happened. . . . Write me a few words in regard to the welfare of all. May God Allmighty for Christ's sake bless you all. We shall yet come together in our Father's house. Your Affectionate Husband, & Father, John Brown.

". . . PS Yesterday Nov 2d I was sentenced to be hanged on Decem 2d next. Do not grieve on my account. I am still quite cheerful. God bless you all. J. Brown."

In a small wretched wooden house on the outskirts of Chattanooga, Tennessee, a young fellow with a thin face was sitting at a table, writing. His mouth was a twist of hate and savage exulting. In the next room, the kitchen, a short graying woman went heavily about her tasks; she had hopeless wounded eyes.

"Sir—Although vengeance is not mine I confess that I do feel gratified to hear that you were stopped in your fiendish career at Harper's Ferry, with the loss of your two sons, you can now appreciate my distress in Kansas, when you then & there entered my house at night and arrested my Husband and two boys, and took them out and in cold blood shot them dead in my hearing, you cant say you done it to free slaves, we had none and never expected to own one, but has only made me a poor disconsolate widow with helpless children. While I feel for your folly I do hope & trust you will meet your just reward. O how it pained my heart to hear the dying groans of my Husband & children, if this scrawl gives you any consolation you are welcome to it.

                                                    Mahala Doyle.

P.S. My son Will Doyle whose life I beged of you is now grown up and is very desirous to be at Charlestown on the day of your execution, would certainly be there if his means would permit it that he might adjust the rope around your neck if Gov. Wise would permit it."

Later the thin young fellow read the letter to his mother in a high and quivering voice. When he finished she shook her head. "Don't send it, Willy," she said. "It can't help us none. And he has his own dead 'uns now, his own sorrow to eat at 'im. Don't ye send it."

At night he slipped out and sent it.

In a New Jersey village a dark little woman, who had been reading the newspapers hungrily, exclaimed to her Quaker husband: "Brandon, there are wounded Abolitionists in that prison at Charlestown. I must go and help them."

"Thou, Rebecca? Folly! Thou canst give only a poor help."

"We have talked all these years against slavery, and now somebody has *done* something. These men have risked their lives. I must go south."

She went south, bearing cakes and bandages. She got to Governor Wise: That old man and his young soldiers needed a sister and a mother to solace them, would he allow her to perform a mission of humanity? He saw no reason, said the Governor, why she could not. He would permit no woman to be insulted even if she came to minister to one who had whetted knives for their mothers and babes.

The old man, when he heard that a woman was coming to see him, said: "It will arouse suspicions. Thank her, and tell her to stay off. I am comfortable, all my wants are supplied. I am not sick enough to be nursed. I don't want women here. I've won a calm, and they will only unman me." But the dark little woman came; and Brown was gentle and unfretted with her.

"My wife bakes this kind of tart," he said after she had opened the big box with its half-crushed contents.

They talked quietly for an hour.

"Will you be able to sustain yourself during the long days you are shut up here?"

"I can't say what weakness may come over me. But I don't believe I shall ever deny my Lord Jesus Christ—and I should deny Him, if I denied my principles against slavery."

"Some say you have been moved by a feeling of revenge."

He raised his head quickly and gave her a startled look; he flushed. Then, sinking back on the bench, he slowly said: "I never had a feeling of that kind. . . . It may be that my actions have not always been right. . . . But in all the wrongs done to me and my family . . . in Kansas . . ." (a faint pain shadowed his eyes) ". . . I never . . . had a feeling of revenge."

At the end of the visit he rose to shake hands with the Quaker's wife. The chains rattled on the floor; his face was white and tired. It was better, she said, to die for a great idea than to die of a fever.

"Aye, it is better. . . . Tell my friends outside a calm peace seems to fill my mind by day and night, I sleep peaceful as an infant. . . . Greet all those for me who love their neighbors."

There were other visitors to the cell.

Governor Wise came. He did not bring this time his haughty platform manner. They talked, a man to a man; they understood each other swiftly, and knew respect.

Did Captain Brown have any communication to make other than he had already made?

No, but he would answer freely every question which agreed with honor and would not involve others.

Were there any little things which would add to his comfort here—he could have them.

No, sir. He was very comfortable. He was in charge of a noble jailer, like the one who took charge of Paul and Silas.

Could he, Henry Wise, be the confidant of any special trust or hope? He would do all in his power to carry it out, let it only be consistent with his duty and service to his Commonwealth.

Sir, that was exceeding generous. . . . Yes, he had a request to make. He wished his own body, the remains of his sons and the other Elba farmers who had been killed at the Ferry, to be delivered to his wife Mary, for burial in the Adirondacks. Could this be done?

It would be done, said the Governor.

They shook hands. "I give you my blessings, sir," said the old man.

Virginia clergymen often visited the prisoner. They would pray with him, they thought; they would convert him from the ungodly error of his ways.

"Do you believe in slavery?" asked the old man.

"I do, under the present circumstances of our laws and custom."

"Then I will thank you to leave me alone. I don't want your

prayers, they would be an abomination to my God. You can pray to your Father that heareth in secret."

Once, to a Methodist preacher he said impatiently, "My dear sir, you know nothing about Christianity; you will have to learn its A, B, and C." Then, gazing earnestly into the other's florid outraged face, he added, "I respect you as a gentleman, of course, but as a *heathen* gentleman."

With Southern visitors other than the clergy he was cordial. "Forgive me for not rising, sir. I'm unable to rise without pain. . . . Yours is a fine State. At one time I had plans to live in it, in Tyler County, but it did not turn out so. . . . I'm rather sorry that I am again in Virginia under such unfriendly circumstances, for it is a fine State. But Providence willed it so, and I'm sure we ought to accept that cheerfully." To a young woman who requested his autograph he said, "I must decline, Miss. You see, hundreds have already asked, and if I should accede it would deprive me of all the time I have remaining to me on earth. . . . And I ought to occupy it differently, it will go so quick. I cannot gratify all, Miss, so you understand, don't you, I must refuse all."

Stevens lay on a pallet in the next cell, with his bloodless face and the throbbing torn body; silent, grimly enduring. Visitors would stop before the bars and stare fascinated at him, as if he were some magnificent animal trapped; his coal-eyes would gleam back defiantly. Young women would leave the jail with the sense of him clamoring in themselves; they could not forget easily those dark lost eyes, the curling blue-black mane and the shaggy beard, the exquisite voice, deep, pure (for sometimes, feverish, he would sing low to himself: *The Blood Came Twinklin' Down* or *Ev'ry Time I Feel the Spirit*). Later, one of these young women would go before the Governor in Richmond, to beg for his life. But Aaron Stevens would mount the gibbet.

John Cook, the "lark's" young husband, had been captured in Pennsylvania and brought down to Charlestown.

Edwin Coppoc, John Cook, white persons, John Anthony Copeland, Shields Emperor Green, Negroes . . . the 16th of December . . . *hanged by the neck till dead . . . dead. . . .*

Samuel Pomeroy of Kansas was admitted to John Brown's cell. They were old friends of the Territory days; Pomeroy had been a Free-State chief. *"In prison ye came unto me,"* said the old man, gripping the other's hands.

They talked. The Kansan kept looking hungrily at the wide chimney of the cell. Suddenly he whispered: "You remember the rescue of Doy from the St. Joseph jail. Do you want your friends to attempt it? I've been in touch with Higginson."

And John Brown answered; as he had to young Hoyt, as he had to Thomas Russell, the Boston judge who had visited him on the day of his sentence; answered:

"I am worth now infinitely more to hang than for any other purpose."

With unconcealed sorrow the Kansas chieftain took leave of Brown. But first the old man learned from him that Higginson had gone to Elba, that Mary Brown was on her way south. "No!" he cried; "that must not be!" He called for paper and pen; agitated, he sat down at once to write.

And Higginson in Boston received a telegraphed message. "For God's sake don't let Mrs. Brown come here! Send her word wherever she is!" The message was relayed, it reached Mary Brown in Baltimore, just as she was about to leave for Harper's Ferry.

"I felt it," she said quietly to Miller McKim—he was a leading Philadelphia Abolitionist, he had escorted her down into Maryland; "no one knows John like I do. He won't be moved if his mind's made up."

She returned to Philadelphia with McKim. A letter came for her, forwarded again by Higginson:

"Dear Friend . . . and if my wife were to come here just now it would only tend to distract her mind TEN FOLD; and would only add to my affliction; and *can not possibly* do me *any good.* It will also use up the scanty means she has to supply *Bread* & cheap but comfortable clothing, fuel &c for herself & children through the *winter.* Do persuade her to remain *at home* for a time (at least) till she can learn further from me. She will receive a thousand times the consolation at home that she can possibly find elsewhere. I have just written her there & will write her CONSTANTLY. Her presence *here* would deepen my affliction a thousandfold. I beg of her to be *calm* and *submissive;* & not to go *wild* on my account. I lack for *nothing* & was feeling quite cheerful before I heard she talked of *coming on.* I ask her to compose her mind & remain *quiet* till the last of this month;

out of pity to me. I can certainly judge better in the matter than *any one else.* . . . God bless you all. . . . Please send this line to my *afflicted wife* by first possible conveyance. Your Friend in truth John Brown."

And now Higginson too felt the adamant, the fatality. To Ohio, to New York, to Kansas, the word went out, heavy with sorrow:

"Project abandoned."

 CHAPTER III

And Signs Like Flames

"A NOTORIOUS Kansas horsethief," said Stephen A. Douglas; "a criminal who will rightly suffer on the gallows for his crimes."

"John the Just!" exclaimed Louisa Alcott.

Old Brown will be executed for treason to a state, reflected Abraham Lincoln. We cannot object, even though he agreed with us in thinking slavery wrong. That cannot excuse violence, bloodshed, treason. It can avail him nothing that he thinks himself right.

"They are leading John Brown to execution in Virginia," breathed Henry Wadsworth Longfellow to his diary. "It will be a great day in our history: the date of a new Revolution—quite as much needed as the old one. This is sowing the wind to reap the whirlwind, *which will come soon.*"

In town halls and churches from Maine to the Territories men gathered agitated, held meetings.

In New York, a vast one: "Be it resolved . . . that we regard the recent outrage at Harper's Ferry as a crime, not only against the state of Virginia, but against the Union itself. . . ." An ex-Governor spoke; the Mayor presided. There were three overflow meetings in the streets. Emergency police forces kept a difficult order.

In Boston, a vast one. When the doors of the hall were opened men and women were swept in, some without touching the ground with their feet. Wendell Phillips was a brand of passion. Garrison spoke; Ralph Waldo Emerson. ". . . The new saint, than whom none purer or more brave was ever led by love of man into conflict and death . . . who will make the gallows glorious like the cross. . . ."

In the Virginia Legislature: "The South must stand forth as one man and say to fanaticism in her own language—whenever you advance a hostile foot upon our soil, we will welcome you with bloody hands to hospitable graves!"

"The Ferry raid presses on the approaching conflict," said Horace Greeley; "and I think the end of slavery in the Union is ten years nearer than it seemed a few weeks ago."

Governor Wise was at his desk in the Virginia capital; harassed, distraught. Daily by the hundreds the communications poured in upon the Richmond desk—warnings, counsels, threats.

"Pardon the old man, it is expedient, do not make a martyr."

"Hang the old man, give us our revenge."

"Take his life—and we will take yours."

"Declare him insane, shut him up as one does a mad dog."

Desperately Henry Wise sought in himself the right way. The days were clutchings at his brain, sleepless he tossed through he nights. He was at once febrile and strong-willed, mercurial and stubborn; these inflooding exhortations swept him this way and that, but let him once make up his mind and nothing would turn him from it. Desperately, for his conscience's sake and the continuing life of his beloved Southland, Henry Wise sought in himself.

Suddenly he decided.

First: *John Brown was not insane.* Whatever the dark record of his heritage might be, the old man himself had escaped the taint. True, he was too fiercely exalted to be of "normal" mind, he was a fanatic certainly; but equally certain it was that he must be counted responsibly intelligent. Henry Wise had talked with the old man, he remembered the startling interview in the paymaster's office just after the raid ("No man sent me here. It was by my own prompting and that of my Maker"); he had read and been profoundly moved despite himself by the letters from the Charlestown jail: no madman had ever talked and written thus.

Now Henry Wise entered in his notebook: "I *know* that he is sane; and remarkably sane, if quick and clear perception, if assumed rational premises, and consecutive reasoning from them, if cautious tact in avoiding disclosures and in covering conclusions and inferences, if memory and conception and practical sense, if composure and self-possession are evidence of a sound state of mind. He is a fanatic, but a man of courage, fortitude and supreme honor; a bundle of the best nerves I ever saw cut and thrust and bleeding and in bonds. He is responsible for his act. *I will take no smallest step to have Old Brown pardoned on grounds of insanity."*

Second: He, Governor Wise, would not be swayed by appeals to expediency. (". . . To hang a fanatic is to make a martyr of him," had warned a Southern editorial; "and fledge another brood of the same sort. Better send these creatures to the penitentiary and so make them felons. Monsters are hydra-headed, decapitation only quickens vitality and power of reproduction." And again: "Dare you do a bold thing, my friend?" had written Fernando Wood, New York's pro-slaver mayor. "Have you nerve enough to send him to States Prison instead of hanging him? No Southern man could go further than myself in defence of Southern rights, but yet were I Governor of Virginia, Brown *should not be hung.* And in such a course my conduct would be governed by sound policy. The South will gain by showing that it can be magnanimous to a fanatic in its power. The man is the crazed tool of Abolitionist scoundrels. *Do not make him a martyr. . . ."*)

Governor Wise's answer went out: "I have duly received and weighed every word of your letter. Now, listen to me, for my mind is inflexibly made up. . . . These men have been scrupulously afforded a fair trial, with every opportunity of defence for crimes which were openly perpetrated before the eyes of hundreds and as openly confessed. The crimes deliberately done by them are of the deepest and darkest kind which can be committed against our people. Brown the leader has been legally and fairly tried and convicted, and admits the humanity of his treatment as a prisoner, the truth of the indictment, and the truthfulness of the witnesses against him. He has been allowed excess of counsel, and freedom of speech beyond any prisoner known to me in our trials. It was impossible not to convict him. He is sentenced to be hanged—the sentence of a mild code humanely adjudged and requiring no duty from me except to see that it be executed. I have to sign no death warrant. If the Executive interposes at all, it is to pardon. And to pardon him I have received petitions, prayers, threats, from almost every state in the Union. By honest patriotic men like yourself I am warned that hanging will make him a martyr. You ask: Have you nerve enough to send Brown to States Prison for life instead of hanging him? Yes—if I didn't think he *ought to be hung*. I could do it without the quiver of a muscle against a universal clamor for his life. But is it wisely said to a State that she had better spare a murderer, a traitor, because public sentiment elsewhere will glorify the criminal with martyrdom? I say to you firmly that I have precisely the nerve enough to let him be executed. He shall be executed as the law sentences him, and his body shall await the resurrection without a grave in our soil. I have shown him all the mercy which humanity can claim. . . . Yours truly, Henry Wise."

But still the communications poured in. Letters, telegrams, threats, warnings. Damn Judge Parker, the Governor groaned, why had he let the old man live so long, given him a whole month? The very thing Wise had feared had come to pass—the countryside, the whole nation was seething with a huge ferment. And Wise cursed himself too: why had he not proclaimed martial-law after the raid, and executed the traitor under a court-martial! A panic began to grip the Governor.

"I have seen between 30 & 36 men," wrote T. A. B. from Ohio; "all armed with Colts Six Shooters & a species of home made Bowie knife, well calculated to do Exicution. They will cross the river near Cisterville with 200 others and arrive Dec 1 for Ferry rescue. . . ."

From Cleveland the United States marshal forwarded a letter: ". . . and they have 9000 desperate men, and boast that he will not be hanged."

Philadelphia reported: "5000 men armed with Pikes rifles and four cannon."

Detroit warned: "8000 men . . . Dec 1 . . . new style carbines . . . 10 shots a minute at the jail guards."

Governor Henry Wise marked these communications: "Contemptible Nonsense." Governor Henry Wise wired to President Buchanan of the United States: "I have reliable information . . . convinced that attempt will be made to rescue prisoners. . . . Places in Maryland, Ohio and Pa. occupied as depots and rendezvous by

desperadoes. . . . We are kept in continual apprehension of outrages from fire and rapine on our borders."

Two days later Colonel Robert E. Lee, United States Army,
arrived in Charlestown with three hundred artillerymen from
Fort Monroe. A thousand militiamen from neighboring towns
bivouacked about Charlestown. Four hundred men from Richmond and Petersburg were ordered in, with cannon. Proud serious-
faced lads arrived from Lexington, cadets of the Virginia Military
Institute, under a Professor T. J. Jackson. Charlestown was like
a town besieged. Troops were quartered in the churches, the
schools. In the court-house the guns were stacked outside the
counsels' railing, and knapsacks and canteens were piled upon
the bench. Even the graveyards knew the hobbed boots and the
clangor of steel. Mounted patrols ranged every precinct of the
county. Sentries were stationed a full mile beyond the town; it
took an hour and forty minutes to post the guard.

Night after night mysterious fires licked at the winter sky.
The barns of three Charlestown citizens were burned down; the
three citizens had been on the jury which had doomed an old
man to the gallows. The fires continued throughout November.
There were strange rifleshots outside the windows of prominent
townsmen. Mayor Green ordered all strangers to leave Charlestown, under pain of arrest. (Young Hoyt was among these; he had
failed, the old man had stood against his purpose like stone, but
the lawyer-stripling left with a strange sense of fulfillment, with
"I am worth infinitely more . . ." echoing in him, like an exulta-
tion.) And now the little town was a single throbbing body of
dread. There were frantic rumors of invasion, sudden alarms
shuddering through from house to house. The troops would fall
hastily into line, the cavalry would go rushing with cries and
ringing hoofs through the cold dark of the night.

(The South's very heart was beating in that little town. The
dread, vague, almost nameless, the ominous sense of some vast
fate beyond this special moment, hung dark, hung over the Tennessee mountains, over the red baked fields of Georgia and the
cotton lands leaning hotly close upon the waters of the Gulf. That
mad thrust of an old man and some boys was like a knife un-
sheathed, the knife of the North thrusting for the Southland's
heart, murderously singing: blood, frenzy, insurrection. Twenty-
two evil little creatures had stolen down into their land; they

≡ * 348 * ≡

were as a snarl and a threatening footfall—a beast which was half a nation crouched ravenous and waiting.

Men of the South, be ready, let us be ready, let us fight for our land and our life and the ways of our fathers!)

The gallows-day was approaching. Governor Wise sent orders to Major-General W. B. Taliaferro: "Keep full guard on the line of frontier from Martinsburg to Harper's Ferry, on the day of Dec 2d. Warn inhabitants to arm and keep guard and patrol on that day and for days beforehand. Prevent all strangers and especially parties of strangers from proceeding to Charlestown on Dec 2d. Station guard at Ferry sufficient to control crowds on the cars from East and West. Be prepared, if situation requires, to tear up railroad tracks. Let mounted men guard outposts. Two companies to keep crowd clear of outer line of military. Form two concentric squares around gallows. Have extra strong guard at jail and for escort to execution. Let no crowd be near enough to the prisoner to hear any speech he may attempt. Allow no more visitors to be admitted to jail. . . ."

And in the Charlestown lock-up, full in the midst of the dread and the rage, the old man with the flowing white beard and the sabre cuts calmly spoke and wrote, and the words went out. (A hundred reporters sent him living and etched into millions of wide-flung homes. Now he was doing this, saying that; yesterday he had written his will: could the rights of his stricken family be respected in regard to all his property not of a warlike nature?—today he was requesting a plain pine coffin for the last rest of his body.) And the nation listened.

"I am only walking now as God foreordained I should walk. All our actions, even the follies leading to this disaster were decreed to happen ages before this world was made. . . . And God will not forget the work of his hands."

"Let them hang me. I forgive them, and may God forgive them. For they know not what they do."

Calm little words. And the nation listening (on the 28th of November 1859 a brief obscure note in the newspapers says that Washington Irving is dead), the nation a vast gripped gaze; with here grief, and there a fury of hatred, but wonderment everywhere (across the Atlantic waters Victor Hugo is saying: "The eyes of

≡ * 349 * ≡

Europe are fixed on America. The hanging of John Brown will open a latent fissure that will finally split the Union asunder. . . . You preserve your shame but you kill your glory"), wonderment everywhere and an inner searching. For those little words speak deep beyond themselves, they seem in a torn bewildered land to hold some serene yet passionate mystery of faith: *I, John Brown, will go without fear, with a great shining peace in my heart; I will show men how to die for truth.* Calm little words, inescapable, like fingers pointing; little ghosts of words haunting the thoughts of men: *Where do you stand? what do you believe? We can no longer go as fools in a blind wilderness. This people in our midst, this dark prostrate soul will shape our life or our death. Americans, brothers, which way are your eyes turned?*

Darkly on the horizon creep the deep low sounds; louder, faintly louder; as creep the sullen mutterings of a distant storm.

The voices of grief and revulsion rise, from the North the South from the farthest West in the land of the brothers tragically cloven.

And in the sky there are portents, and signs like flames.

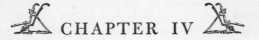 CHAPTER IV

Come, Mary, Gather Up Our Bones

MARY BROWN, after receiving the plea to remain away from the Charlestown jail and "not to go wild; out of pity to me," did not return to her mountain home. "I'll abide my husband's mind," she said; but she stayed in Philadelphia, with the McKims, and waited; waited with desolate patience for the word that in the end she knew would come. It came. "Mary, if you are equal to the undertaking of seeing me before I suffer; if you can afford to meet the expence & trouble of coming on here to gather up the bones of our beloved sons & of your husband; and the Virginia people will suffer you to do so; I am entirely willing."

She showed the word to McKim. The Abolitionist said that she must write at once to Governor Wise, she must get his permission. She flushed. "I don't think I can do this . . . good enough," she said. Of course not, answered McKim gently; she was under a terrible strain; might he tend to the request for her? She could approve it.

"Governor Henry Wise: . . . and I beg for the mortal remains of my husband and sons . . . for decent and tender interment among their kindred . . . Mary Brown."

Would this do? McKim asked, gentler still. Yes, it would do, she said; and wept softly; and soon was calm again.

In Charlestown, Major-General Taliaferro, commanding the Commonwealth's troops, received a telegraphed order: "Sir: when John Brown is executed on Friday the 2d proximo, you will place his mortal remains under strict guard and protect them from all mutilation. Place them in a plain coffin and have them taken to Harper's Ferry, there to await the orders of Mrs. Mary Brown who has a duplicate of this order. You will also allow the bodies of her sons, who fell at Harper's Ferry, to be disinterred and taken by her or her agent or order. Respectfully, Henry Wise."

(Close by the waters of the Shenandoah, Oliver Brown lay in an unmarked grave, together with eight of his comrades. It would be beyond her heart's strength to look upon him, for identification. . . . The remains of Watson Brown had been taken to a Virginia college for preservation as an anatomical specimen.)

Mary Brown left for Harper's Ferry with the McKims and Hector Tyndale, a young Philadelphia lawyer. They arrived on the night of November 30th; they stayed at the Wager House. Only Mary Brown would be permitted to go on to Charlestown, the others would have to remain at the Ferry. (Her friends were virtually prisoners; eyes watched them ceaselessly. Once as they took a turn about the streets to ease the sickening strain of waiting, a mocking bullet whined high above them in the air. Twenty-six months later, on February 7th, 1862, a Major H. Tyndale, commanding the Twenty-eighth Pennsylvania Infantry, would, under superior military orders, burn the arsenal town of Harper's Ferry. A squat stone engine-house—where once, on a morning of white ravelling mists and a hush over the shining rivers, a cracked voice had called "Calm, men; sell your life dear, sell it dear!" and blue-tunicked Marines had come swarming with bayonets and sledges—the engine-house would stand through the flames.) Now, on this first day of December, Mary Brown left her friends at the Ferry hostelry, and stepped heavily into the waiting carriage. She was dark-veiled. A captain of militia sat beside her. The carriage, with nine cavalrymen riding as an escort, wheeled off into the cold gray day, swiftly along the Charlestown road.

And while these things were going on and the gallows-time approached, a little inner world settled deeper into its final peace. The old man was "dayly & hourly striving to gather up what little I may from the wreck." He sat writing, writing, all through the days, and far into the nights, until his eyes would fail. Jesus Christ, he told himself, had taken from him the sword of blood, and had placed in his hands another—the "words, words" he had despised so long were now become his very strength. Aye, he would speak to the heart of his land (only yesterday he had read in the newspapers what Emerson had said: The slaveholder believes while he chains and chops John Brown that he is getting rid of his tormentor. Does he not see that the air this man breathes is Liberty? that it will be breathed by thousands and millions?) So the letters, even as his days forever diminished, went out steadily, to relatives, to friends, to public-men, to strangers.

"I have been *whiped* as the saying is; but I am sure I can recover all the lost capital occasioned by this disaster; by only hanging a few minutes by the neck. . . . I cannot remember a night so dark as to have hindered the coming of day, nor a storm so furious or dreadful as to prevent the return of warm sunshine and a cloudless sky. . . . May God for Christ's sake ever make his face to shine on you all. . . ."

"I have asked to be spared from having any mock; or *hypocritical prayers* made over me when I am publicly murdered: & that my only religious attendants be poor *little, dirty, ragged, bareheaded, & barefooted Slave boys;* & Girls, led by some old grey headed slave Mother. . . ."

"It affords me some satisfaction to feel conscious of having tried to better the condition of those who are on the under-hill side, and I am now in hopes of being able to meet the consequences without a murmur. . . . Did not Jesus of Nazareth suffer death on the cross as a fellon? Think too of the crushed Millions 'who have no comforters.' *I charge you all* never to forget the griefs of the poor that cry & of those that have none to help them. . . . Farewell. Farewell."

Often, Avis the jailer, reading in accordance with his duty these letters of his homeland's enemy, would look forth unseeing through tear-filled eyes.

And now, on this deepening afternoon, the last before the hanging, Avis the jailer stood before the old man, and said: "Captain Brown. Your wife is here."

 CHAPTER V

I Wish Carven

MRS. AVIS, a tall faded woman, led Mary Brown into a private room of the prison structure.

"I must ask you to take your coat off, Mrs. Brown," she said, hesitantly, not meeting the other's eyes. "Those are my orders."

She began to run her moist fingers through the garments of Mary Brown; then slowly over the soft heavy body.

"How is my husband's health?" trembled Mary Brown, all unheeding, as in a dream.

"His wounds are healing nicely."

When the searching was over, the jailer's wife stood there, fumbling her keys in the big moist hands. "You . . . mustn't think . . . we're glad," she said.

"Can I go in to see him now?" asked Mary Brown faintly.

"Come."

Avis was waiting in the corridor. He led Mary Brown to the cell-door. He unlocked it.

John Brown was standing half-shrouded in the darkness by the further wall, beneath the barred window. A taper was burning on the table. The iron door clicked shut behind her; the footsteps faded. . . . She moved toward him. He took two steps forward, the chains clanking.

"Oh, John."

"Mary."

They stood clinging to each other, weeping. A minute passed; two; they clung weeping.

But soon they were quiet. They sat by the table, and quietly talked: a gaunt bowed man, in carpet slippers and seedy black trousers, with a white beard falling away from his breast; a pale heavy woman, dressed in black.

"I'm glad you came, Mary."

"John . . . it's a hard lot."

"Be cheerful, Mary. We must all bear it in the best manner we can. I think it's all for the best."

"Our poor children."

"Aye . . . aye." They sat. His bony hand stole across the table, found hers. Through the hands their hearts flowed, they clung in their hearts. "But we'll not be separated forever, wife. We'll come together in another house."

Then anxiously he asked: "Tell me, Mary, do you blame me? Have I given you too much to bear?"

"I have no blame, John."

"No," he said, and his eyes shone. "Our sacrifices are not at all too great."

He began to talk about the Elba home. Had the crops matured well this season? How were all those yet living? Was Martha carrying her baby well? Once suddenly he groaned, "Our poor shattered children." But this did not last; he went on quietly. God, he said, would be a husband to the widow, he would be a father to the fatherless. . . .

". . . And now, Mary, let me say a little about educating our young daughters. I know it doesn't become me to dictate in this matter. I have little right to meddle now in your worldly affairs—I have done so poorly in them. But still, you know, Mary, don't you, I have not lost interest in my daughters." So let them be told that he wished them educated for a plain life. He did not at all mean an education as miserable as he or she had got; he meant enough of the learning of schools to enable them to transact the common business as well as the common duties. Let his daughters be useful though poor, let them know the music of the washtub and the needle before the music of the piano. Aye, he wished them to be "matter of fact women."

She nodded brokenly as he spoke. Her eyes went again and

again to the chains that galled his ankles beneath the heavy white-wool socks.

"They say it'll be tomorrow, John. Will it be tomorrow, John?"

"I'm peaceful, Mary. I've had a long life."

Footsteps sounded harsh along the corridor. . . . The militia captain called through the bars: "You will have to leave soon, Mrs. Brown. Your carriage goes back in half an hour."

"Why," the old man said. "Surely my wife will be allowed to stay this night!"

"No. Mrs. Brown must return to the Ferry."

The old man leaped up, went clanking half in a limp to the bars; one of his slippers fell from his foot. "But you can't do this. It's a little thing. Why, tomorrow we'll be apart."

"I'm sorry. My orders won't allow it."

The old man stood there, quivering in a sudden rage. His hands gripped the bars, they were white circling gnarls of bone. "Orders!" he cried with scorn and pleading. "Orders on this night!"

Mary Brown went to him. She put her hand on his arm. "Don't, John," she said. He glared at her. Then he dropped his hands from the bars. He turned; stooped to pick up the slipper; and limped weakly back to his bench by the table.

"I ask nothing of you, sir. I beg nothing from the state of Virginia. Carry out your orders. I'm content."

The officer went silently away. . . .

"I want to read this to you, Mary, before you go. It's my last will. I wrote it this morning. . . . Listen with care, Mary. I wish it carried out, exactly. . . ."

I give to my son John Brown Jr. my Surveyors Compass & other surveyors articles if found also my old Granite Monument now at North Elba . . . Said stone Monument to remain however at North Elba, so long as any of my children or my wife; may remain there; as residents.

He gave her a slip of paper. "This is what I wish carven on the two sides of the stone, Mary," he said. "I have left blank the day of birth of our Watson and Oliver. I have marked their deaths, but you will remember better than I their day of birth. . . ." Then he went on reading the will:

I give to my Son Jason my Silver Watch with my name egraved on iner case. . . .

≡ ∗ 355 ∗ ≡

I give to my son Owen Brown my double Spry or opera Glass & my Rifle Gun (if found). It is Globe Sighted & new. I give also to the same Son Fifty Dollars in consideration of his terrible sufferings in Kansas: & his crippled condition from his childhood. . . .

"Do you hear, Mary? Is this clear?"

"Yes, husband." She was silently weeping, with upturned face.

I give to my Daughter Ruth Thompson my large old Bible containing family record. . . .

I give to each of my GrandChildren that may be living when my Father's Estate is settled: as good a copy of the Bible as can be purchased at a cost of $3, Three Dollars each . . . all the Bibles to be purchased at one and the same time for Cash on best terms. . . .

The voice went on: *I give . . . I desire . . . It is my will. . . .*

"Do you hear, Mary?"

"Yes, John. Yes."

And now it was the time for them to separate. He held her hands, and said, "Mary . . . I hope you will always live in Essex County. . . . Get, if you can, all our remaining children together. . . . Impress right principles, Mary . . . to each succeeding generation."

He bent; their lips touched, trembled together.

"Now go, Mary. . . . God will be with us. . . . Good-bye. Good-bye."

"Oh John. . . . Good-bye."

Mary Brown began the long dark ride back to Harper's Ferry. There she would wait through the night; tomorrow she would take up the body.

John Brown sat writing his last letters. When he had finished these, he read a little in his Bible. . . . Then he slept.

CHAPTER VI

My Dearly Beloved Wife, Sons: Daughters, Everyone

As I now begin what is probably the last letter I shall ever write to any of you; I conclude to write to you all at the same time. . . . I am waiting the hour of my public *murder* with great composure of mind, & cheerfulness: feeling the strongest assurance that in no other possible way could I be used to so much advance the cause of God; & of humanity: & that nothing that either I or all my family have sacrificed or suffered: will be lost. The reflection that a *wise & merciful, as well as just & holy God:* rules not only the affairs of *this world;* but of all worlds; is a rock to set our feet upon; under all circumstances: *even* those more severely *trying ones:* into which our own follies; & rongs have placed us. . . . I am endeavouring to 'return' like a 'poor Prodigal' *as I am,* to my Father: against whom I have *always* sined: *in the hope;* that he may kindly, & forgivingly 'meet me: though a *verry great way off.*' . . . Oh do not trust your eternal all uppon the boisterous Ocean, without *even* a *Helm;* or *Compass* to *aid* you in steering. . . . My dear young children will you listen to the last poor admonition of one who can only love you? Oh be determined at once to give your whole hearts to God; & let *nothing* shake; or alter; that resolution. You need have no fear of *regreting* it. Do not be vain; and thoughtless: but *sober minded.* And let me entreat you all to love the *whole remnant* of our once great family: 'with a *pure heart fervently.*' Try to *build again:* your broken walls: & to make *the utmost* of every *stone* that is left. Nothing can so tend to make life a blessing as the consciousness that you *love: & are beloved:* & 'love ye the stranger' *still.* . . . Be faithful until death. From the exercise of habitual love to man: *it cannot* be very *hard: to learn to love* his *maker.* . . .

John Rogers wrote to his children, 'Abhor the arrant whore

of Rome.' John Brown writes to his children to abhor with *undiing hatred,* also: that 'sum of all vilainies'; Slavery. . . . And now dearly beloved Farewell: 'be of good cheer' and God Allmighty bless, save, comfort, guide, & keep; you, to 'the end.'
Your Affectionate Husband & Father
John Brown

CHAPTER VII

As a Fool Dieth

THEY LED John Brown out to the porch of the jail. (Inside, the young fellows whom he had brought to the threshold of death— Emperor Green, huge, ebon-glistening, with dumb anguished eyes; proud Copeland the Oberlin student, slender and straight as a javelin; black-bearded Stevens, former army-deserter; the Quaker boy Edwin Coppoc, now suddenly weeping; slim dark John Cook, the husband of the "lark"—they stood by the bars, listening to the fading footsteps, hearing still the echo of his "Good-bye, my men. God save you all." Only one he had not bidden farewell. Hazlett; who had been captured in the Pennsylvania hills and extradited to Virginia—illegally, for there was no proof that he had been among the raiders. To the very end the old man and his comrades would not recognize him, in the hope of cheating the gibbet of his young life. "I do not know him," they said again and again as they were questioned. But Hazlett too would go to his death. They would all go.) They led John Brown out to the porch of the jail. An officer, a sheriff, and Avis the jailer, led the way. The old man limped in the midst of the four guards, with his seedy black trousers and the white-wool socks showing above the loose carpet-slippers; his arms were pinioned close to his body. The air was sharp and pure; the morning sun flooded the street. Soldiers. Soldiers. Bayonets gleaming. Cannon grimly trained. Tramping feet. "I had no idea," the old man said, "that they would consider my death so important."

≡ * 358 * ≡

In the road, between files of militia, was a big open wagon with a team of white horses. A pine coffin was in the back. The old man as he went down the steps of the porch handed a small paper to the officer. Then he climbed into the wagon, helped by the sheriff; and sat down upon the coffin. Avis sat by him. The sheriff, an undertaker, and the driver, were up on the front seat. The officer in silence read the scrawl:

"I John Brown am now quite *certain* that the crimes of this *guilty land:* will never be purged away; but with Blood. I had *as I now think:* vainly flattered myself that without *very much* bloodshed; it might be done."

The scaffold rose against the morning sky. It was well beyond the town; in a field of forty acres, on a hillock yet in grass despite the winter. Fifteen hundred troops were massed about in a great hollow square. From the ends of the field, howitzers were trained to sweep every approach.

(Behind the gibbet, standing in line with Company "F" of the Richmond militia, was a young actor. John Wilkes Booth.)

The wagon, with its escort of cavalry and marching men, came wheeling slowly around the bend of the road. The old man on the coffin beheld the vast swept Shenandoah sky; the white clouds low over the northern woods; and looming far off to the east and the south the misty Blue Ridge Mountains.

"This *is* a beautiful country," he said. "I never had the pleasure of really seeing it before."

The wagon drew up on the rise; creaked into the troop-square; halted. A command rang out; the files veered in a swift and precise evolution; a bristling passageway was formed from the wagon to the gallows. The old man climbed down, unassisted. He walked without an order to the structure; went slowly up the ten steps to the platform. There he stood—a little bowed, the white beard ruffled in the wind—looking out to the low surrounding hills where the people would be gathered to watch Avis and the sheriff ascend the platform.

The old man shook his jailer's hand. "I have no words to thank you for your kindness," he said. "Farewell."

He shook the sheriff's hand. "Farewell," he said.

The sheriff drew a white cowl over John Brown's head. He adjusted the thin tarred rope about his neck.

"I can't see, gentlemen; you must lead me."

They placed John Brown on the drop.

The troops of the escort deployed into their places. The minutes went by; the troops wheeled, marched, countermarched. Twelve eternal minutes went by; the muskets rattled, the ground shook beneath the tramping feet. John Brown, soldier of the Lord, stood still and erect.

"Do you want a signal before I spring her?" whispered the sheriff.

"It does not matter. Only do not keep me waiting too long."

The maneuver was ended, the last Virginia soldier was in his place.

A hush now hung . . . the fields, the sky, the men were hushed. . . .

Colonel Preston of Virginia raised his hand. The sheriff gripped tighter his hatchet. He stood forth, poising himself. His arm heaved, steel gleamed in an arc, the trap crashed, the rope spun through, the rope jerked and shivered . . . shivered . . . shivered. . . .

Silence.

Clear, calm, Colonel Preston's voice now rose: *"So perish all such enemies of Virginia! All such enemies of the Union! All such foes of the human race!"*

 CHAPTER VIII

Rest at Evening

JOHN BROWN's body hung on the gibbet for thirty-seven minutes. . . .

Then the Charlestown surgeons came forward. The body was slowly swinging with the wind. They put their arms around the body to hold it steady; they held their ears at the breast to listen to the heart. They pronounced the body dead.

Then the military surgeons listened at the breast.

Verified. John Brown's body was dead.

(In distant Albany they are firing a dirge of one hundred guns.)

The simple pine coffin was placed on a special train of two cars. Fifteen Virginia citizens volunteered as a bodyguard to see that no harm befell the body on its return to Mary Brown. They brought the coffin to her in Harper's Ferry, late on the winter afternoon. By nightfall Mary and John Brown were started on the long journey back to the Elba mountains; the train moaned northward through the darkness.

(In Cleveland, fourteen hundred people are praying together in a black-draped hall.)

The next day, Friday, at noon, the funeral train reached Philadelphia. A great crowd was waiting at the station. Hundreds of Negroes were there—and scores of those hostile ones who yesterday had tried to break up a meeting of sympathy. The mayor of the city had called out two hundred policemen. Now he forbade the brief resting of the body at an undertaker's; ordered the body to be forwarded out of Philadelphia at once, he could not have this disorder in his city. As a feint an empty hearse was driven away from the station; the coffin was secretly placed in a furniture car and borne to the Walnut Street wharf. A boat slipped out, crept up along the coast towards New York. The next day Mary Brown followed, by train, with McKim.

No, she said when she arrived in New York; would they please not ask for public ceremonies. She wanted her husband to come home quietly. So they rested over the Sabbath; and John Brown's body lay at an undertaker's. The face did not have the pallor of death; the rope had left it faintly flushed. He lay as a person in a quiet sleep.

(In Rochester, Syracuse, Fitchburg, the church bells are tolling. In Plymouth and New Bedford, in Concord, in Manchester, tolling, tolling.)

On Monday the journey home began again. Wendell Phillips the orator was now by the side of Mary Brown. Night came; the train reached the town of Rutland, Vermont. A heavy snow was falling; the bells rang out on the dark windy night. Early the next morning sleighs were waiting for the funeral party; the storm had hours ago stopped, but the drifts were high. Thirty men and four women were waiting, with boots and snowshoes; they would walk a distance through the snow, for his memory.

The procession started, the men and women moved slowly and silently ahead of the horses pulling the three big sleighs. Bells sounded again, bells were like silver on the pure shining air. Soon they came to a bridge arching a frozen stream. The townspeople formed themselves into a double line along the sides of the bridge. The men uncovered their heads. The sleighs glided through the silent lanes. In the cold faint distance the bells were ringing. . . .

Just before dark descended they came to Westport, New York. They were now within thirty miles of Elba; but the road wound over a mountain almost impassable, it would take the whole of the next day to cover it. So once more the party rested; and John Brown's body lay in the village court-house, and six young men sat till dawn as a guard of honor.

Again the retinue of mourners started, in carriages now, for a heavy night rain had washed the snows. Hours ago a village lad had started off over the mountain on a swift horse, to tell John Brown's people that he would soon be home.

All that day they slowly climbed the wild winding pass to the summit; and as slowly descended into the valley beyond. The sun was going down when they reached the handful of poor dwellings which formed the town of North Elba; it was night as they came out of the last forest depth, into a dark clearing. They saw lights flickering down the slope towards them. Some Negro neighbors were coming to guide them, with lanterns.

The carriages drew up before the low huddled house. McKim gave Mary Brown his hands. She stepped heavily down. At once from the doorway there came a sharp broken cry . . . and Annie Brown was locked convulsively weeping in her mother's embrace. Then Sarah came, and little Nell; and inside there sounded the wailing of the girls who were widows.

*   *   *   *   *

The next afternoon the small bare parlor was crowded. The Brown family; McKim, Wendell Phillips, a Reverend Young; the handful of neighbors, whites and Negroes. The coffin was on a table near the open door. The face was exposed, the sun was on it. He lay as in a quiet sleep.

"Almighty and merciful God. Thou art speaking to us in the great and solemn circumstances which have brought us here together. Before Jesus Christ, the Saviour of Man, may we consecrate ourselves anew to the work of truth and love for which our brother laid down his life. May we consecrate ourselves to the outcast and the oppressed, to the humble and the least of our fellow-men. Father in Heaven, in imitation of the self-forgetting and sacrifice of the departed, we supplicate Thy special blessing upon God's despised ones. . . . We ask this in the name of Jesus Christ. Amen."

Now let John Brown's neighbors come forward, those who wished it, and look this last time upon him.

One by one they came forward. The Negroes were weeping.

Then John Brown's people stood close by his body, by the face as in a quiet sleep. And Wendell Phillips said:

"God bless this roof. Make it bless us. . . . We dare not say bless you, children of this home. For you stand nearer to one whose lips God touched, and we rather bend for your blessing. God make us worthier of him whose dust we lay among these hills. . . . He sleeps in the blessings of the crushed and the poor, and men believe more firmly in love, now that such a man has lived. . . ."

The short procession from the house to the grave began. Four of the Negroes bore the coffin. Mary Brown followed, supported by Wendell Phillips. Then Oliver's Martha, leaning on the arm of McKim, and little Nell clutching his hand. . . . Bella walking by the Reverend Young. . . . Salmon Brown, Sarah, Annie. . . . Ruth and Hen Thompson. . . . Hen's aged father and mother, parents of Will and Dauphin Thompson lying in Virginia. . . . The friends, the neighbors.

They buried him by the great boulder—at the foot of the letters J. B. which once he had graven in the rock to show Mary Brown where she should put him when he returned. As they lowered the body into the winter earth, old Epps the Negro, his son and two daughters, sang *Blow Ye the Trumpet, Blow!* —the hymn which John Brown had sung at night to his children, carrying them in his arms before they went to sleep. . . . And now it was done.

Night came on. The grave lay hushed in the silence of the mountains.

A NOTE ON
THE MANUFACTURE OF THIS BOOK

THIS EDITION of "God's Angry Man" was planned for the members of The Readers Club by WARREN CHAPPELL, a famous graphic artist who now resides in New York. He was one of the star pupils in the *atelier* of the graphic arts which Rudolf Koch once conducted in Offenbach-am-Main in Germany. He has illustrated dozens of books and designed several type faces. In planning this book, he has made use of a type-face called Baskerville: the letter-shapes of which were cut by the Mergenthaler Linotype Company following the designs originally drawn by John Baskerville, an eighteenth-century English printer. All of the headlines were set by hand in a type called Bulmer, which is named after another eighteenth-century English printer named William Bulmer, although the designs were probably drawn by an employee of his named William Martin. The decorative ornaments were all drawn for *this* book by Mr. Chappell, and cut into lead to be treated as type. And the drawings for the binding and the jacket came from Mr. Chappell's studio, also. The printing of the book was done by the American Book–Stratford Press in New York. The paper was supplied by the West Virginia Pulp and Paper Company; it is noteworthy in that, although it is an inexpensive sheet of paper, it is completely free of the ground-up wood which tends to cause papers to deteriorate.